the **_Love Unaccounted_** series

by Love Belvin

MKT Publishing

~Of course, he wouldn't be outdone...~

"And this works best with your current schedule?"

His eyes ballooned as he exhaled. "Yeah. I'm flexible. I'm gonna make time!"

I didn't hide my grin at his enthusiasm as I tapped into the calendar app of my iPad.

"That's cool. I'll run a few of your dates against hers and arrange for joint sessions, too," I mumbled into my lap, tapping away.

"Is...she as flexible as I am?"

I lifted from my device. The muscles in Trent's face were relaxed, but his eyes told me all I needed to know; it would be an easy fix for these two.

"Yeah." I laughed. "Very flex—"

My words were halted by the ruckus of my office door being swung open. In stepped a tall bearded man dressed in a three-piece wool suit.

Ezra?

Trent jumped to his feet, startled just as I was.

"She's gone," he spoke through gritted teeth.

I sat back in my chair, taken by his nerve. But I can't say I was surprised by his abruptness. He'd come early to today's session.

"I know," was my simple reply.

"You said, we'd work. You guaranteed—"

"I'm with a client, Ezra. You can't just come into my office, throwing your issues on the wrong plate." I gestured to Trent.

"Oh, nah." Trent's eyes bounced between the two of us. "It's gravy. Love, we'll be in touch." He tossed me a quick wave. "Ezra, see you Thursday, man."

Ezra's eyes fell, hopefully in embarrassment. Trent was his parishioner!

His hand extended, and Trent accepted it in a shake. When the door closed, I cocked my head to the side.

"Nice job, Pastor."

"Oh, I gave you that client," Ezra quickly returned.

"No. You referred a client that pushed back several for me to take on right away. And this is how you conduct yourself in front of the two of us. Where's the respect?"

"I am going through a dark affair in my life. He would understand if he knew. She left me!"

I lifted and drop my shoulders, glancing away. "You're in the valley. It's a part of the marriage journey. Get used to it. Just don't set up shop there."

"What's the use of having you if this could be possible?" His brows met at that jab. Then his open hands flew in the air. "Look. I understood full well at the beginning of this venture, you didn't hold the formal qualifications of a therapist, but I'd also researched you, and spoke extensively with your relatives."

I rolled my eyes. "First of all, have a seat while you're speaking to me."

His neck retracted just slightly, and one brow peaked. "Pardon me?"

"You heard what I said. Ezra, I respect you...actually like you a lot, but the moment you come into my place, throwing around your imposing weight, that could all come to an end. I'm overseer here. I'm boss here. I'm leader in this place. You are a client, needing my services. Do you get where this is going?"

"I could have gone to someone else, Love. Someone who would have at least worked it so she would not have left," he threatened.

I sat up in my seat. "I have countless peers on the shelves next to me. Not one would care to take on your story. None could have gotten this far with you, and none have my talent to manage you."

"That's mighty arrogant of you." He scoffed, coolly. "I wholly disagree."

"Ezra, don't fool yourself. My specialty is broken people, bringing them to a place where they can experience healthy, long-lasting romantic love. You're kidding yourself if you think many of my contemporaries would be prepared to take you on. Many of them do the cutesy couples with minor flaws that makes for a plot, and have them live happily ever after. *I* take on the impossibly companionable, and work on their internal individual issues many would deem irrevocable."

He leaned down toward me, still standing, and I could smell his fragranced beard. "You clearly didn't do a good job with Alexis."

I cocked my head to the side again. "Who said Lex was the broken one of the two?"

We locked eyes. Ezra slowly stood straight, and I didn't miss when his lips parted in sheer astonishment. That's when I found myself in Lex's shoes: eye warring with a warrior. The beast. Ezra was, without effort, intimidating. His presence alone had a heavy weight, an air of power and fearless leadership. And while I believed he possessed a high level of knowledge, wisdom had not always been present for him.

"So, I'm broken?" his rasp held a tone of humility.

If I was not mistaken, Ezra had momentarily put down his weapons. If he could only remove the armor, too. I was not in the business of attacking people, no matter how weak their seemingly tough veneers.

"You need lots of work, but the one thing you have working for you is I 'get' you. You're not an overnight success. When I agreed to this, I knew it wouldn't be a short bubblegum love story. I don't do those. I believe in you, but you have to kill some things in yourself to make this thing work."

"Things like what? What do you 'get'?"

My eyes skirted around the room. I stood to get a box that was used to ship a pair of shoes I'd recently ordered. I brought it over to the coffee table.

"This box encompasses your life. It represents the barriers between you and the world—the world being everything that doesn't affect the core of you. Inside this box are all the things that matter to you...the only things you cherish in life."

I gave a nod to confirm he was following me.

"Okay..." His response told of his stubbornness, but I knew he was following.

"Inside the box," I pointed, "is Ezra and God." I gave a brief pause for digesting.

"Outside of the box?" I was surprised he asked.

"...is Lex and everything and everybody else. I'm out there, too."

Slowly, Ezra straightened his spine, backed up, and collapsed on the sofa across from me, on the other side of the table.

"Do you get where this is going? Ezra, your wife is in the same category as your cleaner's guy, mechanic, your dentist, and me, a virtual stranger to you. Nothing or no one else is inside this box, not even your parents. Marriage doesn't work this way. She needs to be in here with you. She's your partner, not a tool sent for your one-sided pleasure."

"One-sided? I am no savage," he murmured.

"I don't believe you are."

"Your readers do." His fingers yanked through his thick beard in a combing manner. His eyes were in the corner of the room.

"My real ones, the ones that trust me to be the author and don't try to co-write *my* stories know I wouldn't have taken you on if you were not good at the core and redeemable." He finally looked at me. "I can work with you."

"I just don't like the way I'm being perceived."

Another client reading my reviews while under my care.

I shook my head, dismissing his anxiety. "Ezra, we're privileged to even be privy to your personal life. Your marriage is sacred: the details that get you to your custom-made *happily ever after* are a personal matter."

He scoffed. "And that's it. It doesn't matter that I'm being dragged through the mud like some caveman?"

"I'm there with you as the author. I'd say your story resonates. The few who have callous things to say are those who choose to pry, is how I see it. My stripes haven't changed. This will be our tenth book, and I'm writing the same length, in the same fashion. It's safe to say I'm established. If they don't like what I present, they can stop reading. Bottom line."

Ezra sat up, exhaled his frustration, and rubbed his palms into his face.

"Ezra, you have to trust me. I master journeys of this nature. Go through the darkness of process. It's going to hurt, but if you want it, let go of those things keeping you from giving her what she needs. Once you achieve that, you'll see brighter days. I promise."

"Okay." He sighed again, flashing his palms that gestured his compliance.

"And please stop reading my reviews. It'll impede your journey. I promise you, I don't lose a night of sleep over them. Either I'm for you, or I'm not. If I'm not, get off my boat. The same can be said for your marriage. Either you want to meet Lex half way, or you don't. If you don't, release her so she can find someone who will account for her wellbeing. Just like my readers, the choice is yours, sir."

Ezra's head swung up, his nose scrunched in disgust. I tossed my head back and cracked up.

"See! That doesn't even have the same appeal as when she says it." I tried calming myself.

"Let me assure you, no one has the same appeal as that woman, Love."

"Good. Great start!" I glanced at the clock. "We're still twenty minutes or so ahead of your appointment, but let's get started."

"It is well," he agreed, sitting back on the couch.

"Where your treasure is, there your heart will be also."

Luke 12:34

~one~

~Ezra~

"'Tis so sweet…to trust in Jesus. Just to take Him at His word…"

I crooned the first few lyrics of Louisa M. Stead's venerable psalm. This early afternoon at my baby grand, my coordinated fingers stroked the Shea Norman rendition, desperate for Him to hear my plea. I needed His attention, and for nearly two weeks, I felt as if He'd hidden Himself from me.

"Just to rest upon His promise…"

I was admittedly in despair, saturated with grief I couldn't extrapolate or conquer. At the piano in my living room, I tapped each key with the passion of never having been a man of chaos or disorder. And now, in this empty house that had never felt so vacant prior to including two occupants, I never felt so hollow.

"Jesus…Jesus, how I trust You…"

My lungs cried my heart's sorrows and appeal, yearning for His face. He'd turned away from me...just like her. He promised me *this*. It was our agreement eight years ago. Our covenant. I'd taken on my due birthright. The ministry. I'd been devoting my every waking moment to spread His gospel: preached anointed sermons, laid hands, counseled, fasted, sought His face, petitioned His hand...sacrificed my flesh.

"Just to rest upon His promise..."

Admittedly, I'd seen more terrifying circumstances, faced even graver turmoil—true menace...greater threats. Risks that were self-inflicted, albeit. Nonetheless, my life could have been taken on casual whim. I'd been spared from subjects who played by a different set of rules. Sinister extremists, whose greatest fear was not being killed but being conquered. I'd been delivered from their hands. *But this...* It was internal combat. I had never before felt the inner conflict I'd been subjected to in recent days.

"I thank You for the grace to trust You more..."

I had to believe He'd deliver me from the traps of this stronghold as well. He'd show up and bring respite—revelation about this quandary that zapped every bit of vitality from me. I had no zest to function. No zeal to impart.

"'Tis so sweet to trust in Daddy... Just to rest upon His promise..."

I sang it from the depths of my need. The emptiness of my ability to hope. *I trusted she was it*. That she had been the *right one*. And now, she was gone. No sign of covenant. That wounded me more than anything. How could I begin to attempt a resolve without Him? This arrangement was *His* doing. She was *His* object for my purpose. I would not make the wrong move; run after and drag her back here to demand she get in line with His will. This was something they'd have to work out without my participation.

I don't know how long I played and sang. I just knew the overwhelmingly deep dolor that weighted my spirit. It was also utterly clear to me these were those 'first world' emotions I'd succumbed to. Why had I felt so afflicted? What did it mean that I'd been counting down to the sweet moments until I would no longer awake to a day filled with grey despair? Grey anguish was worse than black. Black skies are followed by the morning sunlight. Grey hovered with ambiguity of time: you didn't know when your deliverance would come.

"Just to know it was said by God..."

The moment I realized my grieving had been in a manner reminiscent of David's, I closed the hymn, being sure to call upon the rusty discipline of my chords to land strong and with precision. My digits pressed into the keys of the piano just as meticulously. Each stroke slow and drawn out, again describing my glumness.

I sat up on the bench, straightening my spine, needing to prepare to go. I had a call to make before doing so; and therefore, needed to get started. That's when I heard rustling behind me. I turned, not knowing who I expected to see, but in sheer shock of having an uninvited guest.

She stood at the entrance of the room. Her slimming frame resting on a pillar with tears streaming down her face. My shoulders slumped and I turned away from her, unable to stand at this point. For a while, she graciously didn't speak. This gave me time to conjure words of dismissal.

"Tell me everything's fine and I'll leave, believing every word," she whispered.

I wanted to turn to her for assurance, but couldn't bear to see the despondency in her eyes. Her emotional play wasn't for the reasons she spoke of. Her tears were because of what she'd just walked in on me doing.

"All is well. Life can resume as normal," I attempted.

"She wasn't at church on Sunday, and I bet she won't be in the sanctuary tonight."

My nostrils flared. This would not be a docile visit. She came with ammunition, and I was not prepared.

"All couples fight, Mother."

"But not all couples call it quits in under a year."

That's when I turned to her. "No one's calling it quits."

"That young lady started coming to both morning worship services and sat in the same pew each Bible study. She's not by your side as first lady to the pastor of one of the most prestigious organizations on this side of the country. Don't tell me nobody's calling it quits!" she yelped her maternal leverage.

I hadn't heard that screech in years. It had no less effect either. I turned back to the baby grand, taking another deep breath. The last person I needed to see me in this state, carrying out my indiscernibly pitchy emotions via song was my mother.

"She's doing what you've resented me for not doing all these years. She's putting her foot down."

"You have no idea what our problems are," I challenged her with a creased forehead.

"Ezra, you are *my* child! *My* joy, *my* headache, *my* heartache! I *know* it was you who ran that girl away!" She pushed off the pillar, padding toward me with angry eyes. The closer she grew, the more I could recognize a difference in her appearance. My mother was indeed thinner. Her face painted with more makeup than I was used to seeing. She didn't speak for a while, and that irked me.

"I'm not the type of man to run to his mother about marital pangs," I grated.

She rolled her eyes, waving off the notion. "You think that's what I'm expecting? I may have driven all the way out here to see about you two, but I ain't so foolish to believe you're going to give me an ounce of detail that would begin to make sense of the strange man you are." My eyes widened then retracted. She was right. My mother may have never agreed with my personality traits, but she'd always protected me from a world that wanted to dissect my mind. "I made you. I may not get you, but I know the good stock that's in you. I know you're more of Bishop Travois Daniels than you are Bishop Sylvester Carmichael."

A grunt erupted in the back of my throat at the mention of my beloved grandfather. I swallowed it, just as I'd been accustomed to doing. I was grateful for the comparison. Honored by it.

"When did she leave?"

"Who said she left, Mother?" I cringed, accosted.

My mother rolled her heavy eyes, sucking her teeth as she took a seat next to me on the bench. I scooted over to make room.

"Now, I may not be the best example of a wife, but being a laboring mother ain't all that optional when you truly love your child. You're my only one, Ezra. And I may have let you run across the world all those years ago, but I did it believing in that gut feeling I've always had about you. You do what's right. And when it doesn't want to get right, you make it right." She patted my knee, gazing beyond the piano. "You may need time, but you always manage to get people and things in order. Don't fall short of that in your own home, son."

I blinked, stretching my lids. "This one may be beyond my influence," I murmured, intentionally to myself.

She scoffed. "You're a therapist, sweetheart. I'm sure you two were working through it in your own way. Hang on to that, Ezra. It ain't the world's business how you last, as long as you last."

That struck a new course of thinking. Me working *with* Alexis on the trauma from her attack. I'd never considered it, because I hadn't known it was still an issue.

Because you didn't care to assess it.

Perhaps...but it didn't matter to me—*doesn't matter to me.*

We're all new creatures in Christ—

That thought was thwarted by Alexis' haunting words. *"You never pray with me. Never minister to me."*

Christ...

She was right: I objectified my gift. I'd never looked at Alexis as a wife. I'd only looked *past* her, to God for delivering His end of the bargain. I took the gift and ran, so to speak. I viewed her as a blossomed flower, instead of a seed needing to be watered and properly nurtured to grow.

My mother nudging me called my attention back to her.

"I have to go. Need to get cleaned up for service tonight. I would ask if you're okay with preaching, but that's the one area of your life that doesn't seem to be affected. Your father won't admit it, but he admires that about you. You can impart a word in the fiery pits of hell if you think it's going to save souls."

That thought warmed me as she rubbed my shoulder. I was partially dressed in suit pants and an unbuttoned shirt. When otherwise my unkempt presentation would have been an issue for me, being informally clothed in front of my mother while she nurtured me was what I needed.

Her strong regard met mine as she whispered, "I believe in Ezra."

I swallowed hard and jaw clenched, resenting the budding emotion from her dutiful visit. I was no momma's boy, and yet her presence had been weighty. It was a stark notification of how out of sorts my life must appear on the outside. She was covering me in the only way a mother knew to. That mantra sealed the deal.

"And I believe in Ezra."

She smiled, her features weary, but her spirit fiercely bold.

"Before I go..." she gestured to the keys of the piano. *"Amen*, please."

"Mother, I have an important call to make before I leave for service. I don't have time," I attempted fruitlessly.

She'd caught me doing what she dreamed for me since I was a boy. Playing the keys and singing prided her. I could attribute this to the presence of Alexis in my life. I hadn't sung publicly in decades, and rarely sat here and played the baby grand. Today, I felt the need to view this as an instrument rather than a piece of furniture.

Perhaps because of the fond memory of her on it.

"All those years of lessons, young man. The least you could do is give me a few minutes of your craft." She clutched her chest. "I tell the world how my son has the best voice around. It's too bad it's one of your many gifts you didn't pursue." Nodding again, she requested, *"Amen."*

Taking another deep breath, my hands rose over the keys as I tapped the first I thought would give me a good introduction to Andraé Crouch's

Amen. As I began yielding into the number, my anxiety suspended. My spirit man opened to the submission of God when I affirmed that His will was well with my soul. I'd been in this submissive spiritual position for eight years, and while I'd seen His hand as a result, I had my bouts with my own flesh. And not in a sexual regard: flesh can be personified in our conduct and thoughts. Quite often in life, we have to temper our flesh to receive what God has for us. It's in our control and therefore must be our decided execution. Sometimes, we have to take our hands off the matter, simply stretch them to the heavens, and say, "Amen."

"Faith must be...in what you say..."

I no longer felt my mother at my side at some point. And once I was done, a glance around the room confirmed she'd slipped out while I had been caught up. My mother's visit gave me every bit of the revelation needed to, at least, get through tonight's Bible study. I stood from the bench and stretched. The past twelve days had been challenging. My eating, sleeping, and focus had been off. However, I'd been able to manage.

Gaiting out of the living room, en route to my office, I pulled my mobile phone from my pocket and called Montgomery. My fingers combed through my beard as I awaited his answer.

"Pastor," he greeted.

"Any update, Montgomery?"

"Not at this time, sir. There seems to be the same volume of people going in and out, but no calls to the police department or ruckus. So far, they've been able to keep it contained."

"And Alexis?" I asked, needing to be sure she stayed away from the hot spot her reckless father had created.

"She's still at the *Hyatt*, sir with very little movement. She hasn't been to visit the apartment."

"Good." I let out a silent *'thank you, God'* as I arrived at my desk. "Let's just pray this remains the case."

I sat behind my desk in my office, fighting against using the newfound ability to track Alexis' whereabouts by just logging into a website an acquaintance of mine from Oxford created. It was an underground application that had not yet been approved for retail. He sent it out two years ago to a few people in its testing phase. I had no desire to track anyone until the night Alexis went out to the club with her girlfriend, Anushka. That night, I made a call all the way out to Japan to get assistance on how to use this impending software.

This time, I went about keeping up with her in a less direct method: Montgomery. Since Alexis left her apartment to live with me, I had him looking into matters that concerned her and therefore me. The moment she left my home almost two weeks ago, I tightened up my surveillance to be sure of her safety. Yes. I knew where my wife had been staying since the day she left me. Once I was able to drag my body from the corridor floor that day, I contacted Montgomery for her tracking.

It relieved me to no end that Alexis decided to check into a hotel here in West Milford instead of going back to her apartment in the city. She took Ms. Remah with her. Apparently, Ms. Remah left before I returned home from church on Valentine's Day. That action alone led me to believe this was all thought out by my wife, perhaps while I was at *RSfALC*, waiting on them to arrive. Once I could get over the deliberation of the mass exodus, I could be grateful for them not returning to Harlem. That would have been disastrous and difficult to contain.

Still my chest twisted with the feelings of betrayal and resentment that I struggled with daily. I felt more powerless than ever in my adult years. My anger positioned me to pounce with vengeance. My spirit heeded me to sit back and act with caution. Which action I'd lead with, I didn't know from hour to hour.

~Lex~

Holy shit! It worked.

I woke up without the sharp stab of pain in my chest and stirring anxiety in my belly for the first time in days.

Prayer. I tried it. The first night I left the most peaceful place I'd ever called home, I couldn't sleep. I twisted and turned all night, imagining the stubborn, overbearingly controlling, and spiritual Ezra was likely sleeping restfully, assured in his position to move along with his acceptance of my leaving. I had to save face for Ms. Remah, so I rose early the following morning, fell to my knees, and did something he'd advised in almost every sermon: prayed.

I prayed the way he'd taught me. I opened with praise, moved on with my desperate requests, and then ended in praise again. I didn't get obnoxious and greedy with my requests. I just needed the pain of loss to go away. Each time I opened my legs to Ezra since he'd dragged me out of the club that night with Anushka, I now realized I'd been giving him a piece of me. Ezra dangled the possibility of unconditional love in front of my scared heart.

I hadn't realized that until a few nights ago when I soundlessly cried myself to sleep for the umpteenth time.

Ms. Remah and I had been at a hotel since Valentine's Day. I checked us into a double bed, the only type of room available that Sunday morning I decided to abandon the covenant I made with my husband. There was a saltwater fishing conference in the area, and only one room available, according to the front desk staff when I called while tossing clothes in a duffle during a panicking fit. I had suddenly come to the decision when I realized my husband couldn't love me as I had fallen for him. It hit me some kind of hard. After enduring that first night with his frenzied calls and texts, I hadn't heard from Ezra. And this was fine with me. I had more pressing shit to deal with.

I chanced a glance over to the next bed, hoping to have a few minutes to myself to get my head together before I faced her. Too late. Ms. Remah was sitting up on her bed, facing the window. My shoulders dropped.

"Morning," I tried through the morning gravel.

She grunted in response. Her round frame sat slumped against the grey early morning clouds. I rubbed my tight eyes, feeling like shit.

"Another rough one? I know it was for me."

It had been another restless night for her as well. Each night we'd spent here was rough.

"De good doctor say wrong, huhn?" She snorted. "All t'ese years."

No. *That* hadn't been the cause of my sleepless nights, but I wasn't in the mood to cry about a broken heart.

"If it makes you feel any better, waking up was easier than sleeping through the night," I tried.

"Mi old, Lexi," she grumbled. "Back no good fuh de bed."

I sighed. She'd suffered through this enough. This was it. I had to push a little harder.

"I know." I sighed, cupping my forehead. "I swear I won't be upset if you and Oscar went back to the house."

"And leave yuh 'ere to eat burgers all day? Mi go back without yuh?" She tutted, unable to turn back to face me.

My eyes went down to the table where her pet fish swam in his mobile tank. Even he was ready to return home, I would've bet.

"You won't be betraying me. I won't even be upset. The time alone would be good for me. I know you need to go back for health reasons. You can't keep sleeping on this mattress with your back."

I knew her biggest issue was her back. The hotel's mattress was no good for the six herniated discs in her spine. In the fall, for her birthday, I purchased her an expensive ass *TEMPUR-Ergo* bed. It was recommended by her doctor as, not a cure all, but an aide for pressure points, and frame molding.

"What could it possibly be, huhn?"

To make me leave. She wanted to know what terrible thing Ezra could have possibly done to make me want to pack up and go. The thought of permanently leaving terrified me, even after seven short months. He'd given us full rein of his home, giving us the feel of autonomy over it. If it was a calculated act of manipulation, it worked.

"I'm too ashamed to admit it, but he's not dangerous. I don't believe he's capable of harming me, you, or anyone. He had plenty of opportunities to show his hand."

Not to mention I'd given him reason to by trying to spit in his face.

She tutted again. This time I could feel the admonition in it.

"You dun't nuh shame, galy. You dun't nuh tuff calls," she grumbled, her back still to me.

My heart pounded with resentment.

"What if it's because he likes to spank me to get off?"

I could see her chin lifting. "Do yuh get off, too?"

What?

"What does that matter?"

She turned to face me with squinted eyes. "Means yuh like it, too. Men 'ave strong needs, yuhnuh. Ezra got strange taste. If he hurt yuh, yuh go. Mi kill 'em next! T'row mi inna jail!" Her belly leaped with conviction at that. "But if him teach yuh fuh yuh *and* him, yuh grow wit 'em. You American galys. Yuh believe in a...novels and movies." Her arms flagged. "Yuh tink it means real love. Commitment. Sacrifice. Learning." She tutted again, shaking her head. "*You*," she pronounced fully, "together make fi yuh own happiness."

Tears pooled in my eyes.

"But what if that's just his happiness and not mine?" I argued, mouth balled tight with anger.

She shot to her feet faster than I'd known her capable of doing. "You tink I dun't nuh what you two do in de basement? How wild and loud yuh scream, yuhnuh? Yuh dun't tink I see the glint in yuh eyes and de marvel in his around de house when he look pon yuh? But yuh want it de way yuh want it only. He want it de way he want it only. Ezra ah strange mon, but he no monster. Yuh say so yuh self. Grow up! Yuh ah nah baby, Lexi!" she cried.

"What do you know? You've never been married!" I charged back, stinging from her blows.

I did this—married—for her, and now she was telling me I hadn't done it right?

"Listen, likle gyal," she hissed lowly, mouth contorted. "Mi nuh married because mi was de fool, believing it should 'ave been one way. Mi didn't put me first, tinking bout everybody except fi mi! I still live wit regret, yuhnuh. Mi still alone. Nuh help. Nuh companionship. Old, yuhnuh—sick wit nuh body but a girl I dun't birth." She turned to walk away, trying to take a breather, but she came right back in my direction. "Yuh better t'en mi, Lexi. Stronger!" she cried. "You nuh let people in yuh head, but yuh let dem beat on yuh heart, yuhnuh." She shook her head.

"Who?" my vocals quivered. "Who did you let in your head that's made you live with this regret, Ms. Remah?" She tutted, turning away from me. I was partially afraid to push her, and the other half desperate to challenge her. But I wanted to know how she could rebuke me with so much conviction. When had she been in my shoes or in others far more damning? "Tell me! Have you ever loved?"

She planted her fist on the table next to Oscar's tank. Her shoulders curled over as she shook her head frustrated.

"Mi in love when I was a likle gyal. Mi mada and fadda wanted him fi mi likle sister. He wanted mi and mi wanted him long before. We been lovers before then, but nobody knew. Wi parents insisted on dem getting married. It was bad—ah big deal back then, yuhnuh. I left for de States. They pressured him. Mi sister wanted it, too. Nobody knew mi had a baby in mi belly. Mi sister married him and came to follow me. They found me and saw de growing belly. He was angry...told her de truth. Said he wanted to be wit me and iz baby. But she nuh want to part fram him. She threatened to tell mi parents. We dun't want to shame de families. I was in school, by mi self—no man. No help. No money from back home. Mi sister was evil!" she cried.

"She was jealous even doh mi told her they could go on wit each other. He dun't like it, but it was fuh de best. I dun't tink about me heart. I only used mi head back den. Mi gave dem mi baby."

I leaped on my knees from the bed.

Her niece is her daughter?

Holy shi—

"Lillian?" I gasped at the sudden revelation.

With her back to me, Ms. Remah tutted.

"Wait... Does she even know?"

She couldn't have. At least she hadn't told me.

Ms. Remah stood straight, extending her spine. "Grow up, Lexi. Yuh ah nuh pickney."

She wobbled toward the bathroom, closing the conversation. There were so many things I wanted to know, countless questions I had to ask.

Nonetheless, it was clear she was done with the topic of her past. She had illustrated her point of choosing the heart over the brain, though I wasn't clear on which was appropriate in my situation.

"I go back. Mi give yuh time to t'ink, but not fi long."

My mouth fell again. I was happy that she would be returning to her rightful bed, but didn't like giving her the impression that I was a brat. 'The American galy', as she put it.

"It's not just about the weird way he goes about sex, Ms. Remah. As you so curtly pointed out, I seemed to get off on it, too. It's bigger than that. Sex is the one thing he masters. It's all he knows. He can teach a course on it." I swallowed back a cry and whispered, "He doesn't love me."

"Den teach him!"

She slammed the door on me with that one.

I sank back on the bed, my spirit more broken than when I woke up. This conversation established the end to my quiet retreat where no one bothered to question or judge my call. I'd called out of work without pushback, and had furled up in this hotel bed, only leaving for the doctors and the restaurant downstairs. I'd developed a fondness for their burgers—more like an obsession.

It was time for me to come out of hiding. It may not have been the ideal one, but I had a life to pursue. Brighter days to chase. One thing was for sure: I had to return to work. I'd spent enough time licking my wounds. I had to face the music, and try to move on with my life.

Harlem Pride.

~Ezra~

"Here's the membership renewal report Shannon left for you," Monica, a new administrative assistant, informed as she placed a bonded portfolio on my desk. "Oh, and a Tony Dungy called about setting up a meeting with you and Trent Bailey."

Tony Dungy?

I gave a sightless bow. "Thanks."

"Is that all I can do for you, Pastor?" she asked respectfully in tone, but recognizably in a suggestive attempt.

I sat back in my chair and rubbed my strained eyes. I was exhausted and unbelievably wound up from personal, professional, and ministerial matters. The last thing I needed was another unprofessional subordinate trying for my attention. This was precisely why I'd changed *RSfALC*'s business approach. They hired people based on social merit and not competent ones. Monica here was Sister Shannon's cousin, from Florida, who my father hired without an interview. She'd been collecting more and more hours as Sister Shannon had returned to school. Monica received undocumented training and had made it known for weeks she was interested in being more than my professional subordinate without being direct.

"That will be all, Sister Monica. Thanks." I supplied a tight smile.

Rude, I knew, but I was in a low tolerance type of mood. She stood in front of my desk with her breasts nearly bursting through her undersized cotton blouse, and jeans that looked like second skin. And to make the sight more unpleasant were the burgundy *Ugg* boots covering her feet.

"You so quiet all the time." She shifted her meaty weight from hip to hip while playing with her fingers. "I be wanting to talk to you, to see if you need stuff, but you…"

I cocked a brow. "I what?"

"You scary." She giggled, her eyes bouncing between the end of the desk and me.

"Is that right?"

"Yeah." Her southern accent was conspicuous. "Shannon told me you all business, but I know men like to let it hang *some* time." Her eyes were locked into mine now. "You don't have to call me Sister. Monica works. I know where we at and all."

"Do you attend services here, Sister Monica?"

"Yeah, since I started."

"And that was when?"

"'Bout four months ago."

Since I took over.

As if on cue, Precious walked in with her arms filled with files.

"Then you should recognize the moral outfit of this organization." Her forehead creased in confusion, simultaneously Precious stopped in her tracks. "*Redeeming Souls for Abundant Living in Christ* is a Christian-based organization. Inside these four walls, we conduct ourselves as children of the Kingdom by practice and name. We refer to each other by our Kingdom titles. We are children of the Kingdom; brothers and sisters in Christ. If you're inside these four walls, you're engaged in Kingdom business. In here, you're Sister Monica, because we are about our Father's business. That is the only agenda you should be concerned about. As far as me letting 'it hang' while I'm 'all about my business,' you should know it is my Father's business that I'm about. Am I clear, Sister Monica?"

Her lashes fluttered with manic speed and she exhaled deeply. "Yes, Pastor Carmichael."

"I am very pleased. You may leave now."

When the door closed, Precious snorted. "Wow. We're going to stay understaffed if you plan on ripping people in two."

My chin reared. "You weren't privy to the exchange before you came in here, or the suggestive expressions and glances she's doled out over the months since she arrived."

"I'm surprised you were with the way you've been so buried in the books around here." She stood straight, a crease marring her forehead.

"Am I supposed to be doing something else?"

"What I mean is you need to loosen up. I know you're going through with your marriage ending, but it may have helped for you to be nice to her. I'm sure you could use the distraction right about now."

Distraction?

"Precious, I can understand what you're used to when it comes to pastoral conduct and infidelity, but you should know better than to think I'm about those games."

She took a shuddering breath, clearly hesitant about unleashing something.

"Ezra, you did it. You tried to go do your own thing, and went out and got a woman to marry. After a while, I understood your need to try it your way. I've always been turned on by the rebellion in you. But it's backfired this time. It didn't work. *RSfALC* needs strong leadership in the wake of the Bishop. We don't need an uptight pastor who can't function because his wife doesn't understand her role."

"And what role is that?" I asked, fighting my incredulous reactions.

"Knowing when the Monicas of the world can actually be a help when things at home aren't right," she argued, holding her ground.

I hadn't seen this offensive side of her since my days at *Pepperdine*.

"Is that what The Good Bishop has brainwashed you to believe? That it's okay to entertain the Monicas of the world?"

Though it should've been no surprise, my heart was breaking for her. These were souls that my father had misguided through his immoral practices over the years. My mother, by allowing my father free rein, had encouraged this tainted mentality.

"He's taught me to understand no man is perfect. We've all fallen short of His glory. Even those untamed hearts like yours end up following the rules at some point."

"Following what rules?" my voice had finally elevated.

"Ezra, we could have cut out all of this messiness—the stripper emails, her overall lack of church etiquette! Jeeze, Ezra," she sighed. "Your father doesn't even like her. Your mother seems to tolerate her, but I don't see Mary taking her under her wing, and that says a lot."

I noticed she referred to Alexis' dismay as the stripper emails rather than her brutal attack being rehashed for people's entertainment. People who didn't care for her enough to show compassion, instead they spread the horrible memories of her rape.

I stood to my feet. "And what would have been the better alternative?"

"*ME!*" she screamed at the top of her lungs, scaring herself with the level of emotion she exuded. "I've tried the route of being quiet, compliant, and obedient to everything you asked for eight years now. I haven't pushed. I even went to your wedd—" She lost her breath. "I know we had that big misunderstanding when we were younger, but you should know as a man of God, forgiveness is necessary. I'm sorry, Ezra. I misunderstood you. I didn't know any better. I was twenty years old. You were into things that you had no business fooling around with and tried to rope me into them, and it didn't work. When are you going to get over it? I did!"

Her red eyes rimmed with tears. She was exploding. I hadn't seen this degree of emotion from her since we were in our early twenties, after she decided we were no longer brother and sister-like, and expressed her attraction to me. I never understood the switch. I was a twenty-two year old with an uncontrolled libido that led my decision-making process. The first time I had Precious was one night while I was home on Christmas break during my third year of school. She had been coming on to me so strong since the start of my second term at college, but our physical distance didn't lend itself to much. We kept in touch throughout the years, and I'd cared about her to a great degree. Precious was wildly attractive and smart.

When she visited me in California my senior year, expressively ready to further explore what we'd initiated months before, I tried to introduce her to the world I'd recently subscribed to. It all went downhill from there.

"Look… I'm sorry." Precious swiped her forehead, her eyes focused into the distance. "It's been the pressure of it all: *"Be patient. He'll come around." "You two are meant to be together. Ezra just goes about things his own way." "You're a beautiful, smart girl. He'll see it soon." "They won't last. She's not one of us."*"

Revealing those conversations between her, Marva Graham, and my father reminded me of when I'd lost the last shred of hope for him. Along with Marva, they were the two who put her up to pursuing me as kids. Her desire was manufactured, not even of genuine interest, and it had morphed into an obsession at some point. All these years, my tactic had always been making it clear how disinterested I was.

"I'm almost forty, Ezra. Not married, no kids. The clock is running out on me. I have Seth in my ear, and while that sounds like a silver lining, even his presence in my world leads back to you. Like he can't seem to get over his disdain for you. Now he wants me to come down to Atlanta to help him run the church when Apostle Wilkinson retires next year. I can't leave *RSfALC*! Look at where we are in this transition phase! It's just...too much." She shook her head.

"As much as I sympathize with you, it's not appropriate for me to advise you on any of this other than to say, you have to live your life for yourself, Precious. You have to do what's right for you. It's what I did, what has always been the right move for me."

Her neck swung back. "How has it always been the right thing for you? I don't pretend to know exactly the state of your marriage, but I can surmise your wife isn't working out. She's called out of work all last week and haven't been this week! After this email scandal about her stripper days, I don't see you tolerating her much longer." She stepped closer to me. "Didn't you just preach on Sunday about the signs of God telling you to abandon ship? You said there are things we try to pump life into that God has already expired for our good long ago. Sometimes He goes ahead of us to curse those things that you believe are good for you, but are meant to do harm to you. I could've sworn you were sharing your testimony."

That was a decent summarization of my sermon, but totally out of context for my life.

"Precious, you should know I don't impart from personal emotion when I speak. You know my flesh is dormant while He uses me. That message was not from the experience of my marriage."

Furthermore, one way or another, Alexis and I would be fine. We had to. There was power in covenant. She would come to her senses in due time.

"Well, maybe it should be. Maybe you should look deeper into your own situation to see how it applies. It might save you a lot of time, embarrassment, and money in the long run." She abruptly turned for the door, slamming it on her way out.

I sat back in my seat and rubbed my beard, wishing I could rub the stress and increasing exhaustion away.

~two~

~Ezra~

Go…

I couldn't signal my limbs to move. In the torrential rain and obscure darkness, I sat motionless in my parked SUV. The smoke emitting from an area of the building floated into the rays of the moon, further marking the murkiness of the night sky. My eyes stared blankly at the back of the gray metallic *F-Type*. On occasion, they'd roll over to the entrance of the building in hopes of catching a glimpse of her.

That would kick your legs in gear.

Perhaps if I saw her, I'd muster the balls to snatch her up and talk some sense into her. How long would this go on? What is she thinking? I understood she had no positive examples of marriage around her growing up, and nothing to compare to a truly problem-riddled union. She had to think she was in a hopeless affair simply because she hadn't given it time so she could properly adjust. All marriages endure an adjustment period at some point. Even I struggled with having an unmade bed and disarrayed closet on most days. For neither circumstance did I feel my marriage was doomed.

Venomous anger bursting from my chest forced me to snap the handle of the door, shoulder it open and leap outside. I didn't go far. I made it to the hood of my truck and rested against it, crossing one leg over the other. The moment I questioned my actions in this type of weather, I realized the conditions were acclimated to my mood. Cold and...an unnamed and unfamiliar disposition. My chest tightened at the revelation of an ache, my lungs seized, and eyes blurred. I experienced misfortunes and disappointments in the context of interpersonal relationships: romantic and platonic.

I'd had passionate differences of opinions with professors in my academic tenure; made difficult decisions as a leader in my current role regarding people I truly cared about; had several women I regretfully distanced myself from when I realized they had developed feelings I could never reciprocate, and had seen innocent and harmless women and children thrust into desperate lifestyles that I was appointed to govern—all of these circumstances evoking a deep empathetic regard to varying degrees. I could also extrapolate those sentiments to properly manage them. *But this...* I'd never felt the miscellany of...cutting emotions in my life.

Cacao legs... Dilated eyes when I'm explaining my morning sermon at her request... Full lips, a pounding chest at my touch... Round mounds spread, awaiting my ministrations... Timid vocal chords when asking to be taught how to pray...

"I'M IN LOVE WITH YOU, YOU STUPID, CONTROLLING, SOCIOPATHIC SON OF A BITCH!"

My breathing grew erratic, lungs struggled to keep up with my need for air. I couldn't feel my feet, and abruptly my left palm smacked the hood of the truck for balance. I stood, bent over, desperately praying to stay on my feet for what seemed like an eternity. Slowly, my breathing wound down to a point that ebbed the panic, but my lungs still worked overtime, eyes remained blurred, and my head wouldn't stop its rotation.

"Sir..." I vaguely heard...again. "I said, are you okay? Are you locked out of your vehicle?" I snapped my neck toward a woman of Asian descent holding an umbrella that swallowed her small frame. "I can ask the people at the front desk to call *Triple A*."

I struggled, but successfully stood straight as I possibly could. With a swaying neck, I tried to convince her, "I'm fine. Thank you."

Jesus...

Immersed in embarrassment, I resumed my faculties. I shakily backed up for the driver's door and climbed inside. She backed away from my truck, giving me room to pull off. I berated myself on the way home. Never in my life had I ever become so diluted—so overcome to the point of losing myself unless under the power of the Holy Spirit. That was not the same sensation. What I felt could be likened to hopelessness and a loss of...control. Powerlessness. The last time I felt so lost in helplessness, I was in a wadi in Oman, Saudi Arabia, laid out prostrate, tearfully petitioning God.

How could I be back here?

Before I knew it, I was pulling into the garage of my home. I walked into the rear corridor, not bothering to hang my coat in the garage to let it drain. In the wadi, I left with a solution: a covenant with my sovereign God. Tonight, I left the hotel with empty confidence. I just wanted to lose myself in the obscurity of the darkness in the guest bedroom. It was how I slept of late. I couldn't go into the master suite, except to dress. That was her domain. Her rightful sanctum. It felt so natural and right with her in there.

Just as I was about to turn the corner for the back staircase, the chime on the back sliding door leading to the deck sounded. I reared back and caught a round frame saunter in with an air of familiarity.

Ms. Remah?

I sucked in a breath. "You're here?"

I detested the shriek in my discovery. No real man should be able to produce such a squeal. It was borne of desperation.

"Mi can't?" she contested with her chin in the air.

"Of course you can! It's your home...and hers." I tried squaring my shoulders to conceal my unspoken inquiry.

Alexis couldn't be here. I'd just left her Jaguar at the hotel.

Ms. Remah eyed me warily. Her regard went to my soaked coat and shoes, and back up to my eyes.

"Mi nuh baby, Ezra," she warned with splayed nostrils.

She could visibly see my weakened state. At any other time I'd be embarrassed, feel my manhood was compromised. Tonight, I felt a sign of relief. I may not have verbalized my confirmation of her perception of my state of mind, but her presence, oddly, had been a relieving factor.

The air grew thick as I asserted silence. Similar to her non-biological daughter, our stubborn spirits warred mutedly.

...until I broke.

"I don't know what to do. How do I even approach her?"

She huffed while making her way to the stove for the tea kettle. The kitchen grew silent for longer than I preferred. She filled the pot, set it on the stove and lit the eye while resting on one hip. Out of nowhere, Ms. Remah fired off a string of words in her native tongue, too rich for me to decipher.

She turned toward me with a tough regard never seen from her. "Yuh affi deal wit her good! Or next time, mi kill yuh myself, Ezra!"

I swallowed every ounce of pride for her audacity. By no means was I in any position to challenge her at this height of her anger. No. I actually believed she'd try to take my life with little thought. I managed a stiff nod in assent of her warning.

"In de emergency room, when patients of violent crimes come into the unit, we ask if t'ere's anybody they dun't want to come visit—yuhnuh, for protection. When that young girl came in, she had big scary eyes. When dey asked her questions she answered them with big eyes and little breath. I stood t'ere with de security and asked her if t'ere was anybody she dun't want to come. She said nuhbody!" her voice grew animated, arms flagging. "I asked her why her eyes so big? Why she talk that way. She said because she was a warrior. She couldn't cry. Then she went out from de meds. That girl was in so much pain, yuhnuh!" Ms. Remah cupped her stomach, cringing. "But she nuh cry for a long time. T'ere was a lion in there. I knew it. Never seen nuttin' like it. No mada, no fadda—nobody. She stayed in that bed and controlled di pain from wit'in."

Goosebumps layered my skin, and my stomach turned violently. I could envision my beloved bruised, battered, broken, and alone in that hospital room. Praise God for Ms. Remah having the insight to join lives with her. To cover her. Where would she be now if someone hadn't stepped in? She could have easily fallen into psychosis or severe stress-induced depression.

Ms. Remah's grunt called my attention from the floor.

"Mi never seen di girl so...soft on eh man—never try so hard fuh nobody! She dun't know fi long time, but she felt you here"—she pointed to her chest—"because she thought she could handle you here!" Her index finger directed my eyes to her pelvis. "All she wanted was acceptance from you. With you it was different, Ezra. I dun't nuh what you agreed on. Mi come back from home to see she had a man to marry." Her emotions were springing to life in the clarity of her dialect, contrary to Bishop Jones when he was spirited. "But you!" She sucked in her tongue. "You give her motion in di ocean 'den leave her out t'ere alone in the trouble waters."

Anger filled her eyes.

I sucked in a breath. "I'm trying to understand where I went wrong and how I can improve; you have my word, Ms. Remah."

"Di hotel restaurant. Bacon cheeseburger: lettuce tomatoes, red onions—*nuh yellow*—red onions, mayonnaise, ketchup, and five pickles."

With water dripping from my beard, I nodded. It was a small concession; a wellspring coming from this cantankerous woman. Something that would cause me to be more graceful with her moving forward. I was now indebted to Ms. Remah for the unforeseen future.

That night, the hollowness in my chest was replaced by a spark of possibility. Conceivably, I could gain the reins of this madness in my world. Ms. Remah's return and her atypical perspective gave me the push I needed to confront this madness that was my fugitive wife.

~Lex~

"Hand me those *Max 95s* over there in the corner," I directed while locating the last recorded count on the inventory sheet.

"Ugh!" she grumbled before backing up to the other stepladder. "Is you listening to me, yo? We can run up on that bitch. I know where she be at."

I bit the top of the mechanical pencil as I considered numbers in the back of *Peewee's Champion Runway* sneaker store. I thought I'd seen my last days in this storage room, but he called with a sad IRS story, and, per usual, I came running to assist.

"Here!" Tasche began pushing stacks of six piled shoeboxes in my direction. Thankfully, none collapsed, making a mess I didn't feel like cleaning up. She was frustrated. "This the last one, I think."

She climbed back down and sat on the ladder. I counted them and recorded the number.

"Fuck, Peewee!" I mumbled, rolling my eyes.

Sick of counting the same numbers time after time because his tight ass don't want to put shit on sale for the purpose of moving stock!

Again, I had no idea how he stayed in business this long, only selling less than a dozen pairs of shoes a day. And then with a major chain right down the street!

"Lex, man, I swear to god, that bitch foul for what she did. I liked Ny and all because you vouched for her all these years." She pointed her index finger in the air and spoke with a threatening scowl as she faced the wall. "But I swear, something been off with her, and how she been getting at you for a minute now." Then she shrugged. "Truthfully, it's been since you brought her around. You ever think Ny liked you in the first place? Like *really* liked you?"

The same moment I saw her face me in my peripheral, I caught her implication. The pencil fell from my mouth.

"The hell you say, Tash?"

She shrugged again, her tongue quickly swiping her full chocolate lips. Those raccoon circles around her eyes loosened as she hesitated.

"I on't know, Lex. I been thinking about this shit since you was planning your wedding and shit. Then at Peaches' birthday joint at *Diamond's* that night Ny, was poppin' them bottles and talkin' mad shit." Her mouth balled with visible resentment.

"Talking what, Tasche?" I urged.

"I on't know." She shrugged, staring straight ahead. "Just mad shit."

"Look, Tash, if you think I'm gonna get mad because of it, don't stress yaself. I'm good." I partially fibbed, though it held so much truth to it.

"It's just now... Hind sight is fuckin' twenty/twenty, and I wish I woulda checked her ass then. Maybe this shit woulda never went down. I didn't know she was coming for you like that though. I swear, Lex!" She pounded her chest with her fist. "I took her in on the strength of you. She ain't Harlem World. You and me, we Renaissance High all fuckin' day! You know?"

I got it. My friend was feeling guilty for sensing Nyree's treacherous ways before I did, and not checking her. I couldn't be upset. It was my responsibility. I'd been avoiding doing it myself. Things had been getting tense between Ny and me—mostly on her part.

That fucking Ezra!

When he came into my life, everything got tossed to some damn elusive place. Talk about having your world turned upside down. I'd literally told myself after Nyree's engagement party, when she made a comment about me being so desperate to bring Pablo, and that her mother would certainly sniff out the trash in *both* of us with that decision. I said I would check her on it, but never did because that's when that motherfucker, Ezra proposed. After that, Nyree was no longer a priority: chasing behind this strange and entrancing man had become everything.

I exhaled as I turned gingerly to sit. "Tasche, it was my responsibility to check her, not yours. Like you said, I brought her into our fold. I was so wrapped up in school, the rec, then getting married that I never addressed it...kept letting her live." I snorted. "Didn't help that I couldn't understand where the hate was coming from. I ain't never do shit to her, but stay loyal."

"Nah," Tasche shook her head. "She ain't Harlem World, Lex. She ain't a stay down bitch. That's ya problem, Lex. Ya heart too big for people. You only need to give it to your day ones"—she clapped her hands—"and ya man. Fuck err'body else, yo." Her eyes remained trained to the wall ahead as she gently scolded me.

I gave off a muted scoff.

I fucked up with giving him my heart, too, Tasche. I just fuck up all the time with this shit.

Sudden sadness engulfed me. At times like this, I wondered if my mother were still alive would I have room in my heart to let others come in and fuck things up. If I recalled correctly, her issues alone filled me to capacity. No matter how damaged or broken a mother is, her child will love her unconditionally. Because as children, we know no better. We only know the energy we get from the womb we were developed in. My eyes cast downward.

All in all, I was happy I agreed to meet my girl down here today. She'd been trying to contact me all week while I was holed up in the hotel, licking my wounds of betrayal and guarding my most prized accomplishment to date.

"How did you even find out about it?" I asked with sudden curiosity.

"My daughter's father's peoples go to your old man's church. They heard it from the office people there, or some shit." She tossed her shoulders in the air again. "She remember that shit they did to you because they all know where I work. They know you my peoples and shit."

I nodded. Harlem was indeed small, and especially if you were from here.

"So, what we gonna do? Go through the front or back with this one? Straight up! Tell me when and how, and I'm lacing my shits up, ya heard." She hesitated. "We can't go through the front. That bitch ain't gon' wanna see you."

I shook my head, swallowing back a cry for what I was about to say. I knew my mother would never approve. But before I could speak, Tasche came with an idea.

"Yo, you know she fucks with Peaches like that. I'll run up in ol' girl's mouth myself if she interferes with your ass whoopin' for Ny. Then again, Peaches Harlem World, too. She may set it up for us." She nodded. "Yeah. We can go through the back door that way."

The old and familiar adrenaline rush from planning for a fight sprouted from my chest, shooting to all my extremities. And talking to my girl about rolling up on someone only boosted it. It was a rush that never got old, or less intense. But a roil in my belly competed with it, bringing me back to reality.

"Nah, Tasche." I shook my head.

"Okay," she acquiesced, going into her jacket pocket and pulling out a box of *Newports*. "How you wanna do this shit then? And oh, I want in! That bitch played me long enough when it comes down to you. I shoulda tagged her when I peeped her card."

I panicked at the sight of the cigarette. My senses began kicking in, in high gear. The first decision was to get her the hell up out of there before she started smoking, and the second was to avoid telling her why I would not be beating Ny's ass...for a while, anyways.

"Aye, yo, Tasche," I started. "I don't think Peewee wants anybody—"

"Yo, Lex, baby," Peewee wobbled in the room just in time. "You know I ain't gon' be able to pay you, right—"

His eyes rolled over Tasche, sensing he'd caught us in the middle of something. Lucky for me, Tasche perceived it to be a warning for her not to smoke. She sucked in a labored breath as she stood to her feet.

"A'ight, Lex dawg." She nodded my way. "Get back to me with that plan. If I need to call in late, just let me know, and I'll make it happen." She turned to leave before she could catch my deep exhale. "Peace, Peewee."

"Later, Tasche." Peewee muttered behind her, wearing a confused expression. "So, like I was saying," He tapped his mustache nervously. "I'm not gonna—"

"Peewee, if my motive was money, I wouldn't have come." I sighed. "I'll be done in about twenty minutes. I can tell you now. Shit ain't looking good for you. Your inventory hasn't changed much in three years. You have to knock down these prices to get this shit outta here!" That advice came out harsher than intended.

I was tired and hungry, and just wanted to get out of the dusty storage room. Not to mention Tasche's revelation about Ny never really liking me, and my reminder of how we deal with snakes like her. I was at my limit for the day.

Just when I decided to come out of hiding.

"Fuck!" He grumbled to himself, stomping his foot. "Retros make good money, too."

"These shits ain't retros yet! You got at least seven years before you can start calling them that, Peewee! These kids don't recognize these shoes, unless they're sneaker-heads, and that's a subpopulation!"

"Fuck!" he repeated, eyes cast toward the floor. "These mufuckas really coming after my ass, Lex. They asking for five figures, yo." I could see his eyes glossing over. "I gotta do something."

I took a deep breath.

"I got a source down at the Harlem Times and the Harlem World Gazette." I pulled my bag over for my phone. "Give me dates for the sale right now. And it better be at least two weeks. I have a few other ways to get the word out, too." Peewee scratched his head, confounded. "Peewee!" I yelled, snapping his daze. "Now! Dates now!"

"A'ight! A'ight, yo!" He held his hands in the air, reminiscent of a twenty-year-old, and not a graying man of over fifty years.

"Think about who you're going to get to help you move these shoes out on the floor and closer up in this storage area for quick grabbing. I'm setting the prices my damn self."

"Lex—"

"Fuck that, Peewee!" I hissed with tight eyes. "Your way ain't worked in years. It's my way or I ain't fuckin' with you no more!"

"Okay... Okay!" His palms pumped in the air again. "I can call Sharky in tomorrow."

With my face to my phone, scrolling through my contacts, I demanded, "Tonight. Start moving this shit tonight!"

"Dayum, Lex! Okay!"

"And call Rasul's idle ass. He can use the exercise."

I heard his deep breath, but stayed in my phone.

"Yo, Lex, baby, about 'Sul..."

"Save it."

"But—"

My eyes shot into him. "I don't need his shit right now. I got enough on my plate."

"But this something that got me worried, Lex. He gambling again...with the wrong crew—"

I cringed, my eyes reflectively squeezing shut.

"I don't wanna hear it, Peewee! He's over fifty years old—*your* peer! If you know he's in some foul shit, *you* should check him on it. I'm tired, Peewee! Tired!"

I half meant what I said. I'd always felt my father was my responsibility at the end of the day. The truth of the matter was, I was extremely stressed between that damn email going viral, my nightmares having returned now that I was at the hotel alone, preparing to leave my short termed marriage, and needing a place to live again.

With widened nostrils, and eyes shooting into him like daggers as we shouldered up, I convinced him of my decision.

"A'ight. A'ight!" He backed away. "Lemme go call a few people down here to help me move this shit."

I stood motionless, holding my harsh expression until he left the storage room. I dropped back on a step of the ladder on a deep exhale. He'd unearthed a headache I'd been avoiding for the past two weeks: being my father's keeper.

I stayed at *Peewee's Champion Runway* for another two hours, planning prices, spreading the word on the blowout sale, and laying out a floor plan for the next few weeks in hopes of this plan really working.

It was dark by the time I made it back to my hotel room. I don't think I'd ever felt exhaustion like I had crawling onto my bed. I hadn't even bothered to kick off my boots, coat, or bag. Between the lighting of the moon shining through the dark room and my humming limbs, I was drugged into sleep within moments.

My bladder woke me first—

No. Maybe it was my grumbling belly, or the increasing nausea—

It was all three that had my neck lifting my head from the mattress. I warily shuffled from the bed until I was on my feet. With a few shrugs, I managed out of my coat, and after tripping over the flat floor I made it to the doorframe of the bathroom, holding on for support so I could kick off my boots. I barely made it to the toilet before my urine broke air. It was a close call. Once that deed was done, my head began to spin, threatening the contents of my empty belly.

One…two…three…

"*Foour!*" I groaned, straining to lift from my seat.

I made it to the sink and washed my hands, using my upper thighs to balance me against the countertop of the vanity. I splashed cold water on my face and took a few more deep breaths. As I turned to leave the bathroom, I was able to shed my clothes that suddenly felt unbearably tight. This was unusual for me. I never got sick and hoped it wasn't the flu. Couldn't have been: I was too damn hungry.

After pulling back the comforter and sheet, I crawled into bed, resting my back on the headboard. I needed a few moments of rest before I could pick up the phone to make the call. It would take room service at least thirty minutes to get here with food. Maybe more on a Saturday night. *Fuck!* I opened my one lid to locate the phone. I groaned. It was too far away. I'd have to get up.

Just when I tell her to go back to the house…

I wanted to cry. Feeling the first wave of blues, I wanted to cave to self-pity. I took a few deep breaths. *Not now. Not now. Not now.* It felt as though I didn't even have the energy to cry about being sick and hungry.

A knock at the door snapped my attention.

"Who is it?" I barked.

"Ezra Carmichael."

That name sent a zing down my spine. It was intimidating at first sound. Had she gotten to him? What did she say? I called to set up a meeting with Elle to talk about the church speech and all that, but not Ezra. I hadn't spoken to him since leaving him in the foyer of his home. Was I ready to sound off with him? Honestly...

Hell no!

I was sick.

"I brought food," he rasped through the door.

Without thought, I scrambled to my feet and opened the door. I didn't even look at him before diving back into the bed to cover myself. I was down to only my bra and panties. By the time I settled on the mattress, I turned to see him carrying a serving tray mounted with a metal salver. The same one the hotel uses to deliver my—

"Bacon cheeseburger? Lettuce, tomatoes, red onions—please say they're red and not yellow—"

"...red onions, mayonnaise, ketchup, and five pickles," he assured.

My shoulders dropped for a few seconds before I tore off the lid and was hit with the most delicious smell ever known to man. I ripped open the extra packs of ketchup and splattered them over the plate.

~~~~~~~~~~

~Ezra~

Never before in life had I seen such an enchanting siren devour food with little care of her appearance. She bit with a gusto I had seen in third world countries with impoverished villagers. She chewed with the impatience of a wild animal with little time to feast on its freshly killed prey before other vultures approached wanting a share of the game. Alexis' head hardly surfaced from the plate. So far, Ms. Remah hadn't misadvised. She was utterly engrossed in feeding her face, breathing wasn't a priority. It almost made me forget my agenda, such a fascinating and disturbing spectacle.

"So, she did betray me?" Alexis finally garbled while biting into her sandwich again.

She hadn't swallowed her first bite yet.

"She shared your latest...compulsion."

Alexis rolled her eyes while facing ahead. I switched stances after her third bite that elicited a groan.

"It's time to leave, Alexis."

Her brows shot into the air. "And go where? Harlem?"

"No. Come back to the house where you belong."

"Oh?" she asked with a mouthful. "Is that where I belong? In your dungeon, waiting to be fucked by you? And I'm supposed to be good so long as I have shelter, food, and a car, all paid for by your highness?"

"Don't be ridiculous, Alexis. Most women would pay for your circumstances." I scoffed at her absurdity.

She swallowed and lowered the loaded burger for the first time since it touched her hands. "And not enough would leave. I've spent my career comforting and aiding women in abusive relationships. I'll be damned if I walked right into one with my eyes wide open—"

"So, I've abused you now?" I could not believe the accusation.

"In a...neglectful manner, yeah..." she stumbled in her assertion.

"Why are we reaching for extreme mal-titles to describe a simple misunderstanding?"

Alexis snorted mid-bite. "A misunderstanding," she muttered. "You withholding pieces of my past is a misunderstanding? Especially since I let you do shit to me like tie me up? That's a misunderstanding to you?"

"Mouth, Alexis?"

She swallowed so hard and fast—too hard and fast—that she tapped her throat. "Mouth? You better be lucky I'm not using my damn fists on you! You are not in control anymore, Ezra! I gave you that bit of it. I gave you that access to me, and look where it got me! Burned. So, I don't give a fuck about you not liking my language or you coming here to demand I come back to your fuck pad of a basement!" Her long arm pushed in the air and index finger led it, swinging wildly. "I'm good where I am! Here, I have my life back! Here, I can go back to doing me! Here, is where I don't have to worry about giving more of myself away than someone can reciprocate. So, fuck you and this whack ass burger you tried bringing up here to convince me to go back!"

She tossed the remaining burger back on the plate. My body tensed with heat, anger flaring from my core. It wasn't about the overpriced eighteen-dollar meal, but about her stubbornness. That and she apparently had no clue of the personal hell I'd been in all this time.

"On my dime," I informed with quieted wrath.

"Excuse me?" She snapped her neck to face me.

"This haven you've nestled your 'woe is me' broken spirit in is being underwritten by me."

"What? Please!" Her face distorted in disgust. "I checked in with my credit card!"

"The MasterCard I pay off each month."

Alexis gasped at that realization.

Yeah... I'm still boss here, kitten.

"I never asked you to pay for shit! You demanded to pay off my loans to marry me: nobody said shit about you continuing to do it!"

"I take care of mine, Alexis. You belong to me," I reminded her with smug confidence, now well past the original composed state that I'd arrived in. "So please, mind your vulgarities."

I watched in slow sequence as Alexis' mouth dropped and she froze with disbelief—abhorrence. She pushed the tray from her lap and stood to her feet, squaring her shoulders as she approached me.

"Get your controlling, heartless ass the fuck up outta here." She pointed to the door. "Now!"

After a few seconds of debating, I backed up from where I stood and quietly ambled to the door, shutting it behind me. Why doesn't she get that she belongs to me? *What made that concept so deplorable?* My steps halted and I immediately turned back for the door. The moment I raised my fist to knock, I heard the contents of the serving tray clatter onto the floor. I took a deep breath before turning for the elevator.

~Lex~

Soft knocks at my office door stole my attention from a screen filled with stats and other census data. To my surprise, Mary Carmichael stood there, sporting an unusual perceptive, determined expression with her arms and ankles crossed as she leaned into the frame. She looked thinner, wore heavy makeup today, but was stylish in a tan wide brim floppy hat, faux fur vest, wide leg pants, and heels. Her lips were perched in the air, signaling her mood.

It was Monday and I'd just gotten settled back into work at *Christ Cares*, a pleasant distraction from my craziness. It didn't matter that now was not a good time, I knew from the jump what was in the air. My eyes raced to the few people moving about at the other end of the hall behind her. I exhaled while rolling my eyes closed as I sat back in my chair.

"So, we're going to do this now?"

Mary straightened. Her gold braided metal *Chanel* bag strap stayed in place as her mauve stained nails moved to rest on her hips. She nodded.

My eyes danced around the small office.

"Well, at least, let's go somewhere where we have more privacy." I would not be discussing my personal life anywhere on *RSfALC*'s campus. "But first I have to pee," I informed before swiveling my chair to stand.

~~~~~~~~~

"I know he comes off as brutish, and nothing can get through that thick skull, but...Lex, it's all a part of his protective armor. If you're going to be his wife, you have to find a way to live with it. He's a good man." I rolled my eyes. "*And* if you're good to him...patient with him, you'll have a long and successful marriage. Trust me, you're in a far better position than most women."

I hit her with disbelieving eyes, my tongue swirled in between my lips and teeth behind my closed mouth.

"And what do you consider a 'better position,' Mary?"

Thirty minutes and two delicious peach pastries later, we were nestled inside of some fancy as shit coffee shop on the Upper West Side. Not even ten minutes into our 'daughter-in-love' chat, I'd had it.

"A loyal man of God, who serves his congregation, provides handsomely, and comes home to you every night. I don't know a woman who would turn that down," she shrieked.

"Try a woman who wants more than that, Mary."

"What's more than that, Lex?" she trilled.

"Love. I want a man who is all of those things, but most of all who loves me. All those other things are mechanical. What you described is a...warehouse-made marriage. I need something more."

"Again, what's more?" Her eyes went wide.

"I need inside of him. I could give a damn about what he does outside of my home, for people I don't know."

"But he's a servant of God—"

"I don't think God does either, Mary. What good is a man of God to people who can't reach him. They don't know him. No one does. Scratch that—*I* need to know him. He's *my* husband."

Mary sighed and angled her head, clearly needing a moment. But not for long.

"You guys are still new in your marriage. Do you think every day will be easy? Well, honey, let me tell you... Successful marriages endure time and trials. You haven't made it a year and you're ready to call it quits?"

"Because the stakes are high now!" I hissed.

"*Wha*-what? Stakes?" Her eyes popped and neck jerked. "What stakes?"

"My baby!" I grounded. She sucked in air. "Yes, Mary. I'm pregnant. Now, do you think I have time to be babysitting your son's bullshit?" My eyes closed in shame. I quickly back-peddled. "I'm sorry." I slapped my face into my palms. "I...I just have a lot going on right now, most of it is your stubborn, controlling, manipulative, arrogant son who has no room in his strategically hand-made life for my heart or baby." I stopped once I felt the cry creeping up my chest.

Things went silent for a while. The both of us gathering our thoughts, switching up the pace: Mary, likely searching for the next silver lining, and I spent the time realizing how good it felt to share my news with someone, even if it was still the wrong *one*. I had no real symptoms of sickness to speak of validating my condition, so speaking it felt strange, but good.

Some of my most painful days with Ezra were those last few when I realized in Arizona my robot of a period had not come, but I'd been spotting. In the bathroom, while Ezra waited for me to get ready for his night at the youth conference, my mind raced with why I had been spotting lightly. I'd never experienced that. As unbelievable as it may sound, I knew something was off. There was a problem, and yes, one possibility could have been me being pregnant. My cycle never changed, and since having sex regularly without protection, I'd been more in tune with myself. Being with Ezra did that. It was much of what drew me to him. He highlighted the beauty and power of my body.

After checking into the hotel when I left him, I found a doctor. Ms. Remah couldn't believe it either. Still can't, but I knew she was happy for me. I was concerned about someone else. A baby was the last thing Ezra and I needed on our hands. He had me on a head-trip all of our marriage.

It all happened so fast: the shit with Seth Wilkinson, and then seeing Ezra in Arizona so powerful, overwhelmingly spiritual, and influential in a room of 14,000 people. In Arizona, people were screaming their resonation of his message, jumping and running in the spirit, and falling out from the reception of his potent words. *That* Ezra intimidated me as much as the beast, the cerebral scientist, and scholarly therapist. I was married to all the masks, and none left room for a baby.

And sure enough, here I was. Pregnant.

"Did he tell you he doesn't want this baby?" Mary asked, her face haunted.

"No."

"Then why would you think—"

"He's made it very clear he doesn't want children." I got straight to it.

I'll never forget his words at Stenton Rogers' house. They were painful.

Mary palmed her forehead, accepting the truth of her incorrigible child.

"What did he say when you told him?" She couldn't even look me in the eye.

"Nothing. I haven't told him." Then her eyes appeared. "And neither will you."

"But—"

"Mary, I understand your need of viewing your son as 'normal,' and as much as I would like that, that's not my job. It can't be my role in his life. He's a grown ass man."

"But he's my child, and a mother's job protecting her child is never done: you're about to learn this." She gestured to my flat abdomen. "It will always be on my shoulders to have him be well-adjusted. There has to be something I can do. Or at least don't penalize me for caring to!" It was her turn to grate. She even rolled her eyes. "Ezra may not be perfect, and trust me, he's broken no one's heart more than mine. No one has wanted to smack him upside his head more than his mother." She rocked her head for good measure. "But I know in my spirit there is more good in him than bad. Now, I understand you have to look out for you, but as long as I have air in my body, I will want the best for my child. I want to see him settled before I shrivel up and die."

"But that doesn't give you the right to meddle in my life. I'm my own woman, and Ezra ain't the type to tolerate that either."

Mary chuckled in spite of herself. "No. He isn't." She supplied a wry smile. "And I don't suppose you are either."

I answered with my eyes. Mary was possibly not all that crazy.

"But you have to tell him about this ba—"

"I will." I stood from the table. "At my pace, when I believe he's ready." I began gathering my trash.

"When will that be? You can't wait—"

"Listen, Mary, I'm starting to like you, but I could never respect the way you handle your own marriage. Leave mine to me. Whether he likes it or not, Ezra will hear about this baby soon. But not from you. Like I told you at the *Girls Not Brides* fundraising gala last year, I can promise to keep an open mind about getting to know you and helping you get to know him. Or shut you out completely...from your grandchild's life."

Those dark ebony eyes ballooned again and she stood from the table with her purse clutched in her arm. "You would do that?"

"Of course I would. You just said a mother's job protecting her child is never done. I won't have controlling people like your son or immoral folks like you and Sylvester around my child. These issues have to stop!" My tone was more pleading than demanding.

Things went silent as we played the stare down game.

Wouldn't it be like Ezra's mother to do this!

But just like with her son, I wouldn't back down. Already I was over this family and their fucked up antics.

"What are you gonna do about the church and this email thing?" She tried a new angle.

"I'm taking my time on deciding that, too. I have priorities, and the church isn't one of them. My peace of mind comes first." My hands rubbed over my flat stomach.

"Well," Mary's eyes skirted to the floor. "At least let me buy you a few more of those peach pastries you inhaled as soon as we sat down. Girl, I need to go lay down! I feel a migraine coming after this conversation."

She didn't wait for my reply before snapping her neck toward the register and walking off with her chin in the air. I'd guessed that was the one power move she could make today. All others were shot down by me.

~three~

~Lex~

    The place was immaculate—the lobby, elevator, and halls alone. As a kid, I would always wonder what the inside of this place looked like. I couldn't believe I was finally seeing it. I wished Tasche was with me. She would have been souped as hell. Gassed about me knowing someone who lived in *Trump International*. I had to get my excitement under control. I was here on unpleasant business. Business I wasn't sure I wanted anything to do with.

    I rang the fancy doorbell and took a deep cleansing breath. I tried to put my game face on. The door opened to a Hispanic woman dressed in a maid's uniform. She smiled.

"Hi. Is Elle home?"

"Si!" she answered as she nodded, backing away to let me in.

    As soon as I crossed the threshold, I saw Elle jogging toward the door with a face brightened by my presence. I'd never seen her underdressed. Her blue and white tie-dye leggings, matching fitted tank, and sneakers gave it away. Elle was small, not really having a need to work out, in my opinion.

"Hey, Lex!" she smiled. Her blonde curls messily pushed back from her face by a headband.

"You work out?" I tried for small talk; the business was soon to come.

"Yeah. Just came from a run. I didn't know if you'd actually come this time." Her tone turned cold and eyes hard, at that apparent jab. My smile fell as well. She pivoted. "Come on back. I had food prepared in case I got lucky. *And I see I got lucky.*" I caught the inflection when she sang her sarcasm.

I wasn't in the mood, but had to face the music. So I followed her to the back of the massive apartment. It was fancy as shit, too. Tall walls encasing were just as broad as the floor-to-ceiling windows. The living room was well dressed with lofty furniture, an open room next to it with a huge pool table centering it. I didn't see any personal pictures on the wall, just large framed artwork. The kitchen was spacious as well with a floor-to-ceiling window.

Elle invited me to sit at a bar table, comfortably sized for my height.

"Nice place."

"It's my boyfriend's," she shared while pulling a bowl from the fridge. "Thanks. I hope you eat shrimp and avocado because it's what he made for us, and I can't cook for shit."

Her slender frame whipped across the kitchen, collecting bowls, utensils, and glasses with an air of familiarity. It made me wonder if that was how I moved around Ezra's kitchen, which was just as elegant as this one, only bigger.

She exhaled when she finally made it to the table.

"I hope you can't smell me. I have a meeting in Philly after we're done." She began clamping salad with serving tongs to serve us. "I can wash before that one. At least I know I won't be stood up."

"Oh, cut the bullshit," I hissed, massaging my forehead.

Elle paused, her arm midair. "Nice language for my first lady. You sound tougher than you were at your place," she clowned me. "You know I finally joined *Redeeming Souls* on Sunday." She dumped a portion of the salad in my bowl. "Oh!" she chirped. "You wouldn't know that because like a coward, you weren't there. Did Ezra tell you when he got home?"

I swallowed hard, my eyes shooting off sightlessly.

"Hold up!" Her tone turned distrusting, panicked. "Did you guys change your mind? Are you not going to work this out?"

"I don't know," I supplied with little confidence.

"You don't know?"

"No. Look… Things are really up in the air right now for our marriage—for my life. I just wanted to come see what's being asked of me."

"I think first you need to figure out if you're going to stay married to the leader of the largest church in the north region of this country. This ain't the type of thing to close your eyes, squeeze, and shoot about. I can swing it either way, but I need you to be absolutely sure."

"I don't know!" I exclaimed with my palms in the air, suddenly feeling weighted. I wasn't of that church culture. I only wanted to do what was right. The last time I saw him in my hotel, I could give a fuck about right or wrong. "What's he saying?"

"When I spoke to him about us meeting here today, he asked that I give him direction from there. Are you guys even staying in the same house?"

I shook my head, my fork pushing food around in the bowl. Elle sat back and sighed loudly, tapping the table with her short, oval nails for good measure.

"Lex, give me something! Please!"

I knew nothing about her line of work to know what she was asking for, but I didn't like the demand in her tone.

"Look! I gotta lot of shit going on right now—"

"Shit like what?" Elle gasped. "It's my job to either make it go away or help you manage it."

I shook my head. "Shit like where I'm going to live in the next week or so, and if I'll have a job, what that'll all mean for a woman who rides for me like a mother, her health issues, and what to do with my bullshit ass marriage."

I stuffed my face with the salad. It fucking danced on my palate, it was so good.

"So you *don't* want to remain married?"

"I don't know! I feel like a damn fool for not saying no, I don't want to be married to that son of a bitch anymore, but it's not that simple."

"Okay. So why *wouldn't* you want to be with him? Hey…" She neared the center of the table. "He's not into anything scandalous, is he?"

Scandalous?

"Yes!" I decided on sarcasm because I was losing it.

That question wasn't from Elle, the dutiful public relations professional Ezra had hired. It was from Elle, the client and now parishioner. My life had been reduced to his masks again.

"What?"

"The fact that I'm in love with a man who doesn't love me any more than he does you. He only values me more because legally, my pussy is his, Elle."

"Oh, thank God!" she breathed and fell back into her chair.

"Thank God? Now can you see why I couldn't get up in front of thousands of people that Sunday and declare something that was one-sided?"

Elle straightened. "Thank God Ezra is one of the few without major scandal. I've trusted my spiritual leadership and emotional well-being to him. I've never sensed anything fishy going on with him, unlike most of the men of God I've encountered in my life. It's just good to know." She fed herself a forkful, unbothered.

"But it's not okay for my life to be shot to shit. Is this meeting now over?"

Elle's exotic eyes raked up to my face, but she chewed at a casual speed before swallowing.

"I can't fix your marital issues besides having a few choice words with him about being pigheaded. I can, however, give you time to figure if you want to continue on with him. Just keep in mind if you do, you have to be prepared to address his congregation alongside him. There's no other way around it."

Silence engulfed us as we ate. There was so much I wasn't telling her and wouldn't. I sort of hated myself for still protecting his privacy. I could never share with anyone how Ezra liked to tie me up and spank me for his pleasure...and mine. Sometimes I lied to myself and said it would expose my dark pleasures, too. But the truth of the matter was, I was still that person wanting to please people who didn't give a fuck about me, or at least enough. That was shameful.

"Is it that bad?"

My eyes traveled over to Elle.

"What? The salad is good. Your old man is good for something," I garbled.

Elle tossed her head back and hooted loudly.

"How old are you?"

"Twenty-nine." I frowned, confused.

"Interesting." Her brows hiked. "My old man is good at lots of things, including me." She winked. "I've been married before, and even now, living with a man, I know it can be difficult. Sometimes he comes home and isn't much for conversation as we sit at a quiet table for dinner. But the moment we hit the bedroom, I have his dick either rammed into my mouth or ass—no pun intended." Her eyes retracted. "When one of his sports teams loses, he's in a pissy mood for two days, three if his dick isn't either rammed into my mouth or ass—no pun intended—to help him off the ledge. But these are just quirks to his personality. And if I can be honest, he's got the shorter end of the stick, because I can be a real bitch to be around when I wake up to a dark moon instead of the bright sun that shines over everyone else."

She battled depression…

That's why Elle saw Ezra. This revelation made her more palatable. I didn't need to be around 'Perfect Patties' or princesses who didn't know shit about dark days. I could use someone real enough I could cop my shit to. I may not have been diagnosed as depressed clinically, but I damn sure had my fair share of blue days.

Elle shrugged as she continued, her face to her bowl. "If you decide to throw in the towel, call me. I can help you through that, too."

"Thanks. But I can tell you this: If I do decide to play nice and stand with him before his church, I'll write my own script. Something where I'd be able to sleep at night, feeling true to myself and *RSfALC*."

"Those are always best." Her face bloomed into a smile.

"Hey," I decided to switch gears, "you know those long dresses with matching capes in the Erika Erceg line?"

"Yeah. That gothic looking shit?" She stuffed her face. Where it all went, I didn't know.

I cleared my throat, embarrassed. "Yeah. I need a few of those in different colors."

"Cool. Anything else?"

"Just don't break me with the fee. I no longer have First Lady spending privileges, if you know what I mean." I bit my bottom lip.

"It's not like you're asking for the high end designer versions available on JAGMisha.com. I can get you one in each color for no charge. I wish you'd burn them, though." She looked me in the eye. "But I know there's no chance of that happening."

I smiled cheesily. "Two in each color, please. You know my size."

Elle rolled her eyes, clearing her generous bowl.

~*Ezra*~

As the tea tray was placed on the coffee table, I studied the intricate designs of the kettle and that which corresponded with the mugs and saucers they lay on. I couldn't help but consider how the byzantine print mirrored the design of life. How involutedly woven the designs of our lives are because the Master Potter has multidimensional views our simple minds cannot extrapolate. Even I, as a man of science and psychology, could not understand all human behavior. But He could, and He still hadn't shared the complex design of my current quandary.

"You know your mother picked out this tea set?"

With my chin resting on my palm, I peered up and across the coffee table to my father. His eyes were big and filled with animated lust as he spoke while Sister Monica turned to leave. The moment she closed the door behind her and we were alone, that habitual coquettish smile disintegrated into a harsh grimace.

"She brought this after visiting *Basilica of Sant' Apollinare Nuovo*. I sent her women's group over there in the early '80s. She came back 'cultured'." He snorted, pouring himself a cup. "This was a part of that *new* her." He sat back in his seat and noted, "But it was worth the cost and new pompous behavior. She was the first lady of a powerful organization. She knew the role, played the role...was bred into *this* philosophy. That's why it's important for us to marry our own. Doing it unequally yoked could have irreparable and embarrassing backfire. Do you understand, Pastor?"

I didn't speak, just offered him a respectful regard, my patience for this inevitable natter waning that quickly. He'd only arrived twenty minutes ago. It surprised me how long this conversation had been deferred.

"Listen, Ezra," He sat up in his seat, placing his elbows on his knees, no longer interested in the tea suddenly, though he'd ordered it. I studied his plaid suit, purple clergy collared shirt with the chain running from inside the shirt to the inner pocket of his jacket. He looked...official, authoritative—influential. "This isn't a situation we can't gain control of. If the girl doesn't want to be in this no more, we can have her go quietly. I have my lawyers on standby. Got a plan in place whereby she signs a nondisclosure agreement after we give her a couple of hundred thousand—"

"And what?" I asked, disgusted by the navigation of his proposal.

"And you can move on. I know you told me a year ago you need a wife. And I get that, son. A man my age and tenure gets it. But you have to trust me when I tell you the woman has to be of the right breed. She has to know her role...her job here."

"Which is?" My conversation with Precious came to mind.

He straightened his spine and spoke with incredulity. "Which is to make you look good. That is the simple role of a wife. She is to complete your outfit, Ezra. I don't know if what you wanted was a woman who you could build up so you can have a certain liberty, but you can have that and more if you choose strategically." His tone had turned emotional at some point.

What he didn't know was I had been strategic. I consulted God on this venture, and we had an agreement. I kept up my end of the bargain, and thought He had, too, until this. Alexis had gone AWOL, and now the church knew. It was one thing not to have addressed the email scandal on Valentine's Day and to have her sit out that Sunday. However, it was an entirely different matter to have her miss Bible classes and the following Sunday as well. And to make our ambiguous marital status even more opaque, she hadn't been to work all week.

Needless to say, it had been an incredibly stressful week or so. And indisputably one of the darkest hours of my life. This was bigger than a woman: this was about God silencing Himself on what should be a period of His guidance toward recovery. It was also about failure. I'd failed myself, my church, and my parents. Though I was sure he couldn't read it, I was sitting across from my father without wind in my sails, incredibly wounded by this event in my life. He was now in a position of superiority in our constant battle of wills. I wouldn't confirm it, but my father was now sitting high, looking low...at me.

"Precious—"

"No!" I growled, and was sure to measure the upspring of my words. "Absolutely never in my life will I join with Precious Graham. And that is an unequivocal never."

"That misunderstanding is in the past," he whined from a wrinkled face. "You two are adults now. No miscommunication at this age."

"We were adults then. I have been able to move on, and with her working so close to me at the capacity you requested. That was my sole compromise. Nothing more should be expected."

"Precious understands pastoral ministry, she grew up with it all her life." He was referring to him being her example, as if she were raised in his home. "She will understand your need for...Alexis from time to time. She will know when it's appropriate to travel with you, and how most often it ain't. She gets discretion, son."

I shook my head, unable to believe his stamina in this argument. But it did strike one provoking thought. *Is that where I'd gone wrong with Alexis?* Not having her travel with me? I didn't have a problem with her tagging along. I just didn't want to bore her with the humdrum of church propaganda or worst: overwhelm her with it. With Alexis, we were supposed to chart our own path. If that was a term she wanted to negotiate, I was open to it. I'd even invited her out to Arizona. That was when I realized having her with me was an added benefit.

I exhaled, my eyes lolled over to my spirited father. I saw the moment he was met with the revelation that he'd made no progress with his immoral agenda. He stood, pulled his jacket together to clasp its buttons. A stalling maneuver.

Typical.

"I know you have that conference call with the head *C.O.O.L.J.C.* bishops for Holy Convocation week. Congrats on that by the way. Nothing makes me more proud than seeing my son's name announced as a featured speaker. That's not a' everyday achievement. Not even something me or your grandfather, Bishop Travois Daniels, have ever done. It's a task you need peace in your mind and heart to prepare for. You don't need the chaos of your home, or lack thereof. So as you sit on that call, I want you to think about something." He rounded the table gaiting slowly, making a show of it toward me. "I will leave you with this: *The son said to his father, 'Father, give me my share of the estate.' So he divided his property. Not long after that, the son got together all he had, set off for a distant country and there squandered his wealth in wild living. After he had spent everything, there was a severe famine in that whole country, and he began to be in need. So he went and hired himself out to a citizen of that country, who sent him to his fields to feed pigs. He longed to fill his stomach with the pods that the pigs were eating, but no one gave him anything.*"

My muscles tightened all over. My father was chafing the Word to apply to our embattled relationship. I could feel my jaw clenching to the point of popping. He was labeling my decisions to travel the world to discover life on my own as me being the prodigal son, aimlessly wandering around, engaging in a high-risk lifestyle. And he was more correct than he'd ever know. I had been.

"*When he came to his senses, he said, 'How many of my father's hired servants have food to spare, and here I am starving to death!*" He continued. "*I will set out and go back to my father and say to him: Father, I have sinned against heaven and against you. I am no longer worthy to be called your son; make me like one of your hired servants.' So he got up and went to his father. But while he was still a long way off, his father saw him and was filled with compassion for him; he ran to his son, threw his arms around him and kissed him. The son said to him, 'Father, I have sinned against heaven and against you. I am no longer worthy to be called your son.' But the father said to his servants, 'Quick! Bring the best robe and put it on him. Put a ring on his finger and sandals on his feet. Bring the fattened calf and kill it. Let's have a feast and celebrate. For this son of mine was dead and is alive again; he was lost and is found.' So they began to celebrate.*"

Luke 15:11-24. Or at least my father's rendition of it. If it was not clear how insistent my father was about me terminating my marriage with Alexis, it had now been made sound. Though the story and lesson paralleled, he couldn't be more wrong about the application. How arrogant of him to believe he was the Father I'd humbly returned home to.

He gave a dramatic pause. One I didn't think I'd survive without jumping to my feet and ushering him out of my office. Out of my life for good, no matter how preposterous the impulsive thought was. We may not have seen eye-to-eye in my youth, but I'd walked a straight line since returning home years ago. I hadn't given him any ammunition to use against me, conceded to his every request. Until I chose my wife. I felt violent at the implication that I'd somehow brought this on myself.

His hands gripped my shoulders from behind as he sneered over my head, "You are not always right, Pastor. You may have all those fancy degrees, flashy titles, mystic ways about you, walked a straight line in these past eight years since you've been home, but *no* man is without sin, and all have fallen short of His glory. Good day, Pastor." He smacked my shoulder before heading to the door behind me.

~Lex~

I stepped out of my car at *RSfALC* and shut the door. My stomach toiled with anxiety as my eyes roved up the building, all the way to the steeple rooftop. Congregants scuffled all about in the large parking lot, even in the streets blocks away. They were bustling in for the eight o'clock service at the largest and most powerful church in Harlem, New York, seemingly anticipating yet another eventful occasion. Little did they know, I'd be a part of the event this morning. I let out a long breath. I had to get through this. It was the least I could do. I started my conscious amble to the rear entrance.

Just feet away, near the doors, I saw a conspicuous head of blonde natural curls standing in a tan, ankle length shearling coat. She didn't recognize me right away as her tense frame held still in the frigid February air. Her gloved hands rubbed together as she examined the incoming droves of saints in search of me. Her attention so rapt, I was able to walk directly in front of her.

I saw the moment relief washed upon Elle's glowing being. She exhaled and slightly rolled her eyes.

"I told you I'd come," came out nastier than intended.

"You told me you'd come two weeks ago today, too. Remember?" she tossed right back, matching my tone. I could have sworn to seeing a slight rolling of her eyes. Then they softened. She gestured to me with her chin while giving me a onceover, inspecting my assigned wardrobe. "You ready?" I knew the question was more about the task ahead; that Elle was always about her business. I nodded my lie. "Let's go. We only have five minutes before showtime." She turned on her heel.

As I swallowed hard, I told myself perhaps I deserved this. I did leave them hanging on Valentine's Day. But I was in no way prepared to handle something of this magnitude, considering the state of my relationship with Ezra.

Right away, I noticed the security guard a few steps ahead of Elle, clear a path. My heart pounded all the way to the double doors of the *Bishop's Office*. As we approached the long hall, the noise of the crowd quieted and there were fewer people around. Inside the reception area were a few bodies: Ezra's entourage and another face I didn't recognize. Just as we passed through the doors, Sister Sharon was there accepting our coats. Then the office doors ahead opened. Amongst the figures coming out was him. Ezra strolled out, and I noticed he wasn't as entranced as I'd seen him in the past, minutes before speaking. It reminded me of the itinerary.

Two services to get through, I reminded myself, exhaling my nervousness.

His eyes landed on me and slanted a bit. My eyes shuffled over to Elle the moment she spoke.

"We're just a few minutes out, but if we can clear the room so I can speak with Pastor and First Lady..."

In seconds, the room had emptied out. There was only Elle, Ezra, me, and another man ending a conversation on his cell.

"That was Jamie," he informed. "He said the cameramen are on hold, praise and worship is closing, and she's in place."

Okay...

So, the guy worked with Elle. But doing what? He was handsome: warm brown skin, defined eyelids, close beard, and well dressed.

"Are you ready, Carmichael?" he asked Ezra. His reply was an affirmative nod. "And you, Lex?"

My face wrinkled.

"Lex," Elle snorted, understanding my concern. "This is Jackson Hunter, my boss." Ezra cleared his throat conspicuously. "...*and* boyfriend!" she quickly amended with a forced smile. "He's here assisting me."

"...and Ezra," Jackson chimed in, offering me his hand for me to shake. "Are you clear on what your statement will be to the congregation?"

Though I did take his hand, my mind hadn't caught up from the introduction that seemed to have happened so quickly.

I felt the dry smile cover my face as I finally put motion in our joined hands. "The surprise delivery of the exotic flowers that caused the gooey, giddy, and helpless smile. That's you," I murmured. Elle's hard eyes shot into Ezra. She never skipped a beat. From the corner of my eye, I caught Ezra licking his lips while regarding the floor. "It's nice to meet you, Jackson, and yes, I'm prepared with what I need to say."

I took a deep breath, applying a generous smile as I turned to Elle.

"Good girl. Let's do this," she thundered before turning for the door.

On our way up to the sanctuary, I wondered how Ezra did this journey to the pulpit with all these people, about twice a week. From the short period of time we'd been together and he'd been preaching full time, I knew Ezra would be zoned out these few minutes before he hit the stage. Apparently his crew, too. The elevator ride and troop to the sanctuary was made in silence, except for the speakers that flowed with the happenings inside the parish.

Elle and Jackson were typing away on their phones and giving one another occasional communicative glances. That shit made me nervous, reminding me of how I was about to address thousands of faceless people. His people. My heart began to pound and shaking hands gripped the aluminum waist rail on the elevator. I felt my chest heave. Then I felt warm flesh cover mine, pulling it from the fierce grip. My eyes fell on a left hand with a platinum wedding band. I scanned up to find Ezra still regarding the floor, but signaling his presence with a squeeze. Slowly, his head rose and eyes rounded over to me. His face was expressionless, but regard was very much present. He was comforting me.

The bell tolled and bodies began to file off the elevator. The live music grew louder as we neared the buzzing source of energy. Ezra never let my hand go while we approached the sanctuary doors. As soon as they opened, a clipped microphone was instantly fastened to his robe, and we drew closer on the stage. The lights from the pulpit were almost blinding. Thank god the music was slowing. I immediately located Dwayne, who was keenly looking for his cue from Ezra.

Ezra released my hand a few feet from the podium, signaling for me to stand in place as he continued on. When I glanced around the large stage for Elle and Jackson, I saw them in the wings of the pulpit, both eyes stapled to me. Elle pumped both her palms in the air and then gave the thumbs up. It was confirmation that I stayed where I was supposed to.

"Good morning, people of God," Ezra's usual deep, self-possessed, and rasped tenor trickled through the speakers. The way he announced himself on the pulpit always had an effect on me. This time I felt it in my belly.

Don't touch it! Every muscle in my body tensed. Ezra walked over toward the other side of the stage to get the microphone Dwayne was handing him. Those two communicated in silence seamlessly while up here. "Do you mind if we deviate from the standard order of service?"

The crowd responded in a way that encouraged him.

"I have a special pulpit guest this morning, whom I'd like you to hear from," Ezra continued. "I've not been remiss in dealing with the news about the seedy email that circulated two weeks ago." The mention of the word *email* had my pulse beating in my ears. "I needed the time to tend to my wife's feelings about it first, as she's my priority. Amen?" his delivery was so calm—so cool and unbothered.

Ezra had an easy comfort in front of people. He was a natural in the spotlight, unlike me. I couldn't keep my knees still.

"*Amen,*" echoed throughout the colossal room.

Ezra smiled warmly—disarming even me. His eyes raked over to me, and waved me over to the podium. With weighted feet, I trekked over to him. There was a mix of ease and anxiety in doing so. I innately followed instructions given by this man. He was a natural leader. A commander. It was the subject matter that brought about the anxiety.

"*Redeeming Souls*, please receive my incredibly enchanting wife, Alexis Grier," he rasped gently, his timbre echoing powerfully throughout the sanctuary.

Ezra moved slightly to give me room at the lectern and handed me the microphone. But I was too caught up in his eyes to begin my script. Things went quiet, my nerves at play.

"So, what? I'm now back to being a Grier? No Carmichael?" I asked, kidding: my nerves were that bad.

Ezra's brows furrowed, confusion flashed in his eyes in the quieted room. I cocked my head to the side, waiting for an answer, and that's when his expression shifted to amusement. His eyes sparkled anew.

"Sweetheart," rumbled from the back of his throat as he adjusted the mic in my hand to align with my mouth. *Always in control, this man!* "You will be Mrs. Ezra Carmichael until you leave this earth. I wouldn't have it any other way," he declared effortlessly.

That shit stole my breath. My mouth dropped and eyes popped as I stared him dead in the eyes.

The room going up in appraisal of his vow broke my attention.

Maintaining that amused gleam, Ezra lifted his brows, prompting me to get started. It reminded me of his controlled state. No matter the occasion, he was always aware...and bossy as hell.

I turned to the audience, who was still in an uproar from our exchange. I took a minute to collect my thoughts as I fought through my own spell of sorts. My eyes darted over to the dignitary section where I saw Mary standing with her hands crossed at her pelvis, wearing the biggest smile. Next to her was Ezra's father, scowling eyes filled with doubt. Precious and her mother were behind them, both with fixed gazes on me.

"Good morning, everyone," my voice carried weakly over the microphone. Still, the audience responded positively. "You know, it's not easy being the wife of a pastor, much less a man of God like your pastor, Ezra Carmichael, here. You want to walk in what he believes just as faithfully as he does. Well, when it comes to Ezra, that's almost impossible. He's decidedly committed every day. He submits himself through prayer, fasting, and meditating as an act of worship, and covers everyone under the sound of my voice every day. It's what he was raised to do. His parents and grandfather instilled the Word and the walk in him, and he wears the banner proudly *every day*." A glaring applause ripped through the sanctuary in perfect time.

I needed to pace myself. My words were heavy. And true. As the crowd quieted, I nodded to show I was with them before continuing.

"And then I came along. A woman having grown up in the Harlem struggle. Like many of you, I've seen dark days. I've been poor, unemployed, living from check to check, sometimes without parenting or guidance in my youth. And yes, I even worked as a waitress at a strip club, trying to make ends meet. It was not the safest environment for a young woman my age to be in, and that was proven. But I was able to move on with my life and make better decisions. I began a job with the city and went back to school. I worked hard to put the ordeal behind me, and I have. I worked my *Harlem Pride*."

I slowed another moment to take a deep breath. Elle was clear on pacing my output to give the perception of calm and control: two traits Ezra owned.

"I even happened upon a man. A good man. A man of God—" before I could continue, the parishioners began shouting their excitement of where I was going. I forged ahead, feeling powered by their encouragement. "A man of God who didn't hold me to my past. Instead he saw goodness in me— greatness, in fact. He made me his wife, and *that* is validation of how God sees me." Before I was done, applause exploded in the air. I could hardly hear myself.

Ezra peered into me, intently. I saw the beam in his eyes I couldn't identify. I didn't want to explore it, so I continued.

"Unfortunately, not everyone is happy when you are. Some are even malicious enough to expose things you've conquered to exploit you. But that didn't happen and it won't happen, because I am not that young victimized girl, lost in despair. Today, I am a victorious woman who stands next to *your* man of God"—I noticed my pitch rising, trying to be heard above the screams and yelps—"being covered by the same decided commitment to ministry, the Kingdom, and our Savior." I ended with a nervous smile.

I'd gotten through it though I didn't think all of my words were heard over the applause that erupted in the building. I handed Ezra the microphone and sterilely nodded my completion of the assignment. This was all I was told to do for both services. Ezra took the microphone and pulled me into his hard frame by the small of my back. The surprise of it all snatched my breath away. His warm lips and wiry beard met the side of my face. I shivered, suddenly overcome by an emotion I was all too familiar with: needing approval.

Was he thankful that I saved his face for his organization? Yes, it was my mess that caused it, but it looked bad on him and his family. No matter what I argued in my head, I was still taken by the security of his arms, the hardness of his body, and the dizziness from his scent.

"*Redeeming Souls*, please welcome our good sister in Christ and close friend, Grammy-award-winning recording artist, Yolanda Adams!" Dwayne excitedly announced across from us.

The crowd went up, this time in a rowdy manner. You would think a fight broke out with the amount of shouts and gasps resounding. At that, Ezra let up, removing me from his clutch at casual speed. He turned to position himself next to me, but still not taking his piercing eyes from me. I, however, managed to. Down below us, in front of the steps, at the opening of the stage was a tall curvaceous figure. Long auburn waves covered her back as she held the microphone to her face. She finally turned around, smiled and winked at Ezra just before belting out the first of her notes.

Holy shit!

I know Yolanda Adams! Even the heathens knew her. The dancers at *Rusty's* would strip to her song, *Open My Heart*. Disgraceful, but true. I would catch her morning radio show every now and then, not to mention her performances on BET's award shows. She was fierce!

Yolanda Adams is here...

RSfALC would have celebrity guests from time to time, most I didn't know, but I never expected her to be here on today. Then it hit me. I turned back to look for Elle. She stood in the wings, next to Jackson, both with their shoulders poised and spines straight. She winked at me. *Yes.* This was orchestrated—all of it, including my speech. Not that I could see anything wrong with it, it was just that I couldn't believe I was involved in a public relations tactic.

"Are you okay?" Ezra whispered in my ear.

I swallowed, now facing ahead. "Whose idea was this?"

"Elle made the recommendation, and I pulled the strings."

I nodded with an open mouth. Ezra clasped hands with me as we watched Yolanda's performance from behind. It didn't matter, her vocal chords could be experienced from a mile away and still be felt. I didn't recognize the song or lyrics, but I listened intently. She sang about coming through trials and temptation through attacks by the devil, but being kept in the midst of it all. I could tell right away even the song choice had been strategically selected. I wondered if she knew that. By the way she sang with visible passion, it didn't matter. As she ripped through notes, the congregation got wrapped up right away. I didn't see a sitting party from my vantage. Even the balconies were filled with emotionally stricken people. Dwayne and the *RSfALC* mass choir backed her vocals. It was amazing.

Ezra gripped my hand as the lyrics, notes, and melodies turned dramatic. I slowly turned to find him with his eyes closed and head slightly bowed. He was praying...or something. He was a preacher, and in church, which meant he was caught up somewhere. I'd admired Ezra for his devotion to his role and relationship to his God. He was unwavering when it came to Christ. I envied that dedication.

My attention went back to Yolanda. The words shooting from her chords transformed from usual church verbiage to true soul-touching phrases the common man could recognize. I *had* been kept. Throughout the madness of my father's prison stints, my mother's mental episodes, and my bouts with loneliness when I had neither; I had survived. I became independent once I lost my grandmother and had to face the coldness of the world without the comfort of family. I had seen women who didn't have the fortune I did over the years. They didn't find jobs or were inspired by the prospect of an education to save them from poverty. Hell, my friends were still in that struggle: look at Tasche. However, before Ezra came along, I had been pretty fortunate. That couldn't have been by my doing alone. What made me different from everyone else? Why had my life taken on a different path?

Yolanda's delivery grew more lively during my introspection. The crowd was there with her, caught up in the spirit of her message. Ezra's head faced the floor, chin now burrowed into his neck, and hand still clenched over mine. And when Yolanda sang about thinking she was going to lose her mind, my eyes squeezed in a painful memory. I refused to get emotional. I was up here to do a job, and that was it. I chanced a peek over my shoulders for Elle. I sucked in a breath when I saw her head burrowed even deeper into her chest than Ezra's. Jackson held her with one arm, consoling her.

I need to get off this stage!

The moment the last noted ended, I was directed off the pulpit, leaving Ezra to take over. I didn't hear much of what he said. I joined Elle and Jackson in leaving the platform section of the sanctuary. The moment we were off the stage, I could feel my limbs again. The pulpit was surreal.

"Yolanda Adams," I whispered with balled lips, my legs moving swiftly to keep up with theirs and the security directing us. "That's a bit extreme, don't you think?"

Without looking at me, she returned, "We needed an immediate diversion, one bigger than your address. According to a statistic, the first few seconds of impact after a major event, lessens the significance of the prior in the minds of those who witnessed them both."

This is crazy! My face fell at this. *These were real professionals handling the shit storm Nyree caused!* How much was he paying them?

"You did good, Lex." I glanced up just in time to catch Jackson's endorsing wink.

If he said it, I guess I did.

"Your reaction to him saying you'll be his wife until you die was priceless!" Elle smiled with big eyes. "I didn't think you had it in you to adlib. I mean, Ezra owns a stage, so it was no surprise for him to follow up. But you led him to it." She regarded Jackson. "This is good."

"Those were my nerves at play, not my genius," I murmured, rolling my eyes.

"So," Elle spoke lowly, slickly. "Timothy Griffin, the criminal court judge who's running for a seat on the Supreme Court, is Nyree's father-in-law."

I shrugged my shoulders unconcerned, not having a clue who he was or giving a single fuck about Nyree or her in-laws. I was having a time dealing with my own in the moment, thanks to her.

We moved briskly to the doors of the sanctuary where I would sit in my usual seat, thankfully. Elle thought it was important to appear business as usual. Me sitting with Ezra's parents would be an obvious act of diversion, or so she said.

"Yeah, well, let's keep with that magic. We have the eleven o'clock service to address."

My face didn't pick up until my eyes landed on a beaming Lilly, welcoming me with pride. She offered me a secret high five once I was planted in my seat. Validation from her had always been welcomed.

But still…

My life was completely fucked up, and I still had one more service to get through.

~four~

~Ezra~

The Sunday following addressing *RSfALC* regarding the email disgrace, my spirit felt abrasive. My actions were the same. To those around me, my regimen remained intact, preparing for the eight o'clock service. I even arrived earlier to meet with the camera crew about Viacom's latest rollout for enhancing the broadband for telecasting. I was disoriented, but responsive throughout the conversation. My sermon had been absorbed, deeply embedded into my psyche and loaded in my belly. I prayed with my staff, and even had a few minutes to pray alone before being escorted to the sanctuary. My body was prepared to implement what it was created to do. But my spirit was under duress.

When I mounted the stage as Dwayne and the praise team closed their praise and worship number, he eyed me for his cue to begin to bring it in. Typically, I could measure the atmosphere from the time I walked into the room. I could determine how easily the Holy Spirit could navigate in the created climate from the praise and worship portion of the service. It was my job to make the climate conducive for Him to dwell and be pleased. If it was not, I would have him extend the final number, typically a ballad from the choir, and include words that would induce compliancy needed for the right environment. Sometimes I'd take extreme measures to balance it out; it all depended on what was in the atmosphere the audience brought in collectively.

This morning, the parishioners were ready: their temperament at a level where God could reign and pour out His spirit. However, His vessel was not aligned. *I* was incredibly off. I gave Dwayne the signal to extend the song, and flawlessly, he instructed the choir. I stood at the pulpit, arranging my tablet and Bible, placing my beads above them. My eyes, in spite of me, rolled up and over to where I knew she'd be sitting. My heart raced with each second until my regard landed, afraid that she wouldn't be there. Since when did that matter to me? I even had a flash thought to demand that, moving forward, she sit with the dignitaries to the left of the pulpit where I could easily locate her.

I squeezed my eyes shut at that ill rationale.

She was there. My shoulders dropped at the speed of my lungs being emptied in relief. Alexis sat as tense as I felt, while observing me with pensive eyes. Her hands were clasped together at her lap over her tablet. She'd been following my every scripture reference since the fall. I quietly observed this over the months. It hit me when she began timidly asking questions about them. Alexis no longer attended services to appease her impending First Lady role. She had even surpassed the purpose of attending out of curiosity of my role as the primary speaker of the house. She now attended in need of the unadulterated Word, just as those around her. The only difference was that it was her pastor, whom she'd 'fallen in love' with, delivering it. I couldn't begin to understand what that all meant, but I could certainly comprehend her genuine reasons for attending church. She was a soul in need of healing and guidance; something she didn't receive at home, where her pastor governed as well.

Alexis' bashful eyes diverted in diffidence before returning to me with less confidence. She had never been able to turn off her attraction to the conundrum that was me. At one point in our relationship, it thrilled me. Today, it baffled me. *Is that what's causing the rift in our covenant? Does she want me sheared open for her to easily read?* I, once again, found myself confounded by this woman, which meant my resolve had been compromised, and *that* was now interfering with the calling on my life.

My God…

It had finally hit me. For the first time in my life, I did not want to impart the word of God. I wanted to be someplace else, wrapped up in self-pity for the circumstances in my life. This was not me.

Dwayne caught my attention in my peripheral.

Christ! Not now!

I was not ready. I had to think fast. We were under strict guidelines from the television stations we broadcasted to. I realized this as Dwayne eased over.

"Pastor, Karen is here, making her way up to the sanctuary. She asked for words before you speak."

I glanced down at my watch for the time. *Isn't this just wonderful!* I groaned internally. I loved First Lady Sheard, but detested diversions in itinerary.

"She's in the building?" I asked with more snip in my voice than what was fair to Dwayne. He was just the messenger.

He nodded, eyes filled with apology. That's when I saw a group of people to the left of the stage, at the dignitary section. Karen had arrived, greeting my parents, senior elders, and reverends. She moved hurried and spiritedly. I rose to the podium, as I could, that quickly, feel the shift in the sanctuary from the change in program.

In no time, Karen was on the pulpit approaching me with a disarming smile. She pulled me into an embrace.

I realized as she did, she uttered, "Thank You, God," before taking to the microphone.

"I don't like these things. Dwayne, come bring me a portable mic," she drawled in her soprano pitch, still not acknowledging me.

I'd known Karen for over a century. She's a four-time, Grammy-winning gospel recording artist, who travels all over the world, spreading the gospel through song. Her husband and I are well acquainted. Karen is more like family, as she and my mother are very much good friends and have been since well before she married. This has to be understood to explain how she is one of very few who could abruptly disrupt a service at *Redeeming Souls for Abundant Living in Christ* and not be thrown out on her face.

"Praise God, *Redeeming Souls*," she exhaled into the microphone once it was handed to her by one of our stage guys. "I don't normally do this, but I move when the Spirit of the Lord prompts me to." Her southern and child-like manner of speaking always reminded me of Dolly Parton's, and I never failed to tease her about it over the years. "We're going over to *Praise Tabernacle* in Queens this morning and I said, '*Lord, how're we gonna make it all the way to Harlem before RSfALC starts their first service?'* And you know what He said to me?" The church responded in a manner of encouraging her to continue. "He said, *'Daughter don't question me. Be obedient.'* And here I am. We called Sister Shannon, and she reminded us how Pastor Carmichael ain't like Senior." The congregation responded to her humor. Karen shook her head. "Uhn-uhn! He don't like surprises in the program." Karen cackled along with the audience.

The laughter went on for so long, I was able to observe even my parents and clergy were in agreement with her by the animation of their chortle as well.

I could be known for worse things…

I didn't like the diversion from the itinerary. Last week, we had to do it to address the failed scandal concerning my wife. To do so, we had a celebrity performance; Karen here would be no different. *Redeeming Souls* had been an established church for decades, and it was regular practice to have recording artists and well-known preachers visit. I tried to balance that activity with measuring when we'd have those figures here. This church was a conduit to salvation: a private oasis, purposely controlled for the welcoming in, healing, and repairing of souls. I didn't welcome the reputation of a celebrity church.

"Well, Pastor, I have to be obedient." Karen continued with suppliant eyes. "The Lord was dealing with me about you in my sleep since last night, in my hotel bed. I know I haven't checked in with you since your wedding, and we didn't get a chance to really talk at your momma's birthday party back in October because you were so busy working the room. But me and First Lady Carmichael talk every week, and she came out to Detroit last month, bragging about her Ezra." The church found humor in that as well.

I didn't. My mother was overly loquacious, especially with her closest girlfriends. More than that, I was deathly curious about what God had revealed to Karen, and wanted her to get to the point. As one God constantly used in the prophetic realm, I was very much accustomed to abruptly delivering a Word to people.

"Now, He wasn't clear on the reason," Karen admitted. "but He told me to show up and sing this song." She turned to the band directly behind her and nodded, apparently cuing. "I'll start off and you can pick up my key." Ahmed returned her nod. "Dwayne, you can pick up when it's time. Okay?"

Dwayne nodded, though clearly as lost as I was. Karen had blessed us in song on countless occasions, and had fellowshipped with us after service just as many times. She was familiar with Dwayne's keen talent enough for them to feed off each other. It was Dwayne's incredible gift as a musician and singer.

"Praise God," she whispered into the mic with her eyes closed, seemingly prepared to start.

I stood back to give her the stage, my mood no longer rigid, only curious. I waited along with the congregation.

"Oh, the glory…" she belted dynamically, clearly moving into a place of worship. "…of your presence. We your temple…give you reverence. So…arise to your rest…"

Swiping my beard with my palm, I recognized, right away, the psalm: *Oh the Glory of His Presence*. The song had been covered many times over the years. A powerful worship tune in its own right; however, when Karen belted it, you had no choice but to yield your spirit and open your soul to make room for His indwelling.

Ahmed and the band began the music, and not too long after, the choir sounded. The three entities had gelled that seamlessly. Only God could do that on a whim. Hardly two minutes into the song, my eyelids collapsed as I allowed Karen to guide us into His presence. The authority of the song and urgency of her vocals commanded you into meditation. Her gift was that anointed. It didn't matter how many times Karen had performed here. This was my band, not hers to have such an instant assembly to.

Absorbed in the holy atmosphere she created, my disposition began to ease. I apologized to God for my stubbornness, and confusing contentment with motivation needed to carry out His will. I didn't have to be happy to serve: serving was what I was born to do. Just like a layman with employment, you show up to work no matter what you feel like if you want to get paid. Only in the Kingdom, God instructs us to "*enter His gates with thanksgiving and His courts with praise.*" It does not matter what my life circumstances were, God was still going to get the glory, and His people still needed shepherding.

That's when it clicked.

Karen's assignment was to come here and grab the reins of the atmosphere for me, a foul-mood shepherd. I'd slipped. I'd allowed my circumstances to overtake me. My situation with Alexis had finally caught up to me. For these four weeks since we'd been separated, I had not accepted culpability in our failed marriage. I hadn't been reacting as a leader should. I'd been focused on her decision to end our covenant instead of considering my contributions. As leaders, rarely are we faultless when our governing entities go awry. When there's total duress, there is a link, in some form, to our governance.

As Karen sang the church into a Holy Ghost frenzy, my thoughts went to a friend of mine, whom I'd been in touch with increasingly since my beloved left our home. She wasn't a licensed practitioner. Though advanced in education, she had no formal training in the psychology or psychiatry; yet she'd been known for assisting couples into formal, loving, and lasting relationships. I met her two years ago through her relatives; fellow men and women of the cloth. She was not a clergy member, but was very much a part of their circle.

Yeah... A licensed professional seeking guidance from a non-licensed practitioner.

I'd only agreed to see her years back because I grew dismal about the covenant I'd made with God years ago about my calling, and she was the only person I knew who could understand marriage in the spiritual realm. I didn't totally agree with her ideologies regarding the dynamics between men and women in relationships, but could certainly understand the ones about the role of a woman married to a man of spiritual leadership. She had been comprehensive on the subject matter.

I reached out to her to update her on Alexis leaving, and she said something to me that had been left unsettled in my spirit since.

"Ezra, you relegate everything—including your wife—to a box, and the only two things inside of that box is you and God. You can't have a flourishing marriage if your wife isn't situated inside of that box and seated next to you and God. If God, in fact, gifted her to you—which is possible, biblically speaking—He didn't do so for you to interface with her like an object that can be tossed outside a box like your job, your education, your ministry, your martial arts, and your relationship with those outside of your home. That's a good practice to manage all those things, and not have them overtake you. But your wife is your equal. You can't be completely satisfied in life if you objectify her. She was created to help you, to take on your big world with you. Now let's say He did send her to you, do you think you're maximizing on her by consigning her to one place in your life: your sandbox? Is her only value in your life to physically feed you, and not mentally stimulate you, or spiritually back you? Is that all God created this bright, tough, apparently well-rounded—if she's been surviving in your contrasting world—loving, and nurturing woman for? Think about it! God is all-knowing, but you're not His only child. You're not His end all and be all. Ezra, you're good, but you ain't all that, sweetie."

Needless to say, I left that conversation offended and predictably angry. I refused to digest her counsel, and secretly viewed her position as rejection just as I had Alexis'.

How arrogant of me to carry that foul temperament to the sanctuary, not 'feeling' like serving God's people? Shame, humiliation—*sheer embarrassment*—is what I suddenly felt.

I found my arms outstretched and my face to the floor in exaltation as I stood motionless but for my mouth moving in praise. Karen stood next to me with an encouraging hand on my shoulder, belting out the lyrics that rebuked my spirit, as well as inspired my motivation to impart this morning.

I understood from that moment on, I had to develop an approach to gain the reins of my own life. I had to earn the role of leadership from Alexis. I had to win her over wholly. I had to account for the gift God had given me. Alexis was right: I had to somehow account for her love.

~Lex~

"And..." I glanced down at my notes on the conference room table. "I think that's—*Oh!*" My head shot up, scanning the table. "The safe house proposal was submitted to my mentor today." The small room when up in applause. There were even a few air fist pumps. "In fact, just before this meeting. He promises to have it back to me by the end of the business day tomorrow." I giggled in delight of their support on this. "So we all know how I'll be spending my weekend. It's due to the board on Monday morning so that it can make it to their agenda this month."

"You kick ass!" Eduardo declared. "Yo, could you imagine if *Christ Cares* expands like that?" he addressed Tamara, another outreach worker. "You really should be worshipped, mami."

"After the shit she's been through over the past few weeks, that board better cut us a break. We need it as a team. Plus, Lex, you been working so hard all month for this."

I cringed at her first statement. It took that small mention to remind me of the specific reason the board possibly wouldn't approve my proposal to use one of their many unoccupied properties in the city for emergency housing. Yes, I'd returned and addressed the email scandal, but they were still unsure of me. They had to be: they barely knew me. And even if Ezra could throw his weight on it, I wasn't too sure he'd want to, considering our separation.

"This could mean a lot for Harlem World. One hundred-seventy beds and community rooms? Shit... We need to start thinking about what we gon' do if they shoot us down." Larry, another outreach worker, twisted up his lips.

"You mean, as in counter their decision?" Richard, the program's crisis prevention counselor, sat up in his chair.

"Yeah!" Larry snapped his neck at no one in particular. "'Cause we got too many people in the city, still struggling to find a safe place to sleep at night. And the damn city gives priority to women with children. Last I checked, men have the same level of poverty and homelessness as women. If society would just change their old-fashion views on gender roles, we could have more equality." He sucked his teeth, ever so dramatically on closed rolling eyes before they reached me. "That's why I got your back, Lex. Even though you married to the pastor, you look out for everybody."

"Sure do!" Melanie announced in agreement.

Eduardo followed up with, "Gotta agree, Lex-Boogie."

"Actually, I don't. I only look out for the less fortunate," I admitted. "They have quieter voices in a heavy commerce-driven society."

"I don't think any of us here are any different, Lex," Richard's usually calm voice boomed through the small talk amidst the table.

It was my cue. After leaving Ezra on Valentine's Day, I called out of work for two whole weeks like a coward, unable to face my colleagues. I was really fucked up in my heart, my head, and compromised body. Richard called, and was able to encourage me to not allow too many days to pass before facing my team. He explained it would work against the reputation I'd been building before Nyree's email went out and they didn't know I was Mrs. Ezra Carmichael. After an hour long chat with his calming demeanor, I returned on Monday. The first day was hard as hell, especially with Mary's unannounced visit. But I'd been making it through the week, and getting lost in the safe house proposal helped.

"So listen, guys,"—my eyes fell to the table—"I guess it's time for me to address the email situation." I sighed after the room quieted. My heart raced so hard, I could hear it. "First, let me start off by apologizing— addressing my marital status." I took a deep breath. "I purposely kept that from you guys because I didn't want to be given your respect from the door because of who I'm married to; I wanted to earn it right out the gate. I know what it's like to feel like you're being looked past for someone who doesn't have the merit to do the job in question. I didn't want you to think this was that type of party." I was able to pull my chin up. "I know my shit: I worked it for almost a decade and then went back to school for the formal training of it. Marrying the leader of this organization didn't get me here. Trust me; he made sure to tell me." I snorted. *The motherfucker even made it hard for me to get here.* I could never forget that interview. "As for the email: I'm sorry you all had to see that. It—I swear to you—is a part of my past that if I could do over—"

"Don't you *even*!" Larry shook his bowed head.

"Nah, Lex. You ain't gotta go there," Eduardo declared. "Not for nothing, that's how we know you legit."

The other people at the table nodded and uttered words of agreement all at once.

"That's right. I know *Rusty's*," Larry shared. "I know the type of clientele he keep. That's probably where your passion come from. Working as a dancer made you a damn good social worker, Lex!"

"Damn, right," Richard offered loud enough, over the other approvals.

"Yup!" Ms. Baker cut in. "I can now look at Mr. Carmichael with more respect. He ain't too good to marry a real Harlem thoroughbred." She slapped palms with Melanie as the room busted out laughing, including me.

"But wait!" I tried slowing down to speak. My hand raised in the air. "I have to make this one thing clear." We all calmed down. "I didn't strip." I pounded my chest. "Much respect to all the strippers out there hustling to find their way. I ain't never mad at nobody's hustle, but that's what fucked—" I cringed. "That's what bothered me so much after my attack. I wasn't there enticing them as some of the articles suggested, and like what the girl who sent the email tried to imply. I was waiting tables. I didn't interact with them." I took a deep breath. Memories of my inner thoughts during that period came flashing forward.

"Uuuh!" Richard straightened again in his seat. "As Larry said, we don't need you to rehash it for us. We're just glad you're back." He gave the table a cursory glance to prompt their approval.

It was unnecessary. They were clearly on one accord.

"Lex," Eduardo cleared his throat as he started stacking his papers as though preparing to leave. "It's a done deal. As long as you're healthy and happy. We're good, babe."

"Yup," the ladies sounded.

I took a deep breath to calm my emotions. They were being gracious about this thing. I checked my phone for the time.

"Hey, that's it for today. It's almost two. You guys take the rest of the day off, and I'll see you tomorrow."

We all had varying hours, but most times, some of them didn't take a lunch because of being that entrenched in their roles. When Ms. Bethea explained to me last holiday season the parameters of dismissing my staff early, I made sure to implement it as often as ethical. They were a hard working group, rarely slipping on their posts.

After the shouts of approval, we all filed out of the room. As I took to the stairs to head down to the second floor, I could feel the start of hunger pangs. Pregnancy somehow intensified all of my senses. I was looking forward to a hot shower and a fat ass burger from the hotel's restaurant after picking up Ms. Remah's prescriptions after work. Unlike my staff, I wouldn't be leaving early. I had two interviews for an administrative assistant scheduled for this afternoon. Ann had been able to identify two candidates she believed would be a good fit for our team. We needed one as our new funding increased our workload and marketing needs.

As I ambled down the hall toward my office, my phone vibrated on my portfolio.

Ezra: Would you be available for dinner after service this evening? I would like to see you.

My heart stopped and my feet lost their rhythm. I stumbled.

Again?

After addressing the church two Sundays ago, Ezra and I had dinner together, and it didn't go so well. I didn't think he'd want to see me so soon. This felt awkward. I didn't recognize the place I was in with Ezra, and probably because I knew shit about marriage. If we were just dating, I would think this was where we'd break up. But we weren't dating. Legally, we were still very much bound to each other. *Bound.* That word made me think about bonded. And bonded made me think of bondage. And bondage in the same context of Ezra made my body react in ways that were inappropriate for where I was, and worked against the fact that we were separated.

Shit!

Entering my office, I pushed the door, but not hard enough for it to close shut. If I had, I'd sure be rubbing one off at my desk. I knew this because I'd done it once or twice at the rec. Instead, I sat down and returned his text. This was no easy feat for me. My feelings for Ezra were so unsettled. One minute I hated him, and then in the next beat, my heart would bleed for him. Like this past Sunday at church. From the moment he hit the pulpit, I wasn't used to the feelings that came over me of sharing the heavy load he obviously carried with him. His broad shoulders hung lower than usual. There was a thick crease between his brows as he struggled internally. He sat down when he hit the pulpit, something he wasn't known to do. Dwayne threw far more glances in his direction than I was accustomed to seeing on a Sunday morning. And for the first time, on the stage, Ezra seemed unsure. That small show of being a mortal human was what softened my feelings for him. He seemed lost and nothing like the demanding man in my hotel room last week.

And the way he folded when that lady came and sang. I knew if anything could break Ezra down it was anything church or God-related, but... His vulnerability that day on the pulpit was crippling. He sobbed without tears while mimicking the submissive position. I took that thought with me as I replied with as much courtesy as I could gather.

Me: They're saying a storm should be landing tonite. Might not be a good idea for me to drive in that.

I rolled my eyes at my soft attempt at saying no to him. It bothered me to reject him. I sure as hell hated when he'd do it to me, but I couldn't give a damn about appealing to Ezra's feelings anymore. My right hand went to my flat belly. I had something...someone far more important to please. *My miracle.* Flutters erupted in my belly at that thought. My eyes went adrift in the corner of the room.

Damn. I'm having a baby!

That controlling fucker had gotten one off on me. If anybody could impregnate *my* womb it would be him. I chuckled quietly in my office.

Goddamn him!

Ezra: I wouldn't imagine having you drive that late. We can have dinner at your new favorite eatery.

The hotel? That was considerate. But it was also now impossible for me to say no. My shoulders dropped. I missed the house—terribly. How could I not? But I'd been enjoying being in the cut. There was no pressure in that small room where I could pig out, sleep, pray, and rub my belly excessively without worrying about being caught. It was my private joy. I was also on a timer for when the world would know. Either I had to tell Ezra, Mary would run her trap, or my growing belly would tell on itself.

Shit!

"*Life as a shorty shouldn't be so tough...*" Or is it "rough"? The lyrics popped into my head. I couldn't remember. My mom used to blast *C.R.E.A.M.* all the time in the house.

The buzzing of my phone broke my thoughts.

Ezra: Please don't make me beg, Alexis...

Damn, Ezra!

Me: Sure.

"Are you happy?" I asked out loud.

"About what?" I glanced up to Ms. Bethea's twisted expression.

I cracked a smile. "Marital issues," I replied, shaking my head.

"Oh." She smiled. "Wanna ride over together for our first interview?"

I checked the time. "Oh, wow! Yes." I began gathering my things. The interview was being held in the *Grace Room* at *RSfALC*. Their space was actually more impressive than ours here, which is why they held all interviews over there. "Let me just grab a few snacks to nibble on. I kinda rushed through lunch," I muttered, scurrying to get ready.

"Take your time. I'll meet you downstairs," Ann offered before leaving.

My phone sounded again.

Ezra: I am well pleased, beloved.

I froze at that reference. Why did that name still affect me so?

Because you're in love with him no matter his stupid-ass-ness.

I exhaled hard as I grabbed my things and stomped out of my office.

I experienced another thought-provoking sermon by Ezra during Bible study that night. He spoke about God being more concerned with holiness versus happiness. Ezra explained happiness is a state of mind, a temporary sensation that, for most, can change the moment a small detail of life goes awry. This is why God's focus isn't on keeping us happy.

Some guy named Paul in the Bible said he could find contentment in any state. "*I know how to be abased, and I know how to abound. Everywhere and in all things I have learned both to be full and to be hungry, both to abound and to suffer need. I can do all things through Christ who strengthens me.*" I made sure to record these verses in the fourth chapter of Philippians, because it spoke to me, too.

In my search for happiness, I always came up short. Even with Ezra: there were times I felt the fortune of our marriage—plenty of times I could see the benefit of being by his side. But then he'd turn around and do something '*Ezra*' that caused me to wonder how could such opposition exist in one person. Yes, I knew my husband was by no means perfect, I just expected more from him as a pastor and well educated professional. Why those accomplishments raised my expectations, I didn't know. Ezra was just like every human man I'd encountered, only his flaws varied. The question was, could I live with them as his wife. I wasn't so sure.

But why? Was it because I was chasing happiness instead of something deeper? Something God wanted me to focus on rather than my idealism of marriage and life, in general? *What is happiness anyway?*

According to Ezra, holiness is a lifestyle God's people should adapt to, aligning their lives with his will while on this journey. He said many people shun the idea of holiness, believing it to be too limited in terms of what is or is not acceptable Christian living. Instead, he encouraged us to view it as putting parameters around sin to keep us safe and at low risk of sinning.

Apparently, holiness is a long-term practice and goal, rather than a short-lived state of mind like happiness.

"Hebrews 12:14 says, '*Make every effort to live in peace with everyone and to be holy; without holiness no one will see the Lord*'," he informed. Ezra's delivery was smooth, unrushed, and well measured in the quieted sanctuary. His voice was so commanding at some points, I had to stop recording my notes to gaze up at him. "Happiness is a fleeting state of mind. Holiness is a long-term goal that leads to everlasting life."

It amazed me how he was able to come up with such relevant, educational, persuasive, and impactful messages. And I swear, for me, he was the exact opposite of his father. I had to keep in mind this was just my opinion because back when Bishop Carmichael preached every service, the congregation got with him, too. But with Ezra it had been different.

Ezra didn't shout out his words for affirmation or to incite people to jump from their seats. He somehow guided us into his sermons to think and consider life application. And by the time he was done, I guess folks wanted the tools he spoke of so badly, they shot from their seats for him to pray that they got them. *Shoot!* Several times since being married to him, I'd been tempted to go up for prayer myself. Of course I never did, thinking it odd and not wanting to throw him off his game—if that were possible.

Tonight, his flow was just as smooth as usual during his sermon, but in between him praying for people, I saw signs of exhaustion. He moved a little slower. He didn't give his occasional smiles when he spoke to some requesting prayer at the altar. It seemed to be all about business up there.

Lilly tapping me to let me know Sister Shannon was at the end of the pew calling for me broke my attention. Sister Shannon did her index finger swirl to let me know I needed to grab all of my things. I immediately figured this was Ezra, making sure I was ready to leave at a decent time for our dinner. I hugged Lills goodnight before leaving my seat.

I waited outside of *the Bishop's Office* while Ezra changed out of his robe. He didn't take very long, but as I waited, I witnessed the bodyguards assigned to the office tell at least five people Pastor was unavailable to speak and they should make an appointment with his assistant. That was awkward, but I was grateful: *we* were hungry.

The door opened and my hand flew to grab my purse from the seat next to me before standing to my feet. When I met his eyes, I stumbled.

Goddamn, Ezra was a fine chunk of man without even trying.

He wore a charcoal wool suit with a gray turtleneck. It was a rather informal look for him and the suit jacket had just one button. His overcoat was tossed over his right arm where his hand was tucked in his pants pocket, and he carried his leather satchel on his left shoulder. He walked over, his eyes intently on me. My whole pelvis area vibrated with a new type of excitement never felt before. Those eyes. There was something in them that had not been there on Sunday when we last saw each other. His left hand rose en route to my face before retracting. Instead, it went to my wrist—his right hand joined in. And he did something he hadn't in a while. He circled them. Only this time there was no seduction, it was intimacy. His eyelids were heavy, but not with lust. Ezra was preoccupied with something. Something other than disproving me or mesmerizing me. I didn't know how to feel about that.

"You hungry?" he rasped.

My mouth hung open. I had to swallow to speak.

"Starved."

"I'm quite famished myself." He cracked a smile that caused a tightening in my core.

My eyes diverted. *What the hell, Lex! Get it the fuck together!*

"Let's go. I've been told the winds are kicking up."

He took me by the hand and led me out of the building and into the parking lot. Ezra walked me to my car before taking off to his truck with security hovering. I followed him out of the city, and even learned a short cut to the hotel. The whole ride there I tried schooling myself on how to act around him. I couldn't fall back into my old feelings for Ezra. We weren't the same people. I would not fall further for him, risking it all. What was more important was gauging his mood. At some point I had to tell him about my bundle of joy. By doing so, I also had to prepare myself for the ultimate rejection. It would certainly come.

I parked next to Ezra at the hotel. He waited for me as I got out of the car. The wind was brutal and the first of the rain and hail mixture had begun to fall. Ezra took me at the hand again, leading me to the doors of the hotel.

Once we entered the lobby, while brushing off his overcoat, he asked, "Would you like to go to your room to get cleaned up before dinner?"

I thought about it, but quickly decided against it. Shaking my head, I murmured, "No thanks." I was too hungry to delay it.

We walked over to the restaurant entrance inside where we were taken to a table right away and given menus. The place was pretty much empty. I'd guessed not much was popping in the countryside of Jersey this Thursday night while shaking out of my coat with Ezra's assistance. He handed them over to the hostess.

The waitress arrived and introduced herself. "Let's start off with some drinks. Can I offer you a cocktail?"

Ezra's eyes arrived at me with invitation. My stomach flipped, and I found myself swallowing hard. "Just a ginger ale, please."

"And I'll have sparkling water," Ezra added.

Quickly, the waitress responded, "Okay. Let me go grab those for you."

"Pardon," Ezra called out when she turned to walk off. "Could we order now as well? She's pretty hungry."

"Sure," she replied. "What can I get you?"

"She'll have your bacon cheeseburger: lettuce, tomatoes, red onions—please be sure they're red and not yellow—mayonnaise, ketchup, and five pickles." Ezra questioned his accuracy with his eyes. I nodded, hiding my shock.

He remembered...

"That comes with fries," the waitress informed.

"Yes. Your steak fries will work," he advised. "And I'll have your fish of the day broiled, a baked sweet potato, and your house salad."

"Okay. I'll get that right in and bring your drinks."

Ezra nodded his approval before turning to me. He seemed to study my face from top to bottom for minutes long. It was weird, but so was my enigmatic husband.

"How's the social service wing of *Christ Cares*?" he finally spoke.

I lifted my eyebrows. "It's been my lifeline. The staff is great; Ann's been supportive...Precious has been ghost." I shrugged. "What more can a girl ask for?"

When my eyes returned to him, I found Ezra nodding. "Good to know."

"What do you have her busy with anyways?" I asked, curious about why she hadn't been lurking around much.

I'd seen her a couple of times since the email blast, but there was not much to say, though we worked in the same building. The last time Precious had been ghost like that, Ezra had forced her on a hiatus.

Unenthused, he stretched his forehead. "I haven't assigned her anything rigorous. I imagine her scarce presence is due, in large part, to the fact that she's dating. She's been spending lots of time in Atlanta."

"With that Wilkinson dude?" My eyes grew.

Ezra's attention went to pulling out his vibrating phone. He glanced at it while answering, "It can be anyone's guess," without emotion. His face was hard, filled with exhaustion. He silenced the phone before placing it on the table and regarding me again.

"How are you, Ezra?" Something was off with him. "Have you seen the doctor?" Maybe he was coming down with something this winter.

Slowly, he glanced up, eyes meeting mine, and his elbows landed on the table while his head angled slightly. "I don't believe it would take too many guesses to describe my current woes, Alexis."

Our eyes were deadlocked. I noticed he didn't detail his problems that I knew involved me not being home with him. That provided a level of comfort for me. I wouldn't have been able to tolerate a begging man. I was not in his home because I decided not to be, and no amount of convincing could fix that. Ezra going that route would have ended this dinner before it began.

Our drinks arrived. I gulped down a few sips hoping to settle my rumbling stomach. I knew nausea would set in soon if I didn't eat. The soda helped a little. I was able to focus on contributing to a conversation.

"How's Mary? The last I heard from her, she wasn't feeling well. She said she had an appointment with her doctor this week."

Ezra pushed his glass back. "She was in the E.R. this week. They kept her overnight."

"Oh, my god!" I gasped. "Is she okay? I didn't know!" Shock couldn't begin to describe what I felt.

Mary said she had some health issues she'd been dealing with, but never did I think they were serious enough for random emergency room visits. *Shit!* I needed to call her. I couldn't imagine Bishop providing the patient care someone recently admitted into the hospital required.

Ezra's eyes, which held something unidentifiable, stayed on me. He didn't blow off my sincere melodramatic response. "She was dismissed the following afternoon, so I can only put my faith in her physician's decision."

I leaned into the table, afraid to inquire. "You think it's related to those migraines she gets?"

Since the first night I met her, Mary struggled with some sort of head pains. She never spoke of it in detail to me.

"All she said was 'old woman crisis' and not to worry about it. It's very indicative of a woman her age: Very closed off and private about health concerns."

"Mary ain't old!" I snorted on a whisper. "She may be stubborn with answers, but that woman has more life than you know. I'mma call her and see what's going on."

Ezra snorted this time. "Good luck with that," he murmured.

"Shoot! That's the least she could come clean with, considering how much she's in my ass—I meant butt."

Ezra chuckled, his eyes downcast at the table as he fingered the condensation on his glass. "Is that what you call it? I call it meddling."

I sucked my teeth. "Call it whatever you want. Mary's gonna cough up some 411."

A soft smile formed on Ezra's face. It was one that met his eyes as he regarded me with a slanted head, totally relaxed in his seat. I couldn't help but return his gaze. I wanted to know what was behind it. This was another mask he was giving me. It wasn't predatory, lust-filled, admonishing, or loaded with agenda. I wanted to ask, but didn't want to give him another opportunity to reject me. I made a promise to myself to knock that shit off. If he didn't want to offer me more than a home and an incredible fuck, I would just walk away from him altogether. And I did.

Just then, the keys to a piano sounded. A smooth and charismatic voice announced himself and informed that he'd be playing no matter the harsh weather outside. I twisted in my seat to find the source. I found a suited man, sitting behind a black piano in the corner of the restaurant, playing with rain pouring behind him in the oversized windows. I didn't realize the restaurant had live music. I'd also temporarily forgotten about the coming storm. It had been announced for a few days. I didn't pay it much mind because it was supposed to clear by late morning tomorrow. I'd told Ann I may be in late depending on the severity of it. The city would only see harsh winds and mild rain.

I turned back to face Ezra. "Hey," His eyes moved from the entertainment. "You gonna be okay getting home?"

"We don't live that far from here, Alexis," he rasped, reminding me of the hour growing late. Ezra was tired.

"Yeah, but the house is almost a thirty-minute drive." I knew this when I'd decided on the place. "And with the way trees fall into the road around here, that may be risky." I was genuinely concerned.

"Alexis, I have an SUV. I'll be okay. Besides, I'm enjoying your company," he supplied resolutely. "Unless you prefer I leave. I don't want to impose on your privacy."

I shook my head as I went for my soda. "I'm fine as long as you are."

"And here we are." The waitress appeared, delivering our food.

My plate hardly met the table top before I went for my bun to remove it and pour ketchup all over. I was engrossed right away, suddenly feeling hunger pangs that weren't there seconds before my food arrived.

"Would you allow a few minutes to express grace?"

I glanced up to find Ezra's eyes filled with humor. I dropped my burger, feeling like shit. Had I really forgotten my morals after leaving the pastor's house for only a few weeks?

I met Ezra's open hand and my pelvis leaped at the heat of it. I can shamefully admit that while he was doing his due diligence as a believer, all I could think of was what it was like to have those hot palms against my bare back when he had me bent over, thrusting into my core, or against my one nipple when his moist lips were on the other, or at the back of my neck when he was pumping his thickness into my mouth. Damn. Being here with Ezra conjured those same thoughts I'd been struggling with and thought I'd buried, knowing sex with my husband was bad for me: it weakened me. Fucked with my Harlem Pride.

But fuck!

That one time after the R. Kelly concert when I rode his ass in the living room with the inspiration from the show, he was so caught up, he dug his nails in my ass as I dropped down on him. I didn't feel it right away. I was too busy riding out all the pent up desire I had from the conversation I had with Tasche and another girl she invited while we walked out of the show. They agreed they didn't know a single man who could bring what R. Kelly was selling in his music. I silently disagreed. I knew I had a fucking freak at home that could top anything appealing I'd ever heard. I just didn't know that freak was home sleeping while waiting for me. My pussy dripped the moment I smelled him when I came through the door. And when I saw his big body stretched out on the furniture, I knew I couldn't wait until we got upstairs and undressed. I managed to pull him out while he was still asleep, taking him into my mouth. I was a little tipsy, but didn't give a damn. I was on a mission to make good on what I knew Ezra could bring. And by the time I sat on him, the same big hot hands that I was now holding had been on my back. His nails softly scraping down my torso until they met my hips where he clung while my walls swallowed him in—

"Alexis..." his rasped tone ripped me from my thoughts.

My eyes opened and just as I was about to counter his Alexis with beloved, I realized I was gripping his palms. His thick, bushy brows were hiked inquisitively.

My face froze as the big question hit me. Why hadn't Ezra tried to fuck me yet? Where was his manipulating seduction? Why hadn't he demanded me to his bed?

The fuck? My face fell.

It's not that I'd been so preoccupied with sex, considering all that I now had on my plate with my at-risk employment, walking away from my home, and a damn miracle pregnancy. Trust me, I'd had my rough nights with need, but I'd forgotten all about this incredible draw I had to this man. My husband. I forgot how my body responded to his mere heat. I was now so damn hormonal that it pissed me the hell off how he hadn't expressed his need for me: the sole need he'd ever admitted to having of me.

"Is everything okay, Alexis?" His face was still screwed with confusion and...worry?

I shook my head, suddenly frustrated. I couldn't. Wouldn't! You don't get over a broken heart by giving it back to the one who had recently shattered it. Besides, he'd never wanted it in the first place.

He only needed your body, remember?

I sighed. "I'm good."

I picked up my burger and my appetite automatically resumed. I stuffed my face with juicy beef, crunchy vegetables, and dripping sauces. It was my heaven. I had little control around these burgers. It left no room for decorum. I realized this when I caught Ezra's deadpan gaze on me when I was midway into it. My eyes went wild. That was until he cracked an amused grin.

"You're making me envy that cow," he rasped before forking his sweet potato.

I glanced down at his healthy plate and saw no traces of fat juices.

"Well, that's just one of us. I don't envy diet food. Gimme some fat," I informed before going for my next bite. I quickly stuffed in a steak fry.

Ezra's head tossed back as he laughed hard.

I continued with my plate as I enjoyed the smooth tunes ringing from the piano. Ezra did the same, occasionally tossing a glance over to the corner of the room.

When we were done, Ezra flagged the waitress for the bill.

Feeling wonderfully satiated, my hands went straight to my midsection, and I rubbed my belly contently.

"That good, huhn?" Ezra's eyes signaled my midsection.

My hands fell.

"Is that all for you guys?" The waitress was at our table. "I'll settle this for you quickly. It's coming down pretty bad out there. At least two of our staff called out, and the news reports are saying it won't let up till around seven in the morning." She leaned into the table. "I don't mean to sound rude, but you might consider getting a room here. My boyfriend works in emergency services, and he texted me saying they'd been called already to an accident on Brewington."

Brewington Road was one of the main roads in the area. That *I* knew.

"Thanks for that update," Ezra supplied before she left with his card.

Our eyes met again in muted exchange.

"Alexis, I will be fine driving home. Please don't worry." He retrieved his phone from the table to place it back in his pocket.

I knew Ezra wasn't the type of man that liked to be pushed. In order to hold my tongue, I diverted my eyes back to the piano. The guy was still going, so engrossed as though the weather didn't faze him at all.

"He probably has a room." Ezra read my mind.

"There's nothing like peace of mind," I threw back at him.

When I thought he'd return my sass, he only smiled and redirected *his* eyes.

Ezra?

"Here you go, sir. Please sign the top copy. The bottom is yours to keep." She handed Ezra a pen only for him to pull out his own. "And folks, *please* be safe. It's ugly out there."

"Thanks," Ezra and I returned out of sync.

We collected our coats from the hostess up front and headed into the lobby. I watched uneasily as Ezra adjusted his overcoat while observing the downpour outside from the massive windows. It looked scary-dangerous out there: all you saw were sheets of rain falling from the sky.

He turned to me once all fastened. "Please call Ms. Remah to check in on her. Let her know I just left and will be there in less than an hour. I'll give myself extra time on the road."

Glaring lightning struck and the few patrons and front desk staff gasped. A man drenched from the rain burst into the lobby through the revolving door, out of breath.

"Four!" He held up as many fingers. "Four damn stalled cars. Two in an impact, one turned over, and another in a ditch—and I'm coming from only two miles up the road!" His face was red from the neck up; he was so distressed. "You can't see anything out there!"

That's it!

"Just come upstairs. You know I have two beds," I offered Ezra.

His eyes flew from the man who was removing his hat, uncovering his soaked silken hair.

"Alexis—"

Damn it, Ezra, I may be upset with you, but I don't hate you!

I spoke over him. "I'm not explaining to Mary and the *RSfALC* community how I let you drive out there in that shit! It's just a few hours, then you're free to go about your merry way." I voiced my concern.

Ezra sighed. "Are you sure? I don't want to intrude. I can even get my own room if that would make you feel more comfortable."

What?

And there it was... That's what I'd been getting from Ezra!

Humility.

It was in his eyes since we left *RSfALC*.

We stood in the middle of the lobby with locked eyes, desperately trying to read one another. He didn't want to bogart his way into my personal space. That was so unlike the beast I knew who snatched me from Harlem and dragged me up here to the woods under the guise of covenant. The man before me was gentle and considerate.

I sighed, eyelids collapsing. "Ezra, you're my husband, not a random man I met at a local Bible study tonight. I can endure one night with you. I'm not in any danger." *Well...my heart is an endangered species when it comes to you.* "And let's be real, you're footing the bill for the room anyway."

After the longest period of silence, Ezra rasped, "Okay. I'll take your extra bed."

Why did that relieve me? Was it because it was the right thing to do or because deep down inside I needed a night with him? *And not for sex!* I didn't need to return to that lustful fog he could entrap me into. I didn't know why I was okay with doing this. I tossed this over all the way to the elevator and down the hall to my room.

When I opened the door tagged *Do Not Disturb*, I stretched my arm, inviting him into my new home. Quietly, Ezra strolled in, bringing with him all the grace and confidence he'd always carried, even with this new docile demeanor he portrayed. I closed the door and paced further inside, stopping next to him. The place seemed smaller with Ezra here. His eyes perused the standard room. They stopped across the way and I followed their path to the extra bed that was Ms. Remah's. My eyes collapsed in shame. The bed was mounded with a suitcase, a duffle bag, and layers of clothes.

I watched as his eyes landed on the bed I actually used, closer to where we stood. My shoulders dropped this time. The comforter, sheets, and pillows were in total disarray. I was embarrassed. Ezra hated an unmade bed. In my defense, I'd forgotten to remove the door tag so the room could be cleaned. My head was so busy with finishing the proposal, I rushed out of here with a one track mind.

I cleared my throat as I shuffled over to the bed, straightening the pillows. "Take off your coat and get comfy. I would offer you a night cap," I joked while pulling up the sheets and comforter, "but I know you don't drink. *ESPN?*" I offered nodding toward the television.

Ezra didn't reply. With heavy eyes, he began pulling off his coat. When I was done with the bed, I followed suit, coming out of my clothes while he used the bathroom. I exhaled deeply once the door closed. I sent a text to Ms. Remah to check on her. I needed her to know Ezra wouldn't be going home tonight, either.

When Ezra ambled out of the bathroom, I held my pajamas in my hand as I motioned to my bed, "I guess you're stuck with me tonight. Try not to express too much disappointment. I sleep on the left side, as usual." He snorted before loosening his tie. I murmured, "Get comfortable."

I made my way into the bathroom to pin up my hair and shower. Even my bones were tired. It had been a long day—including an unexpected turn of events. I couldn't believe Ezra was here with me. And I wasn't annoyed by that strange fact.

After my shower, I lotioned and threw on a flannel gown that looked more like a shirt than pajamas. When I opened the door, Ezra was in the bed, shirtless watching television. He flipped it off when I toed out. I dropped to my knees to pray, something I'd been doing for some time now. My life had been so up and down, I needed to develop some consistency to keep from going crazy. I didn't recite long prayers. I did as Ezra taught me, which was naming my request no matter how big or small. Then I ended with thanking God for all the good things about my life, no matter how big or small. It had been a therapeutic practice for me.

After killing the light, I climbed into bed, shuffling into the mattress and pillow until I found comfort. I immediately heard and felt Ezra twisting himself, but what surprised me was the nearing of his body heat. I wanted to panic. It was a decided choice. Until his scent invaded me, coating me with warmth and familiarity. It teased me with that feeling of normal, because that's how my world had been for months being in his home and under his guardianship. I felt him at my back, almost molding into me. That was until he eased a throw pillow at the small of my back and ass, separating us. His hard, wiry legs hit the back of mine and his strong and hard arm reached over my side, resting on my waist as his hand splayed over my abdomen. My belly leaped in surprise. And it was that immediate feeling of belonging that had me easing into the spell of sleep in no time.

I felt warmer than usual. Like every damn where. I didn't want to focus on my high body temperature or other senses. I only wanted to return to sleep. I tried recapturing my last conscious thoughts, hoping they would hurl me back into the dream I'd awakened from. I couldn't recall the details, only that they were warming and...arousing. There was only one subject matter that could arouse me at this point in my life.

Ezra.

That's what I smelled. His delicious scent assaulted my nostrils. My lips separated, groin stirred, secreting my sex. My breasts felt unusually heavy, nipples tingled something fierce. I felt a dense muscle twitch against my ass.

My eyes cracked then bulged. I told myself to calm the hell down. Ezra stayed with morning boners. It's a guy thing. I tried stretching in place. That only intensified my state. *Fuck!* If I didn't release this shit, I'd be hurting for days! I knew this because it's what led me to rubbing them off again last week when I couldn't take it anymore. The difference was this level of horniness far exceeded what'd I'd been feeling while alone. Ezra was here with me.

I checked the clock on the nightstand, noting the lighter tone of the rain outside. It was 6:18 a.m.

I jerked my neck back toward him. Ezra was still asleep. I couldn't believe it. It was over an hour past his usual wake up time. Yet he was here in my bed, dead asleep without a care in the world. *Hell! Back at home, I'd have to beg to see him in bed at this hour.* That simple fact pushed me over the edge.

I shuffled around and pushed him until his back hit the mattress. Ezra's eyes flew open as I was pulling down his boxers. I saw the moment they trailed down.

"Beloved..." his morning hoarseness pleaded.

It wasn't a simple task, but I managed them down to his legs with roughness. Then my eyes focused in on his standing erection, sprouting from a bed of hairs. I swear until Ezra, I'd never seen anything so masculine and beautiful than his dick. Our eyes locked over it; his, a mixture of shock and curiosity, and mine in uncontrollable excitement. While his weary eyes held mine, I scraped my top lip as I contemplated. I wanted to push him into my mouth and suck him dry, but that would've been too much like old times. I didn't want to fall back into the old groove with Ezra. I needed something new or nothing at all. And I knew if I played this wrong, we'd find ourselves back where we started.

No.

I reached for him, grazing my palm lightly over the thick veins of his swollenness. I don't know which beat harder and faster, my heart or clitoris. Shit! I wanted him so bad. My left hand joined, stroking him now in a particular rhythm. I was exploring him, something I'd never done because my impulsive ass jumped in head first. Ezra was absolutely beautiful, alpha. Even his dick stood dominantly. His thick head that I vividly recalled being so smooth against the bed of my tongue was carved perfectly.

This fat edge is what brought me to climax countless times, I thought as my thumb traced the rim of his cock.

His hands rose, reaching for me as he rasped, "Sweetheart." His face etched in tortured pain.

"Don't!" I warned. His hands and arms froze mid-flight, just inches away from my heaving chest. "My rules. My way," I gritted. Our eyes locked as my heart thrummed with anxiety never felt. Ezra had never let me lead in the past. It was always his rules. I'd never been able to explore his body. Yeah, I knew my husband had pronounced abs, but I'd never been given a moment where I could see them tremble in arousal as they were now. "Hands over your head. Grab the edge of the mattress!"

Slowly, Ezra's arms reversed in direction, and his hands dug beneath the pillows until I could see the big balls of his triceps. His face was tight with an unknown emotion, but I held my footing. I had to.

"If you move, I stop, Ezra! Don't test me," I hissed.

His eyes softened in acquiescence. My hands automatically moved to grab him, and stroked him rhythmically, enjoying the way his abs leaped each time I reached his bulbous head. Ezra sucked air through his teeth, tormenting me.

"Beloved," he cried out in a tortured whisper.

"Don't!" I warned, more nervous than angry.

I was so damn aroused. Ezra did that shit to me! He got under my skin without trying.

"Baby," he called to me with eyes so slanted I could barely see his pupils, "please let me touch you. I won't do anything you don't want me to. I just need to feel you."

Holy shit! I'd never seen him beg. Ezra had never been so needy.

My groin twisted, my pussy dripping as a result.

"You don't get to touch! You wanna feel me?"

"Yes, baby." He nodded, bushy brows meeting.

"I'll do it *for* you. You move an inch and your ass is out of here!" I warned.

I scooted up his legs and sat so my sex touched his. I pulled my pajamas over my head, tossing it on the floor. Ezra sucked in air. My eyes bulged at the sight of my hard and dark chocolate nipples that were damn near black. Seeing them in the same visual as his bare skin did shit to me. I was so wet, I could feel it on my ass. My finger swiped against myself and a string of desire pulled away, linking it to my cave. Ezra caught it, and his whole body went rigid. I rubbed my wetness onto his erection.

"*Oh!*" he moaned.

Excited at that reaction, I swiped more and rubbed it onto him. I kept doing it until I had enough to stroke his full pipe. The sounds he made came from the pit of his belly. I wanted him inside me so bad, but refused to do it. The moment I let him inside, was the moment I would lose. His dick had special powers. It was best he was outside. I had no idea I could be so devious. I gripped him tightly, trying to mimic my sex. I don't know how close to it I was, but he eventually began thrusting with me. He lifted his pelvis so high, his dick brushed against my clit. My body jerked, but I quickly recovered and scooted closer. Ezra was so long that I could grind onto him and stroke the top of him all at once.

Goddamn… My head rolled back.

I was so damn wet, my rolling hands never went sticky or dry. It was pure gel against muscle. His hardness rubbed against that bundle of nerves. He felt incredible in my hands and against my sex.

"Kitten!" he whispered intoxicatingly. *He called me kitten!* That thrilled me. I needed to hear that odd term of endearment. Especially while seeing his hard chest muscles bunched between his arms as he clenched the mattress while he grinded into me. "I'm about to come."

"Hold it!" I yelled harder than necessary.

He wouldn't ruin this for me. I wasn't ready. I could've come long ago, but he'd taught me how to hold and control them. I pumped him and grinded, studying the free fall of my breasts and my hair, that somehow loosened, brushing against my back. I kept going, thrilled by holding his virility in my hands as I squatted over his big hard body. No pastor, no engineer, damn the therapist, fuck a domineering husband…he was now my subdued lover.

I struggled to open my eyes, but when I did, I caught Ezra's eyes squeezed shut and his tongue roved over his top teeth, from canine to canine.

That was my undoing. I felt the first wave of my orgasm and within seconds, I bucked into him out of sync with my hand movements.

"Kitten!" Ezra cried and his body jerked violently.

"Shit!" I screamed. "I told you to hold it, damn it!"

As my groin began its release, I watched as the head of my husband's cock squirted his essence into the air. It was my most erotic sight. Intimacy like never before. Addictive. I tried catching some of it with my hand but couldn't manage it all with my own fall over the edge. My head rolled back, and I could only anchor myself with the firm grip on his erection. I came so unbelievably hard I didn't know how long I was lost in ecstasy. Our shrieking moans erupted together as we rocked into each other. Ezra and I cried out until shouts turned into whimpers. I thrust against him until I could no longer. And when he sucked in air again, I knew he was too sensitive to touch, too, and I released him. I collapsed onto the bed next to him, unable to open my eyes, and relieved to not have landed on the floor or on him, hurting myself.

I listened to our ragged breaths, suddenly recognizing the contractions in my belly, my post-orgasmic satiation evolved into concerned about the baby. Was that too much? Is it okay? So many questions racing through my mind. My hand went directly to my belly, not caring that he was next to me. My new reality came crashing in as I tried catching my breath.

"Alexis," Ezra rasped, still gasping for air.

"Yeah," I replied half-heartedly, my mind on to more important things.

"Would you mind catching a show with me?"

My face wrinkled. That was the last thing I expected to hear.

"Show?"

"Yes. *Phantom of the Opera*. I've been wanting to see that since learning there're several cast changes. I'd like it if you could attend with me," he murmured gently, still gaining his breath.

What the fuck?

When did we turn this corner? Did I want to go out with Ezra? I was supposed to be flushing him from my system after all, not inviting him to my room and then semi-fucking him. The proposal seemed in earnest, and I didn't want to hurt his feelings.

Feelings?

Ezra had no feelings! But I wouldn't be a mood buster. That was his game, not mine.

"Sure."

"Sure?" he echoed in disbelief.

My eyes roved over the ceiling as I rubbed my belly, studying the slowing of my throbbing core.

I don't think any major damage has been done. The lingering contractions slowed. Definitely calling my GYN about this. Until I get the green light, I'm staying the hell away from Ezra since I couldn't keep my hands off of him after spending one measly night together.

"Ezra…"

"Yes, beloved."

"You need to go."

There was a small break of silence, but not a moment of regret on my part. I didn't know what Ezra had in mind when inviting me to dinner last night, but if it was to appeal to me, he had to start with my heart, and what we did had to do with lots of my body parts, but not my heart.

"Okay," he gasped before leaving my bed.

~five~

~Lex~

I studied my circling thumbs while sitting on the exam table, wearing nothing but a gown and trouser socks.

I should stop and get a manicure after I leave here… But then I'll be starving and sick by the time I reach the hotel. That won't work…

My mind ran with what I should do. Everything now revolved around me not getting sick, or me eating, or me not giving away my pregnancy, or thoughts of him. Ezra. It had been four weeks since leaving him, and I still couldn't get him out of my system. I resented myself for being so weak when it came to Ezra. How could you still want a man who marginalized your…existence? Ezra put me in a damn cage. Unless I was fucking him, I was useless. Who could be in love with a man like that? Then to add insult to injury, I was carrying his baby—his *unwanted* baby.

Ezra not wanting this baby wasn't an issue for me; I could take care of my child on my own. It's my blessing to have. Me still wanting Ezra was the issue. Me still craving him: his touch, his instruction, and his satisfaction had me convinced I needed my head and heart checked.

"He should be in momentarily, Lex."

My head shot up to the nurse, reading my chart on the other side of the room. I smiled nervously, realizing I'd been called out from another stream of thoughts about Ezra.

"Thanks," I barely whispered.

I needed to get my thoughts in order. I had to be sure my baby was still okay. Fucking around with Ezra this morning wasn't a good idea no matter how good it felt. A silent giggle slipped from the back of my throat. I'd conquered the beast and made him my bitch. *Damn!* I'd never seen Ezra so needy and...yielding. In those few minutes, I could have gotten him to agree to anything I asked. But it was useless. The one thing I wanted from him, he wasn't down with. Ezra didn't want an emotional relationship with me, just a physical one.

The moment my eyes rolled at that thought, the door opened.

"Hey, Lex!" Dr. Richardson strolled in, and I sighed my relief. He had to be in his early forties, and seemed to be smart and have a good bedside manner. He was compassionate and informative during my first visit when he confirmed my pregnancy three weeks ago. "Wasn't expecting to see you until next month. What's going on?" he spoke with his nose in my file.

"She's concerned about contractions during se—"

"Does sex hurt the baby?" I blurted, nervous as hell but in no way embarrassed. "I mean... I know I can have sex, but like...orgasms. I have them a lot...and they're like...really intense. I need to know if I should give up sex altogether"—*or more specifically, not have Ezra touch me because let's be real, Ezra is synonymous with orgasms, and he ain't worth the health of my baby*—"because I can."

My words shot out of my mouth so fast, with so much passion, I didn't realize Dr. Richardson and his nurse were laughing—more like snickering. My mouth dropped. I didn't get it.

"Well." His thin lips twitched, fighting humor. "Ummmm..." Dr. Richardson turned to the brunette nurse, who wasn't as good at hiding hers. He combed his fingers through the strands of his jet-black silky hair, trying to compose himself.

I motioned with an extended neck for him to get on with it.

"Okay." He shook his head. "First, it's great to know you have an awesome sex life. I don't think any of my patients have ever described theirs in such a manner. Be grateful for that level of chemistry between you and your husband." He gestured toward my wedding rings. "And trust me when I say he wouldn't be a happy camper if I were to advise you against sex. October 20th is a long ways to go without it." He smiled warmly. "Sex is fine at this point in your gestation. You're not one of my high risk patients. Also, the baby is well cushioned and not engaged in the act at all. If you don't experience pain or discomfort, all should be well." He then scoffed, "So long as there are no extreme measures...like air suspensions, chain whipping, fisting or—" his words grew short from the shattered expression on my face. "Are you a member of the BDSM community?" I saw the blood drain from his face.

"Yes and no. My husband is—was." My eyes closed, frustrated.

"You're divorced?"

"No."

"He's no longer part of the lifestyle?"

"I think." I managed to open my eyes again. "Yes."

His forehead wrinkled. "I'm confused, Lex."

And quickly I supplied. "I am, too."

"You're just twelve weeks. Are you two considering terminating your relationship? Will you no longer have sex with him?"

I shook my head. "He'll want to." I could tell by how needy he was this morning. His body rocked violently underneath me as he came. It was a dangerous explosion. As much as it empowered me and swelled my ego, Ezra's vulnerability scared the living shit out of me. That was too much damn power I held this morning.

"And you won't?" His eyes were wild, dancing inside of mine, searching for clear answers.

The room went silent. Then Dr. Richardson covered my hand with his cold one for comfort. He probably thought I was a battered wife. What I couldn't say was that although my husband wasn't in love with me as I was with him, I still craved him sexually.

But maybe Dr. Richardson knew that.

"Okay. Let's start with what you cannot do."

I scraped my bottom lip between my teeth and nodded, desperate for any professional advice to protect my baby.

~Ezra~

"No paddle ball?"

I examined the empty tennis table across the room. The center net was down, and no paddles or balls in sight.

"Two idiots fighting. What started over a book led to the table." Yaroslav gestured with his head over to the table, his eyes moving intermittently from there to the television, watching the news.

"You weren't..." I hesitated respectfully, something I'm not known to do.

"One of the idiots?" He snorted, amusement in his eyes as he regarded the television. "I have been an idiot for enough of my adult years, Ezra. I try to retire that title under the custody of your government. My temptations are beyond these walls and gates."

"Well, that's good to know. I am happy to learn I didn't make time in the heart of my day to come scold you about a day room fight with your neighboring cellmate." That was my subtle way of inquiring about his request for my visit.

Yaroslav didn't react to that. I decided to be patient. This was not a typical request of his. Usually he waited for me to visit him here, even if I'd allowed a few months in between like I did after my wedding last year. He understood my schedule, and the erratic nature of my business. His lifestyle had once resembled it, no matter how illegal it was.

Minutes later, I watched as the two inmates who were here when I arrived left out separately. One had been reading a magazine, and the other was watching MSNBC along with Yaroslav. At this point, I really needed an answer. I had a meeting with our youth coordinator in less than two hours. It would take that amount of time to get to the bridge then cross over it at this time of day. As it stood, today would be a long and tiresome day for me.

"Radovat'sya," he uttered, facing the screen as we sat along a wall.

Radovat'sya? Radovat'sya? My mind raced for recollection of that term. I was not well schooled in Russian.

Rejoice...

"Why?"

Slowly his eyes rolled over to me. "I did as you advised."

Initially, I was puzzled. Then when I realized the man next to me was just as stubborn as his age was high; I instantly knew.

After expelling heavy air, I asked, "You wrote her?"

Yaroslav's regard went back to the news suspended in the corner across from us.

"What made you change your mind? After all these years..."

He pulled in a grand breath through his hairy nostrils, fortifying himself.

"Because after eleven years of being away, nothing has changed for me," he answered in his thick brogue.

That explanation was confounding. To my knowledge, Yaroslav had never met his daughter. How would that drive his motivation to finally contact her?

"What would you expect to change, my friend?" I tried a specific approach.

He finally returned his gaze to me, and what I saw in his eyes defied every steely fiber I thought created the ironclad man I'd known for nearly seven years. I saw intolerable pain and debilitating fear in Yaroslav Kazlov.

"My need of her has not lessened."

I felt my face harden. This did not make sense. *What need?* How could one need someone they'd never met? He'd only seen her through occasional pictures over the years.

"How could you need her? After all these years... What could she do?"

His eyes slowly closed, and I saw the shiver that undulated his over six-foot frame. After a few seconds of silence, Yaroslav wiped the coat of sweat sheening the receding area at the front of his head.

"Redemption from the damnation of my actions toward her."

Still plagued with bemusement, I at least felt confidence in our meeting on the same road. We would intersect at some point.

"For not reaching out to her until this point in her life?"

Yaroslav took another breath. He, too, understood we were missing one another in this.

"Carin has tried to contact me since my trial. I have all her letters; many are still unopened. I started reading them weeks ago and—"

His budding emotions prevented him from continuing. My mouth literally fell, beard meeting my chest.

"Kazlov," I swallowed, closing in on his proximity. "Your daughter isn't old enough to have been writing you since your trial. She was in utero for part of it. I know you understand this, which means we're not talking about her. And if she isn't the person you wrote, that means your letter was addressed to—"

It was his turn to arrest my words. "Carin, her mother," he elaborated slowly, his chin to his chest as well. Only his posture was a display of vulnerability. "My daughter—our daughter's name is Cajsa. It is Swedish like her mother's, and has the same meaning: pure...chaste." He sniffled tearlessly. "Only unlike her mother, she will never be ripped from her sobriquet. She will remain...untouched until she says." He sipped his coffee.

And they gave the diagnosis of Antisocial Personality Disorder...

He'd just manifestly confirmed my rejection of the diagnosis my more seasoned peers tried to give him all those years ago. I loved when God substantiated His word. I had to measure it against my raging flesh that would like nothing more than to expand my ego.

"She was only fifteen when I met her, you know?" His deep timbre broke my trance. His eyes were upon me. "Carin. She was just days after toddlerhood. She was...beautiful. Hardly developed, she had no particularly stark womanly features. It was all in her eyes. There was a fierce warrior in them. Something that couldn't be broken. My men took her and three other women in her family, from their home one night. My general had an ongoing feud with her uncle. Carin wasn't supposed to be there. Her mother had not come to retrieve her the night my men accosted the household. They killed all the men in the house, including her uncle. Drunk with victory, they took the additional step of bravado and acquired the women. A trophy act." He shrugged apathetically. I was sure this was common behavior for settling scores for a man like him.

"When they brought her back to my compound, I almost didn't see her. This was my general's score. His spoils. But I caught those ocean blues when I walked through the holding cages where we detained our prisoners. I saw the flash of fire behind them. At first the baroque animal in me wanted to devour her. Shred her to pieces to exterminate that defiant spirit in her." He sucked his teeth and exhaled, consumed by the memory. "Her little body trembled at my feet. Her touch on my hairy shell vibrated in delicious fear. Her tears tasted of the best mors! The faint pants of torture her lungs produced as I explored her milky skin." He stopped to breathe.

My God...

"It was the first time in my life I realized I was created to connect with someone else. When with her, I felt purposed beyond any of my operations or attainments. The way my demons would yield to her uncontaminated virtuality, and calm. She learned to love the darkness of my essence. I forced her to. She fought me outside of my bed, but inside she endured the darkness that governed my world since a young mal'chik. I spanked and pleasured, broke old wills and planted new ones that suited me." He sucked his teeth again. "There were some things in her that were not available for my brutality. Some things God gave her in her mother's womb that would not falter at my control." He pointed to his head.

"Within months, the other women I used to entertain my proclivities bored me. Then I started to need her to sleep." He chuckled. "This kroshechnyy...itty bity thing. My big body needed it to shield against the nighttime torment. She needed me to live, and I needed her to sleep. Doesn't seem like an equitable barter." He snorted, head rocked. "Well…" he sighed. "I had to travel, and figured I could take my sleep aide along with me. After a couple of years of that we came here for business and after, recreation. I had no idea I was being set up by an associate, and… You know the rest of my story."

Yaroslav turned to face me again.

"I haven't slept since my apprehension."

Christ…

"I don't follow. She was a slave. I'm sure you had scores of them. Their tenacity varies." I knew this from working in that line of business for some time. Specific and strategic tactics broke strong spirits in human beings. Whether implemented at a physical or psychological level, people can be broken. "Carin was just the first to challenge your experienced hand." I wasn't convinced of much beyond that.

His dense wiry brows lowered to cheeks.

"I… How do you amerikantsy govoryat?" He considered. "I fell in love, Ezra."

My head swung back of its own volition, eyes shot from my skull. I had to quickly gather myself. Open displays of shock had never been my preference. I despised surprises, particularly from people I considered myself well conversant with.

"You fell in love with her?" I couldn't believe the words spilling from my lips.

This couldn't be.

Yaroslav confirmed in his typical casual manner: he didn't refute it. He sat motionless in his seat, chin laying on his chest demonstrating his aged profile. His shame. He'd discovered the one frailty that disproved his harsh and formidable reputation of profiting from a trade involving a class of citizens thought to be the weakest of the land: women.

I'd never subscribed to oppressing women. I viewed them as equal in value, just counterparts in societal roles: women cannot do what men were fashioned by God to do. Conversely, men could not exist functionally nor flourish without women. Each are created with purpose. I despised how my father marginalized my mother. But in that moment, I realized I'd become desensitized to their emotional needs while living amongst cultures that didn't value women beyond their bodies.

"She wrote back. After all the brutal handling of her body and heart, she wants to marry me."

Could I become any more amazed than I'd grown since the start of this conversation?

She wanted to marry her captor? This was a man who bought and sold women—young women—in sex trafficking. He'd kidnapped and, I'm sure, murdered to defend his business. No, I did not believe he was a psychopath, but he certainly didn't adhere to many identifiable social norms either. This development was significant in Yaroslav's progression. However, it highlighted significant elements about me.

"I'M IN LOVE WITH YOU, YOU STUPID, CONTROLLING, SOCIOPATHIC SON OF A BITCH!"

Alexis…

My eyes closed in rebuke.

In spite of Yaroslav's brutality and life as a captor, Carin still wanted to marry him. Despite my manipulation and unleashing of the dark beast in me, Alexis still fell in love with me. The irony in both cases demonstrated the delicacy and unyielding strength in women. My friend here had to continue seven years of his eighteen-year sentence to make good on Carin's faith in him. I, gratefully, didn't have the barrier of age, time, or distance.

"Kazlov!" The guard shouted from the doorway. "You better wrap this up if you want grub."

Yaroslav turned to me, his eyes lit anew. He stretched forward to gain his feet, straining the whole way. Once standing straight, adjusting to standing on his prosthetic leg, he looked younger, lighter. Something in him had been renewed.

"At my age, I cannot afford to miss many meals." I stood to meet his height. He extended his left hand. "I don't know what will be done with Carin," he shared with wary eyes. "But I called you here to tell you, I chose to live the life of abundance that Jesus promised. You were right. That letter was where it started. You be well, *moy drug.*"

I matched his left palm with my right, usual for me, as I am left handed, too.

"Why don't you wear a prosthetic for your right arm?"

Yaroslav's gaze traveled to what was available of his right arm. He scoffed.

"Carin said it hurt her too much when I…disciplined her." He shrugged. "I laid it down, never using it again."

"Concession…" I mumbled, more to myself.

Nodding my goodbye, I watched him turn for the door and toddle out. Years of decisions and regrets rested on his shoulders, possibly now dissipated because he decided to live a life of abundance. My mind spun with more revelations than I could handle at one time.

~Lex~

"A damn rabbi?" My chin—hell, whole face tilted toward the ground. "Get the—" I caught myself. "heck outta here, Annie. You've got to be kidding me." My voice was too calm for the shock I was in.

She shrugged her shoulders with casual speed and an unbothered facial expression, revealing her usual off-the-cuff persona.

"But you don't want him anymore?" I asked, disbelieving.

She shrugged again. "He fucked up with that proposal shit, Lex," she whined.

"But he's willing to leave his faith for you...practically broke all the rules to be with you! And you said you wanted to be with him forever, Anushka!" My calm had disappeared.

My god, how heartless!

She tossed her hands in the air. "Well, what in the hell am I supposed to do, Lex. I'm no good at this type of thing!"

Finally, some emotion!

My phone went off while I eyed her suspiciously. This chick was really a piece of work. As crazy as it sounds, I began to see her parents' struggle with her over the years.

Mary: Hi sweetie. Just checking on my babies.

I snorted. Mary had been texting every other day since our last heart-to-heart.

Me: Laying it on thick again aren't you Mary?

Mary: Hey. I'm gonna be a glamma. I can lay it on as thick as I want. I'm so happy Lex!

Panic struck my chest. *Why the fuck did I open my mouth to her?* I couldn't expect a woman like Mary to keep something like this on the low.

"What's wrong, Lex?" Anushka asked, concerned.

I shook my head.

Me: If you want to stay happy you'll keep this between us until I can tell him.

I sighed, eyed the walls of the small African heritage boutique, *Yorùbá*, where Anushka now worked. It took every ounce of discipline not to bust out laughing at the idea of her working here. A pan-African bookstore, it sold clothing, coffee, and tea, and had great Wi-Fi. The place was small with a stench covered by heavy incense and the oils they sold.

"That Mac is dope, girl!" Anushka noted.

"Thanks. It's Ezra's—well, kinda." I rolled my eyes and shrugged myself.

"What do you mean, kinda?"

My phone buzzed.

Mary: Don't worry sweetheart. Your secret is safe with me. I'm just praising God until you're ready to share it with the world. Just promise me one thing.

Me: What?

"Lex…" Anushka called out expectantly, reminding me I was in someone's company.

"Oh! What did you say?"

"I saiiiid," she dragged out while sitting up in her seat. "What do you mean by it's kinda Ezra's?"

"Oh! Well, he bought it. Right after Thanksgiving, he bought like four laptops at once to see which one 'suited his needs'," I used air quotations. "This one didn't make the cut." They were all laid out on the dining room table one day, and I played with them all: a Dell, HP, Samsung, and the MacBook. I found myself engaged in the Mac, exploring its features in relation to the iPad and iPhone. I must've spent too much time on it, because I glanced up to see Ezra finishing packing up the last of the rest. When I told him I'd get off of this one, he said it was unnecessary. He'd decided on the HP and I could keep the Mac. It was just like that. That simple. He didn't even bat an eye. Although I hadn't thought about that day in a while, it always stuck with me, because I wasn't used to people giving me anything. "Ezra peeped me playing with it, and gave it to me." I shrugged with my neck.

Mary: That you'll keep my grandbaby healthy by treating yourself well. You're stressed and that's no good for either of you dear. I'll keep you lifted in prayer. Got to go!

My mouth twisted up, wryly. If I allowed myself to be fooled, I could get caught up in the maternal offerings of Mary Carmichael. I had to shake it off and remember the lifestyle she played a part in by tolerating it.

"That's nice," Anushka remarked dreamily, something I'd never heard from her.

My forehead stretched. "What?"

"That he takes care of you like that. That's why I gave Darius a chance—more like forced my way into his peripheral." She giggled.

"What do you mean?" This conversation just turned interesting.

"Hold up." She hopped to her feet. "Got a customer."

I snickered to myself before I continued my web search for something, and I didn't exactly know why.

"Y'all got them meditation beads…the red, black, and green?" some guy inquired behind me.

"No. Sorry. We have other colors, but those sold out right away," Anushka managed a regretful tone.

That's when it clicked. I typed in a Google search and ended up on *David Yurman*'s site. Within seconds, I located the perfect gift for him. The moment I laid eyes on it, I decided why I wanted it for him. It was a *'meeting in the middle'* gift. I'd molested the man and kicked him out of my hotel room! Last Friday morning was still on my mind. So much so that I found myself rubbing one off this morning at the memory of his triceps bunching when he squeezed the mattress over his head. I knew that was a difficult experience for him. Ezra was a damn control freak. In the moment, it felt good turning the tables on the dominant lover in him. But afterwards, and certainly after leaving the doctor's office, learning everything was okay with the baby, I'd suddenly felt guilty.

My hands mechanically rose to my belly.

"Ugh!" Anushka's sigh rerouted my reach. "That guy acting like he really couldn't do any other color beads? Really?"

Smoothly my hands reached out to the keypad to continue with my order.

"Anyway," I spoke as I typed. "You were saying why you forced your way onto that poor man's cock."

Anushka rolled her eyes. "I did. I really did. And, Lex," she perked up. "I knew it would be big and it was. It's a little on the short side, but damn it's a sausage I could like... chew on!"

"Ewww... Annie," I groaned.

"I know... Not a great visual. He hated when I said that. But yeah... After you got married to the minister guy, I said I should try something new. I didn't know which religion, but you know how I am about my brothas. There's this sandwich spot in Brooklyn I go to from time to time. And there's an Israelite Rabbinical Academy across the street. I'm used to sitting at the window, eating and people watching. I get a kick out of watching the Jewish dudes come in and out with their little kippahs." She laughed, and I rolled my damn eyes.

"Then one day, this fine ass brotha stepped out. Big guy like yours, lower cut beard, but with glasses. Damn, Lex dawg! He was fine!" That made me smile along with her. "I dropped my *Brooklyn Beauty* in the plate and ran out with it to him just before he closed the car door."

"And what did you say?" I asked to break the heartsy-eyed look she suddenly wore.

"I asked him was the sandwich really kosher. I lied and said it was my first time at the restaurant, and I didn't want to be fooled."

"And?"

"And he threw a disturbingly handsome glare to the plate in my hand then to the restaurant. He said it was a legit place and therefore food. I told him I was studying religion at Medgar Evers, and was seriously considering Judaism."

"Does Medgar Evers even have a Religious program, Annie?"

"Shit if I know. I had to think on my feet. The weather had just changed in November and I was freezing my ass off: I'd left my coat in the restaurant!" She gasped.

"And he bought that?"

"Yeah. And not to mention my Victoria's Secret Bombshell that had my cherries sitting right, girl!"

"Get the hell outta here, Annie!" I waved her off. "And that worked?"

Her jet black eyes widened and she snapped her neck B-girl style. "I had his number that afternoon, and his dick in my mouth two days later. My cunt had to wait another week, but my mouth kept busy. I didn't mind. I really wanted this. I wanted something deep...real, you know?"

I busted out laughing to the point of tears running down my face. Anushka sat on her crossed legs in the chair, unable to hide her amusement. I'm sure to her this story was crazy as hell, too.

When I was able to calm, I tried to re-direct the conversation. "So, you two started dating hard from there, to the point you introduce him to your parents? That's huge for you!"

It was. When she called me last night, giving me a brief rundown of her disappearing act, I couldn't believe she met a black man she had the balls to take home to her parents. The best part of the story is they hit it off well.

"Yeah," she rolled her eyes. "And that's when shit went haywire." Her back slammed into the chair.

"How?"

"Because if they like him, he's too close to societal norm. That doesn't work for me."

"But he's a damn rabbi, Annie!"

"A black rabbi! That's a double-doser. I wanted them to know I could make a great life for myself even if I went against their cultural grain." She pouted like a child.

"But you just said you wanted something real and deep. What do your parents have to do with that?"

"It was too much. I never imagined marrying someone my parents accepted."

"What's wrong with that? Apparently they aren't the racist asses you convinced me to believe all these years."

"The hell they're not! They have to be. That shit don't go away overnight. Indians only marry Indians—traditionally." She shrugged.

"That may be true, and even then I could understand people marrying their own—culturally." It was my turn to shrug, defeated.

"You did!" Anushka lifted a curious brow.

I shook my head. "No, Annie, I didn't." That admission saddened me, especially when I thought about what was in my belly. I had no idea how I would raise my child alone, considering who Ezra was in church. How long would I even continue to go to *RSfALC*? When would we divorce? *Do I want a divorce?* "Ezra and I aren't cut from the same cloth, and that makes marriage that much harder. It helps to be of the same mindset to create a world together."

"So, you're saying I'm right? I should've broken things off with him when my parents embraced him?" Her eyes filled with an unidentifiable excitement.

I shook my head while closely regarding her. At times like this, I didn't understand Anushka.

"No," I answered slowly. "I'm actually saying what you did to Darius ain't cool at all. He told you he'd leave his faith for you. Religious leaders take their beliefs seriously, and he was willing to put his to the side for your childish ass, beefing with your parents. Let that shit go, Annie. This ain't a real world problem," I echoed an Ezra statement.

"What the fuck, Lex dawg?"

"He fell for you, and all you cared about was some stupid, age old beef with your mom and dad. This man was minding his business, going about his life when you interrupted him on your own selfish agenda. He did shit with you that went against his grain, his rules. He wanted to marry you." I shook my head, too angry to yell. "And you dump him because your parents like him. That's some crazy shit, Annie. Think about it."

"But—"

"No. But nothing," I shut her down and proceeded with my online order.

The moment I clicked **Place Order**, I shunned myself for scolding my girl for breaking an innocent man's heart with her own selfish agenda. I was that innocent party, purchasing an expensive beaded bracelet for a man who snatched me out of my world with his selfish agenda, and didn't have the balls to even love me.

Some habits are hard to die...

"Ummm… Lex," Anushka croaked. I peered up to find the sullenest expression I'd ever seen on her. "I'm…ummmm…" She swallowed. "I'm going to call DDD now."

"Oh." I sat up in my seat. Her less lax manner of speaking and tender vocals told me she was in a place. She said *going* and not her typical *gonna*. I closed the laptop and slid it into the bag. "I need to get back to the office anyway. My lunch was over twenty minutes ago."

"Yeah. I'll lock the door behind you. Hopefully, Ayodele won't ride past anytime soon and see the sign up," she muttered behind me on the way to the door.

I couldn't believe she left *Saks* for this place. I was sure she wasn't making the same money. But that was Annie: random and risky. I wouldn't feel bad or apologize for digging in her ass. Yeah, Darius' heartbreak mirrored mine, but my friend was wrong. Her stories of sexcapades were one thing: fucking around with someone's heart was another.

"Hey." I turned to her. "What does DDD stand for?"

With her chin to the floor she murmured, "Donkey Dick Darius. It's what I call him."

My mouth dropped, and I tripped on my way out the damn door.

~Ezra~

"Changing the traffic sequence is a must. It would just be a matter of selecting a new one," Marcus, *RSfALC*'s logistician, advised.

"And getting the folks used to it." Paul, the head of our traffic control, argued.

Marcus sat back in his seat, scratching his forehead. "Having good men on foot out there, and an announcement from Pastor, along with printing it in bold in the weekly programs for about a month or so should do the trick."

Paul tapped the conference table with his fingers as he eyed Reuben, his second in command, with dubiety. They needed to map out a new traffic route in the main parking lot. It hadn't been done in over a decade, and followed by the parishioners in the same amount of time. However, due to the significant increase in Thursday and Sunday attendees, and three recent incidents in the parking lot, we had to meet to discuss strategy. Marcus' eyes roved over to me, messaging his doubt in their competence. If I were honest, I'd admit to their inability to address this. Paul and Reuben had been in their current roles for almost ten years now. They were of my father's cabinet, but rolled over to mine by default: theirs wasn't a pressing role.

I allowed my silence to communicate for me. I'd been sulking for days since leaving Alexis' hotel room, still unable to wrap my brain around what happened between us. It was all wrong. I was all wrong. For days, I'd been feeling something reminiscent of sub drop, only I wasn't a submissive; hadn't been since starting out. When Alexis demanded I leave her hotel room, I acted without thought and left, fearing the consequences had I not complied. Physically, it was good to get a release, and with her. Emotionally, I felt run over by a steam roller truck.

And this wasn't about sex. I'd come to the revelation the moment I left her hotel room Friday. When her busy fingers awakened me that morning, I hadn't expected to lay hands on her at all. In fact, since she left me on Valentine's Day, of all the desires for things to resume to normal, none had been about sex. This was bigger than physical gratification. At some point since marrying her, I'd developed a connection with my wife that went beyond the bounds of copulation.

I didn't hear from her the rest of the day on Friday, but did catch the rear of her as she entered the *Grace Room* here on the main property. She and Ann Bethea were interviewing for an administrative assistant role. I wanted to wait around until she was done, but felt in my spirit it was best to give her space. The following day I didn't hear from her either. My Saturday was loaded with ninjutsu training then officiating a wedding. By the time the day winded down, I was back in that sub head space. Just when I built up the nerve on yesterday to call and leave a message with an invitation for lunch, Alexis replied via text she couldn't make it because she was meeting Anushka. Each time I considered her decline, my stomach toiled with waves of dejection.

"What I wanna know is what's been the cause of all these new folks coming to *Redeeming Souls*? I mean…" Reuben exhaled animatedly. "I mean, just a year ago, we could be out of here in under forty minutes!"

Marcus snorted. "Our social analysis team, procured by the younger Carmichael here, says the first sign of the influx began when a certain young, attractive, poetic articulatory speaker began taking over Bible class. Further studies attribute it to the mainstay of said speaker," Marcus joshed—alone.

Paul and Reuben studied his slick smirk quizzically while I issued him the familiar blank stare. Marcus, a wiseacre *Harvard* alum, had been in logistics for almost a century. A seasoned man well over fifty years of age, he headed up his own small logistics firm when I took him on two years ago. I needed methodical eyes on the church, not just spiritual—that aspect we had well covered. I opted to use scientific savvy to make the church more attractive and marketable. My ultimate goal was to win over souls, but first I had to intersect with them. Hiring these professionals identified a target audience, and from there, His Majesty took over. While Marcus was paraphrasing, the studies conducted by a contracted analytic firm did, in fact, conclude my presence at *RSfALC* had impacted church attendance.

"Well, I don't understand all this fancy-pants talk. I ain't never heard of such thing from Bishop Carmichael!" Paul asserted.

"Yeah!" Reuben followed up. "Now, those three accidents and other things is because of all these newbies coming in. They just need time to learn the ropes."

"Bishop always let us do what we needed to do as long as certain folks had special parking. C'mon, Ezra," his tone turned pleading. "Don't start changing stuff on us, too."

"We're under a new world order here, gents," Marcus teased, distastefully.

Poor joke for Christians, Marcus...

I was sure as an indoctrinated Roman Catholic and converted Buddhist, he understood the implications of that statement in a Pentecostal organization. It was of his nature to ruffle feathers, especially those of his aged cohorts who didn't match his educational achievements. He could be extremely antagonistic, and his most prized target was my father.

I closed my portfolio and stood to my feet. "Deacon Brown, Brother Williams," I glanced at Paul and Reuben respectively. "Please draw up a new traffic sequence and submit it to Mr. Devereaux by Wednesday, close of business day. That will give him plenty of time to test it out and shoot it back to you for tweaking. I'd like to have the new pattern in place by Bible study, next week."

I turned from the table aware of both older men's dazed expressions. This would be their test. If they could not draw up a simple plan of vehicular evacuation, then it would be time to replace them. Marcus was on my heels; I was sure sporting a taunting smirk and certain swag to his gait. It was his thing.

We moved on to a meeting awaiting us in the *Mercy Room* with my vision-casting board. They were a group of qualified individuals handpicked by me to bring annual God-ordained goals for the church into fruition. We met quarterly for assessment, revising, and further planning. I did not walk into one of my most valued initiatives in the ideal headspace, but I had to get through it nonetheless.

By two that afternoon, I was in the *Bishop's Office* going over quarterly reports of all the *RSfALC* auxiliaries. The desktop screen blurred in my throbbing eyes, frustrating me while I was trying to decipher numbers in proposals. I was terribly unhappy with the first quarter reports. There were no impressive outcomes in ministry—at least not to my standards. I matched what I saw on the screen with the summary forms submitted in the meeting.

Jesus...

I tossed the document on the desk and rubbed my eyes with tented hands. A headache was looming; I could feel it between my tear ducts. *And I was exhausted. Christ!* I had been sluggish a lot over the past few weeks, unable to focus for long periods.

Soft knocks at the door sounded.

"Come in—" I brushed my hands down my face and she came into my field of vision.

I believe I stopped breathing for a few seconds, air caught in my lungs.

"The door was open." She cracked a soft smile.

I could almost discern her amusement of me.

"I see," I hardly let out.

She nodded toward my desk. "You're aging, you know."

"Pardon me?" I was confused, and jarred by her presence.

Her hair was pulled back into a ponytail, displaying her smooth and flawless cacao cheekbones and long neckline as she held her coat in her arms. Her lips were painted red, but subtle. She wore a long fitted black dress with a matching duster, and black suede riding boots. The added inches from the heels appealed to me. Alexis was the fiercest feminine creature in my eyes.

She gestured again to my desk then to my computer monitor. "You're forty, squinting, and irritated while reading. You may need reading glasses." I felt my face drop. She shrugged. "I had to take my father last summer, when he complained of headaches, blurry vision, and having to hold words a mile away from his nose to read them."

Alexis stepped into the office and tossed her coat on a companion chair facing me. She stepped closer to my desk, but did not sit in the available seat.

"Well, I can assure you, I'm not as 'aged' as Rasul," I replied, not liking the man's name on my lips.

"Ah!" she sang without spirit while tilting her head. "But you're too old to be his son. You could be his younger brother."

"Yet somehow I'm young enough to have married his daughter," I argued coolly.

"His very young daughter, who's ten years younger than you." Alexis cracked a haughty smile.

Not that I am dissatisfied, but... "And what brings you here this afternoon?"

Your mere sight has cured my cranial pains.

"Checking up on my safe house proposal." I frowned, bemused. "It was submitted for your committee today."

Going to the mountain of documents I trekked back from that meeting, I located the title.

"Is this your creation?" I asked thumbing through the pages.

Alexis nodded proudly. "Mine with the help of my staff. So...what do you think?"

"I haven't reviewed it yet. I just received it this morning."

"I can wait." She backed up for the empty chair and sat, crossing her legs.

Brushing my palm over my beard contemplatively, I glanced from her to the proposal. "There has to be at least fifty pages there."

Also, I didn't want to attempt to read it in front of her. I'd have to hold it so far from my face to make out the words.

"Something like that." She shrugged. "And I happen to know you're a speed reader."

"And you also just witnessed me pulling it from the bottom of the pile. It's going to take me some time to get to it."

"No, it won't," she informed mechanically, and reached over to pushed it closer to me. "It's right underneath your nose. See." Alexis pointed while sitting back.

"Are you using muscle to push your way to the top of the list, Alexis?"

"It's Mrs. Carmichael to you."

"Today?" My brows met.

"Until I change it." Her eyes immediately diverted, confidence deflating.

What does that mean?

"You've lost me..."

What a choice of words.

"I'm well learned, Pastor. You're an efficient man when it comes to getting what you want. You did it when going after your many accomplishments and when you pursued me. All I'm doing is mimicking your determination. I want *RSfALC* to open a safe house." Her eyes were now fixed to mine.

"And you've resorted to barging in my office, making demands?" I was amused.

"Well, let's be real…I could resort to more convincing methods with you and get two safe hou—" Her eyes fled into the distance again once she realized what she let slip. "I'm sorry."

"No offense taken." I studied her, relishing her presence; it was so unexpected and refreshing. There was so much hanging in the balance of our future, but I felt my confidence returning after that exchange of powers on Friday. "I'll make a deal with you." Her eyes arrived to mine. "If you agree to going out with me on Friday, I can have my feedback to you by Monday morning."

I asked her on Friday morning just before she kicked me out, but wasn't specific enough. This time, I wanted an official yes. Just when I thought I'd moved too fast, Alexis' eyes lit up. But then, quickly, I caught the moment she sobered.

"A date? That's all?"

I can't speak of those things I'd do to gain your trust in me…

She'd think I was crazy. And for her, I couldn't deny how insane I was.

I lowered my chin as my brows lifted. "I could ask for blood. I'm sure that's just as enjoyable as the rest of you." I removed my regard to avoid her reaction, but I heard the hike in her breath.

"Okay." She stood, reached for her coat. "But no hanky-panky, Pastor," she noted while leaving my office.

I let go of an aching breath once she closed the door behind her. My kitten was displaying minx-like qualities.

~six~

~Lex~

Ezra picked me up in a limo from my hotel. We headed straight into the city for Midtown to the theater. Ezra was characteristically quiet the entire ride, only holding my hand as a sign of companionship. He kept his regard out the window with his bearded chin in his cupped hand, his elbow against the door. It wasn't until we were inside removing our coats did his silent act crack. As I pulled out of my wool cape and revealed my bodycon, I could hear an imperceptive, "*Christ*..." from his unmoving lips.

My eyes dropped down to my body where I saw a simple fitted maroon dress, falling to my ankles with a matching cape. My belly was flat underneath my breasts, boosted in my usual padded bra. But apparently Ezra saw more, I thought as I chewed on my bottom lip. My eyes flitted all over except on him. When he was able to gather himself we sat for the show.

Phantom of the Opera wasn't as good as *The Book of Mormon* in my opinion, but the production was fantastic. I think *The Book of Mormon* was a simple enough concept for a regular Jane like me, and this show was a bit ritzier in nature and art form. Still, the experience was wonderful. I could now see why Ezra enjoyed Broadway; it was a complete escape with high energy being acted out live. Ezra sat stock-still throughout the entire production, not reacting to the excitement. It was how he'd behaved last fall at *The Book of Mormon*. Strangely, I knew this was how he enjoyed himself: no fanfare involved.

Leaving the theater, I oddly felt a little closer to the mask of Ezra Carmichael. The sliver of victory thrilled and concerned me. I wasn't supposed to care about getting to know him beyond what he'd shown me in all the months of being married to him. I shouldn't have cared. This was just about getting him to read my proposal for *Christ Cares*. But why did I feel more while walking at his side to the waiting car?

We pulled off in the limo and my stomach growled fiercely. It was well past my snack time when Ezra picked me up, and of course, a fact I had to keep to myself. That had been the downside of expecting: not being able to share with the world the progression of it. We pulled up to a restaurant for dinner. It was *Cipriani* in SoHo, and suddenly my mood switched.

As we stepped out of the limo, Ezra asked calmly, "What is it, Alexis?"

He must have seen my face fall, something I didn't mean to happen.

My hand went to my belly, and I quickly rerouted it to my chin, scratching as I answered, "I just didn't know we were coming here, is all."

"Where did you think we'd go?" He stood patiently in his camel wool overcoat and *Burberry* knitted skully.

His eyes were expressive, but not intense. Brows thick and narrowed. His lashes long and curled. Lips were full and coated with balm. His shoulders unbelievably broad and manly. My eyes fell as my stomach growled silently beneath my cape.

"Well," I squealed. "I don't know…" That was a lie. I did know, at least, what I wanted. "*DiFillippo's* maybe?"

Ezra snorted. A soft and undefined smile spread across his face, his tongue swiped against the inside of his cheek, exposing a few of his pearly whites as his eyes went into the distance. I didn't know how to read that. Was I pushing him? I understood I was secretly pregnant *and* demanding.

"I actually have a palate for it as well. I tried denying myself because I was just there yesterday."

Really? My eyes widened. "You don't strike me as a craving type of guy—well, for food, anyway."

Ezra snorted again at that jab. "Come on. Tribeca's just across the way." He stretched out his hand and moved toward the limo.

Once at *DiFillippo's*, we approached the hostess who smiled at the sight of my husband.

"Back again?" She beamed brightly.

"Good evening," Ezra rasped, his eyes blinked, and he chuckled more humbly than I was used to seeing from him. "I'm without reservation."

"Just for dessert?" she asked. "I can get you a space at the bar."

Ezra shook his head. "I'm trying to impress a lady tonight with a full meal."

"Oh, so no quick order of crème brûlée? It's a packed Friday night." She winked. "But let me see what I can do. The pâtissier is being nationally recognized for that recipe and a few others for the franchise." She went for a phone there at her station.

My big eyes turned to Ezra. He murmured, "Maybe I understated my frequency here."

My mouth dropped. "You've been coming for the crème brûlée?" I breathed.

Ezra stretched his neck, masking his embarrassment.

"One of a string of bizarre behaviors for me of late," he spoke so low, clearly not wanting me to catch that.

"Okay," the hostess called for our attention. "We have something in the back." She gave a reverse chin nod. "He'll take your coats, and then I'll lead you. This way." We followed behind her in the packed place. En route, she turned and offered, "You know, one of the owners, Mr. Azmir Jacobs' wife is rumored to be why he bought into the company a few years ago. We started off with just one restaurant over in California, and when she had the crème brûlée and fell in love with it, Mr. Jacobs bought controlling shares in the company. It was his vision to expand. He got that basketball player, Stenton Rogers—I believe his name is—to invest and now we're here, Philadelphia, Miami, Houston, and other places they're developing. Funny thing is, apparently the basketball player's wife loves the crème brûlée, too." The brunette middle aged woman laughed.

Ezra and I caught eyes and shared one, too, but for a different reason. I'd never heard of Azmir Jacobs, but the ball player she mentioned was one of Ezra's best buddies. Of course, Ezra would never say. That wasn't his style. And I liked being in the know, on the low.

We were seated and the waitress came over to take our drink orders.

"I can actually give you my food order now," I interrupted her spiel about coming back with our drinks and taking our order then. Ezra's eyes shot up to me, gleaming with shock and amusement. He wasn't angry, but definitely taken aback. I was too damn hungry to care. "I'll take the frittatine di pasta, and for my main course, shrimp scampi."

My mouth watered as I called off my order. *DiFillippo's* shrimp scampi was nothing ordinary. It was mixed with fresh spinach, clam bits, and cherry tomatoes. *Damn!* I was starving and excited about being there.

"Okay." The waitress moved to take my menu.

"And caprese salad," I jumped back in. *"For him, of course!"* I asserted, when everyone's eyes at the table grew wide. "The big guy eats better than I do." I shrugged.

"And you," The waitress asked Ezra, thankfully glazing over my piggish slip. "Marisol made it clear what your dessert will be. How about dinner?"

"I'll have the swordfish piccata." He handed over his menu.

"Two!" I called for her attention. "...of the crème brûlée." I tried a polite smile. Then my eyes met Ezra's as she took off to fill our orders. "Sorry about that. You should never order on an empty stomach."

Ezra's brows and palms rose at the same time. "It'll be good to see you eat something other than a cheeseburger." He chuckled.

I rolled my eyes at that, fighting a smirk. My fingers drummed the table, filling the transitioning air. I didn't know what to talk about with my husband.

"So, what's your plan?"

"Plan?"

"Yes. You've left the house, and you're staying at the hotel. I don't believe it will be forever. At least, my bank account flinches at that prospect."

"I should, to make you pay," I hissed playfully, still trying to hide my helpless grin.

"I deserve worse," he supplied softly.

My eyes flew to his face. Ezra's expression was somber. He wasn't faking humility; neither was he fighting it. Did he really understand what he'd put me through? I didn't want to go there, afraid of what I'd find.

"I don't know," I murmured, honestly. "Being at the hotel is sorta like a security blanket. It's not back in the city..."

"And yet not at my home, where you were unhappy."

With wide eyes and parted lips, I nodded. And so did Ezra.

"You know," he started. "I've never formally apologized for the things I've done to make you want to leave."

My eyes squeezed closed as my stomach twisted.

"Is that what tonight's all about?" I peered into his eyes. "To ask me to come back?"

"Beloved, if having you back in my home would be as simple as an evening of the arts and fine dining, I would have done that the night you left me." He quieted as the waitress placed our drinks and the caprese salad before us.

How, oh how, I wish I was having a glass of wine for this conversation. My feelings for him were so unsettled.

When she left he continued, "I've broached the subject of you leaving over the weeks, but I realize not once did I apologize or express my regret without motive. A man of my calling and conviction shouldn't have a wife at the point of leaving. It's apparent I was reckless in some way: I am sorry for that, Alexis."

My shoulders dropped along with my squeezing eyes this time. I had no intention of throwing all his shit in his face. That had never been my style. In fact, I was so far removed from my anger during this wonderful 'date,' I'd forgotten about the controlling and manipulative beast.

"I don't want to drag this thing out. It just didn't work out is all, Ezra." I shrugged, cutting into the fresh mozzarella and tomato.

"That's not okay. I asked you to trust me, to take this journey with me, and ultimately, I failed you. I failed us, and for that I am truly sorry and gravely regretful."

A cry built in my throat at his sincere regard searing my damn soul. I wasn't used to *this* Ezra: the remorseful one. I'd resolved to never seeing eye to eye on our issues.

The frittatine di pasta appetizer arrived at our table. My tongue nervously traced my lips, too nervous to care about smearing my lipstick, or the food between me and the infectious man.

"Listen, Ezra, my *at*-attack was…horrible—far more than I let on to anyone. It took years for me to walk with my head high around the city. Took even longer for me to be intimate with a man. And when you came along…" I stumbled, suddenly finding my moist hands below the table, rubbing heatedly together. My chest pumped with haunting fear and helpless pain. "Let's just say I found you far more attractive—magnetic than any man in life. And I let you do things to me that I could never feel so comfortable doing with another man. The dildo that first night…" My eyes went away from the table. "The ropes, floggers, restraints, horse crops—all of that went against my fear. The memory of my…horror." My eyes returned to his. "But I wanted to be what you needed so much—and not to mention how naturally my body responded to it all in spite of the terror warp it could throw me into. I did it because I… I thought you didn't know. To find out you did know, and still pushed me..." The cry shot up my throat at that, closing off my ability to speak.

Ezra's lids collapsed and he lowered his head, his thumbs circling the corners of his eyes. For a while he didn't speak. I mean for a *while*. I continued with his appetizer then moved on to mine, inhaling the deep fried spaghetti, cheese, and Italian sausage balls. I used the silence and food to help me rein in my emotions. This marriage shit was work, and here we weren't technically together anymore. It wasn't until well after our dinner was served and I had been digging into my main entrée that he spoke.

Over my heavy chewing I barely heard him rasp, "I enjoy anal play." My head shot up. Ezra's earnest glare was on me, and not in a salacious manner either. "Not to have it performed on me, but on occasion, I like to explore pleasure in that way with a woman. I haven't in years, obviously, but when I learned about your attack, I knew that would not happen anytime soon in our venture, if at all. And the reason I bring this up is to illustrate how, yes, I knew about the vicious attack, but not even that could deter my desire of you. I will admit to my extreme attraction to not just your striking physical traits, but also your tough exterior, your brash determination, independence, your wit, intelligence—in spite of your lazy discourse—and your ability to level me beyond my titles."

My mouth fell again, this time filled with half chewed food.

"You never had to 'fit in' with me, Alexis. You were always it. You were her; my gift from above. Something promised to me years ago." He inched closer, over the table. "Bruce Montgomery, a member of *RSfALC*'s security team and law enforcement veteran, handed me your file the night you agreed to be my girlfriend. It took me a few weeks to actually review it."

"And I bet when you did, you regretted hooking up with me and asking me to marry you," I whispered on shaky lips at the discovery of a stranger learning of my nightmare.

This was fucked up!

Ezra nodded silently. "I read it before placing the ring on your finger." *Shit just got real...* I swallowed hard. "Alexis, I may keep my marriage separate from my ministry to my detriment, but I do believe we are all new creatures in Christ. It's one of my mantras. God's grace and ability to forgive and forget our transgressions is one of my favorite features of His. And in your case, you did nothing wrong. There was no transgression to forgive, making it simple to look past your attack. Honey, I didn't see a former bartender or a victim. I didn't see a helpless 'round-the-way-girl caught up in her circumstances. I saw a victorious lamb, who fought against all odds and beat them by not getting caught up in the legal or social services system as a dependent. I saw a fierce warrior who frustrated me with the spewing of a few words of rejection while making my dick hard delivering them. I saw no horror. Not an ounce of inferiority or fear."

I didn't want to believe his words. After years as being called a dike boy, bald head, ugly, black tar baby, pit-bull boy fighter, and head on sticks, among other evil names as a kid, I couldn't accept his lenses.

Countless tears dropped down my face, and my shoulders trembled.

"And? I know you saw more than that. You fucked me worth more than that," I hissed.

And that was why I didn't want him to touch me the morning after he'd stayed the night in my hotel room. I didn't want to be used for his pleasure. I used him for mine.

His lids collapsed. "And I saw the most amazingly feminine body I'd ever laid eyes on. Your small tits and narrow waist made that bottom look like it was bursting." He shook his head, face deadpan, and eyes distressed. "I met this beautiful cacao beauty name Lex from Harlem World. And Lex had this big ol' booty." An unnamed emotion bloomed in my chest that quickly. "Her boobs were on the smaller scale, fitting the palms of my hands, and that was perfect for a booty man such as myself. I mean, it looked to be sprouting from the bottom of her spine. And the first time I touched that booty—"

"Shut the hell up, Pastor!" I bit out.

And he did.

My heart trembled, and lungs worked frantically. Aside from his attempt at comedy, there was nothing insincere about his actions tonight. Ezra was not running game. This realization confused me. He'd been apologizing with this conversation, but not demanding I return to him. He wasn't trying to control me. Shit, I didn't even believe this was a typical move of manipulation.

I was finally ready to look at him again, my eyes piercing him for a hint of deceit. After a few seconds, I exhaled, rolling my eyes.

"My booty bigger than Keisha's?" I asked, recalling his sense of humor rearing at the hotel last fall.

It was here again. Ezra was using comedy, and at an inappropriate time. A needed time.

With a straight face and unmoving beard, he answered, "Astronomically bigger. Way softer and a curvier plump at the bottom. And when she walked, her booty didn't jiggle at the bottom of her mounds like yours do. And I'm pretty sure hers doesn't taste sweet like yours either. I mean, your booty tastes like a mixture of peach juice, fresh pineapples, and lemon zest," he breathed with flared nostrils.

"Ezra!" I screamed then tried covering my mouth with a napkin.

He didn't falter in facial expression for a long while. Then I saw that one cheek hike as he went for his food.

Still unable to calm down, I picked up my fork and swirled pasta around, in a spoon. I couldn't slow my belly for shit. I couldn't believe I was here laughing my ass off with Ezra. It had to be a dream.

As I stuffed my mouth, unembarrassed by my god-awful table manners, I heard Ezra across from me.

"Alexis." My eyes met his. "I *am* very sorry for all I've done to misplace your trust in me, and defile our marriage."

That was it. No promises to do better. No asking if we could try again. His motive was made clear. Ezra wanted to confess his sins, and this time, it was *me* giving the needed approval as I nodded my acceptance.

~Lex~

The next afternoon—more like late afternoon, I was surprised when Ezra called and asked if I wanted to play chess.

Chess.

The hotel lounge had a nice board down in the lobby. I was also surprised he knew. I'd been out all day with Ms. Remah, running errands for her, starting with a doctor's appointment. I even treated her to lunch and grocery shopping. I knew that was a task she was capable of doing herself, but I needed some time with her, still feeling awkward about her being at Ezra's without me. I still hadn't visited there yet. Though Ezra had relieved something in me with his new approach, I wasn't ready.

After agreeing to him coming over, I rushed into the shower to wash off the zombie-like nap I took after I was done with Ms. Remah. I clipped my hair up in a high and braided ponytail so I didn't have to be bothered with it. I didn't know what to throw on, not wanting to dress formal, and not having all my clothes from the house. Luckily, I was able to find a black sleeveless maxi dress, the same one I wore when his parents came to have lunch with us last summer. By the time I received Ezra's text that he'd arrived in the lobby, I was on the elevator headed down. I stepped off the elevator and headed toward the bar lounge where we agreed to play.

Oh, my gooood—

He looked good as fuck! Even two women walking past, heading toward the elevator had a disruption in their stride as they stole a long and appreciative stare of him.

Ezra wore understated, yet powerful colors and rocked the hell out of them. Dark grey pants, a white dress shirt under a black V-neck sweater, and the merlot *Allen Edmonds* wingtip dress boots I bought for his birthday. I purchased them online while out in Arizona when I woke up to an empty suite. At the time, I didn't know I'd be leaving him days later. Man, had we come a long way from the days of me shopping for my husband. His presence both aroused and saddened me.

"Ready?" he asked, unaware of my mixed feelings.

"To kick your ass?" I sassed, a subconscious decision to overthrow my attraction to him.

As we sat down, Ezra pulled out a cloth pouch filled with chess pieces.

"Oh," he grumbled, suddenly reminded of something. "I've completed your safe house proposal."

My face lit up and chest expanded with excitement: good and bad.

"And?" I scoffed.

Ezra paid a few minutes to organizing the board without uttering a word. Then he glanced up at me with a blank expression.

"It was good."

"Good?" My eyes liked to pop out of their sockets.

"Yes," he answered with his attention fastened to the board, still arranging the pieces in the meticulous way Ezra does. "Impressive in fact. I'm very hopeful of it getting approved by the board."

"The board? You are the board! That's why I submitted it." My face tightened with anger and confusion.

Ezra sat up in his chair, reading my face. "The board you submitted to is my Vision Board. It is a group of leaders in our church who have approved auxiliaries, and carry out goals set by them and me, jointly. For what you're proposing, we'd have to submit it to the *RSfALC* board of trustees, as it requires major funding."

"And how long is that process?" I demanded, spirit suddenly broken.

Ezra subtly shrugged. "Approximately six months. Their next meeting is next week, and that agenda has already been set."

"Aren't you on the board?"

"Yes, but I have an equal vote to all twelve other members. There is a democracy to our system."

My eyes fell below, and I felt engulfed by disappointment. Ezra and I began our game of chess, and the silence helped me air out my thoughts. I really thought I'd have an answer by next week. Hell, I didn't know if I'd even be employed by *Christ Cares* by the time this process could get underway. Sadly, this project was the one thing keeping me motivated and distracted from my real problems. Without it, I had nothing to focus on other than my failing marriage and homelessness.

We played several games, and three hours later, we were still in the empty lounge, able to hear our moves on the board. Ezra gently made his plays. I slammed my pieces once I decided their destinations. It didn't matter; I only won one of three games, and was on my way to losing the fourth.

"Shit!" I grunted, slamming my pawn on the board.

"Beloved, you're not thinking hard enough," Ezra advised with neither frustration nor sensitivity.

"I am!"

"You started out with The Queen's Gambit strategy—*wonderful strategy, by the way.*" He nodded his appreciation. "But this opening is inarguably one of the most common openings in d4 d5 games. The white sacrifices a pawn for rapid development, and typically gets his pawn back. You did that. However, this is an extremely dated opening technique, going back to the 1400s. I've been able to build a strong defense against your plays from your strategized, but predictable beginning." His brows met and head angled. "Why are you so distracted? What has your mind, sweetheart?"

"I'm just trying to be a better opponent, Ezra!"

He motioned toward the board. "Not with these mediocre attempts, you're not," his tone soft, unflappable.

Ezra and I began something we hadn't in all the time we'd been separated. We eye-warred. His regard was soft, seeking, and determined against my icy glare. During that unaccounted time, my feelings surfaced in spades, most I didn't understand. But I could identify my boiling anger.

I broke.

"I'm fucking frustrated!"

I had been for weeks. My norm had once again changed. When I decided on companionship, I happened upon a man wanting to marry me within months of knowing each other. The month after I got my degree, I lost my job. As soon as the job I desperately needed for months came around, I lost my home. And the moment I found a pet project to distract me from my latest epic failure, I learned it would take months to progress. Oh, and did I mention I was carrying a baby my husband didn't want? My life had been too much of a fucking rollercoaster. I was exhausted from all the adjustments needed to survive each change.

"You have no idea how difficult it is to learn something new that challenges you!" I grated, out of breath, face tight, and eyes wild.

It was a wonder Ezra didn't react to my meltdown in the deserted bar lounge. I had to look a damn sight; I felt like one. But he didn't lose an ounce of his cool as he sat back in his bar stool unaffected.

"Teach me something," he proposed on a cool rasp.

I felt wounded by his insult. "Like what?"

Ezra's head straightened while his eyes locked into mine. "How to love you."

I shook my head and scoffed, not believing where he was going with this. "You don't teach people how to love, Ezra. You're too old to be taught."

The air between us held staggered, silence ringing all around.

"On the contrary, I can be taught at my age. What cannot be altered is my willingness to learn; that's already covered. I want to love you, Alexis. The way you deserve to be loved. Just tell me what to do."

The air held motionless again. Our eyes met, transmitting so many unspoken words and unexplained energy. The tension thick enough to choke on. However, one thing was made clear in that moment. Ezra had been trying to win me back. This was different from the unexpected apology last night.

When he dropped me off last night, Ezra walked me into the lobby and to the elevators. He planted a soft kiss on my forehead, and oh so badly I wanted him to circle my wrists with his adroit fingers. I wrapped myself in a fetal position that night, holding my budding emotions against the coldness of the mattress. I finally gave in to my withdrawals of having a warm body of companionship next to me at night. The lack of one had never bothered me before Ezra. But that was the problem: there was an Ezra era. And though it was fucked up in many respects, he was in every sense a husband. A leader in our home, he particularly desired me, and wanted me around. He was a provider and a strong presence. I lied all those times I told him I felt unwelcome. Ezra made me feel welcome every day. It was the adjustment to having a peculiar roommate that challenged me. But this man damn sure made it clear his home was mine. And now... I didn't know what I had besides an empty hotel room.

My face tightened, eyes blurred from burgeoning tears.

I gritted out barely audible, "Make me feel something normal. Something reliable. Something I know!"

With that, Ezra leaped from his seat, covered my trembling frame with his, creating a hard shield from the coldness of my new, unkind world. I could feel his heart beat wildly as he smothered me. I pushed my arms up against his steely bubbled chest, until my palms reached the wings of his beard, pulled his face down, and our lips met. My mouth instinctively opened to him, not giving a moment to warm into the embrace. I couldn't give a shit,

Ezra felt like everything in my arms again. His smooth slivery tongue swirled in my mouth fluidly, initiating a rhythm for my untamed lips and *my* eager tongue. Each round I tried sweeping my tongue down his throat, desperate to fuse with him. To fight against the emptiness inside my chest.

"I want to submit to you," he managed against my wild lashes.

"How?" I heaved, not wanting to spare more than a moment to breathe.

"The only way I know how. And what I don't know, you'll teach me."

My arm swung over his thick shoulder, across his back, pulling him into me. My legs opened to him on their own accord, my pelvis itching to smack against his. I don't think I ever needed him more. I don't think I ever needed any*one* more.

I felt his fingertips inching up my thighs, my dress hiking with them. Ezra hooked my panties, pulling them down. My ass anxiously lifted, assisting his agenda, a moan escaped my throat. My mind had drifted away to a familiar place where there was just Ezra and me, making indisputable magic.

His body began to descend, immediately causing me to mourn his lips. Cool air replaced his emanating heat as he dropped to his haunches in front of me. That heat transferred to my pussy the moment his mouth hit my gelled core. My feet pushed against the footrest of the barstool, my body leaped in my seat, and I let out a cry. One hand slapped against my mouth and the other against the back of Ezra's head, sandwiched between my thighs. His tongue twirled from the top of my slit to the opening of my canal. My pelvis pushed into his face, inviting him to me. I couldn't understand the level of sensitivity, but I felt the drag of his tongue on each nerve cell he graced. My body jerked in fits each time he applied pressure. When his tongue finally met my clit, my body mechanically danced against it. I thrust on his muscle as his palms cupped my shuddering hips, and he ate me beyond good sense.

My orgasm hit me seconds later. An oncoming force I knew would be monumentally torrential. I feared we would be found out, not from the sounds flying from my mouth, but those my vibrating body would make as I exploded on the chair and in Ezra's face. It hit fiercely, small whimpers escaped my sealed lips, breasts bounced wildly through the tank of my dress, and my shoulders jerked so severely. I was numb to everything but Ezra. I floated for so long, I had no track of time.

Finally, Ezra's head drew up and I couldn't focus my eyes to meet his regard. He stood gracefully to his feet and took me in his arms again. My body wouldn't slow its judders. Couldn't. My heart shot through my mouth, volcanically discharging a screeching cry. I was undone in more than one way, exposed in the lobby of the hotel while he was still put together. I immediately hated the disparity. It was our usual. I was always the vulnerable one between the two of us while Ezra kept his bearings. Would I always be this defenseless against him? I fucking hated it.

"I fucking love you," I spoke with my lips pressed into my teeth, trying to tamp down my emotions.

Lex is a fuckin' warrior... My dad would chant.

I didn't feel much like one against Ezra. Ever.

"I know, kitten, and I am so grateful for it." His arms tightened around me, and mouth met my ear. He rasped, "I can't lose it. I don't want to share it or exploit it. I want to reciprocate it all."

Our eyes locked again. We stayed in that position for countless minutes. I couldn't move until I got my emotions under control. I refused to cry. Ezra didn't deserve that.

When I felt I was good, I was able to whisper into his chest, "Please stay with me."

"I don't have to. I didn't—" He hesitated. "It wasn't my attempt. I don't want to give you the wrong impression of my need. It's not for sex."

Need?

I pushed at him until he released me. He moved back to examine me. I collected the chess pieces and grabbed his coat. On my way to the entrance of the lounge, I gave a reverse nod for him to follow me.

I didn't turn around until I stepped onto the elevator to press my floor. Ezra was right behind me with his head hung low and his hands tucked in his pockets.

I had to get used to this new humble Ezra.

~Ezra~

I didn't want to leave her. Refused to breathe hard or out of sequence, fearing I'd awaken her. Alexis appeared most peaceful while asleep. Rest wore well on her. And when she did it in my arms, it brought undeniable peace. It made me feel steady. In control. As she lay beneath me, fully bare with one knee hiked as she covered her belly with her arm and hand, I felt an incomprehensible pull to her.

For a few weeks now, I'd been more relaxed in my approach to her. I so desperately needed her to trust me again. To believe in me anew. Last night was one of the best of my life. She'd let it all go for me to have her. I didn't fully unleash. The beast had to remain at bay. That facet of me would, in fact, have to be buried if I wanted a future with my wife. And now there was nothing I wanted more.

As we indulged into the morning hours, and I dived into her, I saw things. Felt things. Some were great and others were chaotic. There was a clutter of divides my beloved had been carrying. Much of it I was unable to decipher, but the biggest was her measure of need for me against that of her trust. She spread wide for me, and met every thrust with fervent anticipation, but she hid her face when she ascended. Because of this, I knew I had work to do. I needed this set right. My life depended on it. Alexis was my cynosure for happiness and holiness. For my ministry and destiny. She was a loaded gift that held all the cards.

I glanced up at the window just beyond the bed, across from us. It was still dark out, but I had to prepare to leave. Carlos would be in front of my house at a quarter to seven, ready to drive me to *RSfALC*, and there were a myriad of things that had to be done before then to prepare for morning worship.

I shifted to pull my arm from underneath her slumbering body. Alexis immediately stirred. Once I was able to sit up, she turned to face me. Her arm draped over my lap. My cock lurched. I exhaled silently. This was not working in my favor. Of all days we fell into each other's arms, it had to be on a Saturday night. I closed my eyes in the darkness of the room, giving myself a few moments of contemplation for how I would quietly and weightlessly leave this bed unnoticed.

"You're leaving?"

I glanced down, hardly able to make out her silhouette.

"Carlos will be by the house soon."

"Shit!" Alexis jumped from the bed. "It's Sunday! Are you even prepared?"

"I completed my sermon before I asked to come over last night."

Christ. I was relieved she couldn't detect my smirk in the dark.

"O-okay…" I could sense her patting down her hair, next to me. "I guess I should start getting ready, too." She mused out loud to herself.

"I would like to see you at the tabernacle today," I spoke into the quieted air. "I would also like to see you again tonight."

My dick twitched again.

"O-okay…" Alexis shrieked, clearly surprised at my admission.

"Well." I inhaled. "I must go."

I turned for the floor, and quietly located my clothes in the dark, my chest twisting with each layer I applied. I didn't want to leave her. Not now, and not like this. We had so much ground to cover. Our first time together after being separated was a huge milestone I wanted to gain traction on, not to abandon her, and leave opportunity for regret to set in. Alexis didn't move an inch as I dressed, but when I said goodbye after opening the door, illumining the room from the hallway lighting, I did catch the hesitant wave of her hand.

~Ezra~

"I need to get going. I have a doctor's appointment in twenty minutes." She coughed again. The umpteenth one since we'd arrived at *DiFillippo's* for a late lunch this afternoon. "My soul is just rejoicing at you and Lex working out your differences. Now, I can rest easier at night."

She rocked back and forth in her seat across from me. A contented smile across the concave of her narrowed face, her eyes cast down on the table. My mother wore a thick layer of makeup again. This had been her look for months now, and while spending time in her presence this afternoon, I had to at least inquire about her health. She had a paid cosmetology team that traveled with her to assist with her presentation. A supererogatory accessory to her First Lady status, but certainly one that caused me to wonder about the less than stellar art job on her face and apparent weight loss.

"Mother." I placed my elbows on the table, drawing nearer to her, demonstrating the attempt at privacy. "Is everything well with you? Your health...are you battling something I am not aware of?"

Even Alexis mentioned broaching the subject with her weeks ago. Suddenly, I wondered if she had.

"Is this my prophetic pastor asking or my meddling son?" she quipped, a grin playing at one side of her thin lips.

"You and I both know I'm not the meddling type. If anything, I tend to be much more neglectful than intrusive as a son." I raised my brows. "And if I were probing under the hat of the prophet, it wouldn't be an inquisition, now would it?"

"That's funny!" She chuckled, waving her hand. "Lex said something like that...about your neglect of me when I spoke to her last week. It was her way of asking me the same question. I'll tell you what I told her. What you should be most concerned about, as far as my health, is what you two do to my heart when you fight. I can't stand it, Ezra." Her face contorted into a deep moue. "I'm so glad that's been put behind you. Now I can have one less thing to worry about. But I'm gonna continue lifting you two in my prayers: marriage is a journey. You want eternity, not longevity."

She hedged the question, and quite nicely, too. She touched on a sensitive topic regarding her. Eternity in marriage seemed to be her goal at all costs. That was where we differed.

She moved to stand from the table. I followed suit.

"Which practitioner are you seeing that's only twenty minutes from Tribeca? Your local healthcare is a ways from Lower Manhattan."

"Again. Is this my prophetic pastor asking or my meddling son?" she asked, swaying on one hip, challenging me.

My phone went off. A text.

Alexis: *Hey. I know you're working. You busy?*

Me: No work reaches a capacity that you wouldn't be a priority.

"Hmmmm... I wonder who that is." My mother's contrived statement, dubious.

"Nice try at changing the subject," I returned her sarcasm.

"Honey, I'm your mother. I don't need to try. You don't need to know who I go see or where. I got Jesus on my side. You just need to know I'm happy things are good again with you and your wife. You almost gave me another heart attack, and so soon after your wedding."

Alexis: *That was fancy. But thanks. I want to talk about our relationship.*

Me: Okay...

Anxiety spiked in my chest. My stomach curled with fear. I'd been to the hotel several times over the past few days. Alexis and I filled our time together exploring sexually and talking about everything, and very little of the hurtful topics. I thought we were progressing. At least that's how it felt to me.

"You alright, honey?" My mother asked, alarmed.

That's when I realized my mouth was open. I forged a smile and guided her to the main area of the restaurant, away from our table.

"Of course, I am. Even after your skilled evasion." I moved to kiss her cheek. It was unusually cold. "I know you have to go."

"Yes, I do. Sister Shannon's cousin is outside waiting. I heard she didn't work out as an admin assistant at the church. I'm glad we were able to move her somewhere. I needed a driver."

My mother didn't know why I had let Monica go. It was only because of how faithful of a servant Sister Shannon had been that I didn't outright fire her. I had no room for those types of distractions.

"I am pleased it worked out for you. Be well, mother," I bade as she walked off.

"And you, my love," she called over her shoulder. Then she turned her neck over her shoulder to face me. "This was nice. I know you're a busy man, but… Call me sometime so we can do it again…more often." Her tone was soft. Sweet and maternal.

I nodded with heavy brows, absorbing her unspoken admonishment of my neglect. I took a deep breath, watching her thin frame amble to the door. It was another reason my stomach churned. Something was going on with my mother. I had no idea what it was, but what was certain was she didn't want me to know. I didn't have time to tarry over it. A more imminent matter was at hand. I glanced down at my phone and pivoted to return to my table.

Me: This sounds severe. May I ask that you remove your panties for the duration of this conversation? Or should I come do it for you?

It was my way of bracing myself for bad news and inviting myself to see her while we took on this impending tectonic conversation.

Alexis: LMFAO! You showing humor? No. You cannot come see me for this. I actually prefer doing it via text instead. This way you can't jump me.

I cringed at her acronyms for profanity. Then my dick hardened. I wouldn't chastise her when I was torn by her vulgar nature. Everything about this woman turned me on. It was dangerous.

Me: Why would you think I'd jump you.

I sat down at the table. The waiter approached.

"The check and an order of your crème brûlée to go, please."

"Yes, sir, Mr. Carmichael." He gave a neck bow. "Right away."

That dessert was going to be the death of me. I'd never experienced a…craving before in my life. This had spun out of control. Vibration called my attention back to my phone.

Alexis: Calm down pastor. Who said I didn't like it when you jumped me? I just want to say… I'm not in the best place in my life right now but being on better terms with you helps a lot. Another thing that helps is you not asking me to come back to the house. I know you want to but don't. I'm not ready yet.

She was correct. I wanted her back in my home more than I let on. It was my strategy: patience and gratitude for her lowering her guard for me although I didn't deserve it. I actually *needed* her in my home and bed where I could care for her properly, take her properly, and most of all, show her I could change—had changed—so she could trust me to some degree again.

After second thought, Alexis was correct in not wanting to speak about this in person. I wouldn't be able to keep my hands off of her. As it stood, I couldn't gain control of my growing erection.

Me: I understand.

"Here you are, sir. Your crème brûlée will be coming out soon."

I received the check. "Thank you." I nodded before signing.

Alexis: Good. So I have a proposal. Why don't we graduate our title? Like we're not separated anymore. We're together but…

Me: Beloved, no matter how you swing this, you're my wife until you leave or I die.

I needed that to be abundantly clear. Alexis was mine. This I was sure of. She should be as well.

Alexis: *Our rules. Our way. Right? We create our own path E.*

Though I enjoyed her nickname of 'E', I noticed she threw my words of proposal back in my helpless face. This was true, but she was still my wife, and that was the only way I'd have it. Nothing less.

Me: So long as it's understood that I belong to you and you belong to me.

I was sure to word that correctly. My beloved had an issue with my unabashed possession. One that would not change. It was the only way I knew. Alexis was mine: mind, body, and soul.

Alexis: *Yeah but you're not listening. We need to define the rules of our engagement. It'll help me. A lot, E.*

Yet another phrase she'd extracted from my proposal: rules of engagement.

Me: I am listening...

Alexis: *I like sleeping with you. In both ways. I think it helps me a lot. But I like that we do it on neutral ground. When you came into my life it was on your terms and your way. You didn't date me really. Then you moved me into YOUR place. The hotel kinda feels like my place. I like the independence it gives me. That's something I felt I lost when we got married.*

I could feel my blood begin to boil. This was not what I wanted. It was not the direction I wanted us to go. I thought I'd continue to show patience, and she would come back home. Yes, I'd begun sleeping again with her next to me, but I wanted more. Needed all of her, not regression in our interactions. I tried gaining my lungs, my raging nerves had become exasperated in no time.

My to-go bag holding my dessert appeared out of nowhere. I paused at that discovery and the gut punch of her announcement. I didn't know what to return to her.

Alexis: *I don't know how long this would be for. It won't be forever. I just need to feel in control of my life again. At the same time I want you in it. I just need time to figure it all out.*

That admittance of wanting me in her life cured my drowning fears of rejection. It cured my symptoms of hopelessness. That quickly my mood had improved, even if only slightly. I still needed my wife back in our home where we could properly function as man and wife.

I stood from the table.

Me: I'll give you whatever you need to choose me.

So, my beloved wanted to keep at this temporary set up of me coming to her hotel. She enjoyed the rush of the unattached passion. The romantic appeal. It apparently made her feel in control. Giddy? I was still learning the value in that sensation. It held some significance to my wife. I wasn't enthralled by the idea, but had to oblige her. She meant that much to me.

Alexis: *Thanks E. I'll see you around?*

I couldn't help the chuckle launching from my throat as I walked out of the restaurant. She was really working this fantasy. I guessed, after this revelation, I had to work it, too.

~seven~

~Lex~

I opened the French doors to find Thaddeus, and more surprisingly, Lillian sitting outside of the *Bishop's Office*. As I padded in skeptically, I noticed they weren't even near one another. Lills eyes were big as saucers behind her lenses as she sat on the love seat. Big Thad restlessly paced the floor, near the office door.

"Hey," came out hesitantly. "What's going on here?"

Thaddeus paused for a moment, but once he recognized me, he resumed burning the carpet. Lilly stood immediately and eyed me from head to toe, processing my presence. I took note of her scrubs, reminding me of the awkwardness of seeing her here this time of the day.

"Do you know?" she asked, her face filled with concern.

"Know what? I was just about to ask what you're doing here."

Lills little arms shot up in the air. "That's what I wanna know," she whispered forcefully.

"Lilly, honey, are you sure you didn't say anything...to anybody? I mean..." Thaddeus exhaled. "maybe something in passing that would be considered offensive?"

"Thaddy, if you ask me that question one more time!" she whispered across the room.

"All I'm saying is nothing good comes from stirring up trouble. I told you I was gonna take care of this! You have to trust me!" He struggled to keep his tone low, but his authoritative nature came to life.

Oh, shit... Big Thad got some big ones.

"I won't say it again. I haven't said or done anything to anyone but Lex." Thaddeus' eyes hit me. I raised my hands and stretched my face at the same time, expressing my ignorance. "And *why* would he call us into a meeting now when I haven't complained to her about him in a couple of months. Nothing has changed."

Thaddeus didn't answer. He just went back to pacing the floor. I pushed Lills down to sit. First thing this morning, I found an email from Sister Shannon saying Ezra wanted to meet with me this morning at ten. And now I see these two. I didn't know what to say. It had all been said. The three of us had been summoned by Ezra. I was just as blindsided. Ezra agreed to the new terms of our relationship last week, but he hadn't been by the hotel in two days. I had no idea of his state of mind.

After a few minutes, the door opened, snatching our attention. My curiosity turned into anxiety. That was until I recognized Bishop Carmichael strolling out, holding his hat and overcoat in his hand. His impassive eyes scanned the waiting area. He offered a nod to Thaddeus, who greeted him formally. When he saw me, he squinted.

"Good morning, Bishop Carmichael," I tried, unable to look him in the eye for long periods.

I was sure he thought it was because he intimidated me. I knew it was because I couldn't stand him.

"Lex," was all he said before moving toward the doors to leave.

Lills nudged me from the side. I replied by rolling my eyes. I much preferred that encounter, or lack thereof, to something more explosive. I knew he didn't think I was good enough to share his last name or have ranking in the church he'd turned over. That was Ezra's doing and problem. Not mine.

"Pastor Carmichael is ready for you now." Sister Shannon's eyes scanned all three of us, confirming we were a part of the same appointment with our fearless leader.

Lills paid me a final questioning glance before following Thaddeus into the office. The moment I stepped in, I could feel the staleness in the air.

It could have come from either Bishop, who just left, or the man occupying the office. Both men could rouse that type of energy.

"Please close the door," Ezra ordered without looking up from his desk.

Seeing I was the last in the office, I did the honors. Thaddeus stood, but motioned Lillian to sit. She still wore her coat, as did I. I guessed we were too distracted by the mystery to take them off. The heat from the building was no competition for the suspense in the air. That and his incredible presence. *Shit!* Ezra had the talent for intimidating while looking good as fuck. He wore a dress shirt and tie under a burgundy V-neck cashmere sweater. His beard was thick and appeared longer for some reason. His hair was lined with rigid precision, and his big globular shoulders were pronounced in this appearance.

At some point, Ezra placed his elbows on his desk, lacing his fingers before him. His chin remained toward the desk, but eyes regarded Thaddeus and Lills.

"I'm sure you're all wondering why I called this impromptu summit. I won't hold you long. I just want to let you two know I've had a change of...heart about your relationship. While I still do not approve of the timing and the way it has been presented, I can no longer use my influence to stall what you two are adamant about doing. With that being said, Minister Brown, if you would like to marry Sister Lillian, I will give you my support in any way I can." Ezra stood and offered his hand.

Thaddeus moved closer to his desk to receive him. Lills head bounced between the two with a hanging mouth. And I stood off to the side, stock-still, not believing what I'd just heard.

"Thanks, Pastor," Thaddeus spoke so low, I could hardly hear him as they embraced over the desk.

"It's nothing at all, Minister Brown."

"*Wh*-what? Wait!" Lills stood from her chair. She shot wild eyes back to me before going back to Ezra. "Are you saying you're cool with us getting married?"

Ezra shrugged with his hands. His lips twitched beneath his mustache.

"So, what changed your mind?" she demanded, her eyes returned to me quickly for answers.

I had none, was just as shocked as they were. Thaddeus may have been playing it cool in front of his pastor, but I knew he was happy as hell to have the weight lifted from his shoulders.

"As you are aware, there have been a few turn of events that have happened in my life. I've had the time to process a few things I needed to let go of. This is one." Ezra supplied. "Thaddeus is my armor bearer. We spend enough time together that I feel his spirit when it's lifted or troubled. I could sense the tension for months now, though his unparalleled respect for my seat would not allow him to revolt. It's time for me to clean house internally. Getting rid of something that wouldn't directly impact me or my life is one. More specifically, if your marriage fails or flourishes, it wouldn't affect my entry into heaven. Your marriage can be strategic and powerful for the glory of God or it can be a quick and fading relief for your flesh: either way, it's your decision to make alone."

Then his eyes strained intently. "But I do implore you to wear the banner responsibly. You are sheep of this flock." His eyes skirted over to Thaddeus. "Leaders of this house. Your conduct as man and wife will be a reflection of this organization. Wear the banner with dignity or you will be held accountable."

"It's well understood, sir." Thaddeus' voice was saturated with so much emotion, he could hardly be heard, but shaking Ezra's hand again made his acceptance clear.

"Wait!" Lills demanded again. "I can't believe this. You're saying it's okay? He doesn't have to feel guilty anymore about wanting me?" There was no humor in her tone or face. She seemed too shocked to even be excited. Lillian shook her head. "Uhn-uhn!"

"Lillian!" Thaddeus snapped.

Her little body shifted to him. "No! I'm sorry that you can process this so easily, but I know the stress you've been under. I know the rejection I've been feeling from this man—my church—because of this!" Her head jerked back over to Ezra. "Do it now."

Ezra's head angled. "Pardon…"

"Lil-li-an!" Thaddeus warned again.

Again, Lills looked him square in the face and uttered, "No!" She turned back to Ezra. "Marry us now. Here. I don't want no take backs. If you're cool with this, go all the way."

My mouth dropped.

Ezra's cool eyes went straight to Thaddeus. Thaddeus didn't know who to focus on. His eyes bounced back and forth between Lills and Ezra.

"We-well… I think Pastor Carmichael has done enough here today—" he tried.

"Are you saying no?"

Quickly, Ezra retorted. "I am not saying that at all."

Right away, I could see the sincerity in his expression.

"Well…" Lillian pushed more.

The room went silent. Ezra's eyes studied Lillian's adamant ones and Thaddeus' hesitant yet pleased ones. I could tell Thaddeus wanted this wild and unexpected act Lillian was demanding. His big round frame teetered with tangible excitement. I tried quieting my breath, deathly concerned about Ezra doing something he never does: go back on his word.

Ezra picked up the phone and asked Sister Shannon to join us. She was there in seconds, looking around the room. My disbelieving eyes bounced all across the room.

"According to the state, a marriage ceremony may not take place within twenty-four hours from the exact time a marriage license was issued—" Ezra was interrupted by Lills.

"That's man's law. I'm talking about doing what's right in the eyes of my God, Pastor."

The office went quiet again. Ezra yanked at his beard, I could tell he was uneasy about being goaded by little Lills. I had her back, for sure. But I also knew you could not push this man. A bear will eventually fight back— attack. Even Thaddeus threw daggers at his impending wife, warning her of her risky action, and scolding her at once. I knew in that moment, these two were quite a pair. Lills took no prisoners, and Thaddeus held a certain respect and etiquette for his shepherd. I knew this would eventually happen: Lillian and Ezra going head to head. I had just hoped to not be around. I'd looked the beast in the eyes before and got away, but not unbruised.

Apparently on this day, the sun shined in Lillian's favor. Because twenty minutes later she was named Mrs. Thaddeus Brown, and had endured a sloppy kiss from the man himself to make it official. Shannon clapped with uncontained joy. I could understand why. Thaddeus was a likeable guy. My face hurt from widening in shock as Ezra officiated their unofficial marriage. I couldn't believe what was unfolding before me. And now I smiled so much, my heart was bursting in my chest.

"Thank you, Pastor!" Thaddeus turned and grabbed Ezra's hand with animated force. "This is truly the happiest day of my life— Hey!" he shouted, one arm shot up in the air. "Thank you, Jesus! Hallelujah!"

My head jerked back, surprised by that emotional outburst. Shannon echoed his praise, encouraging him. His pastor remained quiet, offering an amenable smile of comfort, crossing his hands at his pelvis. Lillian resumed her post at her unofficial husband's side with a tear-stained face. She rubbed his wide back as he continued to praise God for his new and unexpected marriage—and I was sure his pastor's breakthrough.

Without being told to do so, Lillian urged Thaddeus toward the door. He was still caught up in his emotions, but he followed her. Shannon went next, and I turned to leave behind them.

"A few more moments of your time, Alexis," I heard rasped from behind me.

I turned to Ezra, his eyes on the computer screen.

"What are your plans for tomorrow night?"

I shrugged, answering without thought. I still hadn't fully processed what had just taken place. "I thought about skipping out of work early and doing something different."

Ezra's eyes arrived on me. "Different like what?"

I shrugged with my neck and brows, feeling the blues being dumped on my shoulders. "I don't know...maybe go to an art gallery or something. Just something different...something...mature."

I'd been feeling stuck in between worlds. I wasn't a carefree adolescent anymore, but neither was I an accomplished adult. *I'm living in a damn hotel for crying the fuck out loud!* I needed to do something...mature and cultured.

"Is there a particular gallery or type of art you're interested in?" he asked with a peaked brow.

I shook my head, my eyes hung low. Things went quiet. It was official: within an hour, I'd gone from curious, to confused, to shocked, to elated, to now just sad.

"I have a governor's fundraiser to attend in the evening, and would like for you to come along. I don't plan on staying long."

My lids stretched. "Another fundraiser—I don't have anything to wear to something like that unless I wear the same gown from the *Girls Not Brides* event or Adele's—"

Ezra shook his head and snorted, his eyes going back to his screen briefly.

"I'll have something sent to you. Or," His eyes were on me again. "you can come home to pick it up."

He tried it, and I wasn't in the mood. I shook my head, backing away from his desk. I had to go.

"You know my shipping address," I uttered over my shoulder, on my way out the door.

~Lex~

"You were less formal here," I gave my unsolicited two cents on our way to the waiting car.

Ezra stopped and opened the door for me to get in. I caught his quick signal to an oncoming Carlos that he'd had it. Once inside, I waited for Ezra to join me from the other end.

"Compared to what?" he asked when settled in his seat.

Ezra reached in the dark for my hand as Carlos pulled off. We'd just left the governor's fundraiser where we stayed all of thirty minutes. Ezra was in and out with his agenda. Several people tried to corner him for conversation, including the First Lady of the state. Ezra was polite with his abbreviated demeanor until we were ushered out. But I'd paid close attention to his delivery. I always did. Ezra was that fascinating on a microphone.

"Compared to Adele's event last summer, when I met her. You were more…corporate-like with your prayer. Tonight you let your words…linger. You were more expressive." I shrugged.

"Did I not include Jesus' name at Adele's launching?"

I nodded. Ezra always used Jesus' name when praying and speaking.

"Then I argue one didn't exhibit more quality over the other."

My eyes explored the lights of the city beaming through the darkness of the sky. "You were different, but not in a bad way. Just more expressive, I guess."

Ezra squeezed my hand. "Praying at Adele's event was more for her. She really has her hopes high for her shoe and clothing line, so she'd have any magic, mystical, or holy acts performed to grant her that. She called on me because she believed in me more than Christ. So, I went and delivered a prayer appropriate for the occasion and people. Tonight, there were a few Christian leaders there who are closely affiliated with the governor. It was in fact, them who encouraged my invite. I pray according to the spirit, and I can discern the level of receptiveness in a room. Either way, at the events, I never endeavor to be preachy. That can be reserved for sermons."

I nodded in the darkness of the car. He was right: Ezra's etiquette at these events never mirrored his pulpit persona. He was always professional, but true to his cause. It was admirable and intimidating.

"Do you ever get scared? Like…freeze up before you go on? You speak in front of really important people."

"I used to. Even now, I can spend moments before in self-judgment, measuring if I qualify to be a messenger of the Word."

"What do you mean?"

He turned toward me a little more. "Recently, I've become more conscious about my righteousness. I really want to be the man of God I say I am, and definitely what He's calling me to be. So, I examine my actions and decisions with a heavier conscience than I did even a year ago," he rasped.

"What makes you do that?"

I couldn't detect an ounce of doubt in Ezra. He was the most self-assured person I knew.

"Encountering you, and realizing how blemished I am."

I sucked in a breath. My eyes shot open so wide they hurt.

"Ezra…"

"Don't." His left hand topped my left that lay clasped in his right. "It's not a bad thing by far. It's actually been quite…revealing."

It was difficult to gauge the sincerity in that revelation in the dimness of the car, but there was something unfamiliar in his voice that concerned me. I'd never heard it before. Neither was I used to Ezra admitting to error in his ways.

We didn't speak after that. I spent the time wondering what was his angle. Why did he invite me to this event? Why get dolled up for just thirty minutes? The arrangements to have a gown and shoes delivered to me, and for me to dress, do my hair and makeup took longer to implement than the time we spent there. This was bizarre.

The car stopped at a gated property in Brooklyn. The iron railings were high with giant trees standing against them. Ezra nodded to Carlos as we neared the gate. There was a man standing at the entrance of what looked to be a garden from just behind him. He greeted us with a nod and motioned us in with his arm.

Once inside, I saw a beautiful garden lit with tea lights wrapped around trees like a vine. The lights were small in size but bright in density, lighting the whole garden. There were flowers hanging from trees and sprouting from the ground I couldn't name, but was immediately blown away at their vibrancy. The smell of food hit me a few feet in. The place was pretty big. It was difficult to measure the entire size because of the rows of trees and flowering bushes wrapping around, creating a maze. We walked and walked, and as we did, I couldn't believe the expanse of the beauty and colors I saw. I was not a flower person at all. Couldn't even name a single one outside of a rose, but this was truly amazing.

Ms. Remah would die!

A woman dressed in black slacks, a white dress shirt and a burgundy vest smiled brightly at our approach. Suddenly I felt warm in my cape.

"Mr. and Mrs. Carmichael, perfect timing. Your food is on its way out." My eyes shot up to Ezra. He offered a wry smile. "This way please."

We followed her through a shorter path that opened out into a—

"Outdoor movie theater?" I breathed.

My feet stopped. I couldn't move. This seemed too much like a setup. The screen was huge and already displayed previews of up and coming flicks like a real theater. And a few feet before it was a high table set for two with two large, plush recliners on either side.

"Sweetheart, the food is being served." Ezra urged me to continue forward.

"Food?" I asked in total disbelief.

What the fuck?

"Yes. The sushi may not chill but the actual dinner that will be served immediately after will," he advised softly. "Here. Let me take your coat."

I felt the weight of my cape being lifted off. Ezra handed it off to the dark haired woman along with his own. We continued on to the table where Ezra led me to sit. The chair was high off the ground, and I had to take a few steps up to sit. The fabric was a warm microfiber that was welcoming at the end of the winter. In fact, my shoulders were bare in March, and I wasn't freezing my ass off. Ezra knelt down and removed my shoes.

"We want you comfortable for the show," he mumbled then placed my heels next to my chair.

"How is it that I'm not cold?"

"Because the grounds are heated, beloved."

He took a seat across from me and we both faced the ginormous screen. A big warm blanket was laid over me. It smelled fresh and felt brand new. I looked over to Ezra to see he had declined one for himself. And sure enough, sushi was placed at my side of the table. It was a small assortment of sushi and rolls, sauces, wasabi and ginger.

"Are you going to have some?" I asked Ezra who seemed content facing forward toward the screen.

He turned to me, glanced down at the sushi tray.

When those curled lashes lifted upwards, he rasped, "Are you going to feed it to me? I know nothing about Japanese food."

Those lashes were how I knew what mood he was in. The one cheek that rose from his bearded face confirmed it. I couldn't help but divert my eyes in sudden and recognizable embarrassment, and giggle. When I was able to look at him again, both cheeks were up. Ezra was smiling. Sincerely.

I took to the chopsticks and fed him a roll, something cooked. Raw sushi wasn't for the faint of heart. In fact, I stayed away from some of the pieces myself, remembering the doctor's orders.

The area darkened, and the movie began. My eyes flew to Ezra once I recognized the opening of *Coming to America*. It was one of my favorites. A classic. Ezra slowly turned to face me. His regard soft, and eyes squinting. He had known. I sucked back an unexpected cry I was able to catch before it became public.

Goddamn hormones!

I may have pretty much escaped morning sickness, but things like this reminded me of my condition. I cried too damn much as of late. Dinner was delivered just as Eddie and Arsenio reached the barbershop. A big ass burger for me with fries, and a fish dish with steamed veggies for Ezra. Without thought, I stretched my right hand over the table in search of his. Once he felt my touch, he joined me, bowed his head, and mouthed grace. We ate as we watched the remainder of the movie. While the burger wasn't as hitting as the hotel's, it was great. The clarity of the picture on the screen and the awesome sound heightened the experience. At the last half of the movie we were served popcorn. Even that was delicious.

Once the movie ended, I felt sad. I didn't want that feeling of surprise and being made to feel special to end.

"Did you enjoy dinner and the movie, beloved?" Ezra hummed while we walked slowly through the maze of flowery trees and bushes.

I nodded, afraid to even speak because I'd cry. And it was more than that. I was now horny. Mega horniness came with the pregnancy. But I wasn't sure if this bout was my usual hormones, or it had arrived at his surprise here.

"I did," I breathed, laying my head on his shoulder as I held the hem of my long gown.

We didn't speak once off in the truck. At first I feared him ending the night before I was ready. I wouldn't have minded it if it meant him spending the night. But with Ezra I wasn't so sure. He didn't spend every night with me, and my gut told me it was because of what I told him about enjoying the independence having the room gave me.

Fucking big ass mouth!

Soon I realized we weren't headed to the bridge or tunnel and let out a quiet sigh of relief. That realization gave a huge relief to my humming body. I rode in silence while being tortured by his scent. When the truck stopped, so did my heart. This had been an eventful evening I didn't want to end. He didn't speak to explain as he helped out of the truck.

Ezra held the door open for me to enter one of the tallest skyscrapers I'd seen in the West Chelsea Art District. As I brushed past him, I glanced up to find his intense eyes stapled to me. Immediately, I became overstimulated by the vibrant colors and striking architecture. There were silver metals, woodwork, colorful canvases, and strange objects I couldn't identify on display, right there at the entrance. Ezra didn't give me more than a moment to take it all in. He grabbed my hand and led me deeper inside. I caught when a guy dressed in all black gave Ezra a nod.

"Carmichael," Ezra supplied as he returned his nod.

My curious eyes scraped every corner in sight. Art wasn't my thing, but I felt like Cinderella, living in a fancier realm than my own. I wanted to absorb it all. When I felt Ezra pulling off my coat, I assisted, distracted by the vitality of the room. I couldn't believe how lit I was so late at night. It was after eleven.

"Pastor!" I heard shouted from behind me. "Glad you're here."

"No damn *pastor*!" Another semi-familiar tone rang out, sounding en route to us. I began to turn toward it. "It's Ezzie…or Ezra to you!"

Then I saw them…both.

Adele. Seiko.

It was a total surprise to see them. Adele's tall and mahogany frame strutted over to us quickly, seemingly in a rush. She grabbed Ezra into a tight embrace, kissing him on both bearded cheeks. He handed our coats to a smiling Seiko.

"I'm so sorry I have to go," her accent flowed huskily. "Not that I was invited," she hugged and air kissed me. "Vladamir is waiting for me at JFK. We're flying out to Monaco tonight." She brushed her palm down Ezra's lapel. "But it seems like *we* never get a proper moment together, love."

"We'll set something up," Ezra offered noncommittal, bored even. He stood straight, smoothing down his tux jacket.

Ezra was being a dick to her. But she didn't seem to be phased…at least not much.

Adele's darkly aligned honey eyes hit me. "I bet he doesn't get fucked often with that wicked attitude, huhn?" Her accent was thick as hell, but I caught that jab.

I tried stifling my laugh, not knowing if it was appropriate.

"Nice, Delle. Real nice, sweetie," Ezra droned, still appearing unaffected as he bounced on his hind thighs, his hands now laced at his pelvis line.

Adele took Ezra at his cheeks, squeezing them, speaking just inches away from his bush of a chin. "Vous êtes si méchamment voulez me." Then she quickly kissed him on the cheek. "Asshole!"

"Et pourtant, vous êtes ici me aider avec ma bien-aimée," Ezra returned to her.

She rolled her eyes before jerking her head to the guy in all black. "Être sûr de ne pas ouvrir les portes jusqu'à dit," she ordered in another language over her shoulder. He nodded and uttered his acknowledgement.

"Enjoy the gallery, Lex," Adele bade. "And be sure to give him some *chatte* before it's all said and done. Okay, love?" She rolled her eyes at Ezra with that, and strutted off.

"Always a pleasure seeing you, Adele," Ezra called behind her.

"I think you were kinda rude to her." I tried swallowing my laughter.

"Yeah, well..." he rasped, pursuing the exhibits.

"What language is that you guys were speaking?"

"French."

Hmmmmmm...

The guy who we met coming in had us follow him around a corner. We stopped at an elevator where he used a key to call the car. It took a few minutes, but when the doors slid apart, it opened to a carpeted glass room. The space was contemporary, and could squeeze in a dozen or so adult bodies. Inside were two chairs, a small table topped with bubbly, and a metal ledge on one of the glass walls. He stepped in first, scanning the area, for what I didn't know.

With a thick accent, he advised, "No paper for notes."

"I think we'll be fine without them tonight," Ezra murmured, waving me inside.

"Okay." The guy stepped off the elevator after pushing a code into the panel inside.

The doors closed, and my eyes met with Ezra's. The car began its rise. He nodded to the doors opposite the glass wall. We had a three-quarter view of the gallery, and could see the many exhibits on each floor.

"This is soooo cool," I breathed, unable to hide my amazement.

"We'll stop on each floor for a few seconds before continuing our ascent. If there's a particular floor we want to spend more time at, we can press that red Hold button on the panel. I nodded, still stunned by the many colors, palettes, and frames along the wide walls. Considering the hour was late, there sure were quite a few people inside, observing the exhibits closer than we were. The lighting inside was low, giving way to the illumination from each floor.

"Sooo cool," I found myself breathing again. "Have you been here? Is that how you knew to bring me?"

From behind me, Ezra answered, "I attended the grand opening two years ago." I turned to face him, surprised by that answer. "Adele's on again off again boyfriend, Vladimir Smirnov, owns it. It's one of six for him across the globe."

I turned back to the main view. "Are they all this nice?" I whispered. "The elevator and all—" My words halted at the sounds of Alina Baraz & Galimatias pouring softly through the speakers.

My eyes popped and palms slapped my opened mouth. "Now, I know this isn't a coincidence!"

Ezra smiled. "No." He shook his head. "It isn't. Now,"—he motioned out into the gallery—"I'm not sure of the design of them all, but I do know Smirnov claims to have distinguished and high-profile clients who prefer privacy as they view and shop, hence the panoramic view elevator."

My mouth formed an 'O' as I turned back to the gallery. *This is what the rich do.*

Then I heard him in my ear, his warm lips brushing against my lobe, and the shooting heat from his protective build against my back.

"We have twenty-six floors until we reach the top. My question to you is will you be perusing the fine art outside while I am in here exploring the finest exhibition of your exquisite body?"

I could feel my gown being lifted, the heavy material pulling from my legs, causing my mouth to drop. Ezra's hot hands were fingering my legs then thighs until they reached my panties. My lids collapsed and forehead fell onto the cool glass at the shock of his actions. Ezra was about to fuck me in public. And my helplessly horny ass didn't have the balls to stop him. Didn't want to stop him. How could he, that quickly, have me revved up and ready to go?

I felt the pull of my lace panties, and heard the beginning of them ripping from my hip bone. Even that slight nip aroused the receptors of my skin. He turned me to face him, backing me up to the metal ledge. Ezra took me at the back of my head and pulled my lips into his, consuming with his mouth then tongue. Our mouths danced in a way that melted me to the core.

The fuck this man put on me? I questioned as I pulled him into me even more, and he pushed my thighs open.

A moan leaped from the back of my throat the moment he slipped inside of me below.

"You cannot—" Ezra grated before going for his tie. Quickly he unknotted it from his neck and roped it around my mouth, gagging me. "You can come when you need to, but you cannot make noise, kitten!" he whispered into my neck before grabbing my hips again, plummeting into me.

My head swung back meeting the glass, my thighs opened for more of his hips. When he thrust and filled me to the hilt, my breaths shot out in shorts. Ezra angled his hips somehow, and started with hard and short drives into me, hitting hard enough to make my stomach bump into my lungs and grunts to shoot from my mouth. It was pure bliss. His tongue swirled in my mouth so damn seductively, I couldn't decide which action to concentrate on. In no time, I was on sensory overload, easing into the new rhythm he drove into me with. His hips plummeted even higher, hitting a bundle of nerves I never knew were there.

"Oh, fuck!" I whispered hard through the tie, my words garbled. "I'm about to come already!"

The moment I realized that was his plan all along, and why he held such a close proximity with his thrusts, I imploded almost painfully. My groin stirred so hard, I felt those damn contractions in my belly. This time I didn't automatically freak out. I rode out the pleasure and awkward sensation, both so present. But the damn orgasm shot threw me the loudest. The alarms in my head were so sharp, glaring. I could hardly breathe, much less hear the deep pushes shooting from my gagged mouth.

"...beloved," Ezra whispered directly in my ear. I missed the beginning of it, as his warm lips were moist and teasing.

As he continued to speak, I couldn't hear the words against the harsh explosions. My orgasm continued to roll in my groin over and over and over.

"...birthday, baby."

Huhn?

I caught some of *that* message.

Does he know?

My eyes fought to focus against the orgasmic haze. With my mouth hanging, I was finally able to see Ezra's molten eyes, slanted by his recent release.

"What did you say?" I was able to make out with a covered mouth.

I felt him at the back of my head, releasing the tie. His fast delicious breaths swept against my face, carpeted jaw moved again, this time slowly.

"Happy birthday, Alexis," he breathed, but worded clearly. "It's just after midnight." Ezra cracked a one-cheek smile.

"You know—*knew* about my birthday?" I screeched, nose flaring.

"Of course I do. You're my wife, beloved."

My face wrinkled some kind of ugly, no longer able to fight the growing cry. It burst silently through my lips, tears streaming down my hiked cheeks. Ezra gripped me by the face.

"Hey...hey!" he whispered. "Don't do this! Please."

I couldn't help it; neither did I know where the explosion of emotions came from. But each cry rang from my belly. I felt so raw.

"You know I can't bear to see you cry and not know why, sweetheart," he whispered against the soft music again. "Please talk to me."

My eyes shot deep into his. "Why can't you love me?"

Ezra's mouth dropped, and when I thought he was stumped, he spoke. "I do love you—dearly."

My head shook vehemently. "Not like that. Why can't you love me the way I love you?"

With wide eyes, he uttered, "I am loving you like you do me right now. This is me, Alexis. Wide open. No façades. No masks. No guises. It is me. With you. In this moment. Melting into your loving spirit. Needing it."

I felt my eyes widen painfully. I sucked in a deep breath ricocheting around the elevator.

"Ezra!" flew from my lungs like a cry.

His eyes ripped from my face, out into the gallery above me. I didn't mean to embarrass him, and could feel his vulnerability emanating as sure as I felt the heat of his thick frame between my quivering thighs and against my heaving chest.

"Okay!" I whispered, trying to gain my lungs. "I won't push you for more again." I was desperate for him to stay in this moment with me. It was so beautiful. Felt so right.

"No!" he gritted, looking down on me. "You can have it all, Alexis. It's just...me." His nostrils widened, his lips balled as he peered out into the gallery again, his arms astride me, palms planted against the glass. I felt cocooned by his tuxedo jacket. Protected. "This is the one thing I've yet to conquer. But I have it. I just don't know how to express it in a way you'll feel it."

I do feel it. Now.

Ezra, the man who soared in everything he pursued—academia, science, therapy, imparting, leading...fucking—was no good at expressing matters closest to his heart outside of Christ. That was one thing he lived— *breathed*—and shared generously with the world. But his core of vulnerability, his soul, is what he hid.

My legs began to feel numb around his waist. I needed circulation and to calm my lungs.

"I think this ride is over, Pastor."

I pushed against him, trying to move. Slowly, Ezra eased out of my holding and assisted me to my feet. As I shuffled my gown down and into place, Ezra pulled himself together, too. I gasped when I turned to find him knotting a condom.

"How the hell did I not feel that?" My brows met and mouth hung open.

Ezra winked and made some clicking sound with his mouth while punching a button on the wall panel. "I am a talented man, Mrs. Carmichael. It's all a part of my magic."

I scoffed. "Like the magic trick you pulled having public sex? We could be arrested for indecency." That last part wasn't delivered with as much sass.

Ezra promised me public sex last summer. I hadn't forgotten. I was just as damn freaky as he was, allowing him to fuck me in plain sight.

"Now, there was a bit of a magic trick to that, too, beloved. These windows are privacy glass with one way tinting." He pointed to the glass ahead.

My mouth dropped even more. "I thought…"

"You thought I'd take my wife in public where people can spectate? Beloved, I've done a lot of wild things in my past, but that is one thing you'll never have to be concerned about being revisited with you. Your body is for my viewing pleasure only."

I rubbed the back of my head, slightly embarrassed about exposing how far I'd go with Ezra if he pushed me enough.

"Hey…" He lifted my chin with his index finger. His nose rubbed against mine affectionately. "We're in this together. I push, but I also protect. I'll never expose you."

"I'm yours?" I asked, knowing pre-split it would have been his closing statement.

Instead of speaking, Ezra nodded, his eyes searing into me hesitantly. He didn't want to scare me. Ezra had no idea how promising that claim felt. The elevator chiming and doors opening snatched my attention.

Ezra led the way out. Right away, our coats were handed to us by a new man dressed in a shirt and tie. Ezra shouldered into his wool camel overcoat and pulled on his matching knit wool skully cap. He then helped me into my coat before leading me toward the entrance. I turned back to the elevator, watching the short, dark haired guy inspect the car space. Ezra, ahead of me, stopped at some point.

"Is all well, beloved?"

With my attention on the elevator, I asked, "What was that Adele said to him before she left?" I recalled her barking orders just before saying goodbye to me.

There was a slight pause before Ezra rasped, "To be sure to not open the doors until told."

I snorted quietly, my head swinging over to him.

"This was all planned—the dinner, movie, and," I did a reverse nod back toward the elevator, "the show."

A wry smile cracked on his darkly bearded face, the sensual slant returning to his eyes. "I hope you enjoyed your birthday." His delivery was hesitant.

My bossy man had never been so humble. It warmed me all over.

"It was the best goddamn birthday ever." I couldn't help my smile.

It really was the best birthday I'd ever had. Even beat my tenth when Jacob Collins, my crush, showed to my surprise birthday party, and my mom didn't suffer an episode.

"And for that, I am happy." Ezra's full smile bloomed. He pulled me at the hand. "Let's go, beloved. It's late, and I have a flight to catch in less than five hours."

My face fell.

"You're leaving town?" My shoulders dropped, too.

"I have the Holy Convocation Conference this week. I was supposed to arrive yesterday, but delegated my minor role. I have a seminar this afternoon."

I gasped. "You did that for me?"

Ezra pulled me into his hard body. "I did it for us."

The shit that exploded in my chest at that answer. I'm sure it was something I shouldn't have felt. It damn sure was something I'd never experienced. I wanted to wrap my arms around his big frame and tell him I loved him, but didn't want to make the event awkward. Ezra had given me a lot of the real him. It would be some time before I could process it all. But for now, in this moment, I wanted to enjoy his openness.

"Thanks, Ezra," I breathed, gazing directly into his pools of chocolate that somehow sparkled to me.

In response, he asked for my hand with his own. When they met, Ezra tucked me beneath him as we took off to the waiting car.

The best fucking birthday in my life!

~eight~

~Ezra~

"There has to be something that can be done. You've noted for weeks the increase in traffic coming in and out of the apartment."

I trekked the steps of the jet at Teterboro. My phone clutched to my ear, and the other carrying my duffle bag. The steward greeted me on my way inside, offering to take my things.

"Pastor, we're operating on so many non-official surveillance intelligences here. As of now, we have nothing that would hold up in court or a lawful arrest. No cops have been called, and on the surface, there's been no foul play."

"But we know a non-legal occupant has taken up residency in there, and is selling illegal substances."

"Unofficially," Montgomery tried to reason with me.

I dropped into my seat, the unfamiliar and unsavory feeling of helplessness tightening around my neck, choking me. I exhaled, mind racing with solutions.

"Montgomery," I adjusted my tone, reining in my anger, remembering I was in mixed company on the plane. "my wife cannot visit that apartment. She cannot walk in unknowingly on Rasul's wretched bootleg drug operation. I'd willingly lose my lawful rights if she's harmed in this."

I caught Thaddeus and Greg, a security guard, entering the cabin, and grew even more irritated. I had to end this conversation.

"That will not happen, sir. We have someone out there at all times, keeping an eye out for her. They're to notify me immediately. You and I have a solid plan."

"A tentative one," I growled, annoyed. I couldn't continue. I had to go. "We'll continue this conversation when I return. In the meantime..."

"You'll be contacted immediately, sir," he asserted.

"Good night, Montgomery." I ended the call.

"The floral arrangement will be delivered to Elder Winfrey's family tomorrow at ten, Pastor," Thaddeus informed as he sat across from me. I acknowledged him silently while pulling out my handheld devices and laptop. "Three-hour flight, huhn?"

I nodded, checking my alerts from my phone. I hadn't slept yet. After leaving Alexis' hotel room at three this morning, I'd run home to finalize my packing and spent time in prayer before coming to the airport. After this call with Montgomery, I knew I wouldn't wind down to sleep for some time. This was going to be a long trip.

"You look...well adjusted, sir," he noted as I pulled out of my overcoat. "Is that a new *Maison Margiela*?" His eyes were lined with easy contentment behind his thick frames, something unusual from him.

"No, Minister Brown. Same coat."

"Well, you're keeping it clean! Looks brand new, sir." Thaddeus' commentary was atypical and excessively complimentary. "Is that new? Looks like *Gucci*."

I froze, my regard shot up and over to him. His eyes were on the black onyx spiritual beads bracelet on my exposed wrist.

"No. It's a *David Yurman* Alexis gifted me," I delivered slowly, suddenly struck with a revelation.

"Very nice. That Alexis has taste that suits you, sir." The smile on his face could match the circumference of the earth.

Odd how garrulous Thaddeus was this early in the morning, but something more glaring hit me.

Alexis was right. *I am a label whore.*

It was a subconscious trait, but clearly recognized by others. It seemed as though each time Alexis shopped for me, it was from a designer's collection. I never required it, and honestly didn't feel easy receiving expensive gifts. I privately questioned her decisions and cost factors.

Now, I get it. She thinks high end is my speed.

She couldn't be more wrong about me. I am truly simplistic, preferring to indulge in my own vanity endeavors alone and on occasion. It's a personal vice, not a means of social stratum. I had to share that with her in case it was cause for her feeling inadequate in my life.

"So, how is First Lady Carmichael?" Thaddeus asked with his eyes and vocals.

I straightened in my seat, settling my suit jacket around. "She's well," I returned with an air of confidence.

And that became clear in the moment, too. I'd returned to the confident lover and spouse Alexis needed. Folding to an insecure leader would further exacerbate the unstable state of our marriage. It had taken some time, but I was now back to exerting my control over our passion. She'd needed it as much as I had. Last night was demonstration of it.

My intent was to see her off to bed then leave for home to prepare for this morning's departure. However, Alexis' constant blushing, suggestive whispers, and groping from the back of the limousine to the door of her hotel room where she lowered to her knees and took me into her mouth caused an excursion in my itinerary. It took some time because I stayed in my head so much, but my kitten summoned my explosion in her mouth. The way her eyes rolled back as she swallowed my seeds had me arranging her on the table in the room and returning the favor.

Greg calling me from the other side of the cabin to hand me a folder interrupted my thoughts. I took the folder and shuffled in my seat, shifting my weight to my hip to camouflage my threatening erection. *Christ...* This was insane. A simple mention of her name made my mind take flight.

But she was insatiable last night. And wet. Jesus, she was unbelievably wet and pliable. It had only been six weeks since our separation, but I could swear, since that first night I had her after playing chess in the lobby of the hotel, her pussy was more cushioned, responsive, milkier, and eager. It was like a customized suction pump, made just for me. I couldn't get enough of her. And apparently, she couldn't satisfy her edacious desire for me either. After Alexis exploded in my face, and I caressed the last of the vibrations in her thighs and abdomen that were around my head, I helped her off the table.

"I'm going to undress you for a shower then put you to bed before I go," I told her as I unzipped her gown.

Alexis collapsed into my chest and wrapped her arms around me until her hands lowered to my glutes. I could hear the air pushing from her lungs as she moaned.

"Stay with me."

"I can't, kitten. I'm not done packing."

She groaned her disappointment again.

"Well, at least shower with me. You can do that. You're dirty with me all over you," Alexis purred, entrapping me with her feminine power.

It was an easy decision.

"I'll shower with you then put you to bed. But then I really have to go."

She giggled, pushing me with her shoulders toward the bathroom at two in the morning. I wanted to remind her she could easily avoid this problem of separation by returning to my home where she belonged. I chose wisdom instead. When Alexis was ready, she would return. I had to put my selfish logic aside and apply patience. It wouldn't kill me. This was nice: playful pushing from her soft strength, more groping with her small hands, and chomps from her teeth on my flesh while I undressed, all while she tittered like a silly teen. This was all reminiscent of a traditional display of giddy romance. It was her demonstration of loving me. It thrilled me to no end.

In the shower we kissed. God, Alexis kept folding into my body, not wanting an inch of air between us. And I couldn't kiss her enough, suctioned her obvious need of me through her mouth. Before I knew it, my erection created a groove between our bellies. That arrival both electrified and concerned me. Confirming my reluctance, Alexis gasped at the stark presence and tossed her meaty thigh over my waist, offering herself to me again. How could I resist her determined pout as she ground on me, driving me wild? Her last two orgasms of the day were given in the shower. I had no need in receiving another in there: Alexis had given me much more with her vulnerability and unabashed desire for me.

"Yeah, Lillian is well, too."

That statement and the sudden judder from the plane beginning its run, slammed the brakes on my reverie. However, Thaddeus' enthused smile hadn't altered. As I studied his amused and elated expression it hit me. *He was giddy.*

Thaddeus has lain with his wife…

He had to. That was the only way to explain his bizarre, verbose nature this morning. If I'd learned anything in working with him over the years, it was that he was not a morning person, and hated flying during daylight hours. He actually used to be terrified of flying until he understood how often it was needed in his role. He's far more agreeable during evening and redeye flights.

I found my head angling, and I nodded. "I am pleased to hear that, sir. Believe it or not, your level of satisfaction truly matters to me."

"Oh, I'm satisfied, sir!" His head nodded repeatedly. "Well satisfied!"

My head angled even more as I pondered the possible double entendre. Was he referring to sex with his new wife? As our eyes locked—my scowl against his exuberantly brightened expression—Thaddeus nodded, obviously smitten by his new bride. My eyes faltered and shoulders dropped. This was not a topic I was comfortable taking on with my armor bearer. My small troupe of confidants like Stenton, and to a degree, Bishop Jones, perhaps, but not Thaddeus Brown. At most, I could advise technical pointers, but nothing that would involve the visual of him or his wife bare.

"I am pleased to hear that as well." I tried for a smile, albeit tight.

Thaddeus leaned toward me for privacy. "I just want to tell you how much I appreciate your change of heart. You have no idea how right on time it was. The devil sent all his workers for me. I stood on the Word, believing God would provide that way of escape. And through you, He did. I can't say thank you enough."

"There's no need to thank me. I am grateful for your dedication to my ministry, and only want the best for you." I offered my hand, which he accepted, and sat back in my seat.

I opened my laptop to get some work done for the lab. There was never a time where I felt accomplished, always something to tend to. I would work on reports until sleep caught up with me or this flight was over. I rubbed my face, feeling the strain behind my eyes already. It reminded me to make an appointment to visit an eye doctor. I adjusted the swivel tray at a distance for my sight before getting started.

"You know…" Thaddeus started. "It would be nice to have someone to reach out to for…"—he cleared his throat—"private matters. Especially seeing I'm right behind you in terms of length of matrimony and all. I've been told you could offer a few…creative pointers, sir?"

My face fell. Thaddeus' expression grew alarmed, but he quickly retracted, and calmed. He perused the cabin to see who'd been listening.

I cleared my throat and lowered my chin. "What kind of creativity are we speaking of, and why would I qualify to be someone with expertise?"

His head rocked side to side as his mind turned over his next set of words.

"Girls talk, sir." It was Thaddeus' turn to lower his chin for implication.

"Specifically about what, Thaddeus? About being called every night while I'm traveling to say good night, or about surprise floral arrangements being delivered to her job on random occasions?"

"No, sir," he virtually whispered. "About being aggressive in the bedroom and…initiating intimacy in public?" he asked rather than stated.

Thaddeus was unsure about this conversation, as he should have been. It was highly inappropriate for us to have, as well as my wife and her girlfriend, Lillian. I was fuming underneath my cool veneer.

"Minister Brown, I'm sure all the girlie chatter was newly wedded sensual discovery Alexis wanted to share with her friend. It happens to the best of us." Thaddeus smiled suggestively in spite of himself, confirming he'd in fact crossed into that passage with his new wife. "It will likely die down soon enough like every other new…undertaking."

He nodded, respectfully.

Christ…

I couldn't even downplay the topic of sex with Alexis in mind! She had better not *ever* get over what I do to her! I took a moment to calm myself. *If Alexis were here I'd take her to the back of the cabin, gag her then flog her soft flesh until she dripped of her desire for me for this infraction.* Things like recklessly speaking about our trysts incited the beast, what I had been trying to keep dormant in me for the sake of my marriage.

My phone chirping broke my attention.

Alexis: Is Magic Missile available?

Me: Pardon?

Alexis: I'm sorry. I'm looking for your dick

My eyes mushroomed at the device in my hand.

Me: So, it has a name?

Alexis: A muscle that brings me to my knees like that must have a proper name (pun intended) Plus it feels like a magic trick every time you fuck me

Of course that compliment would disarm me.

Me: Why would you say that? Is that what you think I do to you, beloved?

Alexis: Fuckin? Its what we do

Alexis: I miss you

She didn't wait for my reply.

Alexis: A lot

Christ! And she was okay with admitting to missing a man who did that to her? Admittedly, I'd never been one for mawkish semantics when it came to sex, but I never imagined doing that with her. I had always cherished Alexis' body and cared for her enough to think more of her presence in my world. My scalp tightened at the visual of the girl who loved everyone responsible for cherishing her without reciprocity. She deserved more than that.

Alexis: And not just for your Yogurt Slinger either

Me: Yogurt Slinger?

Once the analogy came to mind, I shifted to one hip and crossed my leg. I brushed down my beard with my palm and exhaled. This woman drove me crazy, and I wouldn't be honest if I said I was okay with it. I felt things for her that were dangerous.

Alexis: Need I explain what its like when you blast off in my face?

My temperature spiked instantly.

Me: Alexis…

Alexis: Okay I know You gotta go Just wanted to tell you I miss Magic Missile and love you #GiddyGirlOverHere

Giddy. There it is again.

That had been her word for traditional romance.

Me: That is not what I do with you…with my wife. We have to come up with another name.

Alexis: What? Fucking? Don't take it too seriously Sometimes I like being fucked by you Well…lots of times

I slapped my face into my hand. Thaddeus' description of how I handled her aggressively during sex came to mind.

Beloved, you're so much more than that to me…

And there went that confidence I'd just regained with her.

Me: Please. Try another one.

Alexis: I don't know many terms E Making love doesn't suit you

Me: Sounds like heaven to me.

And it did. I wanted it to be the same for her.

Alexis: Fine We make love and fuck on occasion That suits me better Deal?

Interesting. The term must hold some level of endearment for her.

Me: Only if it's understood when I take you, it is a spiritual experience. Every time I enter your sweet walls, I feel and see things in you…in me, for us.

Alexis: That was beautiful Ezra Poetic too Just don't forget to grab my hair and smack my ass a few times when you fuck me…on occasion

The most alarming sound hurled from my belly and flew through my mouth as I had a fit with laughter. Twitching in my seat, I palmed my belly, and I caught Thaddeus' glaring regard.

Giddy. Was that what it felt like?

Me: Alexis…

Alexis: Yes Pastor

Me: I have to go now.

Alexis: I love you

A clear demonstration of God's grace, beloved…

~Lex~

I yawned as I walked into the lobby of the hotel, miserably tired. Hit with a reminder, I went over to the front desk for my mail.

"Good evening, Ms. Grier. I was just about to check out for the night. Glad I didn't miss you before Susan's shift. She'll be alone tonight." Molly greeted with her usual smile. "One sec. Let me grab your things."

"Hey," I was late in returning the expression just before she quickly turned on her heel for a file cabinet.

She returned with an envelope with the hotel's logo on it. "Here are your new keys."

My face wrinkled. "Oh, okay." I glanced down at the envelope absentmindedly. "I was actually coming to ask if my package was delivered."

"Oh! I think there *is* something back there for you. I was so focused on the switch, I forgot all about that. Let me check." She left again.

My stomach growled. I was in trouble, in between meals. Lucky for me, Ms. Remah fixed me a plate to go, and I could dig in as soon as I got upstairs and stripped. My fingers tapped on the counter while I waited. When Molly appeared carrying a package I couldn't fight my smile.

"I'll help you to the elevator. I see your hands are full." She quickly rounded the counter, and I took the lead to the bank of elevators.

"Not those, Ms. Grier. These over here," she called out from behind me. "They're for the suites. The suites are on the north wing."

I was confused.

"What about the suites? I'm in 306, have been since February."

Molly gestured with her chin. "That's why you have those keys."

I glanced down to my hands, to the envelope.

"Why do I need new keys?"

She snorted. "For the new room. You're in a suite now." Her smile shone bright enough to tell me she was being patient with my ignorance.

"I didn't request a new room or a suite."

Then Molly squinted. "Mr. Carmichael called this morning and requested the upgrade. He's the cardholder on file, so we thought it was okay."

"Ezra?" I asked rhetorically as it was unraveling in my mind. Mr. Controlling was rearing his head. I sighed. "I have to move my things from my room?" I was too hungry and tired for that task.

"No. We did it for you. He asked for that, too."

"That fucker..." He wanted me to be surprised so I couldn't interfere.

"Excuse me?" Poor Molly's eyes looked to pop out at any moment.

I shook my head, far more annoyed than Molly needed to see. I moved to grab the package from her. "What room number is it?"

"It's 3060. Right at the corner."

"Thanks, Molly. You get home safely; it's a little icy out there."

The elevator sounded and opened.

"Thanks," she offered from behind me. "You going to be okay?"

"Of course!" I managed a smile before the doors closed.

I rolled my eyes the moment they did. Why would he have my room changed? It was the last thing I needed at a time when I had no stability. Yeah, the room was standard, and the bed was smaller than Ezra was accustomed to, but it was mine. I never asked him to pay for the damn thing.

You never stopped him either.

I groaned the entire way down the hall until I found 3060. The kitchen was lit, illuminating the living room. I grunted while dumping my purse, package, and bag on the table. After pulling out of my coat and kicking off my boots, I pulled my phone from my bag. Anxiety and anger rising from my belly had me ready to explode.

Me: Don't think because we're fucking again and I told you I love you that you can start controlling me. I never asked you for anything. Not to pay my hotel tab or to upgrade to a suite. I don't need you to take care of me. I've been doing it 30 years. If you think sex is gonna put me back in the same miserable ass cage of manipulation I just left, think again!

I dropped on the sofa, stretching out my limbs. This place, although nice, was unfamiliar. I missed my small, sweet, and standard room already. There was no time to dwell on that. I started feeling sick, needing to eat. I moped into the bedroom where my clothes were hung in the closet or neatly folded in the drawers. I stripped, throwing my clothes to the floor then toed into the shower. When I was done, I grabbed my bag of food from Ms. Remah and headed into the kitchen to warm it up in the microwave.

As I watched the timer count down, I thought how I, at least, could now warm up food. But then when I remembered how neatly my clothes were placed in the drawers, humiliation ignited my anger all over again. I ate at the table under only the overhead light of the stove. I wanted to hide underneath the darkness. It was easier to deal with the helplessness I was drowning in. I was pregnant and hormonal. Some days I didn't know which battle to take on, because I couldn't decide if it was the pregnancy making me extra sensitive to shit. But this was justifiable.

I peeled back the covers, wishing Ezra could understand the toll and all the changes having him in my life had come with this past year. What I couldn't share was my fear of my mind turning feeble like my mother's at some point. How much of her mental illness was genetic?

My phone rang just as I got comfortable in the cold bedding. I shuddered, rolling my eyes hard as I turned off the ringer. It was my father. I'd forgotten about taking him grocery shopping today. He'd have to figure it out until tomorrow. I'd just given him a hundred beans last week.

I turned over and found sleep eventually. The room phone ringing from the nightstand woke me. Dazed, I answered the phone.

"Hello..."

"The bed was too small."

"What?" I felt my face wrinkle.

"The first time I got a full night of sleep since February thirteenth was there with you that night during the storm." In my sleep haze, I suddenly recognized the rasp. "Switching your room...it wasn't a move of manipulation. I get more sleep when you're next to me, but I wasn't comfortable in the double bed."

"But this isn't your bed. It's not your home."

"Wherever your address is will always be my home."

That rang familiar. It was what he said to me the night of my horrible interview for *Christ Cares*. Ezra was nothing if not consistent. It reminded me of my anger.

"It was a controlling move, Ezra! I don't like that shit," I hissed, refusing to let this shit ride.

"In retrospect, I can see how it could be perceived as such." He growled. "Christ, I'm trying; I really am."

"Trying? Ezra, strangers folded my bra and underwear! You call that *trying*?"

Bruh!

"I apologize for that. In my mind, I was extending your birthday euphoria," he murmured, sounding like a reprimanded kid.

"Flowers would have been far more appropriate."

"And what about the issue of the small bed?"

"That should have been discussed with me. How do you know I want you comfortable here? Did you forget we're separated?"

"I get you're not ready to come back to the house, but I don't want to be separated anymore. You said our status has changed." That was delivered very childlike, so un-Ezra-like.

It annoyed me and warmed my heart.

"You don't spend that much time here to make that call, Ezra!"

"I want to."

Wh-what?

"Excuse me?"

"I want to spend every night with you. I need to. I need the sleep. At home, the guest bedroom feels more foreign than that godforsaken double bed!"

"Then why not sleep in your bed in the master suite, Ezra?"

"Because it was christened as our bed, and if you're not there, then rightfully I shouldn't be either."

My eyes squeezed shut.

"Don't say stuff like that, Ezra." It was my turn to whine.

"It's the truth," he claimed throatily. He was tired.

I glanced at the clock.

"It's three in the morning. Are you just getting to bed?"

"I'm just getting a moment alone. I haven't been to bed since the last time I slept with you."

"Are you battling insomnia?" I could hear the shriek of panic in my tone.

Ezra didn't answer. The silence across the line did, though. A cry threatened from the pit of my belly.

"I'm not ready to come back," I whispered, struggling to keep the tears at bay.

"You've made that clear. But you didn't say I couldn't follow you. And it's too late to make that declaration," he whispered painfully.

Fuck, Ezra! Just when I'd been prepared for a leveling battle with him, he did this shit to me. I could feel his pain through the line.

"I return tomorrow," he rasped.

"You told me the morning you left."

"And I need to sleep. I have to preach on Sunday."

"You have more than two bedrooms to choose from at home."

"But you'd be in neither. I need you, Alexis."

I exhaled. "Fine. And I need Magic Missile. Just know he's part of the deal and the only reason I'm agreeing to this."

"You drive a hard bargain, beloved."

"And you drive a hard—"

"Alexis!" he warned.

"Good night, sir."

My eyes shot wide and air caught in my lungs.

"I know you have the upper hand in this, but please don't needle the beast, beloved. I am having a time trying to extinguish him from my existence for the sake of our marriage."

I wanted to tell him I didn't want the beast to go away forever. I just didn't want to deal with him outside of sex; he was too punitive and unpredictable.

"Good night, Alexis," he offered soft and slowly, like an unspoken promise.

"Night."

I opened the door after patient knocks caught my attention. It was just before three in the afternoon. My smile bloomed before I saw the person on the other side. Ezra stood there with a duffle bag, garment bag, and two paper bags filled with groceries, looking adorably exhausted. His eyelids were thick; slight redness in the sclera revealed his fatigue. He was still the big formidable and very masculine man he'd been since the day I fell at his feet.

"Magic Missile reporting for duty," he rasped.

I pulled him in by the lapel of his overcoat and slammed the door behind him.

"Groceries?"

"So, we don't have to leave the suite until the morning."

"We can always order room service!" My eyes brightened.

"That, my beloved, is at your discretion. Right now, I need a shower to start to unwind. I brought wine for your compliance."

A nervous tingle coursed my spine at that mention.

"I don't think I need alcohol to blow off what's brewing inside." I tried for my sexiest whisper. Shit, I was so wound up for him. "I only need your Yogurt Flinger."

I grabbed his bags, placed them on the table and showed him to the bedroom. By the time he was showered and dried, I'd put away the groceries and had his luggage in the bedroom. I didn't leave an opportunity for Ezra to go through his bags for clothes. I pounced on him, forcing him to the bed and plopping him into my mouth. I was on top of him, riding us both into oblivion before exhaustion overtook him, and Ezra fell asleep. I ordered up dinner, too bushed myself to cook anything. My heart tore when I had to tug him awake to eat.

After dinner, Ezra watched his fill of news while I lay content in his arms. His soft snoring alerted me of his sleep. He hadn't been lying about being pooped. At some point, I dozed off myself. I realized this when my screaming bladder woke me up at close to five in the morning.

Panicking when I was done with the bathroom and had checked the time, I shook his big body next to me, pressing my palm into his hard chest.

"Ezra, you gotta get up to go home and get ready for church."

After a few seconds, Ezra rolled over, pulling my back into him, my ass into his pelvis.

He whispered into my neck, "Carlos is picking me up here at six."

I felt him stir behind me some time later. Then I was awakened to the sounds of the shower. A warm kiss being planted on my head broke a dream. Ezra's fragrance blasted deliciously through my nose as he whispered goodbye. The next time I saw him was in eight o'clock service where he was, once again, an entirely different being, delivering a soul-stirring sermon to thousands in his flock. I stayed for both services, leaving immediately after the second.

Ms. Remah came out to my car, bringing Sunday dinner. I shot to the hotel to devour it. Just before nodding off for a needed Sunday nap, my heart twisted, missing Ezra. He'd made it clear when I saw him after the first service that he had to go home and have dinner with Ms. Remah. That nipped at me, and not because I didn't want him to. It was because he was displaying the type of loyalty to her that I should have been, but had not been in the best headspace to do. I spoke with her several times a day and saw her throughout the week. She was safe and content, and for that I was grateful. For once, I had to tend to my needs—emotional and physical—before I could extend myself to anyone else.

At around eight that night, Ezra used his key to let himself into my suite, bringing Ms. Remah's potato pudding that hadn't been ready when I picked up my plate earlier. We made love that night and several after. Ezra stayed at the hotel with me at least four nights a week. The others, he felt obligated to be home, seeing Ms. Remah was there. I was grateful. I hadn't stepped foot in that house since Valentine's Day.

~nine~

~Lex~

As I studied the front entrance of the home, my hands vibrated against the steering wheel. My stomach churned and chest pounded. What in the hell was I doing? It had only been seven weeks, and I'd broken. For weeks, I prayed for a new norm, consistency in my ever-changing world. I resented the rollercoaster I was on, and the hormonal changes from my pregnancy didn't help. I was beyond people pleasing, a trait I'd carried since being a child. Tonight, I was needy.

The outside of the house was lit beautifully with soft white lights, a domestic touch by Ms. Remah, I knew. The orangey driveway appeared glossy from having recently been sprayed down. I knew that was Ezra's doing. He hated debris on the sleek surface. I could see the tail of his truck from the open garage door. I turned around and observed Ms. Remah's silver Malibu parked on the opposite side of the house, near the walkway, leading to the back of the property. That sight warmed my heart. It was a reminder of Ezra's acts of kindness toward her.

There was a calming audible arrangement in the air, up here in the woods. I had to chuckle, admitting to loving this country life. I missed this place. *Once a Harlem girl goes rural, she'll never go back.* Technically, I hadn't left. My hotel was minutes away, near the township line. Even being that close, I hadn't stepped foot inside his home.

That was until the day after he stayed his third consecutive night at home, leaving me terribly lonely. It was so bad, I found myself outside, unexpectedly. I took a deep breath and shakily stepped out of the car. Seconds after I rang the doorbell, I could see his thick frame nearing through the wing windows of the front door. Ezra swept the door open with brute force and hard eyes, stepping into the threshold alarmed. His eyes windswept the front of the property as though in search of something.

"Are you okay?"

I fought not to roll my eyes at my weak pathetic-ness, confusing and panicking him.

"I'm fine." I swallowed, hardly able to look him in the face.

Even with his scowl, he was so handsome, it was unfair.

Things went quiet as he searched my face for answers. I saw the instant he thought I was returning. I absolutely was not. Somehow, I could see the moment he registered that, too. Ezra's eyes fell, causing mine to do the same. My eyes raked down his chest, covered in a blue V-neck sweater. He wore dark gray dress pants and black shoe boots. And per usual, he smelled good as hell. I felt underdressed next to him, wearing gray denim leggings I could hardly button, a graphic tee, motorcycle leather jacket, and sneakers.

Ezra stepped aside, "Come in," he rasped hesitantly, still disoriented. "We just sat down for dinner." *I know.* I knew this because apparently Ezra and Ms. Remah ate dinner together when he was not rendezvousing it up with me at the hotel. That gesture secretly made me jealous. "Hungry?"

I shrugged my shoulders and hopelessly grinned. "It'll be a nice change from room service."

"And for my wallet," he murmured, turning for the back of the house.

As I followed behind him to the dining room, my stomach grumbled at the scent of food. We ran into Ms. Remah in the hall. She carried a casserole dish. Her eyes lit up at the sight of me while speaking.

"Oh, mi gawd," she gasped. "Whayuh ah doh yah?" She scurried into the dining room while excitedly speaking her raw patois.

When she placed the dish on the table, her fists flew to her hips and she hit me with the same questioning regard as Ezra, at the door. I smiled embarrassingly like the fool I was. I couldn't explain my reluctance in returning 'home' against my fondness of the place, so I decided not to try. Ezra stood behind his chair at the table, observing our exchange.

"I'm going to wash my hands," I muttered sheepishly on the way out. I was nervous as fuck.

When I returned, they were seated, quietly waiting on me.

"Let us express grace." Ezra extended his arms.

We all linked hands and bowed our heads, something about the act feeling awkward and yet natural. The food was delicious as it always was when Ms. Remah cooked. I ate rather silently while Ezra and Ms. Remah carried on about an article he read about ocean water being a therapy option for spinal issues.

"When a friend of mine in The Bahamas referred me to the article, she said something to the tune of it being effective if the pain is the result of, or related to, a fluid and electrolyte imbalance," he shared.

"Humph," Ms. Remah replied amicably.

"For arthritis patients, salt water supposedly reduces the swelling by dehydrating the cells in the affected area. It's called osmotherapy." Ezra shrugged, his tone just as easy as kicking it with an old buddy. "I don't think there's one sure shot way to cure spinal related issues in general, but there are several noted aquatic treatments."

"Nuh good in dis weather," Ms. Remah countered with her face to her plate, chomping down on her food.

"What body of waters do you have back at home?" he asked himself, eyes in the air. "I bet Innes Bay would be nice right about now."

Ms. Remah's eyes flew wildly up to Ezra. Then they rolled over to me. "See 'em deh." She gestured with her head over to him.

Ezra chuckled. "It's just a suggestion. I actually prefer the hot meals and cantankerous companionship to an empty house."

I smiled in spite of the unintended jab. He wouldn't have to worry about that if I returned home. The conversation continued. These two didn't need my participation for it either. I couldn't believe it when Ms. Remah went into this long story about traveling to school with her siblings and friends when she was a little girl, and the trouble they'd get into, especially her baby brother. He was a daredevil, according to her. Ezra and I were equally amused at the table, listening to her memories.

"Him nasty up himself!" She shook her head. "Gawd," she cried at a high pitch.

Though feeling like a true visitor, I enjoyed my time with them. I also couldn't help stealing glances at Ezra in between. *Fuck, he's handsome!* I didn't know if it was from him having a fresh cut of the hair on his head and face, or simply sitting at this table after we'd cleared our plates.

The beast comes alive at the end of a robust meal for Ezra.

My thighs squeezed together.

Ms. Remah stood from the table, saying she'd clean the kitchen. The moment she left the room, my eyes hesitantly roved over to Ezra. His were already on me, searing.

"So," I sighed to fill the awkward silence between us. "where are you working tomorrow?"

Ezra balled his lips, considering my question. "A staff meeting at the lab before I address a mountain of paperwork. I have a youth program to attend tomorrow evening, so I'll head over to the church early and edit the curriculum for the new believers' classes, then work on scheduling the ministerial roster."

Ezra stayed busy. No wonder he didn't sleep enough. My neck twisted slightly as I inhaled.

I stood to my feet. "Then I should get ready to bounce. I don't want to hold you up."

He remained in his seat, circling his glass with one hand while the ice cubes inside clanked.

Without looking at me, he asked, "You came for dinner?"

My eyes rolled into the distance at that question. "Yeah. It helped."

He nodded. There was a small pause before he stood. Ezra extended his arm for me to lead the way.

<p style="text-align:center">~~~~~~~~~~</p>

~Ezra~

I trailed behind her hourglass frame with my regard to the floor, considering the slump in her shoulders. One of the challenges in conscionable marriage for me—because that was my new journey with Alexis; I wanted our marriage to flourish, not just function—was constantly lowering my level of sensitivity to her moods. My wife didn't fully trust me enough to communicate her fears and concerns. I now cared to know, but could not push for her avowing.

We crossed into the foyer, nearing the front door. She slowed. I, too, halted. Alexis turned to me, her face marred from an internal battle.

I brushed my beard, tamping down my impatience. I wasn't upset, just anxiously curious.

"What is it, beloved?"

"I didn't come for just dinner." She hid her eyes, an act of subservience that, at one time, electrified me.

"Then what did you come for?"

Her chin slowly rose, exposing the delicate ridges of her neck. "Regulation," she murmured, but with determination. "I'm not ready, but... I feel like—" She took a deep breath. "I'm fumbling here. I need for something to feel...normal."

"What's normal?"

"Now?" she asked. "You..." She struggled with that admission, but it was forthcoming.

Her face fell to the floor, and when I thought she was about to crumble in tears, she moved past me, to the back of the house. I followed, passing the dining room and kitchen. When she turned the corner toward the garage door, my hackles raised. Alexis stopped at the door of the sandbox, her back to me, and hand on the locked doorknob.

"Belov—"

"I prefer *kitten*," she spoke with her back to me. Silence rended the air around us, exasperating my breathing. My tongue mechanically swiped over my teeth, mouth pooled with salivated lust. The pounding in my chest rang audibly in my head. "Nothing extreme: no suspensions, choking, or cramping positioning," She rambled like a voiceover in a medical commercial. "Oh, and I just hurt my back...recently, so nothing strenuous on my front or back."

I switched weight from one leg to another, processing her requests. I'd quelled this need of her when I decided to be more for her. Though a disciplined man, I didn't need a relapse with this deep seated, dark depravity in me. There was so much I hadn't exposed her to before she left me. Things that she would likely never know.

But it's who I was. I was a dominant lover, who thrived on control and expressed submission. She was my wife, my addiction, and muse. Alexis needed assurance and confidence at this time in her emotional state. I regulated her 'fumbling' with a power exchange. Just as I was to be receptive to her communicated needs, I had to be confident in addressing them. My chest expanded, masculinity being affirmed and coming alive. My only concern was how to balance her needs against her limits.

In the quietness of the hall, her shoulders trembled and chin dipped into her chest.

"Why are you crying?"

"Because of this...sick need for you," she spoke through gritted teeth.

"It's no reflection of weakness or demonization on your part."

She scoffed bitterly. "You don't love me, and yet I need you. The beast."

"I'm working on being better." I exhaled, honesty saturating each syllable. "For you. He can go away. I'm fighting every day."

"I need better from *him*," she breathed. "Not for him to go away."

I rubbed my beard, askew. Speechless.

"You're flawed..." She sobbed quietly.

Since we're name calling...

"You're my token of perfection." I stood straighter.

"We're hopelessly broken."

'The tongue has the power of life and death, and those who love it will eat its fruit.'

I choose life...

"We're irrevocably bonded."

Taking a deep breath, I pulled out my keys and rounded her to unlock the door. Her head remained to the floor.

"I'll do and be anything you need when you need it," I uttered over her head, our bodies mere centimeters apart. "But I need *you* decided. If you want me down here, be sure. I'll be back shortly for your verdict."

I paced down the hall to the kitchen. Ms. Remah stood over the sink, washing the dishes.

"I could've done that." It was my job, as she cooked.

She grunted. I pulled out a bottle of *Pierre* and took a pull.

"She staying?" Her regard remained in the sink.

"Not yet." After another gulp, I turned to leave the kitchen.

"Mi set 'er dessert on de table to go. Tell 'uh goodnight." I heard from behind me. "Take it easy on 'er down dere."

I turned to face her. Ms. Remah stood still, her back to me, chin over her shoulder, acknowledging me. I nodded though she couldn't see. *She knows about the sandbox.* Instead of questioning how or resenting her knowledge, I'd used that revelation to balance my inclinations, if Alexis was still down there when I returned.

After a few sets of pushups and a quick shower to take the edge off, I strolled downstairs, shirtless and barefoot. I was dressed for the occasion of play and sleep. It was a matter of her decision. But I wasn't so confident she'd stay.

I opened the door, and as I neared the bottom carpeted step of the basement, I saw her small chocolate toes curled tightly. Her knees tucked under her breasts, her bountiful hips spread, and spine lifting and plunging from sensual anxiety as she lay on the oversized purple pillow.

Passing her, I went over to the stereo to power it on. Next, I went about lighting candles and lowering the lights. At the cabinet, I searched for the appropriate implement. I lay the chain of the nipple suctions around the back of my neck and crossed the room for my kitten. The sight of Alexis' head burrowed in her stretched arms swelled my dick instantly. I helped her up from the pillow, standing her in front of me. Her eyes fought to remain open, harsh breaths dispelling from her expanded nostrils. I circled her wrists with my fingers, measuring her anxiety, reveling in it. I moved behind her.

"You know I'm always good to you," I reminded in her ear, taunting.

Her breathing hiked immediately, eyes squeezed shut. I swooped down and licked both her nipples. Slowly and carefully, I applied the suctions. The apexes were darker and more pronounced, in my grossly stimulated mind of late, when I saw her bare. She sucked in air between her teeth at the initial pulling sensation. Her hands crossed over her belly and her shoulders inclined. A soft moan discharged from her throat.

I directed her to the horse bench, arranging her in a sitting position close to the edge after mounting it. The horse bench is also known as the spanking bench. As much as I would have loved to use it in that manner, my spirit told me not to completely yield to my dark depraved nature. Alexis may have asked for this, but I wasn't convinced her needs matched my capabilities. As her dom, I had to consider this. I didn't want to lose her now. Or ever.

"I won't blindfold you; I want you to watch me," I whispered while cuffing her wrists to the bench from behind. "But you *do* recall the rules down here, do you not?"

After several deep and audible breaths, she nodded softly. "*Ye*-yess, sir."

"That pleases me more than you know, kitten. You will do well to not forget any of them." I licked the helix of her ear, biting the lobe. "You want the beast gentle."

I couldn't help the growl in my warning, unbelievably stimulated by the scent, taste, and feel of her. The miscellany of aroused determination and sensual trepidation.

"Are you comfortable, kitten?" I asked, conscious of her back situation.

She nodded, licked her lips. "Yes, sir."

I arranged her feet on the padded leather rails astride the larger one her hind parts rested on, opening her up for me. She sat eagle style, spread for me. Alexis moaned helplessly as her pussy opened along with her thighs in the air. Her spine jerked at the weight of the chain stimulating her suctioned nipples. She squirmed, further arousing herself.

I swatted her with a small leather flogger, targeting her breasts, beating around the suction pads.

"You're cheating, beloved. And you've lied," I advised. Thrashing her exposed sex, she shivered. "You told me you remembered the rules. You apparently forgot the one about all of your pleasure being doled out exclusively by me."

She moaned. I couldn't remove my attention from her breasts. They were...different. Her need to stimulate them drew my focus to them as well. I dropped the flogger and pulled them together to the point of meeting. Alexis slushed in air as my palms massaged them. Her eyes watched me strained when my thumbs flicked around the extended apexes covered by the electronic suctions. I couldn't believe her sudden sensitivity to nipple play. It spurred my desire for exploration. I removed the suctions and swiped my tongue over both nipples. Her head tossed back and pelvis thrust in the air. My hands continued to rub the curves, pushing them together while my tongue danced on her nipples. The puling sounds from her upturned throat drove me wild and inspired me to lash my tongue faster, firmer.

"Ahhhh!" she bellowed harshly. Her body lurched wildly on the bench, rocking it from the floor. "Oh, my *goad*! My gawd!" Her pleas were unintelligible as it was clear she was coming.

I was amazed at this new discovery, continued working away at her breasts and nipples until her body stilled and cries ceased. Alexis' eyes opened possessed and hooded. She, too, had been shocked by that occurrence, but knew better than to speak.

"You didn't ask permission. Perhaps I *should* unleash the beast for your correction, kitten," I murmured.

Her eyes collapsed at my empty threat. I knew she lied about a recent back injury. Her purpose for lying wasn't clear, but the need to do it tugged at something deep within. That wasn't conducive to a trusting relationship. Still, I was determined to prove to her I could temper my excitement down here.

I positioned myself on my knees before her. Her open labia glistened with her fragrant desire. It all intoxicated me. Riled up the beast within. Her erect pearl cushioned in between throbbed with need. My face leaned in for a generous and torturing sniff of her. Alexis moaned and her knees quivered.

"I want you to watch me down here." I flicked her nipple with little care then applied the suctions. Her eyes burst open and she scraped her bottom lip between her teeth to quell her need to scream. "If I wanted you unseeing, I would have covered your eyes."

She nodded over measured moans.

My tongue swiped in her dripping cavity, lapping every inch of her quivering flesh. My head bobbed, tongue lashed, poked, and sucked. The faster I moved, the more of her juices I swallowed. I didn't touch her. I wanted all her sensations between her breasts and pussy. I ate my kitten with zeal, loving her unique taste. This was the core of her essence, her natural scent, and the powerhouse of her femininity. And now she was baring it all to me, helplessly cuffed to the spanking bench.

"Per...mission to come, sir!" sprouted from her lungs.

I hesitated with that call. The dom in me felt it was too soon. The loving husband in me wanted to err on the side of caution. Then I recalled where we were, and at whose request. I knew what she needed. I retreated from her clit.

"Hold it."

She groaned with regret. I smiled, my saturated lips against her lower ones. Seconds later, I dove back in, driving her to the peak again. I, in fact, denied her twice, relentless in my torture over a stretch of time.

"Pa-Pleeas..." she driveled for the third time before I conceded, my tongue brushing in firm strokes against her engorged nub.

"Come now, kitten," I granted, quickly resuming my rhythm.

Within seconds, a tidal wave of her erotic juices shot onto my nose and into my mouth, subduing me. Alexis screamed louder than I thought was safe. I could hear her wrists yanking against the restraints. As her sex vibrated in my face, her belly caved. I took her at the waist, knowing that would have been her inclination had she not been cuffed, I'd come to learn over the weeks of intimacy with her. At that move, I could feel something relax, and she further gave in to her ascension.

I stood, dropping my pants on the way. I entered without preamble, filling her tightness. Only a couple of inches in before there was no give. I lifted her left leg over my shoulder, gaining another inch. Alexis' hand clenched the leather rails, her head falling behind her shoulders as she moaned. I pulled out to thrust back into her swollen and wonderfully wet cavern.

"Christ, kitten," I gritted, unable to breathe. "How long has it been?"

Her breathing could now be heard.

"Speak!" I barked, rearing then giving a low impact thrust.

"Three days, sir," she moaned.

Three days isn't that long.

I removed the suctions slowly, watching her body coil with each relief. I rubbed each nipple with my gentle caress.

"Oh, shit!" she groaned from the pit of her belly through clenched teeth.

At that, her sex opened more. Suctioning me, I sank fully, her pussy engulfing my girth. Her legs shook violently. God, I couldn't believe she came that quickly, and without me fully inside. Pulling out, I kissed her ankle, pride bursting in my chest.

"Let's change your pose. Your joints are probably tightening now."

I released her wrists and helped her off the horse bench. Alexis' head dropped, but I knew she wasn't at her limit. I'd seen her sexed out past capacity before. It had been a while since our last play down here, and I wanted a full run so she could be reminded fondly.

"Come over to the bed," I murmured, taking her at the back of her neck.

I grabbed the suspended hoist on the way and stopped her at the foot. Alexis' eyes held a priapic slant, and I could see her pulse thrum in her neck. I attached the handcuffs she still carried on her left hand, and secured her right before attaching it to the suspended hook.

"Open your legs, kitten, and push back," I groaned at her immediate actions.

She wanted this. And *Christ*... She was a pure enchantress in this lewd position.

I stood back from her, observing each sienna inch of her generous frame. Her body was made just for my appeal. There was nothing small about Alexis aside from those modest breasts—*that still seemed more bountiful than normal*—and the flatness of her belly with a subtle round over curve of her lower abdomen that I'd always thought fondly of. She was a solid femme creature. My muscles bunched in expectation of being buried inside of her soft, wet tightness. My wrists twitched in unbridled excitement as I made her wait—made myself wait for the threat of the beast's arrival to wane so I could take my wife properly.

"*Per*-mission to speak, sir," she squealed, hardly audibly.

My face wrinkled in surprise, then amusement sprinkled in my chest. I was happy she couldn't see my face.

My kitten...always the bold tigress...

"Speak, kitten. And make it quick," I bit out, veiling my true nature.

I was thrilled to hear her voice...down here.

"Are you going to *spa*-spank me...sir?" She amended.

I didn't intend to. Over the past few weeks she'd slammed me for the spankings. Tonight, I thought all she wanted was bondage. Here was a revelation.

"Would you like for me to spank you, kitten," my delivery hoarse, suddenly saturated in desire.

Alexis emitted a shaky breath and I could see the shiver in her back.

"Pleas—yes, sir."

Quietly, I backed up to the workstation. I tried ignoring the violent beat in my chest, the tightening of my balls. Alexis drove me crazy each time she subtly admitted to enjoying sadism. It was not my scene, but giving her what she needed always appealed to the beast in me. The husband and overseer in me. My hand closed tightly over the handle of the flogger I used earlier. I ambled silently back to her.

"How many do you think you need, kitten?"

I pushed out my chest, stretched my shoulders.

"I-I don't know, sir," she admitted. Then her voice turned throaty. "I just want to feel the burn."

The next sequence of movements was in a flash.

"I'll give you four."—*whish*—"You count, starting now! One!"

"Ahh!" she responded to the first lash, her lengthy body bowing, spine curving. "One!" she gritted.

WHAP!

"Shit!" she belted. *"Two!"*

"Come on, beloved. I want to see those maroon welts over the permanent ones melded into your skin."

WHACK!

I loved the sight of her stretch marks. It reminded me of her robust stature. A real woman.

One that isn't breakable under any circumstance.

"*Ahhhh!*" she cried, that thrash bit more in my excitement. My veins pumped viral domination each time my kitten reared her cheeks back to me, begging for more. "*Threeeee...*"

That moan did dangerous things to me.

How could I want her more than I already did? It was as though she had a crushing power over me. One I had no control over or resistance to.

My palms slammed onto my knees as I burrowed in, chest heaving, and sweat budding from my pores. A near miss, but I was able to successfully let the dark excitement roll over me.

She's not ready yet. Slow down!

I bowed my head, waiting out my composure.

"Ez—*siiiiiiir*!" she cried out. Alexis backed up even more, spread her hips farther apart, arched her spine, and exposed her dripping wonderland. "Please give me the last one! It's mine…"

The dip in her vocals was the most licentious I'd ever heard from her. My cock slammed erect in the air at her plea. I stood straight to accommodate it.

"Jesus, Alexis!"

I leaped toward her, unleashed the final blow, and quickly tossed it the floor.

The moment my hands cupped her at the waist she screamed, *"FUCKING FOUR!"*

I slammed into her, thrusting with brute force, needing to feel her glory to expunge the depravities. She immediately curved the small of her spine upward, welcoming me in. I could feel the quivering of her walls. I plunged and thrust and lunged and pelted into her treasure.

"It's what you do to me, Alexis! Christ, I can't control it!" I divulged after some time.

"Me either," she breathed, neck rolled unsteady. "Permiss—"

"Come, kitten!" I screamed, my head dizzy with pleasure, body drenched with perspiration. "Come now!"

"*Uh! Uh!*" she screamed. "*Oooooooooooh!*"

I didn't want her bliss to end. I pounded into Alexis until I could no longer hold out, and blasted my seeds into her quivering canal.

~Lex~

"I need to go," I groaned, my bones aching in protest.

I kicked the sheet from my naked hips.

"No," Ezra rasped. He drew the sheet back up and pulled me into him on the bed. It was easy for my giant frame to glide over the silk beddings. "It's late. I want you to sleep in our bed tonight. I can bathe you and carry you up."

My eyes flew open. *Bath? No!* That was on the 'risky list' from the doctor. The temperature had to be specific to my body temperature. Ezra preferred his baths scalding hot to help with the tightness of my limbs after play down here in the sandbox. I'd already given several restrictions down here. Limiting the beast *in* his sandbox was an absolute no-no. I still hadn't processed how I was able to pull it off.

"I'm not staying, Ezra. I'm going back to the hotel tonight—this morning," I corrected considering the time.

I could feel him go rigid behind me. That announcement stunned him motionless. What surprised me was how quick he rebounded from his anger. Ezra's big body molded over mine, and he pulled me into him tighter. All I could think about was how I would work up the energy to get off this perfectly tempered mattress and drive more than twenty minutes in pitch black to the hotel. *First things first…* I had to get up.

Shit…

This would be hard. I would have to search for my clothes. And my hair. It was all over me and Ezra. As if sensing my thoughts, he pushed his fingers into my scalp and raked back.

"Mmmmm…" I moaned involuntarily.

The things he could do with just his hands…*and mouth…and dic—*

"I miss you."

My eyes shot open again. His warm breath was on the back of my neck, and I could feel the thrumming of his heart on my back. He missed me? Like this? I didn't know what to say. I wanted to ask for clarity, but didn't want to come off as dumb. I closed my eyes, finding comfort in his words. In many ways I felt the same way. Down here was where he'd break down my guard and insecurities with sharp delicious spankings, and turn right around and build me up doling out countless orgasms. Once we were done, he'd cradle me like a baby, wash me, and hold me like I was the most precious thing to him. The whole orchestrated act was so therapeutic, it scared the shit out of me.

"Have you heard from Nyree?" he muttered, softly.

My eyes remained closed. "Nah."

"Have you tried contacting her?"

"No."

"You've not attempted retribution?"

"No." This was getting annoying.

I was wrapped in the most comforting arms I'd ever known and he wanted to ask about Ny's ass.

"Do you want revenge?" he droned quizzically.

I rolled my eyes at that, thinking about Tasche's eagerness to roll up on her.

"One day."

"Not now? Why?"

I shifted on my back so I could face him. "Because she's not a concern of mine now. I actually have real shit to deal with. Pardon my French, but Nyree is a foul bitch. People like her will always be around for payback. The balance of my life won't." His eyes seared into me, processing my words. I licked my lips. "Do you want me to get her?"

Ezra's eyes tightened in pain. "Beloved, I don't want you to lift a finger or waste a breath on her or anyone else that offends you, moving forward. I'm still angered by her actions, but I assure you, Nyree will get her just due. I just want to be sure you're not stressed about it or preoccupied with thoughts that will prove detrimental to you. To us."

Our eyes locked. I almost fell into that helpless place with him where I was vulnerable and totally content with putting it all on the line alone, just to be near him. I couldn't do that anymore. My uncontrollable and growing feelings may have been rooted for him, but I had to be sure I could trust Ezra before I could love him freely.

I swallowed hard. "I'm good, Ezra. You don't have to worry about me doing anything stupid anytime soon." That convoluted admission sparked the energy I needed to go. I shifted to sit up. "We can fill our time talking about more important things."

Ezra sat up on his pillows and linked his fingers behind his head, opening up the bubbled broadness of his chest. That tempting image boiled my blood.

"What would you prefer discussing, beloved?" he asked, softly sincere.

"I heard about the two women sneaking into your hotel room when you were away last week."

His brows hiked confirming it, but Ezra was unalarmed.

"It was immediately handled..." He was confused about my confrontation.

"And you didn't tell me. Why wouldn't something like this come up in a conversation? We've been spending lots of time together."

"Beloved, things of that nature happen all the time. It's no different from the life of a rock star. The ministry of tele-evangelism comes with its groupies."

My mouth dropped at the casualness of his admission. This was news to me. When Lillian told me a few days ago, even she said this was common. I couldn't believe women preyed on ministers. I mean, I now knew there were some who invited that attention, namely Bishop Carmichael and Seth Wilkinson, but there had to be some who weren't about that hoe-dum life. They were men of the cloth!

"I won't cheat on you, Alexis, if that's what you're concerned about," he murmured from behind me as my mind churned.

Ironically, I believed him. The last concern I had with Ezra was him fucking someone else. The justification of my insecurities regarding other women was what he kept from me. Precious and Natalia… There was some shit with the both of them that he wouldn't let me in on. I hated it.

"I know…" I could barely hear myself.

"Then what's the problem?"

"I just… It's just that…" I exhaled. "It should've been something you shared with me. It's a big deal to me to know you're dealing with thirsty ass women when I'm not around. How would I ever have known? I didn't see any of that in Arizona."

Ezra nodded and his eyes diverted guiltily. "That's because we went through measures to keep it from you. I don't need you distracted by things and people that do not matter. That are inconsequential to us. You're all I'll ever want. All I need. You are my gift, Alexis. I wish you could understand that."

"So, is that why you didn't tell me?" I skipped over his assurances. "You didn't want me to be upset by them?"

"Partially, but yes. Sweetheart, I could spend hours sharing stories of clever women plotting on the pulpit. Women on tour buses, not popping up for hours after pulling off from their city. The one that hid in the shower of my one hotel room and recorded who she thought was me taking a leak. Turns out I had security there hours before my arrival to sweep the room."

"Some sweeping he did." I scoffed, upset about something that likely happened before me.

"He's no longer a part of our security team. He's since been placed in parking lot trafficking."

A giggle erupted from my belly.

"Good for his stupid ass." I slapped my mouth.

"Mouth, Alexis," he implored with a sensual slant in his eyes.

"Nah! He deserved to be fired. What if that were me in there—or one of our kids and she got pictures—"

I didn't stop my diarrhea of the mouth before blurting the wrong scenario. I examined Ezra closely for any signs of anger or knowing why I'd mentioned children. Instead, his eyes softened again. He sat up, inching closer to me, broad muscled shoulders curling in impending affection. His big hand captured the side of my face, and the warmth of his lips made my eyes fall closed. His tongue followed with slow motivation, swirling around my own, urging for a dance. And I gave in to him. I kissed my husband at the sweet and adoring pace he set.

"You said children," he whispered inches away from mouth. I could see the sensual amusement in his eyes. "You no longer believe you're infertile. To God be the glory," he whispered his praise. "That pleases me very much, beloved."

A rush of emotions shot from my core. The tears in tow, preparing to burst from my eyes in rapid speed.

"Ezra—"

My cry was caught by his cushioned lips, and he drank them unknowingly, caught up in his own passion. His big hand gripped the back of my head, feeding me to himself. His tongue applying increasing pressure the more it stroked my own. My spine shivered and goose bumps lifted everywhere.

In this kiss, I could feel his undying appeal to me. I literally tasted his unusual, but impassioned commitment to me. The 'forever' in his attachment to me. I felt his hand raise and graze over my belly. At first, I thought it was an accidental touch until his full palm caressed my flat abdomen.

I pulled back.

"I need to go. You have a long day."

I jumped from the bed, immediately going for the bathroom. When I came back out and passed the bed, I could see Ezra sitting up, only covered by the silver silk sheet. His hand raking his beard contemplatively. When I was up to just my shoes, I headed for the stairs.

"Alexis," he called from behind.

I turned to see him reaching for his pants. Once they were up, he stood still, eyes imploring me. I couldn't move, waiting for it. I knew what was coming. I knew what he'd ask. The one question I wasn't ready for and knew would frustrate me. He hadn't pushed. He didn't demand, and that softened me to him all these weeks of being apart.

"Ms. Remah put some food aside for you. Let me grab it and follow you back to the hotel to make sure you get in safely," he rasped, his words falling with regret and anger.

Ezra was holding back, exuding patience. This was the new mask, the latest one. The one that made me believe we could possibly have a future together.

I nodded, biting my lip before taking to the stairs, up to the main level.

~Lex~

"Christ, Alexis!" he groaned as I pulled my lips as tight as I could into a ring around his stiffness and suctioned while he shot warm liquid in my mouth.

I didn't deep throat him this morning. I wanted him to experience a different ascension. I used my hands and boobs as I started out between his legs. I woke up with Ezra beside me for the second consecutive night. And just like yesterday, I woke up with a puddle between my legs. However, unlike the morning before, I didn't roll over and straddle him. This morning, I wanted him helpless and pulling at my scalp. It was indescribable what I felt when his legs vibrated forcefully around my body. The way he cried, *"Honey..."* at the beginning angered me. Before Ezra, a man could have called me that without a pausing thought from me.

But now...

Now things were different. I knew how little his thread of self-control held. He'd given me the keys to his knowledge the first time he'd bestowed the moniker on me. Kitten could do shit to him without her hands, just with her obedience alone. Kitten held a magic over him simply by exposing her fear of the beast in him. Kitten wasn't an inferior sex toy. She was a powerful vixen that could have this two-hundred-thirty-pound beast shaking violently around me while his dick was lodged into my mouth.

I skirted up his leg, pelvis, and carved abs, bringing my tongue up against his skin along the way. I lay half-draped over his body. My belly-to-belly days with him were way back in the distance, and too far up in the future, so I settled at his side.

"Beloved, I'm forty years old. I don't think that's a safe way to wake me up anymore," he rasped, his morning timbre firing me up all over again.

"I can't help it," I explained with honesty. "I think it starts in my subconscious, while I'm sleeping. It's like I smell you or something—feel your body heat, and respond to it without really knowing."

"That pleases me, beloved," he muttered out of breath.

"Kitten," I corrected.

Ezra turned to me. His eyes slanted with sincerity. "I am trying to balance your needs against my preference. I don't want to upset you."

"Why would you upset me by calling me my sex name?"

"Because this is not about sex," he rasped, deathly serious. "I believe where I mishandled you was making you believe so much of us was about that."

"It was," I agreed, harsher than intended.

"But it wasn't, at least that's what I realized once you left me."

I frowned. "Okay. Now, I'm confused."

Ezra turned slightly to face me. We were both laying on our sides. "Yes. I thought having you in my world would certainly satisfy my sexual needs initially. That was why I didn't mind you not having the same religious upbringing—I preferred that you not have it. And yes, I did explore the Bondage and Dominance lifestyle with you, one I still crave. But, beloved, when you left me, the last thing on my mind was sex."

"Then what was?"

"At first, it was losing my way. Disappointing God." Things grew quiet. I took the time to process his admission. "It was selfish, I know. But it was because I couldn't see things from your perspective. I'm sure it was because I didn't want to, but now I do. I want to. I need to begin to look at things past my own needs and tap into yours. Even back then, while it was my goal to pleasure you, I did it for my own satisfaction: because I knew I could."

"I guess I can understand selfishness." I shrugged.

"You? Know about selfishness?" He scoffed. "I can hardly believe that."

"Please. Sexual selfishness is my specialty. I realized this since being here."

His brows met.

"Are we talking masturbation?"

My eyes shot wide and mouth dropped behind closed lips. I nodded, my pulse beating out of nowhere.

Ezra's eyes closed and squeezed...in pain? *But I thought this wasn't about sex.*

"How often?"

"Often," I replied quickly. No need to lie.

But I could still hear the beat of my pulse bounce off the pillow. I could swear to hearing his, too, across from me.

"Did you enjoy it?"

I couldn't help my snort. "Of course, I did. No one can please you better than you. And if they do, shame on you." I cracked a smile.

Ezra did not. He actually raised and angled his head from the pillow. "Is that right?"

"Damn right."

I couldn't believe he was asking *me*, the queen masturbator. Ezra may be the sex king, but I knew my way around my body as well.

"Show me," he rasped slowly.

"Show you what?"

"Show me how you pleasure yourself, because if I recall, I distinctly told you, your every pleasure comes from me."

"But we weren't—"

"Unless you are legally dissolved of me, your pussy still belongs to me. So, since you believe you can serve it better than I can, let's see it. Show me."

By now my mouth hung wide open.

What the fuck...

"Now, Alexis!" his demand was crisp. "Do you do it on your back or stomach?"

My eyes fluttered, dazed.

I can do it either way, homes...

But... ummmm... "On my back, I guess," I whispered, confused.

"Okay. Show me." He eyed me expectantly.

I rolled over and lifted my knees. I could feel Ezra shift next to me, too. My hand pushed down my belly.

"No. Here," he demanded.

I glanced over to find him on his back, too, patting on his chest and belly. And there was that sharp command in his request that always appealed to me. It was just as visceral as being aroused by him in my sleep. Without pushback, I shuffled to lay on top of him. Ezra aligned my legs to rest over his and my ass directly on top of his dick.

"Go," he spoke right in my ear.

I could hear the push of air from his warm mouth on my lobe. My hand shot down between my open legs. The pad of my middle finger hit my pulsating clit and I stirred it, at first, gently. A sound of relief escaped my mouth, and I could feel my nipples harden. Ezra's legs arched, bringing mine up with them. His hands caressed my thighs, nearing my pelvis but not quite. I applied more pressure on my clit and increased my speed around it. His fingers hit my left nipple and I could immediately feel the liquid against them. I must have missed when he licked them, but *goddamn* they felt magical rubbing against the nerves of my areola.

"Does that feel good, kitten?" he whispered in my ear.

And there was the name.

My head pushed further back on his shoulder. "Yessssss..." I admitted with closed eyes.

My fingers rubbed with more speed. Then he slipped his right index finger inside my sex.

Oh god!

"Jesus..." he breathed. "You ever feel your pussy quiver?"

I shook my head, barely able to breath. His fingers were still playing at my sensitive nipple.

"Well then, my kitten, you've not fully masturbated. You have to feel what my cock does when you come around it."

"Uh!" I yelped, turned the fuck on.

My fingers sped up and I could feel the stir begin in my groin. Ezra pulled my hand from my clit and pushed it lower down my labia.

"Feel."

He laid his hand over mine, splayed, and guided my middle finger inside. He pushed deeper than I'd known it to go. Then I felt his thumb flicking over my nub. *Fuck!* His speed and pressure were perfect. That's when I felt the first clench of my sex around my finger and his.

"Oh, fuck!" I cried, no longer caring about censuring my pleasure.

"Uhn-huhn..." Ezra hummed in my ear. "This is why only I can touch this pussy. It's why it belongs to me. You can't do what I can do with it."

He pulled our fingers from me, bringing my right hand up to my right nipple.

"Stay right here for me, kitten," he commanded politely on a whisper.

His hand ventured down, this time his fingers landed on my clit, causing a leap in my pelvis. Instantly, my orgasm approached. My ass wouldn't lay on his lap. It stayed in the air as I pushed my thighs against his to raise my sex to his hand.

"Mmmmm..."

"Greedy little pussy, huhn?" he groaned in my ear.

Yesssssss...

Ezra used his left hand on my left breast, his right hand on my clit, and had me occupy my right breast myself. He played and played, and my pussy leaped and leaped. My lungs worked overtime and my groin spun and spun.

"And for my final trick..." he groaned.

His right hand pinned me to him, and within seconds I felt the crown of his dick at my entrance.

"Yes!" I damn near screamed. "Please!"

"Please what, kitten?"

Without any deliberation, I proudly cried, "Sir! Please, sir."

"Very well," he growled before pushing into me from behind.

His long dick worked its way into me while he continued to strum my nipple and clit. Ezra couldn't have been half way inside before my body shuttered in pure bliss. Shooting pleasure rocketed my entire body. My head swung side to side, arms flayed over him, and toes curled painfully. I reached a realm of pleasure never before visited, once again, at the hands of Ezra.

I experienced after quakes from my body's shocked state after being wrecked by an orgasm. For a moment, I couldn't move. My frame lay motionless, splayed over Ezra's big body. My stomach muscles didn't cry out in protest like before. That relief echoed in my mind.

"Alexis," he rasped.

I managed to swallow, but slowly replied. "Yeah." It was more of a helpless squeal.

"Don't touch your pussy again without my knowledge or guidance."

With what he'd just demonstrated how could I argue? Yes, it was my body, but with him, it experienced more pleasure and at a better quality than I could ever produce on my own. I was convinced.

"Yes, sir."

He sighed, turning me over to my side.

"That pleases me very much. Now, we have to get ready for work. You've used my workout time here in bed."

My eyes shot open, though he couldn't see.

I turned to face him.

"Work? But you didn't even come again."

Ezra chuckled, leaving the bed. "It's not just about sex with me, beloved."

~ten~

~Ezra~

I lifted from the kneeling position at the couch, mumbling remnant words of praise after the closing of my prayer. Sitting back on the couch, I rubbed my face, coming down from my worshiping flight, mind slowing from the process. I tried transitioning mentally to prepare for a run down in the gym. My palms brushed from my eyes to the shag of my beard. The second I opened my eyes, my blurred vision fell upon her. She stood in the walkway, leading to the bedroom, wearing a white cotton, strappy pajama gown.

"Whatchu' want for breakfast?" she inquired over a deep yawn, not even bothering to cover her swollen mouth.

"I'll have to pick up something on the road, beloved. I'll be headed out right after my run this morning."

Her tight morning face wrinkled in disappointment.

"Really? You have to be at the lab early or something?" She rubbed the sleep from her eyes.

With my chin resting in my upturned palm, I observed her unkempt morning glory. Even lacking graciousness and feminine refinement, she was captivating. The most enchanting woman I'd ever encountered.

I shook my head. "I have an eye appointment, believe it or not," I murmured.

She gasped slightly. "Eye appointment? So, you really think you need glasses?"

I shrugged my brows. "I don't know, beloved. But I do know this tension in my head isn't going away, and my sudden drowsy spells are growing quite frustrating."

Her face dropped. "Sorry about that," she spoke hardly audibly.

"Your regrets aren't necessary for something you have no control over."

She chewed that lip, deeply contemplating something. Alexis was also the most baffling creature. I had no idea what was running through her mind most times.

"I just remembered. I have to book Ms. Remah's ticket back home this morning," I noted aloud.

I'd convinced her to attend her friend's sixtieth birthday celebration two nights ago. She wasn't sold on me paying for the flight, but I would hear nothing of it. Secretly, Ms. Remah had grown on me. She'd become a pleasant companion since returning to the house. My dear wife's presence could never be replaced, but this time had certainly been beneficial in appreciating my other housemate. Morning coffee and newspaper reading had become a valued pastime for us. Dinner as well; some of our most fascinating dialogues had been derived at the dining room table. Come to find out, Ms. Remah wasn't the cagey specimen I once considered her to be.

"Hey," Alexis called out with mild urgency. "You mind if I tag along? I promise not to slow you down. I can follow in my car."

I was surprised she never commented on Ms. Remah's trip or me paying for it. Those two women were the most independent known to man.

Again, baffling…

I stood to my feet, stretched my arms, back and legs, feeling a burst of exhilaration within seconds.

"Sure," I replied with strained vocals then began past her to the bedroom where I needed to change into running gear. "Hope you decided on which of the two movies for tonight," I grunted moodily.

~~~~~~~~~~~

It was a relief to not have many around when entering the lower level of *RSfALC*. It was a Thursday morning when only staff was in this area of the church. Alexis followed me quietly. I was surprised to have her shadowing, but delighted just the same. I felt gimcrack...just lousy.

...and old. Gimcrack and old.

"Well, Mr. Carmichael, I can't speak to your recent bouts with exhaustion, but I can confirm your need of reading glasses. The straining when reading small letters, and tiredness of your eyes when trying to focus in is because of your need of visual assistance. Your case isn't severe, but yes, you need them."

I saw the timid smile spread across Alexis' full lips over in the corner where she sat observing the entire visit. Though grateful for her discretion, I regretted bringing her along. This was something a man married to a woman ten years his junior should do alone. I didn't want her to perceive my aging as a sign of frailty. I was still her dom. Still in control. Could still bring her to tears, drown her in orgasms. I was still capable of leading her to pleasure beyond her wildest dreams.

"So how does this work?" I growled, in spite of myself.

Dr. Inoke chuckled. *"It's simple. We have a selection of reading glasses out front. You can choose from there, or purchase a pair of your preference outside of here. We can also order a pair for you if you'd like. Reading glasses are easy to come by."* His demeanor remained upbeat.

It made me want to ask him if he wore reading glasses and if his old lady was relatively youthful compared to him, and how did he fare with functioning as an old man every time he had to read off a menu.

"I have a few minutes to peruse your assortment," I grated, resentful.

My god, I'll be at the table reading the menu with glasses alongside my parents! Where would be the age differential?

"It's a natural progression of aging, Mr. Carmichael. Everyone needs them at some point," he continued with amused concern as we trekked to the area of his practice where the exhibit of glasses was. *"And with today's trend, spectacles are worn as an ornament...a fashion accessory, not necessarily a needed visual aide."*

Just as I was about to supply a snarky remark, I felt a small hand on my back rub up and down. I glanced to the right of me and found Alexis at my side, her regard straight ahead.

"Those," was the first word Alexis spoke since we'd arrived.

I tried on the third pair of glasses the optician recommended 'based on the shape of my face'. Her decision was delivered throatily, her smooth mahogany neck extended from her shoulders. That assertion was stark. The room quieted and all eyes fell upon her. Alexis recoiled, her hands rose to her mouth, and she let out a coy giggle.

"Fine," I conceded through gritted teeth, eyeing myself with contempt in the small mirror.

God, I hated this ordeal!

We left the optometrist's office, and I was the recipient of a pair of squared black plastic framed reading glasses that weighed heavily in the pocket of my coat. I walked Alexis to her car, kissed her briefly, then took off to my truck for the city.

Retrieving the documents waiting in the box outside of the door, I entered my office, leaving the door open for her. After placing my coat on the hook and unbuttoning my suit jacket, I thumbed through the documents while rounding my desk. I tossed a glance over my shoulder to find Alexis on my heels. Startled and not wanting to knock into her, I stumbled back toward my seat.

"You think wearing reading glasses makes you old." It was a statement as we stood virtually toe-to-toe.

"I'm just not in the mood for another adjustment in my life right now. I'm sure you can appreciate that."

She nodded, her nose rubbing against the fibers of my beard. A dangerous act of affection at such an inappropriate time. I yearned for her passion. Her soft hands brushed down my chest, past my abs.

"This is an adjustment I find hot, Pastor."

I chuckled softly at her desire to placate my vanity. I even placed a chaste kiss on her head to close this conversation on my need of reading glasses. Having Alexis this close, presenting her seductive mien could only prove frustrating to me. She was my addiction. I wouldn't tease myself, had a long day ahead.

Her small fingers hooked beneath my belt. When I thought she was just going to playfully pull me into her, I felt her grip at the buckle. She pulled the belt from its loop and detached it quickly. My face hardened as my eyes fell to her hands. She unbuttoned my pants, slid her hand beneath my boxers, and grabbed my mushrooming erection. The heat from her soft hand had me swelling in no time. Her head bowed to my waist as she fisted me. My line of vision was blocked by her hair. The motion of her hand and the smell of her mane had my control fleeting. She pushed me back into the chair. I landed harshly and peered up to her expectantly.

Alexis licked her lips, fingers combing her hair to one side. She lifted her long dress, exposing her thigh high boots encasing the chocolate wonder of her toned thighs. Visuals of us at *Jux Supper Club* in her *Jimmy Choos* flashed through my mind. She lowered to the floor at a leisurely pace, her long legs spread as she rested on her haunches. Her panties exposed lewdly for my viewing pleasure. She reached over to push my pants down enough to pull my steely erection from the covering of my briefs.

"*Bel*—" I cleared my throat. "Beloved, we're on consecrated ground*sss*..." I hissed at the sight of her tongue trailing under the head of my erection. "...the tabernacle."

"If I can agree to the sandbox, you can relent to the *Bishop's Office*, sir."

I sucked in a breath. She was serious. We were doing this. Here. A burst of excitement ripped through my chest.

"Christ, Ale*xissss*..." She managed to cup my balls, her mouth wrapped around only my crown.

"You looked so fuckin' hot in those specs," she whispered, blowing on me.

My jaws clenched, balls filling. "Mouth, Alexis," I warned through gritted teeth.

She extended her tongue, spreading it against my shaft. "I'm using it, sir," she teased coyly.

"Jesus!" I breathed.

"*Shhhhh*..." Alexis hushed. "I'm 'bout to fill it."

At that, her mouth opened and dipped my cock. She took in as much as she could and clutched the rest from the base. Her face contorted, *god*, she was so focused on the task at hand. She plopped me out and drove just my head into her mouth, sucking as her tongue thrashed. Her hooded eyes opened and met mine. My kitten was seducing me. She was communicating the sincerity in her feelings about my aging process. It had in fact turned her on, seeing me into this maturation passage. I was still her dominant, though it was her exerting feminine power to stroke my ego. My head swung back, hitting the chair. I gave in to her talents, needing a co-pilot to take over.

Her insistence on this revealed so much. I was stressed. As sure as my sacks were inflating, building, gathering, preparing to explode, emptying my reservoir—pressure from ministry, work, and my delicate marriage—life's stressors had been mounting. The defeat in it all was that none would go away anytime soon. I'd been offloading things I could get around: counseling, duties around the church, delegating roles in the lab, and even my quiet time I'd always coveted. It was all to accommodate the newest and weightiest phenomenon in my life: my gift.

My left hand bounded her gathered hair, gripping it at the roots to navigate her oral plunges over me.

She'd been worth the adjustments. She humbled me, pushed me past my limits, and challenged me. There were so many concessions I made to accommodate her. To better myself in order to receive the gift God had bestowed. The terms of our covenant. And even on a day when I began to feel the defeat of my failing vision, a natural aging process, she'd turned my silent groans of woe into those of pure bliss.

My right hand enclosed both her fists jerking me, demandingly, adding even more pressure. My blurred vision cleared to the small mole on her slightly angled neck. My toes locked, hips bucked into her head, and seemingly every muscle in my body tensed painfully. I tried to hold back, not fully sold on releasing under this roof. But her dedication made my struggle for modesty difficult. And to make matters worse, Alexis moaned. She could feel my pinnacle arriving as I thrust ruggedly against her tongue.

Then, I was hit with a revelation. Here was my gift at work. She was my garden of pleasure. My private retreat from my calling and work. It was far more than a physical escape. Alexis was my emotional and spiritual haven. She had been created to inspire me beyond what I was to the masses. She had been on 'my' inside, gated away from all the stressors. This was us, restoring what was ailing in me. I let it go, breaking the levee that held the growing reservoir. As I shot into her mouth, Alexis massaged my sack, and I could feel weights falling from my shoulders as my muscles loosened, and gratitude for this unspeakable gift I'd been granted. Hot air burst through my mouth, pulse beat loudly in my head, and my spine jerked several times before collapsing.

The room spun swiftly, and I fought against my faculties to regain my equilibrium just enough to lift my head. Heavy breathing filled the room, mine more of a disturbed pattern, and Alexis' from roused excitement. Her dark eyes were lined with unmitigated lust, sensual accomplishment. She'd topped from the bottom, the reins of my emotions in her hands. At the control of her influence. This was a power exchange I would have never thought would relieve me. Balance me. I'd been thrown askew again. The need to take back that power and subdue her at the groin grew and raced up my spine. Countless images flew through my mind. Once again, I found myself in that split second of time to make the right call.

The sound of the door opening tore my attention from a kneeling Alexis.

Precious strolled through the office, a mountain of folders clutched in her hands. She headed straight for the coffee table to put them down, not peering my way until she straightened. She glided toward my desk, a smile in tow until she grew closer, registering my compromised state. Undoubtedly, my ragged breaths, strained expression, and lax positioning in my chair alarmed her. On autopilot, she drew toward me. Her mouth fell when she could perceive the wooly strands of my wife's wild mane. Precious gasped when their eyes met.

Christ...

I didn't know she'd be here at the church today.

Alexis didn't move, squatting stock still. Precious' eyes roved over my bared loins, moist from my wife's secretion. The sequences moving so swiftly, I didn't have time to move myself, to at least cover my exposed dick. Precious cupped her face as she backed up in search for the door. A mewl discharged behind her palm, en route. She slammed the door behind her.

Alexis' and my regards met. There was a serene slant in her eyes, I could perceive over my heaving chest.

"Well, there's another scandal waiting to break," I mocked hoarsely, still unable to move.

Calmly, Alexis began to arrange my clothing, tucking my softened cock back into my briefs. She stood to allow me to do the rest.

"I'm sure far more scandalous affairs have gone down in the *Bishop's Office*," she advised unbothered.

I stood, bringing her into my chest.

"Are you okay?" I would not have my wife demonized for being designed to suit my needs, no matter how unconventional they were.

She snorted softly, rolling her eyes. "Getting caught going down on a man happens all the time. Being caught going down on your husband is bawse status." She supplied a one-cheek smile and shrugged.

Alexis really hadn't been affected by that imposition. I gathered her into my arms. Though it was probably best to not further our intimacy after being walked in on, my need for her exceeded decency. I took her at the back of her head, covering her mouth with mine. Her insouciance to this religious culture once again inspired me. A pang burst through my chest at the need to want to protect her from everything and everyone. If I could hide her in my bosom from the adversaries of life—the sharks of my world—I would do it without thought. However, this was no damsel in distress. This was my Alexis with Harlem Pride. She was my warrior, capable of fighting anything or anyone rising against her. Including me.

God, I have to be better for her...

I pulled back, took her at the sides of her face, relishing the priapic slope in her eyes. Her regard was beyond sexual, it was admiration. And it felt unbelievably exhilarating coming from this cacao goddess.

"We're still on for that movie right after work, right?" she murmured, my hands still holding her head.

I nodded. She had no idea how much I was now looking forward to it, to have her all to myself again.

She kissed me, planting her warm lips to mine once again.

"Gotta go."

I nodded again, contented into silence as I went about arranging my clothes. I watched her straighten her dress and finger her tresses before grabbing her things to leave. She didn't look back before closing the door behind her, making it clear, Alexis was decided on demonstrating her tarrying desire for me despite witnessing my aging.

After taking a few minutes to gather myself when my wife left me to go to work, I tended to the business of the day myself. It felt like a long journey until the end of the day when I met Alexis at the movie theater in West Milford. She waited for me in the lobby, having already purchased our tickets. During the film, I couldn't help but steal gapes of her, watching her reactions to the comedy, twists, and plots as she chewed on popcorn and Twizzlers. We shared my sparkling water, Alexis gulping far more than my share. But I didn't mind. I embraced the moment of contentment for my wife, and savored it with her.

We returned to the hotel suite where we showered together and I was able to return her favor of pleasure. Twice. She let me tie her up to the shower knob, and spank her with my wet hand. The impact from our sodden skin made the bite sharper with lighter strikes. I didn't want to hurt her, only to rouse her with the post-pain sensations. Alexis was always game for whatever I asked. She trusted me more than I deserved. In bed that night, I wrapped her underneath me, covering her as she slept in a fetal position. Gone were the woes of not wanting to be here. The gratitude of being anywhere she was engulfed me as I rubbed her shoulder until I fell into slumber.

~~~~~~~~~~

The ringing of my phone tore me from my sleep. My head lifted off the pillow, holding suspended in the air. It rang again before I fully roused, recognizing it. Deep slumber was a fleeting occurrence for me. If I wasn't wrapped around her, it was an impossible feat. Being ripped from it was startling. As a pastor, one should be used to these middle of the night calls; however, I'd routed calls to my ministerial staff. I'd had my days of accepting those emergency calls when I was on the clergy roster. Those days were over for me, only extreme emergencies passed through my filter.

Alexis shifted, partially lying on top of me at some point in the night. I reached over toward the nightstand for my phone, not considering checking the identity of the caller; I was that disoriented.

"Hello," I groveled.

"Ezra!" she cried into the phone.

Alexis' head shot up from the pillow, her heavy eyes fought to open.

"Precious?" My chest began to pound. "Are you okay?"

"Your father told me to call you. Mary's at Mount Sinai. It's not looking good, Ezra. They're saying she's not going to make it."

My face folded. "Make it? What do you mean 'make' it?"

At that, Alexis jumped from the bed and scrambled for the light.

"Ezra, c'mon. You act first and ask questions later." Alexis spoke while frantically going through drawers. "Tell them you're on your way! C'mon!"

The brisk in her tone further alarmed me. Without more words, I disconnected the call and grabbed the underwear and socks Alexis handed me. Soon came other clothing items I tossed on mechanically, internally questioning what could have sent my mother to the hospital. *A car accident at this hour?* Before I knew it, Alexis was pulling me out the door.

~Lex~

"Down the hall, to the right," the nurse instructed before I could part my mouth to ask for directions to the room.

Ezra was finally alert. The entire ride into the city he was quiet, I was sure trying to manage his panic. We rounded the corner and saw a heap of people in the hall, some were familiar faces from the dignitary section of the church. They quickly parted outside of the end room, allowing access.

"Tell Bishop, Pastor's here!" someone ordered.

Just as we met the small group—some dressed in trench coats and slippers due to the late hour—Ezra's father came out of the door. He waved us inside a small waiting room.

"You sit here," he ordered me to a chair. "Come, son."

He took a stunned Ezra at the shoulder walking him to the door that I could tell led to Mary's room.

"This has been a whirlwind turn of events. They called me at the last minute. I had no idea all of this was happening. They say she's been sick for years—" was all I heard before they entered the room.

From the quick opening of the door, I was able to make out a distraught Precious. Her mom stood next to her. There were a few other people in there and a nurse, but the door closed too fast for me to make out everything.

What Bishop did was outlined his family and I wasn't a part of that for him. I felt slighted at first, but relief instantly ruled that out. I may have gotten Ezra to the hospital as quick as I could drag him to the car, but I didn't do hospitals and illnesses too well. It brought back the worst memories for me. The most immediate was visiting my mother in the psyche ward, and then her final trip when she died from a stroke after her last suicide attempt. It also brought back haunting memories of my attack, being poked and prodded after being violently poked and prodded.

Shit!

My eyes collapsed and I felt those dark emotions begin to overtake me that quickly. I rocked back and forth in my chair as I tried breathing deeply. Their close family and friends from out in the hall peeked through the rectangular window of the door that separated us. I had to keep my shit together. Ezra didn't need his wife having an emotional meltdown while his mother was sick.

And Mary! I couldn't wait to speak to her. If she wanted so badly to be intimate with her son, she should start by telling him she was sick. No one liked being caught off guard. She stayed up my ass, and I'm sure she'd do the same with Ezra if he had a more yielding personality. I would have to tell her to just…talk to him. He's a hard ass, but she's his mother; he'd listen to her.

I heard a loud gasp from the inside of her room. Then the door opened and an Asian man and Indian woman, both with white coats, somberly walked out. Two people I didn't recognize followed, clutched in one another's embrace, heading out into the hall. One wailing louder than the other.

What the fuck?

I jumped to my feet to see what was going on in there. There was a longer window running horizontally on the door. Ezra was on the edge of Mary's bed. Tubes ran from all over her body that was exposed, and an oxygen mask was pushed from her nose onto her chin. She looked deathly thin…and old in the bed. I hardly recognized her. Bishop Carmichael faced the window, clearly managing his emotions. Precious stood at the end of the bed silently crying, covering half her face as her mother held her in her arms. Marva's lips were tight and chin in the air, managing her emotions as well. It seemed as though she was there to comfort her daughter.

What's going on?

I backed away when a nurse neared the door.

"She wants him to sing..." I could make out Bishop informing someone in there. "Patty, help him out."

"You can go in if you like. I'm not sure how much longer she's going to hold out," her voice was soft, but eyes detached as she gently touched my arm.

Much longer? That brought to mind Ezra's question to Precious when she called. Before I could question her, I heard the odd belting of a familiar baritone note.

"*Let the church say 'Amen'...Let the church say 'Amen'... God has spoken...*"

It wasn't as strong as I'd heard of him, but just as fluid and controlled in delivery. Ezra was singing. I choked on a cry, immediately struck by the same emotion he had to have felt. The nurse offered a sympathetic smile before walking into the hall. Seconds later, cries ripped through the hallway from those waiting outside the room. My heart began pounding. A woman's shrieking wail made me drop back into the seat the bishop ordered me to. Someone sang the background vocals, backing Ezra up.

What. The. Fuck!

Is this what church folks did? They sang when someone was dying. I couldn't deal. But I couldn't leave. Ezra was in there, understandably shredding in pain. It was in his vocals.

"*Even in the valley...or standing at your red sea...*" Ezra sang.

Precious' cry carried through next. I'd guessed she could no longer keep it in. I stood. For what, I had not worked out yet. I caught a glimpse of Bishop standing over Ezra, cupping his shoulders in support. It was a similar posture to Marva and Precious. I stood on my toes to see Mary's eyes now closed.

Was she? Noooooo!

My chest ripped. I stumbled to my chair, shock consuming. The familiar emptiness after learning a loved one had died returned in spades. My husband lost his mother, the only woman who could never be replaced in a child's life. I knew that debilitating pain. Had carried it with me every day since my mother left me. My arms wrapped protectively around my belly.

"*I need you to say it...when your dream's about to die...*" his voice dipped at that line, emotions toppling, and I could not move to go and hold him.

The first audible cry burst from my sealed lips. I refused to let much more shoot out. I covered my mouth. I don't know how long I sat out there listening to Ezra sing so controlled, but clearly pained. The more notes he belted, the more I understood why Bishop ordered me to stay out here. Ezra's singing was a rare intimate side of him that I'd never been privy to except for that first Sunday he took over preaching at *RSfALC*. I felt like an intruder out there.

The door opened, and Precious and Marva walked out. I didn't understand what that meant. Was it over? Ezra was still singing. Marva's dry eyes skirted over me on her way to the door.

"Uh... Marva dear," Bishop Carmichael called out to her, his head peeking from the door. "Let them know they can leave. We're preparing to go." He looked at me. "You want Precious to call Thaddeus to come get you or can you drive home by yourself?"

I was too distressed to react to his bullshit. I wasn't leaving my fucking husband here like this. Ezra was still in there singing his goodbyes to his mother! He was out of his damn mind. Understanding an answer wouldn't come, Bishop ducked back into the room.

"As you may have heard," Marva spoke in her faux soprano, out in the hall. "Mary Carmichael has gone on to glory. At this time, the family is asking that you go home so Pastor Carmichael can part with his mother privately."

If my eyes weren't so swollen and my diaphragm so jumpy, I would've rolled my eyes.

"*If God said it...*" Ezra continued, his tone more stressed now, his cadence yet determined.

The woman helping him sing exited Mary's room next. She continued singing, "*God has spoken...let the church...say Amen...*"

I swear, this was too much for me to witness. I was so torn with wanting to leave to give everyone their space. But my heart was in that room, crying his heart out.

Mary!

The tears wouldn't stop falling, neither would my belly relax. Mary was dead, unexpectedly. How did this happen? I don't know how much time had lapsed when Bishop Carmichael finally strolled out of the room. His face was taut, expressing sorrow.

"Make sure he has a ride home," he demanded without looking at me.

He walked into the hall and I dropped in my seat, slipping down while muffling my cries. That's when I heard the first rip of emotion in Ezra's note. He began to sob in his intonation, now alone with his mother. The Asian doctor and a few others walked in the waiting area, and I jumped to my feet. My palms shot into the air.

"Not yet! He's not ready!" I commanded, not knowing if they were coming for her body or not, but knowing they would not disrupt Ezra's time in there with his mother.

The doctor nodded and gestured for his crew to turn around. When the door closed, I collapsed on my chair again. I sat out there for longer than I could count. By the time Ezra appeared in the small waiting area, I could see rays of the sunlight from the window in Mary's room. I shot to my feet and crowded his personal space. I didn't know what to do or say, but I knew I needed to share the heat of my body, somehow feeling as though it would provide some strength. Ezra pulled me into his broad frame, wrapping his arms around me. His fingers gripped my back and my hair, pulling it at the roots. I didn't mind the discomfort. I just wanted him to not feel as alone as I had in the past.

I insisted on driving back to Jersey. The ride seemed quicker than the one to the hospital, with my mind racing with questions. How did this happen? Did it really happen? Was this just a dream? The hour of the day provided a bit of delusion, so I couldn't be too sure. The loudest thought ringing in my head was that apparently Mary never told my secret, not even on her death bed. She didn't tell Ezra about my pregnancy. That spoke a lot about her character. It was revealing of her faith in me as a woman to do the right thing. It also brought with it a blanket of guilt for that respect not having been reciprocated. I tolerated Mary, not necessarily basking in the glow of her desire to connect with me. I saw it for what it was and kept her at arm's length. She knew it. And yet she kept my secret.

We pulled up to the hotel well after six in the morning. The bellman was setting the coffee machine in the lobby as we strolled in. Ezra promenaded with his chin low, and I remained just inches behind him feeling some elusive vantage point from there. I wanted to comfort him so bad, but didn't have it worked out as to how.

He dumped himself on the couch in the living room the moment we walked into the suite. I headed straight for the bedroom and to the closet.

"Alexis," he called hesitantly from out there.

"I'm packing our things now. We can check out in an hour."

The decision had been made for me. Our hotel rendezvous was over. It was time for me to return to the house. Our home.

The following days were dreadful. I had no idea of the inner workings of the church culture until then. Apparently, Mary Carmichael was an influential woman to people across the country. We had dozens upon dozens of floral arrangements delivered to the house. It became so inundating, Ms. Remah, who loved flowers, rotated them by date, placing the older ones on the back deck.

Speaking of her. Though she wasn't the most expressive person, Ms. Remah was especially happy to have me back home. She'd been more hospitable, making sure we had meals around the clock. She wouldn't allow us to lift a finger, only permitting me to do laundry because it consisted of Ezra's underwear.

"Dun't ever mek a next gyal wash yuh man's drawers, yuhnuh!" she pointed in my face as she spoke with her usual conviction.

How could I argue with that theory? Though it made me want to ask about the love of her life, who was still married to her sister, and had raised her only child.

Ezra didn't report to work—any of his jobs. He did speak at Bible study that following Thursday, imparting without a trace of grieving until he left the pulpit. It reminded me of his claim of being taken over the entire time he was up there. I wanted to stay by his side every moment of the day to keep an eye on him, but I didn't think it was healthy. People needed their space to grieve. And I had a job to tend to. I'd used a lot of my paid time off the two weeks after I left him.

I felt a heaviness around the house that saddened me. It was from Ezra; I was sure of it. Before I left, he gave so much life to the house, balancing out my timid nature about being here. His self-assured spirit settled the place. Now, with him in the throes of grieving, the place felt heavy and gloomy. I felt a similar atmosphere as a child in my mother's home when she'd return from the psyche ward, drugged up beyond recognition. The place was dull, and I was left to wait out the grayness of the period alone.

Ezra didn't sleep well at night. He'd come to bed late, sometimes leaving after a few minutes, and not returning until just hours before it was time to wake for the next day. It bothered me to no end. One night, I decided to follow him, to see just what he was up to. To my surprise—or perhaps it shouldn't have been—Ezra was on his knees, elbows perched on the love seat in his office, praying. It wasn't at the volume he'd typically take on; I understood because of the late hour. But something blossomed in my chest at the steady cadence of his voice as he spoke a language I wondered if even he understood. Ezra was in pain—in the throes of mourning, and he prayed. It was so unlike anything I'd ever seen. Hell, when my mother died, I did shit I still didn't want to cop to, till this very day. But not Ezra.

His appetite changed, too. Ms. Remah and I both noticed. She began cooking most of the house meals while I was gone and continued when I returned, so she knew his eating patterns. He'd sit at the table, sharing very few words as he used his fork to turn over food in his plate. His sexual appetite didn't change much. Though we hadn't visited the sandbox since I moved back in, Ezra took me every other day. It was a strange but steady pattern, and I wondered what it meant. On days that I got in early from work, I'd catch him in his office, and initiate it before dinner. He never hesitated, and would even let me take the lead. When he climaxed—my favorite part of our lovemaking—he clawed my skin, anchoring himself against his powerful orgasms, and what seemed like more. Ezra would hold me for a little while before silently releasing me to go. Growing to know him, it was not a sign of rejection, just a mark of a job well done. But still, he was off.

As he slept next to me at night, and I'd stay up staring at him in the dark, I had time to reconsider my feelings about my husband. Never again would I complain of his quiet, introverted nature. That state didn't come with emptiness. It was simply who Ezra was, not a mood, per se. *This* was a depressing state that I wanted him out of—for him and for me. I wanted *my* Ezra back.

I needed the beast, but would have to wait it out.

~eleven~

~Lex~

"Someone by the name of Karen's on the phone for you."

Ezra peered up, locating me at the door of his office. He picked up the phone.

"Hello, Karen," he answered. "Yes. Thank you. No, I didn't want her involved in the planning. It seems more appropriate for a relative or close friends if Bishop Carmichael isn't capable of taking the lead. I appreciate you three taking this on. As you know…" he hesitated, clearing his throat, "this has been a difficult time for all."

So, her girlfriends are planning Mary's funeral?

"I've asked Precious and Sister Graham to sit this one out," he continued. "Please let me know if they do not adhere to my decision. Thank you. And please let me know if I can be of any assistance. This homegoing should reflect the woman of God we're trying memorialize. Yes. Thanks, Karen. Yes. God bless you." He ended the call.

Ezra stayed in that position for a while, seemingly reflecting on his conversation with his mother's friend. Eventually he discovered I was still in the doorway. I wanted to tell him that I sent an email to Yanti and asked her to share with Jarabu and the rest of the people in Kamigu that he'd lost his mother, but couldn't quite gather the words.

"Everything okay with the plans?" were the words that formulated instead.

"Yes," was all he gave.

"Anything I can do?" I felt a pang in my chest at that offer.

I was doing it again: extending myself in a situation where I'd only be rejected. If he didn't want Precious involved, preferring family and close friends assisting, why would he take me up on my offer? I should just keep quiet and offer my assistance by way of my sex and mouth. That was where he made me feel valued.

"Yes, actually. They're going to need pictures for her program. My father's sending over photo albums. It would help if you could select ones appropriate for the occasion. I don't believe I'd..."

The moment his words faltered, I intercepted.

"Sure. I'd be happy to. Anything else you need... *Anything*. Just let me know, E."

Just when I was about to back out and leave, Ezra turned to me. He stood from his seat and motioned for me to come inside. To him. The moment I was in his grasp, Ezra engulfed me in his big chest and buried his face in my hair.

"Bear with me," he whispered.

Always... I felt, but was too afraid to say. So I hugged him tighter.

~Lex~

Goddamn, this place is packed...

According to Ezra, *Redeeming Souls* could seat around 14,000 people, but I'd never seen it filled to capacity. Today, the day we said our final goodbyes to Mary Carmichael, it overflowed. From whispers I heard since we arrived, there was seating set up in the basement, and a crowd of people outside, hoping to get in. When we pulled up to *RSfALC*, I could see uniformed police officers directing traffic and guarding the doors of the church.

From the time we were dropped off in front of the church, we were quickly escorted inside where we stayed in a small room near the entrance to wait for Bishop Carmichael. I silently prayed he'd show alone. I literally bowed my head and mouthed words that were more like begging God to not allow this man to show up with Marva on his arm as he laid his wife to rest. Within minutes, we were notified by security that Bishop had arrived. He was a party of one, and I quietly sighed in relief. As we took to the front of the church, two things ran through my mind: the place was packed already, and how this was the same journey I took to marry the man to the left of me, clutching my hand for support.

Ezra ambled up the aisle with his head bowed and brows pinched. This was difficult for him, I knew. I'd lost my mother, too. The difference in my grieving was I did it with a small group at a tiny funeral home. Ezra had to pay his respects publicly, under the watchful eyes of thousands. Did I mention they were recording this funeral? Yup. *Redeeming Souls for Abundant Living in Christ* was a broadcasted organization. Apparently, the power that be decided its official First Lady should be sent off the way she worshipped.

We sat in one of the worst seats in the house for me: the front row. And I understood it was tradition, much of this procession was. It was my role to support Ezra. The moment my eyes hit the gold and brass closed casket just under the stage, my food threatened to come up. It was loud enough to catch Ezra's attention. His red and stained eyes examined me with worry. The sight of them pained me. I had to get it together, hold tight. My husband needed me. I straightened and forged a closed mouth smile. Ezra blinked a few times before sitting back.

The funeral was a spectacular procession indeed. Not before long, I could see why so many people wanted inside the building, and to view the service from their televisions. Countless people took to the pulpit to speak in loving memory of Mary. Most of them I'd never seen before, but decided to focus on them instead of her coffin just before us. One face I did recognize was Ezra's mentor and friend, Bishop Jones. He took to the podium and spoke just as eloquently as he did at my wedding. Like Ezra, he was a fluent orator. You could tell from the stories of comfort he shared, that he mourned with Ezra, who kept his face down much of the service.

Then there were the songs. Some were slow and forlorn, and others more upbeat. Some rang familiar, and I had the feeling, often being sung by the actual recording artists. There was that one woman, Karen, who sang her shoes off. She was the one who abruptly appeared on the pulpit that Sunday Ezra broke down. I could feel grief rolling off her with each note she crooned for her friend.

Then there was the last singer. He stood to a highly-applauded introduction. I didn't catch his name because Precious strutted past me to whisper something in Ezra's ear. He barely regarded her, answering her quickly. I followed her with just my eyes until she disappeared behind our row, into the crowded pews behind. I fought not to roll my damn eyes. Why did she annoy me so much?

"Whenever I crossed paths with First Lady Carmichael out at events, where I sang this song, she would come up to me afterward and say, '*You know my Ezra sings that song, right?*'" The audience responded with amusement as his tone mimicked a nagging woman's. The piano chords trickled in the background. "And I would always say, '*Yes, First Lady Carmichael,*'" he sighed, pretending to be annoyed with her bragging. "And then she always said, '*You sang it real good, though, Marvin.*' And I would tell her I knew I did. I'm a recording artist, have been for over a century. Then she would say, '*But you know, Pastor, my Ezra sangs it better.*' He rolled his eyes. The entire building went up in laughter. I couldn't help but follow.

As I peered over to Ezra, who held his head respectfully, but not sharing so much in the humor, I could see Bishop even chuckling at the joke. *That Mary loved her some Ezra.* Why did this revelation pour like guilt over me?

And she kept your secret.

I sucked in a cry, thankful for the man hitting a note that rang familiar to me.

"*Let the church say Amen...*"

I know this song! It was the one Ezra sang in Mary's room the night...she passed away. My eyes jumped to Ezra, whose regard was down at his knees. I clutched his hand in mine, willing myself strength. I could only imagine the memories this brought him. Why would Ezra sing this song of the millions he knew? And why sing at all? That was weird, but I came to expect strange things from this religious culture. As the man belted out the lyrics, the church reacted in boisterous praise.

I leaned over to meet Ezra's shoulder.

"Why did you sing this to her that night?"

My heart trembled from the bold and possibly inappropriate question. I hadn't asked Ezra anything about his mother since leaving the hospital. I still didn't know how she died. I told myself I would wait until he told me.

"Because she asked me to." Ezra's red eyes strained as he replied.

Unable to help myself, I wrapped my left arm around as much of him as I could from my seat. Ezra leaned into me, receiving my comfort.

~*Ezra*~

"*Who can find a virtuous woman? For her price is far above rubies.*

The heart of her husband doth safely trust in her, so that he shall have no need of spoil.

She will do him good and not evil all the days of her life...

She opens her mouth with wisdom,

And on her tongue is the law of kindness.

She watches over the ways of her household..."

As Pastor Winans sang with his usual moving grace, all I could think about was how little time we truly have with the ones we love. I never saw this coming, had no idea my mother would leave for the other side of glory this soon. There was so much I wanted to give her before she left this side of heaven. She would say I'd given her enough with returning home, settling in a career—or two—and eventually marrying. Still, I knew she deserved more for all the heartache I caused her in my youth, and the neglect she endured recently.

Everyone neglected her. I was no better to her than him.

"I didn't do it. I did nothing wrong!" I shouted.

She met my tone. "Don't you think I know that? You think I would say otherwise if I thought you had a predator's bone in you, Ezra?"

"But Bishop does! He thinks I hurt that girl."

I wanted to cry. I wanted to scream and pound anything and anyone who hurled a wrongful accusation at me.

"Look at me, Ezra. Look at me!" her little hand yanked my chin to her line of vision. "You ain't gotta worry about what nobody says or thinks about you. I'm your mother! You came from my womb! I know what God told me about the baby I was incubating. He said your path would be different, that you would be misunderstood by many. But you were one of His chosen. And no matter what you did, to believe in your gifts and valor."

My eyes and nostrils widened. I felt as though I'd been hit by some unknown force, my hardened spirit coaxed by a calming balm. That's when the tears couldn't be controlled if I tried with all my might. My jaw clenched to a breaking might.

It was Him again. That was His language. His Spirit reminding me of my birthright. For so many years, He'd shown His hand to me in ways that would send most into a crazed fury. Religion is a way of life, but knowing God is a way of living beyond yourself. It's a relationship with a living, supernatural being. He'd disturbed my sleep countless nights all my life. His Spirit would speak to me with warnings, visions, and messages for people that I knew nothing about. I had always been different, set aside. I hated it. Never understood why I was so different. Couldn't fathom why I'd spend time with *my grandfather as a kid rather than my friends or with age-appropriate toys. No one knew to help me extrapolate my peculiarity.*

"Are you listening to me, boy?" her small hand roughly cupping my face.

"I have to go, Mom. I can't stay here. I need to figure me out," I advised painfully. "Losing Jimmy, being expected to follow behind my father, and now this..." I tensed, fortifying myself against the incoming tears. "He believes her. Her mother believes her. They were going to press charges. He wants me to see a therapist!"

"No! They can believe what they want to. I"—she tightened her cupped palms on my face, my bare cheeks and jaw—"I believe in Ezra!"

My eyes mushroomed again. The weight of her words nearly knocking me to the floor. It was the afternoon of my graduation at Pepperdine. I'd just told my parents I wouldn't be returning home to join the ministry as was expected of me. I was leaving the country and didn't know where I'd land or when I would come back. I even told them I didn't know if I believed in the God they did. My father stormed out of my dorm room, exploding in anger. My mother stayed behind as she always did, to salvage what was possible.

"I believe the report of the Lord. I believe in Ezra," she repeated. "Say it back to me!" I don't think I'd ever heard my mother speak from the pit of her belly.

With a pounding heart and confused mind, I uttered, "And I believe in Ezra."

I wanted to give her life the benefits of a son: a career, wife, ministry, and perhaps children someday to cure her chronically broken heart.

You would have loved that, mother...

Trying to tune back into the spirited service, I sucked in a breath and held in the tears I had only shared with her and our God.

~*Lex*~

Emotions were high at *Redeeming Souls* as the choir assisted the man in delivering the soul stirring spirit of the song.

"Let the church say *Amen!*"

It was clear to me Mary was respected and a beloved leader beyond my time at *RSfALC*. A man I didn't know, Elder Peterson, provided the eulogy. Apparently, he was her father's, the late Bishop Travois Daniels', assistant pastor and Mary's godfather. Similar to Bishop Carmichael, he was a hoopin' and hollerin' preacher. However, the personal touch he added to the message concerning Mary was touching.

Her burial at the cemetery was tough. It was for close friends and family only. The location was not disclosed to the public. If I thought Bishop

Carmichael had a large degree of decorum for attending his wife's funeral alone, I learned he had only an ounce when Marva consoled him as Mary's body was being lowered. The few who attended had walked off to their cars, leaving five of us behind: a sobbing Bishop Carmichael, being comforted by Marva, a zoned out and tense Ezra with me melded at his side, and a lone Precious. She was visibly saddened, too. Her face wet from tears and slender frame shuddering as she held herself at the belly. She walked off minutes after her mother and Bishop, somehow lingering. I held tight until Ezra took me at the shoulder to leave.

The first—yes, the first—repast was the public one. It was held at *Redeeming Souls*, in the dining room. It was there that I saw more familiar faces like Elle and Jackson, and Ms. Remah who, stayed behind with Lillian. Stenton Rogers, and his wife, Zoey were there, too. I always found it amazing how close my husband was to one of the most popular athletes ever. Stenton was extremely sensitive to Ezra's mood, eyeing him closely, but saying very little. Like me, Zoey stood at her man's side, observing him to be sure he was fine. It was clear she could pick up Stenton's sensitive state to my husband, too. Ezra wasn't putting folks off, but he certainly was out of character, and understandably so. The two men exchanged a few words that I didn't catch, leaving them to their privacy.

Thaddeus didn't travel very far from Ezra. He, too, allowed him his space to greet other guests or to be quiet if he chose. At one point, I left him for the bathroom. Sister Shannon followed me. It would have been weird to me if I hadn't reminded myself her primary role with me was to block me from strangers of the church. Ezra must have given her that order right after we were married, because she stayed on my heels and kept conversations with strangers politely short. As expected, a few stopped me en route. She escorted me to a private bathroom not so close to the dining room where I relived myself. On the way back, a few presented their condolences, and I accepted them, responding politely.

Just before we made it back to the dining room, I checked my phone absentmindedly. I was shocked to see I had a text and missed call from an unknown number.

Unknown: lex its Jarabu yanti told me about Mrs Carmichaels death my heart grieves for my friend and his family i cannot make it out to see him until next week please tell him I will call with my arrangements

I chuckled at the contrast in writing styles between Ezra, who loved using formal punctuations, and his friend, who didn't use any at all. Jarabu didn't even capitalize the start of his sentences. It was a cute finding. Jarabu really admired Ezra. I couldn't wait to pass the message along.

When I made it back to the table where I left Ezra, his seat was empty. He was gone. I glanced around the large and elegant room and couldn't locate him. Stenton approaching me snagged my attention. His large frame towered me unusually. I had been so used to being shoulder level with most men.

"Lex, I know this is a common offering at a time like this, but if there's *anything* I can do to provide comfort for my guy, let me know."

Zoey walked up on us as he spoke, taking Stenton affectionately at the elbow. My eyes diverted so I wouldn't appear perverted for noticing that small act of affection.

"Yeah. We're going to Spain once Stenton ends his last season," Zoey chimed in. "We're staying for a month. If you think he could use a getaway, you guys are more than welcome to come. It would be great having Ezra with us. That's if you guys don't mind the kids." She offered a teasing smile.

That's when I caught my husband, at first, out the corner of my eye. He was across the room with Precious at his side. His regard was down as it had been all day—his grieving posture—while he spoke to an elderly clergyman based on his tall and decorated hat and long purple robe. It was clear from her proximity that Precious was playing hospitable hostess. Her hand clutched to Ezra's arm as she smiled in on their discussion. Ezra's hands were clasped together. The man was in obvious distress, though holding it together, and Precious thought it appropriate to play public relations relief.

Ezra could have simply declined talking to folks. He was an adult after all. But it would've been good to see him remove the mask of clergy leader at a time like this.

I sighed, my eyes glued to my husband who had been hiding a great deal of pain behind his beard. "At the end of the season is too far away for what he needs." My eyes returned to the Rogers. "No," I hummed in humor. "This would call for one of those chartered flights to Indonesia like next week-type of relief." I chuckled, softening my decline.

"Oh, really?" Stenton's eyes lit up. "We can make that happen. Do you have dates in mind?"

My face fell. I was just joking.

Yeah, I would love the escape with Ezra to give him a reprieve, but it wasn't a plan.

"I can have Srey—Stent's assistant—make the arrangements right away." Zoey pulled out her phone and immediately started typing. "Where exactly in Indonesia?"

"Guys, I was just..." my gaze went back to Ezra. "I couldn't ask you to do that. You don't know me like that."

"Lex, Ezra's my dude," Stenton declared, eyes earnest, imploring.

"It's really no problem, Lex. These two are...different," her voice dropped at that last word.

I had to snicker at that.

Stenton rolled his eyes, cracking a boyish smile. "Not now, Zo."

"I was just…" Zoey rocked on the heels of her feet as she looked away, playing innocent.

I had to laugh at that, too. These two had adorable chemistry.

"Anyway, Lex, it's for my man. And since you're his lady, by extension, it would be for you, too. I can't stand to see him like this. I've lost a parent, and know how rough it can be. I just wanna help."

With my eyes still cast on my husband across the room, now speaking to a small group of people, I nodded.

"Okay," I muttered, my mind racing a million miles a second. "Okay. I'll be in touch."

"Cool. Give Zo your number."

~Lex~

"Alexis," I heard rasped from behind me.

I prefer Beloved!

I silently sighed, but didn't allow my shoulders to drop over the kitchen sink. I pushed the water off and reached for the towel before turning around.

"Yes." I tried for a smile.

"Precious just called. She said you requested coverage for this Sunday and next, *and* the next two Bible studies. You told her I would be out of town?"

His eyebrows bunched, a confused expression lost behind his beard, but I knew.

"Fucking dry snitching first thing in the morning," I mumbled, eyes cast down to my feet.

"Pardon me?" Ezra asked in earnest. I'm sure he didn't catch my words, but he damn sure felt the sentiment.

Releasing a cleansing breath before squaring my shoulders, I prepared for the shit storm. "Yes, E, we're leaving town for about a week. And, yeah, I took the liberty to reach out to someone on your executive board to make the arrangements necessary for your absence. I've also contacted Geoffrey at the lab and asked him to clear your schedule as well. I don't know who you counsel, so you'll have to handle that and your martial arts schedule."

And whatever the hell else you're involved in with your impossible schedule.

Ezra took a step closer, farther into the kitchen. His head cocked to the side, eyes squinting. He wore a gray sweat suit with his gray Jordans, and I assumed he'd had his morning workout. That relieved something in me because it was his normal. But I also knew he didn't sleep much last night. When Ezra left the bed after eleven last night to pray, I pulled out my housecoat and laptop, secretly followed him down to the office, and worked outside the door, letting the melodies of his prayers play the background as I wrote up a work plan for my staff, preparing for my absence. Him getting up early this morning to hit his gym out back was a risk of burning out.

"And where do you suppose we're going?"

"Kamigu," I answered matter-of-factly, with full-fledged confidence I had no idea I possessed.

"Kamigu?" His eyes widened and neck snapped back. "How is this supposed to happen on a whim?"

"With Precious doing what I asked instead of running back to you, stirring up confusion—"

"But I am her overseer, I am the one who gives—"

"And I am your wife." I began toward him until our toes were inches away and I could smell him. He could smell me. "The woman who's responsible for your well-being when *their* eyes are only on the tasks you assign them. My welfare is tied to your strength. You are not at your best after having lost your mother and unexpectedly. I belong to you, Ezra?" I raised my chin to implore his eyes. "Well, damn it, you belong to me, too, and I will not have you breaking down because nobody had the wisdom to give you a break or the balls to tell you, you need it."

"I can appreciate that...I really can, but what you're asking is not that simple. The flight alone is outrageously costly, the expense to stay at the resort is beyond my affordability—our affordability. Yes, clearing my calendar is one steep feat, but the logistics at this late hour are impossible," he scoffed.

I felt my nostrils flair and I stretched my neck on a jerk to temper my response.

"Our flight leaves tomorrow at eleven p.m. Carlos will be here to pick us up at nine. Jarabu is preparing the Queen's Hut for us, because apparently, the King's is being occupied by the Duchess of Cornwall's besties' granddaughter or something—I don't even know who that is. She's finishing up her honeymoon there this week. But he guarantees the Queen's Hut has the very amenities needed for your toys."

Ezra's eyes damn near popped out of their sockets at that.

"Alexis," he breathed, preparing to cut me.

"I prefer beloved for now, but kitten would be more appropriate for the Queen's Hut." I combed the hairs of his beard with my fingertips before turning to leave. "I have to go. I'm taking Ms. Remah to the airport in thirty minutes. Please bring her luggage to the car for me. I'll be headed to work after, and bringing dinner home tonight."

I didn't wait for a reply. I could never survive the rejection of my initiative from Ezra. I had to stand firm on this. Somehow, Ezra was able to talk Ms. Remah into a trip home for a few weeks for her friend's sixtieth birthday, where she would also soak it up in the ocean as treatment for her back. Her doctor said it wouldn't hurt, in addition to the treatment plan he'd prescribed her. She wasn't supposed to leave for three days. Luckily, I was able to move the flight up to today.

It was a crazy day for me with meetings and in-depth conversations with most my staff. I was able to get home in enough time to feed Ezra, pack our clothes, and give him a blow job that relaxed him into an agreeable mood, as I prepared to snatch him from the stupor of depression to a long ass journey over the Pacific.

~Lex~

Air shot from my lips and my thighs leaped higher in the air.

"Ahhhhh!" I screamed from the pit of my belly under the indigo sky, peppered with bright stars.

His head dipped and swung in short successions as my body tensed and abs crunched, preparing to take flight. My breasts bounced in the cool air of the early Indonesian morning. My palms and fingertips pressed into the short strands of his hair, my pussy lifting to meet his slivery tongue. Sweat beads lifted from my pores, the air caressing and cooling my skin. I couldn't help the loll of my tongue hanging lazily from my mouth, the swinging of my head from side to side.

Swipe. Swipe. Slurp. Slurp. Swipe. Swipe—

On the last stroke, with his big hands gripping my hips, pulling the seat of my pelvis to his face, I felt the first roll of my explosive orgasm.

"Shit, Ezraaaa!"

His tongue flicked over my nub without mercy. I could hear his frantic slurping, the ends of his wiry beard, brushing against my ass. Damn, he was aggressive with this one. I shot way into the stratosphere, my body convulsing feverishly. Before I could come down, my lax, dangling frame was lifted in the air, reminding me of his dangerous might. When I was flipped face forward, my senses kicked in, and I fell on my knees. He leaped from the mattress and within seconds, took me at the wrists, pulling me to one of the posts at the head of the bed. My arms were extended and bound together by a wide, flat silk strap. In the next moment, he was behind me, roughly cupping my chin, bringing my face back to meet his musky mouth.

"Mmmmm…"

I moaned senselessly when his tongue touched mine. It still amazed me how much of a turn on it was tasting me on him. After arriving yesterday to Kamigu, and just when I'd been able to doze off in his arms, this is how I was awakened. His face between my thighs, and now his big hard body hovering over me from behind, warming me with his masculinity. His tongue reminding me of our sensual blend. But this kiss wasn't tender. This was no act of affection. It wasn't punishment either. This was the beast taking what it needed. It was my husband's therapy. I didn't mind the roughness, the coarse nature of lovemaking. When he took his comfort from me, I felt impossibly stronger.

A sharp slap bit into my ass. I whimpered at the initial ache then arched my back into the bliss that chased it shortly after. Then I felt him breached me, abruptly, rough, and intentionally crude. I was so wet, I didn't give a damn. As big and strong as he was, Ezra knew the right amount of pressure to apply, getting me off every time.

He rocked, an upward thrust digging through my core. His fangs, biting into my shoulder, and his fingers at the bone of my pelvis on my waist. Each drive into me, melting me for more of him. His lunges were rhythmic, and each impact slapped into my flesh as I gripped the pillar I was tied to, holding on for balance on my knees. When they became more urgent, I could no longer weather against the horsepower, my head collapsed back on his shoulder. Ezra wrapped his big arms around my waist, protectively, changing the impression of his pounding. He rocked with his hot body so close to me now, the mist coating our vibrating frames blending deliciously.

His mouth crushed mine, tongue provoking with lunges down my throat. Eagerly wanting to match his pace, I couldn't breathe at times, that excited about his passion. When I felt the first wave of my orgasm shooting in my groin, my hands clasped the post of the bed even tighter. Sex had always been explosive between us, but Kamigu brought it to a special plateau. The air was different here, our chemistry heightened in this distant land. It was a nice welcome to a home where I knew I belonged.

"You didn't ask permission for the first one, kitten," he growled into my mouth.

I felt drunk, deluded underneath him, pleasantly enduring all of him. This was what becoming one is like physically. There was no space between us. Ezra wanted none. I had no sense to ask for permission to meet my climax because I had no choice in experiencing them. I felt the undulation, was weakened by it. When his fingers began to strum my nipple, I knew he had me where he wanted me to be. Tied up, wound up, intoxicated by his touch, and speechless.

"Uhhhhhh!" I slurred, unable to mumble a coherent word.

"Christ, kitten," he groaned as his upward thrusts propelled to a speed that hurled me over the fucking edge.

I could feel him growing even larger inside of me, intensifying my flight. Ezra held me even tighter at the hips as he shot into me. His breathing turned ragged, heart beating out his chest. Our sweat serving as an adhesive to our troubled souls as we met again deep inside my womb.

Ezra didn't let up until he could gain himself. With his full weight on me sandwich between the post, he lifted to release me. I tried not to panic, barely able to breathe, holding the both of our wracked bodies up. Under normal circumstances, I could appreciate the true analogy of him throwing it all on my shoulders, but there was nothing ordinary about my condition. I had to tell myself this when easily getting lost in my husband's passion. It consumed me, rendered me dumb as shit. Within three tugs, I was released. Before I could register it, I was pulled down on the bed, my back slamming into the concrete of his chest and abdomen.

"Sleep, kitten," he rasped, morning gravel in full affect.

Sleep?

It was four in the morning, and the last thing on my mind was sleep. Instead of getting lost in that alluring sound of his morning timbre, my mind raced with the condition of my baby. I understood it was well cushioned, but I also knew still not being quite twenty weeks yet, I could miscarry. I wasn't out of the woods yet. I didn't want to think about that.

Damn. I can't believe I'm still getting away with hiding this from him!

Under the shadows of the morning sky, I reached for my belly. I rubbed with the motion of my wrist alone, silently praying for the safety of *my* miracle.

~Ezra~

I came into the hut, wanting to quickly change into swimming trunks then catch Jarabu down by the boats to go out into the water.

"Alexis, where are my—"

My steps halted at the sight of her scuffling to her feet. She was on her knees in front of the bed. Alexis quickly covered her naked body under the robe she wore. Her eyes were large, startled.

"I-I..." She swallowed nervously. "I didn't hear you come in."

"What were you doing?" My eyes went to the bed.

"What do you think I was doing? Praying."

"You pray? At this hour?"

She swung her neck back. "Whoa! I do pray," she stated with fire. "Let's start with that. I may not qualify to wear a collar, but seeing that I'm married to a man that does, I think it's natural for me to have a prayer life. And for your information, I pray before getting my day started. I slept in today." She tightened her robe defensively.

Silence rented the air. It had been weeks reunited bliss, but we were back to our stubborn wills warring. As much as I should have been used to this between us, it felt troubling this time, especially since things had been beyond peaceful. Alexis had been my rock during the period of my bereavement. I'd just begun coming out of the fog bleakness.

"Okay, honey—"

"It's beloved," she hissed.

I flinched, reminded of her new level of sensitivity to my pet names for her. Little did she know, right now she was *Manna*. I'd call her that if I felt it would go over well. That was what she represented to me. I knew I'd been low and needed the strength she'd provided. She was an anchor that was helping me move beyond the cloud of grief that I knew would soon become bearable.

"Beloved, I am sorry." My eyes ping-ponged between her and the painting suspended on the wall above her. "You moved so quickly, I thought..."

"That I had something to hide?" Her brows rose. "I don't. I have a lot to pray for is all."

"Like what, beloved?" Panic struck, closing up my throat. "Is there anything I can help you with?"

"No, Ezra. You're not God."

"But is there something I can improve upon?" I didn't care if she could smell my desperation.

I watched as her face fell, her brows met and nose expanded. Then she moved to crowd my personal space. It was an act that instantly soothed me.

"Ezra, you're fine—no...we're fine. But I do have my needs for prayer. Yeah, they include you during a time when you need it, but I'm sure I'll always have a reason to pray."

Of course, she would. The Bible says to pray without ceasing, and aside from that, trouble will always subsist until Christ returns. However, here was when this new and distinctive characteristic of insecurity reared. I needed Alexis. This was something I'd never experienced. Her emotional well-being had to be balanced for me to relax. What she said to me in our kitchen the day before we left was ghostly, because it had been the same for me.

If not more.

She met my lips, her hands cupping the mass of my overgrown beard. Her touch seized my lungs, her sweet breath sent bolts of lightning into my groin. The wings of my back contracted. I prayed she hadn't felt it. Then those hands circled around my waist, pushing up my back. The power she held over me had somehow seemed to multiply. Her tongue moved with a need and confidence I didn't know of her. And when she pulled back, I had to force my eyes to open.

"When you're fine, we're fine," she whispered giving finality to the awkward moment, my siren kitten. "Why did you come in here?"

I took a moment to gather my bearings.

"I'm going out on the boat with Jarabu. I need more trunks."

She backed away, pointed to the dresser across the room.

"There're two more pairs in there. Ida said she'll be by for laundry tomorrow." She turned for the bathroom. "If he's waiting, you should hurry up. I'll be by the pool today, trying to figure out how I'll get back into Yanti's good graces when she returns to the island tomorrow."

"Where is young Yanti?" I asked behind her.

I didn't realize I hadn't seen her over the past three days since we arrived.

"Midterms at school." Alexis shouted from the bathroom. "She's been staying near her campus because of it."

I sighed, moving for my swimming shorts. I would have to let the two women settle their differences alone. I had more immediate subjects to settle, mostly internal. It had been a rough period for me, marked by the unexpected death of my mother. This was difficult to admit to as a licensed therapist. It was more than losing a parent, a common occurrence in most people's lives. This was more or less spiritual.

As I changed into my swimming shorts, my mind began to turn over recent events. Having been a seeing man most of my life, I had never been partial to surprises. This was difficult to explain to anyone without a spiritual eye. God revealed things to me all the time. He'd give me messages of warning and hope for those I covered, and strangers alike. I'd just been recovering from having almost lost Alexis and then came the death of my mother. It still hurt to conceive those words privately. Mary Lynette Carmichael née Daniels would never be seen again on this side of glory. Even as a therapist, I didn't know how to process that.

And Alexis… She'd been a fierce protector and commander during the darkest of my desolation. My wife had more than provided the light I needed to see my way through the gloom. She'd been my beacon. Though I didn't deserve her grace, I admired her courage. She was the submissive in our relationship yet had been able to anticipate my needs over the past few weeks better than I had. Alexis kept me fed, sexed, and protected. Even on the flight here, she'd packed my devices correctly, my clothes were in the luggage before I could stress over what to bring, and she'd even remembered my chess board. She had the stewardess prepare the sleep aid tea to keep me relaxed on the flight. Alexis massaged me after the first few hours, until I fell asleep under her ministrations. She'd been attentive the entire flight.

We slept for the first two days after arriving, adjusting to the time change. Today was the first time I had awakened before Alexis, and went out for a walk on the water where I encountered Jarabu. He caught me up on the happenings of the island, taking my mind off dismal matters. We agreed to take his new boat out. That slip up with Alexis proved to me I had work to do on myself. I needed to rid myself of this paranoia of her discontent and ultimate exit from my life. It was hard when I could feel in my spirit she was keeping something from me. As much as she'd been my pillar of strength, Alexis had also been withholding.

"Are you ready, my friend?" Jarabu shouted in his native tongue, delighted as he waved me on from feet away.

I froze before returning an affirmative nod. I couldn't believe I was here, at the water already. My last conscious thought was ogling the jiggle in my beloved's gait into the bathroom. I hardly recalled stripping out of my clothes to change.

I forged a smile, taking a deep breath. I prepared for recreational time with my dear friend. It was something he'd been requesting for years. Time I, for some reason or another, never made the commitment to until I got married, and even then he was called away to deal with his mother's health. During that visit, we really didn't commune. Similar to my mother, I took my relationship with Jarabu for granted. In my mind, the comfort of their presence would always be there.

Today, I would live in the present of my fortune. I would relish the moment gifted with my loved one.

~Lex~

"Ida, how do you say sorry in Bahasa Indonesian?" I grabbed her arm as she walked past with a loaded tray.

Ida sighed, shaking her head at a pouting Yanti, ignored the question, and walked to the back for the kitchen. My eyes remained locked on my young friend. She was beautiful: bronzed, sun-kissed skin, dark long and thick hair down to her back, and a nice hourglass shape. She'd let her tresses grow in since I last saw her. In just months, she looked more mature.

Yanti rolled her eyes in the air.

"Yanti!" I shouted, my arms shooting in the air, amusement lining my eyes. "You can't stay mad at me forever!"

"How long would it have been before you called me? If it weren't for Mr. Carmichael's mother's passing, I wouldn't have heard from you." She tooted her lips in the air again, tightening her apron.

I made sure to rise early this morning, to catch her before she started her shift. Today was finally the day I had to answer for my neglect. Yanti had been emailing me for months, and I'd been too wrapped up in my feelings to respond.

I shook my head, my face burrowed into my palms. "That's not true. It's just that..." I lifted my head, exhaled loudly. "Ughhhhh!"

"It is what?" she demanded, little chin defiantly in the air.

She was so adorable. But fuck me if my hormones broke unexpectedly and tears pooled in my eyes. I sucked in a quick breath to catch them before they fell.

"It's been a rough seven months, chica. When I was here last summer, I was unemployed. It took a while to find work. Then I had to learn a new work environment and staff. I have to bust my ass to get shit done because my biggest boss is my husband. I can't have people think I got it unfairly. I have Ms. Remah—the one I told you about. I take her back and forth to the doctors and make sure she's settled at the house. I had to adjust to marriage...and I didn't do all that great at it," I resorted to rambling, though it was all true.

Yanti's eyes turned down. Perhaps she was trying to understand.

"But I thought I was your bad bitch, Lex," she whined in her own little way.

On a long sigh, I declared with wide eyes, "Oh, my god! You are. And I'm your bad bitch, too, Yanti!" She still hid her eyes from me. I had to continue to push. "But I did tell you about that R. Kelly concert, huhn?" I offered a smug grin the moment she looked me in the eyes. "Uhn-hnn! Who that bad bitch now!" I slowly nodded my head, displaying all the convincing arrogance I could. "I couldn't believe my girl copped those tickets. It was a private show, too. I was right there in front. His voice live is just the same as it is recorded!"

Yanti's eyes danced. I was warming her up. My plan was to start with words of apology before going in for the kill.

"Yup! And he performed the *Bump N' Grind* remix, girl!" I shouted my excitement, reliving it. I tugged at her arms for a reaction. Yanti's eyes grew, but she fought her interest. "Girl, he thrust them hips just like the video. Ol' Robert still got it. He pulled this one jawn up on stage and had her grinding and shit. I was like... Whew!" I exhaled.

"Really?" she asked warily.

All I did was nod my answer.

"And then afterward, my girl, Tasche, got us up in his face for him to sign a t-shirt we were given at the start of the show." I backed up for my beach bag and pulled out the white tee. "Girl, look how he signed '*my*' name!"

I handed Yanti the t-shirt and watched her cup her mouth. The damn thing fell on the floor.

"Oh, shit!" she screamed over my head as I picked it up for her and shook it out. "Is that my name?" she screamed so loud, people eating at the other end of the restaurant stopped talking.

I gave them a polite bow before turning my attention back to Yanti. I led her to the table where I had my things.

"Have a seat," I offered.

"This is amazing, Lex!" she gushed, giving me a snapshot of the real, pure, and non-urban Yanti that I hardly met. "But don't think we're back friends that easily. Real friends don't forget about each other. That is foul, girl!" She went back to pouting those thin lips.

I nodded solemnly as I reached inside my bag for my phone.

"You're right, they don't. But that's not what I did. How could I forget about you when every day for the past few months, I fought to keep this from my low-tolerance husband?" I tapped until I found the small video clip. "Tasche got us to the back of the building where his car was waiting. If my husband knew his driver, Carlos, allowed this, he'd fire him." I showed her a twenty-minute video taken from my phone of catching the singer exiting the building with his entourage behind him as we begged him to say, "I love you, Yanti." He did us one better and sang it.

"Holy—" she screamed. "Holy...holy sheee*it!*" she shouted, exposing her accent. "Lexi! You did this for me?" One hand cupped her mouth as she held the phone in the other, unable to remove her eyes from it.

I sat back and shrugged. Glancing around, hoping Ezra was nowhere around or I'd have some explaining to do.

"Well, you know." I shrugged again. "It's what bad bitches do, nah mean?"

I didn't feel as cocky as I put on. When I devised this plan to make up with her, the video was the last add. I'd forgotten all about it. I liked R. Kelly and all, but I wasn't fandomania with it. I would never wait for him behind a building at a crazy ass hour just for him to sing a few words at my begging request with his back to me and his bodyguards flexing at us like we were criminals with brawny bodies like theirs. *Hell no!* But at the end of the day, it was worth the risk of my husband's scolding and the dignity we lost doing it. The sheer joy on Yanti's face across from me sealed the deal.

Out of nowhere, she jumped to her feet, pulled me out of my seat, and jumped up and down on her toes while shouting her head off.

Shit, Yanti!

Damn, was she loud and raucous. My eyes shot from my face when she tried to bring me up and down with her.

"Hei!" I heard shouted from across the room, over Yanti's yelps.

Natalia was next to us less than seconds later. Her beautiful face was scrunched up something fierce and she began in some language, clearly ripping into Yanti. Ida was at our other side, seemingly doing the same. Yanti straightened quickly, bowing her head in shame. I wanted to follow suit, and probably would have if it were just Yanti's aunt, Ida, doing the reprimanding. But I would never tuck my balls in front of Natalia's sneaky ass. I still hadn't figured out her fixation with my husband, but was damn sure reminded of it when we landed.

Jarabu met us at the airport this time with his buxom beauty at his side. His eyes beamed with pure joy as they locked onto Ezra and me while we walked down the steps of the plane. Pain struck in them when we neared Jarabu, I was sure for Mary's death. Natalia's lustful glower remained glued to my husband. And when we arrived, they fell in homage. I tried ignoring that, understanding the purpose of this trip was for my husband's mental and emotional escape.

Before I knew it, Yanti turned to me regretfully. "I have to go, Lex. If you're available when I get off, we can 'fraternize'," she hinted the theme of their reprimand.

I sucked in my lips, tucking my chin, and nodded. "Okay." I turned to Ida. "It's really all my fault. I knew she would check in this early, and I wanted to catch her before she started her shift."

Ida nodded, but her glower never left Yanti, even when her niece walked off with her shoulders dragging. I noticed she thought to take the signed t-shirt.

"I'll email you the video, Yant!" I whispered behind her.

Natalia huffed, her nose high in the air. "*Master*—Ezra okay?"

Master? What the fuck was up with that Master shit? Even in her thick accent and limited English, I caught the title.

"My husband is fine. Thank you," I replied with flared nostrils.

Natalia huffed again before taking off, chin still in the damn air. I didn't understand her attachment to Ezra. It was the last thing I thought about when I planned this trip, but the fact never left my head. Ezra had been improving and yet he was still out of it, much to himself. The only person he really spent time with other than me was Jarabu. I found progress in that. Now, I was sensing Natalia had a problem with it.

After watching her leave the open restaurant, I shook my head.

"You," Ida demanded. "Sit here. I be back." Her face still tight.

I obeyed her and sat in the chair Yanti pulled me from. I hadn't eaten anything yet. It was still early. So excited about surprising Yanti—after kissing her ass—I washed up, threw on a sundress, and left the suite to meet her here.

A few seconds later, Ida returned with what looked like a milkshake on a tray. This was strange.

She placed it in front of me, then lowered herself to speak privately.

"You eat bad foods. No good for baby. Eat these now." She paused, struggling for English words while I sat with my mouth to the damn floor. "Nutrients for you and baby. I get peach pancakes and bacon later."

She stood straight to head back to the kitchen.

Snapping to my senses, I called behind her, "Ida!" My heart raced and armpits misted, pure fear coating my tongue.

Keeping her stride to the back, she turned her neck to the side, tossing a brief look over her shoulder while placing her index to her lips. "Shhhhhhh." Then she gestured zipping her lips.

Fuck!

Ida meant what she said about keeping my secret. At least for the next couple of days into our trip, I saw no signs of anyone else knowing, and she discreetly slipped me fruit and vegetable smoothies and decided my meal options when Ezra wasn't around. When he was and she was the one waiting on us, I'd select something healthy, conscious of her eyes being on me. She didn't try to starve me, just included fresh fruits and vegetables and less fatty foods. I rolled with it as I struggled with exactly how I would tell Ezra about my pregnancy before I started showing. I had a touch of paranoia, wondering how in the hell did Ida figure it out.

Ezra still concerned me, but he had a few good days. He eventually began running and meditating in the mornings again on our fourth day back. That was a huge improvement considering he'd only done it once before since losing Mary. His sexual appetite maintained its usual ravishing magnitude. He took me—his words—twice a day, nearly every day we were there. Some sessions were rough and others tender, all depending on his emotional state. I didn't mind. In fact, I loved it all. One thing that did strike me was he wouldn't spank me. I wanted it so badly, not in a punishing manner, but a therapeutic desire. I will never forget what Ezra told me about spankings after the second one he gave me.

"...don't dismiss the idea of a good spanking being a favorable deed. Some thrive from it."

He was right: I thrived on them. They were arousing and cleansing. It propelled my hidden emotions to surface, forcing me to deal with them. You can't address what you bury. Some spankings pushed me into a sensitive headspace where I could feel everything. It wasn't a daily desire, but certainly a dark craving I fantasized about. The orgasms that followed were paralyzing. But now...with the baby, it wasn't a good time to push for it.

Two days after apologizing to Yanti, Ezra and I had just finished making love. My sweaty frame slumped over his big body: my heart just above his, the electrical conduction the two created, slowing to one rhythm. It was the most peaceful quiet as we gazed out into the night sky, my favorite feature of Kamigu. The huts invited the exotic nature of the land inside with glass walls. The Queen's Hut had a whole wall that could retract up, exposing the master bedroom to the tropics.

"Anaplastic Astrocytoma," he murmured over my head, his chest vibrating each syllable.

I lifted my chin to peer up to him. "Huhn?"

"My mother died of Anaplastic Astrocytoma." *Shit...* "Or, as my father termed it, brain cancer. But since he told me the news at her deathbed, I looked into the actual condition. It's a rare malignant brain tumor. Apparently, she'd been in treatment for over a year. Seen countless specialists, underwent several treatments, and sought alternative treatment methods." Ezra snorted. "Even spent a week over in Denmark, undergoing a clinical research trial. Alone."

A sharp pang ran through my chest hearing that last fact.

"She didn't tell your father? Weren't there signs?"

I couldn't believe she went through this...and alone. How was that possible? There was a pause before he answered.

"He said she'd made mentions of symptoms years ago: headaches, dizziness—both of which I was somewhat aware of. However, the seizures she'd had when they were home and alone I had no knowledge of."

"How is this even possible? No one knew..."

I could feel and hear when Ezra swallowed.

"It happens when the two men in your life neglect you—." His voice cracked. Ezra took a few gaining breaths. "If I had spent more time with her... If I would have paid attention to why she needed a driver at her young age... My mother was no high-falutin woman. Yes, over the years, she began to grow into the benefits of her First Lady status, but she was on the lower end of the pompous scale, using her wealth to spread the gospel to women and children. She'd play dress up like the best of the aristocrats, but my mother was simple." He paused for a moment, seeming taken by his own words. "In any case, two of her girlfriends knew."

My mind raced.

"You think that's why she was okay with the Nurse's Ministry? Mary felt she couldn't aid your father the way he needed?" I held my breath, afraid I was overstepping.

Ezra took a deep breath. "Perhaps *a* reason. I believe my mother relinquished her husband to Marva Graham years before that roguish auxiliary came into fashion." His voice faded, inspiration seemed to have drained at that memory.

I hated I even brought up that stupid ass group. I was happy when I heard it was ripped apart and shred to pieces. I curled my leg around Ezra's thigh at the comfort of that. Though I still couldn't believe Mary was a party to that bullshit, I would do anything just to have her call me with Ezra-harassment.

"She was a good woman...Mary," I whispered, eyes captured in the starlight, mesmerized.

I could feel his head move, the ends of his beard meeting my forehead. His big arm enclosing me.

"And so are you, beloved. You're the gift I vow to never neglect."

~twelve~

~Ezra~

"And every day for two weeks, each time he was out at the spring, there would be two—maybe three—people down there, asking to be baptized!" Jarabu laughed.

"I remember," Natalia confirmed, though Alexis didn't follow her language.

"See!" Jarabu pointed eagerly to his wife. "She just said she remembers, too. Possibly two-thirds of the island have been baptized by this man. It was a good time!" He tried calming himself.

I cracked a trying grin as I glanced to the right of me. Alexis supplied an amendable smile, but I knew underneath it, something was brewing. We'd just finished a delicious dinner on the fresco, at one of the smaller restaurants on the island. The sky was pitch black against the moon, celestial fermentation, and tiki torches lining the island. Alexis sat back in her seat comfortably satiated, exhaustion slanting her eyes. Her cleavage sagaciously bountiful in her long floral dress, and her rich dark skin held a bronze from the sun.

God, she's beautiful...and frighteningly addictive.

"And his delivery is so eloquent...words so decisive and convicted. It's beautiful to experience," Jarabu continued, completely passionate in his argument. "My mother cried when she came up for air. She said she felt the power of God all over while under."

He stopped, eyes still beaming with exuberant enthusiasm as he awaited something from Alexis. It was his way of bringing people into a conversation. He didn't understand the aggression in the act. She had nothing to give. My beloved still hadn't warmed to them, more specifically Jarabu's wife. Natalia sat next to him with her hands folded over each other, smiling politely as she had been trained to do. Alexis fought for the same discipline. To break the uncomfortable stretch of expectant air, I pulled a displaced lock of hair behind her ear. That act only proved to be teasing, exposing more of her mink skin.

"Was that her experience when you baptized her, Sir Carmichael?" Natalia asked me.

Before I could answer, Jarabu intercepted with his own question. "Did Ezra baptize you, Lex?" The gleam in his eye still present.

Alexis' eyes fluttered as they retreated to the half-eaten cake in front of her.

She cleared her throat. "No. I've never been baptized."

Finally realizing the circumstance of the table, Jarabu's face turned crestfallen. He wasn't alone on that abysmal slope. My chest tightened with guilt. My wife had never been baptized. How did I miss that?

Alexis' perceptive eyes rolled over to me. "You never asked," murmured hardly audible.

She answered my unspoken question. My eyes danced apologetically in her regard. I couldn't speak to utter my regrets, guilt clasped my throat in a tight grip.

"So," Alexis swung her neck ahead. "Any kids in your future?" The ends of her mouth curling into an applied smile.

But her eyes told everything I needed to know.

~*Lex*~

The rays of the sun pushed through my eyelids. I stirred, rubbed the tightness from my nose before opening my eyes. It felt like I'd just gotten up for my midnight run to the bathroom. I swear I didn't want to leave the comfort of the bed.

All I need is bacon, orange juice, and Ezra.

I rolled over and finally took the plunge, opening my eyes. Ezra. He sat on the edge of the bed, shirtless. I sat up to observe him, unable to help the start of panic setting in. His eyes blank, brows almost meeting, and beard full, and even more overgrown. I didn't mind at all. He was still mourning and was away with me to work through it. Slowly, I started noticing the ringlets of sweat across his shoulders. He sat on the comforter and not the sheet. He'd worked out this morning. This was improvement. I couldn't help the sense of gratitude that spread across my face. I went back to my pillow and stretched my arms and legs while on my side as I stared at him.

"You're going to just stare at me all morning?" he rasped, throatily.

"I can." I wished I could do away with the stupid grin that wouldn't leave my face.

"We don't have time for that." He tossed his eyes to the other side of the suite. "You need to go get cleaned up, but you don't have to shower. You can do that later."

My face wrinkled, grin totally wiped away. "Later when?"

"Alexis, I'm not in the mood for your questions," he muttered, casually leaving the bed. "You have four minutes to relieve yourself, brush your teeth, and wash your face. You can have your banana on the way."

We stopped at the water. I was beyond curious and honestly frustrated with all the suspense, but hadn't uttered a word of complaint. This was his way. Ezra led and I just...followed. But this was a huge contrast to his more reclusive behavior since being in Kamigu. His eyes cast out over the water, wearing a scowl against the sun.

"What's this?"

"Your baptism," he answered with his eyes fixed on the water.

"Baptism?" I glanced at the water myself. "I'm not going out there! I could drown."

My hands went to my belly. This time, I didn't stop en route.

What in the hell is he thinking?

Ezra turned to face me.

"We've been down this road. We're past the trust issue in the water. And I hope we've conquered it in our marriage. I, for one, trust you to a degree I've never dared relying on anyone in life. As much as I've been negligent of your essential needs, I'd like to think for some miraculous reason, you trust me implicitly as well. Am I correct in that assumption, Alexis?" he fired off impatiently.

Totally confused by where this was going I nodded, honestly answering his question. Ezra exhaled deeply, obviously relieved for some reason. He took me at both hands and stepped closer, meeting my toes in the sand. He placed his face aside mine, drawing so close I could smell his perspiration.

"I am sorry for being so narrowly focused in my pursuit of you," he whispered painfully in my ear. "I never questioned our compatibility or the equity in our salvation. I would like to baptize you this morning, if that's okay with you."

My eyes raced in their sockets. This was about the conversation last night with Jarabu. I didn't think it was a big deal, not knowing many people who were baptized. Hell, I didn't even know if Lillian had been baptized. I'd known of Ezra doing it twice for members of *RSfALC* since we'd been married, but I never attended those services. It was apparently important to him, so I would do it.

I nodded. "Yeah..."

"That pleases me, beloved," he droned, still expressing relief.

Ezra led me into the water. With each step we took, the water level rose and my body tensed. Here again, I was out the gate, doing some crazy shit without thought.

"Do you believe God sent his son, Christ, via birth unto the earth to save man-kind from its sin?" Ezra asked softly as we trekked through the water.

"Yes," I breathed, my chest beating.

"And you understand Christ died so we may have eternal life?"

"Yes."

"Before he died, he lived as a mortal human like you and me, leaving a godly legacy as to how we should live until we meet in heaven, a place God has set aside for all those who believe in Him. There are various acts of worship that Christians practice to display our beliefs: some required by Christ, and others, man-made rituals. People following ancient Levitical laws, otherwise known as *Old Covenant*, would have you believe you have to follow a set rules to gain access into heaven to be with our Father eternally. But, beloved, there's one particular event that Christ Himself decreed before His death."

We thankfully stopped when the water met my waist. Ezra turned to face me again. I could breathe again, but my trembles wouldn't stop. The smooth cadence of Ezra's words and potent conviction held me captivated.

"Jesus said in St. John 3:3, '*Verily, verily, I say unto thee, Except a man be born again, he cannot see the kingdom of God.*' In verse 5, He said, '*Verily, verily, I say unto thee, except a man be born of water and of the Spirit, he cannot enter into the kingdom of God*'." He was instructing us to be baptized, Alexis. Baptize comes from the Greek baptizein, which means to immerse beneath. A body is fully buried. The head does not stick out or the feet. Do you understand?"

Reading only his lips while trying to steady my breathing, I nodded.

"Praise God," he soothed, or at least that's what I wanted to perceive it as. I really needed to pray about my inability to separate my lover from my pastor. I was sure there was some perversion in my attraction to this man. "Now, one last thing before we proceed. In Christianity, there is a doctrine of the Trinity: the Father, the Son, and the Holy Spirit. God is of all three entities, and all three are of distinct traits. In other words, they are all key in our journey here on earth—or simply, in life. The Father is the Creator, the Son is the Savior, and the Holy Spirit is the Counselor and Comforter. All are wholly needed and critical. All three powerful and of severe authority. Are you still with me, beloved?"

I studied how his lips moved in small increments, but poured with words that touched my soul. I understood him well.

"Yes," I breathed.

"Very well." Ezra shifted to the side of me, spiking my heart rate again with the sudden move. The last thing I needed was to feel abandoned out in the ocean. He arranged my hands crisscrossed over my chest and placed his big palm over them. His other hand between the wings of my back. "You do trust me, right?" he asked directly in my ear, once again tickling me with the whiskers of his wild beard. My breaths were coming in short, but I was still able to nod. "Alexis, I baptize you in the name of the Father, the Son, and the Holy Spirit, representing the death, burial, and resurrection of Christ—"

My body reared back, and I could no longer make out Ezra's words. I made a quick decision to let go when my weight shifted to the heels of my feet. I let it all go. I submitted to my belief in Christ and how faithful He'd been to me before I even knew Him, and certainly when I wouldn't totally commit to Him. I submitted to the navigation of my husband's spiritual leadership. When my body went under, a balm of peace coated me in the hush of the water. I could hear the melodies of William McDowell's *In* as my frame swayed in the waves. And when Ezra's strong arms pulled me out and held on to me until I could gather myself on my feet, I could feel weights of unexplained stressors falling off as the water cascaded down my body.

"—rise now and walk in the newness of life for you are now a new creature in Christ," I was able to catch from him.

My fist moved quickly to brush the water from my eyes. With a heaving chest, I peered up to Ezra. He wore an expression of pride that could've been missed underneath his messy beard.

"Congratulations on your salvation, beloved," he rasped, peace beaming from his eyes. "I look forward to rejoicing with you in heaven for eternity."

For a while I couldn't speak. I was still out of breath, still reeling from a super-natural experience that felt metamorphic. There was a shifting happening inside of me, and between Ezra and me. I didn't think before I jumped on him.

"Alex—" Ezra yelped before we stumbled in the water.

My subconscious told me it was a bad move for the baby. Luckily, Ezra caught us before going under. I threw my mouth on his as he shifted me to straddle him. He used one hand to cup me from behind and the other caped my back.

"I love you," I giggled into his mouth.

Ezra shared the amusement of my excitement while carrying me through the water and walking us back to shore.

"I love you, too, honey." It was good to see his smile from his eyes, cheeks, and mouth.

"No. I *love* you. It's different," I qualified.

He lost his smile. "I know you do, beloved. And I need it. I need you."

He wasn't ready, and I was okay with it. I was so over the moon happy in the moment, I wanted to tell him every secret I ever held to my heart. No longer could I stand anything between us.

I shook my head, and swallowed, forgetting to breathe in my moment of high spirits. "We have more than that between us. We make magic together...miracles. You don't understand. We—"

"We were wondering where you were!" My neck snapped, startled. "It's past your breakfast time. Jarabu and Natalia are waiting in the main dining room for you. Widya, too!" Yanti screamed from near the loungers on the beach. She waved a small white towel for good measure.

"Widya?" I asked Ezra.

"News to me, too. We leave in two days. She's probably showing etiquette," he suggested before shouting back to Yanti. "We'll shower and be there in twenty minutes. You can order Alexis her usual with a mimosa."

My eyes went wild. "No! No mimosa!" I corrected as he was placing me on my feet.

"Are you serious about refraining from alcohol?" Ezra's scowl had returned.

Damn! This morning had been a breakthrough for the both of us. It was the first semblance of how he was before Mary passed. For a moment, I'd even forgotten about his grieving and was going to tell him about my pregnancy.

I let go of a loaded breath and groaned, "Just for a little while. Trust me, I've had my share of alcohol to call my own fast."

Ezra was on my heels as I moped off toward the villa, feeling as though I'd picked up one of the weights I let go of in the water.

He looks peaceful...

I thought this as I studied him from the living room of our villa. Ezra lay by the private pool, stretched out in a lawn chaise, catching sun in a quiet nap.

I found my hand brushing contently over my belly, my eyes fell to my abdomen. This action always came with conscious thoughts of *"Is it safe? Is there anyone around?"* I'd been caressing my flat incubator of joy a lot here lately, but in private. I glanced back out to Ezra, observing the unkempt beard covering his face. He hadn't shaved in a week. I didn't mind the rugged look. It made him human. Fallible. Like me.

I should tell him now. I could go out there and wake him with the news.

I'm going to be a mommy...

The thought warmed me. My heart stretched in my chest each time I reminded myself of this. I'd only thought about being a mom when I learned I couldn't be. It was one thing to desire something I couldn't have; it's an altogether different experience to yearn for what I could feel inside of me. No, I couldn't yet feel the baby, but my body had been transforming to make room for it. It zapped my energy, leaving less drive for me to take on my day. The baby influenced my appetite and increased my sex drive. *Shit!* Ezra and I always had an explosive sexual attraction to one another, but we'd been fucking like wild hyenas for weeks now. It had certainly been different and beyond the fact that we could now call it lovemaking. *Yes.* We now made love, but often times I'd fuck him because that was just how raging my hormones were because of this pregnancy.

I should go and just tell him.

He wouldn't be mad for long.

No, it wasn't something we planned, but technically we didn't plan to be married either. We just did it. It was unexpected for both of us. Telling him would just hurry the process of his acceptance. I mean…Ezra wouldn't leave me because I got pregnant. Hell…he stayed after the world learned about my attack.

Yet and still, the timing was off. He just lost his mother and was grieving heavily. Ezra had hit so low; I didn't recognize him under the rubble of pain. Each time I thought about Mary being gone, a flutter set off in my belly. I'd like to think it was because she'd known a grandchild had been conceived before passing.

And she kept my secret on her death bed.

My hand stroked my belly again. And again warmth dispersed, shooting to every limb. For me, this baby was a wonderful distraction from the tragedy of bereavement. For Ezra, nothing could likely heal his agony. I knew the pain he'd been wrestling with. I had my bout with it since losing my own mother; and scuffled with it each day since—some days the fight more brutal than others.

So, no. I wouldn't wake him from his sleep with the weighty news. But I could prepare myself to tell him tonight after dinner. This joy I carried would soon burst from my lips. That's how happy I was about having a baby implanted. Right now I would let him sleep, something he hadn't done much of as of late, and what he wouldn't have done had he been back home. Ezra was the hardest working man I knew. He deserved to rest. My bundle of joy would hopefully be here to stay and could wait to be announced later.

A faint sound behind me, from the front of the villa, caught my attention. I shifted in the oversized sofa chair. Beyond the dining room table, close to the stairway leading up to the bedroom, I could see half of a curvy feminine shape, skittishly peeking into the back of the house. I recognized her floor-length orange sundress that clung to her flat belly and wide hips. Her jet black, silky hair fell over her shoulders and around her dejected face.

"Natalia?" I called out alarmed, knowing it was her. "Can I help you?"

She hesitated for a moment. I shifted, turning around even more, trying for a better view. She finally stalked deeper into the room, coming closer. There were dark rings around her ebony eyes and her thin lips pouted sullenly.

"What's going on?" That was the decided question over '*What the fuck are you doing in here unannounced?*'

She didn't speak at first. Her eyes roamed forward until I could tell they found him. I turned to observe Ezra still sleeping, unbothered.

"Natalia, is there something I can help you with?" I asked this time with more bite.

Her eyes fell and closed as she shook her head. "I bring more towels for you." She pointed behind her, to the front of the villa, her eyes still ahead.

My face wrinkled. "Ooookay. Thanks," I croaked. "But next time…please…don't just come in without being invited. We could've been indecent." I flinched internally. That was delivered just as snotty as Ezra would have done it.

But I meant it. This was kind of creepy. I may not have known the culture of this resort or country, but I did know she had some weird reverence for my husband.

"No one tell me problem with him. Jarabu say leave him alone. His mother…die I know," she attempted with a heavy tongue. "But he is very sad…he is sick." Natalia lips trembled.

I shrugged. "He's grieving."

Her almond eyes finally moved to my face. "I want to help. I do what Master Carmichael need," she offered, determined.

It took a few seconds to process her words; they were delivered so spotty and with a thick accent.

Did she…

Is she…

I observed Natalia's small round chin in the air as her ample breasts poked forward, expressing her femininity. Underneath a tiny waist, her wide hips were spread generously as though capable of guaranteeing pleasure to any man she graced. Her posture sent my mind racing.

The fuck?

Natalia was offering her body to help improve Ezra's mood. I understood instantly how she couldn't deal with his subdued nature during his grieving period. She knew him to be the dominant creature that had intimidated me much of our marriage. Her back was arched perfectly—goddamit seductively—her eyes bounced anxiously between me and straight ahead where Ezra lay. Her hands cupped her hips and her ass sat high, perched from her spine.

Oh, yeah. He's definitely fucked her.

At this point, it was undisputed in my mind. I found myself sitting up and choosing my next words carefully, understanding our language barrier. Before this trip, I didn't know Natalia could utter a word of English.

"Have you done that before?" I dropped my chin. *"Helped him?"*

She didn't answer right away. I didn't know if it was because she had to process my words or if she knew the damning answer to the question would piss me off. But her eyes turned pained as they continued to bounce from me to Ezra outside as I faced her. Then I believed the reason was the latter. But I had to be sure. My mouth went dry at the implication and the need to push her for an answer. The longer the distance in the space between our communications, the more anxious I grew.

I ran my tongue restlessly over my lips, my patience hitting a brick wall.

"Natalia!" I barked huskily.

I swear if I didn't have a baby nestled inside I'd beat her ass on GP.

Natalia squirmed in place, her eyes grew wider, shifted wilder. She was visibly uneasy. I couldn't give a fuck about her comfort level. I needed an answer.

Again, I shifted to my knees determined to break through to her. "Answer me, Natal—"

The sliding door sounded behind me.

I heard the familiar rasp of heavy chords speaking a foreign language.

It was Ezra.

My shoulders fell. Ezra took a few seconds to measure the energy in the room. I could tell he correctly perceived the unease bouncing from her and the heat radiating from me.

He spoke again, repeating himself, but this time with urgency in his tone that had the both of us leaping in place. Natalia quickly returned words I couldn't understand. But damn it if I didn't ear-hustle to gather any traces of recognizable terms. One thing I could determine was that same chin lift of determination that she gave me seconds ago while she spoke to him. Her lips trembled in fear and she heaved with her words. Her nipples pushed against the cotton of her dress familiarly.

Natalia resembled me when up against my husband; fearful, but anxiously anticipating expected pleasure. She knew him. She knew the beast. Ezra responded to her in his usual authoritative tone. I couldn't make out much, other than the mention of Jarabu. It was clear to me he was threatening before asking Natalia to leave. She did. Shaken and embarrassed, covering her face, Natalia quickly left the villa.

I jumped to my feet, moving into Ezra's personal space. I snapped.

"Could you *finally* tell me what the fuck is going on between you and her?"

He exhaled, briefly turning away from me. He yanked his beard, his nostrils wide with aggravation. His eyes went from weary exhaustion to tight with anger. I couldn't give two shits. I'd been patient long enough.

"Beloved—"

"Beloved my ass! Something is going on here and I've been nice far too long about this. I've been cool about it, basically bypassing red flags. I've been the dutiful wife, ignoring the way she fawns over you. This woman offered herself to my husband to cure his grieving. No more!" I yelled. "Tell me what the fuck is going on or I swear to god, Ezra—" My words fell.

The room went silent for long seconds. I could hear nothing but my heavy breathing. Ezra's hard eyes were on me, piercing me with audacity.

With a steady rasp he asked, "Or what?"

I couldn't respond, only return his menacing glare. I couldn't back down. Not now.

"You'll leave?" he continued with a frightening whisper. "You'll desert me…again?"

I didn't know where to go from there. His gentle tone disarmed me. Our eyes continued to war.

Ezra's fell, and while his body was still positioned in front of me, his head angled and eyes rolled across the ceiling before returning to mine. "I lost my wife and when I fought with might to get her back, I lost my mother. I'll just suffer another blow, and the one that will probably take me out of here." His nostrils flexed. Ezra tossed his hands in the air. "I am powerless…what can I do?"

There was a long pause.

"When I was being a directionless kid, I found myself in an unusual occupation in India," he began.

"India? You never mentioned being in India. And long enough to have a job there?" I called bullshit.

Ezra flexed his shoulders, showing his impatience for my demanding tone. "India was in between Jerusalem and Indonesia. It is the one stop I don't publicize because of my racy pastime there." He admitted to his omission. I recalled that conversation when I learned about his extensive travel. He never mentioned India. What else was this motherfucker hiding? "I found myself working at a place that's similar to what you know as a brothel. I was an American kid, trying to find himself. And while I was nowhere near rich, my family had the resources to sponsor my idle inclinations. They had no idea what I was picking up on my journey. I made friends with the owner of this place. Let me just put it out there: This town was saturated in sex trade. Either you were a worker or an owner. I was uniquely a trainer. The community was a divide of clean gentle trade and forceful and illegal human-trafficking."

My hands flew to cover my mouth in shock.

Ezra's head turned in shame. The first of its kind.

"While I had my wild days abroad, I'd *never* forced a woman to do what she didn't want to do. Ever! I couldn't stomach unwanted aggression with women, much less participate in it. I'd encountered countless women who'd been forced as young girls years before crossing paths with me. You have to understand that in this particular region, it's a part of their culture for women to become servants, more so at the demand of men. By decent men, they were picked at puberty. The monstrous kind snatched them before they reached menstruation. It was a commerce they were bred into. Some of these women outgrew their youth and became useless to the trade. These women found themselves out on the streets with no protection. An alternative to that risky lifestyle would be to work for the brothel where they were guaranteed security. Only the place was for those with dark inclinations."

"BDSM…" I breathed, understanding how he'd ended up there.

Ezra nodded. "They had no other means of making a living. The owner became fond of me, and eventually offered me a job to train submissives for his clientele. It was his business. But let me be clear"—his index finger appeared—"*nothing* I did was illegal or against their will. There was mind manipulation to retrain their understanding of their bodies and sex. It's a significant component of the lifestyle. By and large, these women had come from violent and abusive environments. They needed to learn how to receive pleasure as well as give it. This was key in pleasing a man. It couldn't always be one-sided. Nonetheless, it was work."

"You taught them to come vaginally!" It was a breathless revelation.

Ezra winced. He shook his head. "Most women aren't capable of that. I wasn't a magician, Alexis. No. I had to find where they were mentally and sexually to get them to a certain head space that would work for the business. This was the game. These women came broken in spirit. They came with vast experience, but severely…wrecked. Their childhoods were chilling nightmares. Inhumane for an American boy like me." Ezra shook his head, his eyes looked into the distance.

"It was my job to repair them just enough to please a man on command. For a couple of years, I trained scores of women. I taught them the formal lifestyle of bondage, dominance, submission, and masochism. Some of them needed spankings. They needed to be punished. It was a preference, but a psychological necessity for them to function at this point in their lives. Some needed to be hurt."

The first tear rolled from my eye at the mention of them needing to be spanked. Ezra once told me I had a propensity to pain. Though I had no clue of it before, he was right. When doled out correctly—sexually—I thrived on pain.

"Again, I did nothing illegal, against their will, or forceful. Although I've had my share of it all, I had my limits regarding pain: sadomasochism has *never* appealed to me. When I would encounter a sub needing that level of play, I'd hand her off to someone…sort of contracted by the owner." He searched my eyes to see if I caught the similarity. I gave him nothing. "Anyway, eventually I met Jarabu. He wandered into the brothel one day and was new to the lifestyle. He enjoyed the women and wanted to learn. His father had died, leaving a luxury island resort and great wealth. His mother had been ailing and he had no respect of this bequeathing. Not dissimilar to me, he was a runner. He wanted to explore and not have the familial responsibility of his heritage. We found ourselves two idle floaters from our native lands with families who sponsored our exiles.

"We became fast friends and I taught him how to enjoy the lifestyle according to his psychological makeup…what he could handle. Most runaways took to drugs or alcohol when they needed to escape. Me, I took on sex. And it wasn't for the physical escape of it, so much. It was the psychological aspect of it that attracted me. Everyone has a role to fulfill…an assignment to keep to. No surprises. I'd always had a keen grasp on the mind. And what I didn't know, I was so curious about, I'd manipulate it to comprehend: break it down to rebuild to what I could understand. This is why I enjoyed bondage. It was a no brainer. This was a means of survival for these women; for me it was a vocation. This was their culture and my option. They came to me with irreparably broken wills, wanting to be led and guided to survive. After a couple years, I had to be honest with myself and admit it should not be perceived as impressive; it was simply feeding my ego."

My mouth dropped. Ezra didn't even notice, so wrapped up in the memory of it all.

"On my nights off, Jarabu and I would explore the town. We visited neighboring villages and their underground activities. One day, in the wee hours of the morning darkness, while in Mumbai, we walked down a road in search of transportation back home. Because of the hour, there were few drivers willing to take the ride. We continued to search until we heard a frightening scream coming from what we'd call a narrow alley. We stopped, exchanging glances to determine should we mind our business or seek the woman screaming, seemingly being beaten. We moved to find her.

"Jarabu found her first. She was being knocked around pretty bad by two young lads who couldn't be older than teens. Jarabu went to swinging on one of them, and I tossed the other before going for the girl. I had to call Jarabu off the kid after I realized he wouldn't let up otherwise. We had to go just in case the one kid came back with more fighters. The woman was bleeding from the face and hurled over, hugging her abdomen. It was Natalia. She clung to me instinctively. Initially, I didn't know if it was because I was bigger...maybe darker, but she physically leaned toward me. Jarabu insisted we bring her back to the brothel. I didn't think it was a good idea considering how rigid the owner was. I explained to him that I was no recruiter. He assured that she'd be with him exclusively, so we ended up bringing her back. Jarabu cleaned her up and nurtured her back to fair health."

Ezra snickered dryly to the floor. "He fell in love with her days after meeting her, according to him. It was ridiculous to me, but I knew him well enough to know I couldn't deter his infatuation of this woman. He said he wanted to keep her forever...marry her. Natalia was so mentally feeble that she didn't put up a fight or express her will for him. The owner gave an adamant no right away when Jarabu approached him after a day or two. Natalia couldn't stay there unless she was a paying customer and Jarabu couldn't stay as a paying customer if he had a woman distracting him from the submissives of the house. So within a week's time, Jarabu took Natalia and brought her home. Here."

Okay. Now the story took on new relevance.

"My life continued. I didn't hear from him in months until one day I got a rare visit out of the blue. It was Jarabu. He came with a timely offer. I'd turned bored with my work at the brothel. Had I continued a week more, I could have fallen into the dark hole of depression everyone in the town had been bred into. I needed to continue on my pilgrimage. So when Jarabu asked me to come to Kamigu with him, it was a welcomed invitation. I'd only hesitated at the inspiration of this invite. He explained Natalia hadn't been faring well in her new home. The culture was different. He had resumed his rightful legacy as the overseer of the island, and that role was just as political as it was profitable. This island was only patronized by elitist. No millionaires, but minimally multi-millionaires.

"He said she wouldn't eat much or sleep restfully. It was bad enough there was a language barrier between her and most of the land. She was timid and distrusting. Outside of sex, she behaved like a caged bird. He maintained his love for her and said he was desperate for help to find a middle ground for them. He was asking me to come and train his wife to submit to him."

"But you said he said sex was not the issue," I questioned.

"Their sex was not about physical gratification. It was a means of communication for them. The start of many forms of interaction and companionship. Natalia's mind needed to be broken—again—and restored so they could connect."

"Shit, Ezra!" I whimpered.

He's a mind fuck. I'd married the master manipulator!

"I left." he tried to state the obvious to quiet my concerns. "When he explained his dedication to Natalia, sharing how he promised his mother a wedding and to be settled to run the island, willfully, it all made for a compelling argument. Jarabu was committed to this woman in spite of my reservations. So, I left for Kamigu and stayed here for just under a year to help Jarabu and Natalia."

"How do you help a man with his wife?" I screamed.

Ezra pinched his nose, letting out a long breath.

"I trained her...to be a submissive, customized for his needs," he admitted with closed eyes. "Natalia and I have a sensual history. But although Jarabu gave me full carte blanche of her body, I've never penetrated her." His hard and determined eyes leveled with mine. "Ever. I may have been depraved and unconventional with my youth, but the 'good ol' church boy' in me still remained to some degree. Natalia was never my woman. I could separate my emotions from the instruction."

"But you've seen her naked..." I whispered breathlessly. "And... she's seen you naked—touched you..." I swallowed back a cry.

"Alexis, I promise you, there was nothing intimate about it. Most times, Jarabu was there with us. Natalia had been severely abused by several men in her time. He wanted equality with her, so the things...the pain she had to incur required his presence and participation because that brought her pleasure. He needed it for their companionship. He had to be coached, too: watch what frightened her and made her go into the recesses of her mind where there was a cluster of rape and violence, how to bring her from those dark places. He needed to know what her dark pleasures were and optimal aftercare for her. How far to push her. What her limits were. Her triggers. It wasn't about me. I can assure you!" he pushed out desperately. Things went quiet. His descriptions were sounding too familiar for me. "The moment I believed they were on level ground, I left. I didn't stick around to do further damage to her psyche. I understood the risk."

And this was why Jarabu had always been welcoming to Ezra. This was why it seemed, at times, Ezra had given him the cold shoulder about returning.

"You knew Jarabu's wife had taken on an unhealthy attachment to you. That's why you've stayed away," my vocals trembled. I couldn't even look him in the eye.

I could hear his deep exhale, though. "Yes. She's made tremendous strides since my first time back, visiting. I didn't even want to honeymoon here: it wasn't ideal, all things considered. But he begged me to come see about his mother, Widya. She'd taken a liking to me, viewing me as the glue that cemented her son here at home. Widya believed if things didn't work out with Natalia, Jarabu would've fled the island again. Her health turned for the worse, and most had given up hope. The timing was parallel with our nuptials. And look at this place," he motioned to the villa and body of water ahead of the property. "Who wouldn't enjoy this landscape? So, I brought you here," his voice cracked, defeated.

My head began its spin again. I had to start to process the heap of shit he'd just thrown on me. But my questions about Natalia had been addressed. No, he was not in love with her, but neither was he with me. What made this shit even more fucked up was she was likely in love with my husband... And so was I. To him, I was no different from Natalia, needing training, only Ezra trained me for himself. Did he view me as broken?

Am I broken?

I stormed off, not having a clue where I was going until I got there. I just needed out of his fucking face before I did something I'd regret. Before I knew it, I'd locked myself in the bathroom and shuffled into the huge circular tub that provided a vista view of the back of the property and ocean. My sulking was followed by hot tears running down my face.

I had been betrayed by my husband again. I was, *again*, a part of his master plan, without even knowing. I was not Natalia. *I am not Natalia!* I was smart, caring, independent—knew how to hustle and survive on my own. Not a bruised and broken woman in a back alley in India!

I lay there, crying, measuring the questions running through my mind about how I got into this shit with Ezra. Once again, I found myself into some shit, being reckless. *Doing stupid shit!* And this was far more complicated than my usual backlashes. I was married and carrying his child. A child he most likely doesn't want. My mind turned to missing my mother. All this time I'd been grieving Mary, but what I wouldn't give to have my own mother here with me in this state. Someone I could get sound advice and comfort from.

A giggle slipped from my dry lips.

My mother wouldn't have had the mental capacity to take on an Ezra Carmichael, who made manipulating minds a sport. That was laughable.

It grew late. I'd watched the sun depart from the porcelain tub. I stayed until I could no longer, my body aching from the hard surface. Slowly, I stood and stepped out of the tub. When I opened the door, I found Ezra sitting on the floor. His head popped up from his bent knee-caps. I could hardly see his eyes in the darkness of the villa, but I could sense his weariness. I could also make out the tray of untouched food next to him.

With hoarse chords he rasped, "Please don't tell me after all this time in there, you've come to the conclusion of leaving me." We both swallowed involuntarily. "Because, Alexis, I can't survive you leaving me. Not today. Not tomorrow. Not next year. You are it for me. I need you. I'll do whatever I have to do: retrain my mind...work with you to restore whatever it is in you that I've broken...your faith in me so you can see that I can change to be better for you. Just. Don't. Leave. Me."

I cupped my face at the recognition of dry tears in his throat.

"Ezra," I breathed, unable to find my voice. "I'm not broken." I focused my eyes on him as much as I could in the darkness of the narrow walkway. "I've never been. I'm not a trainable dog or puppy. I'm thirty years old. The child of a mentally ill woman. The daughter of a career criminal. I've been poor and struggled until marrying you. I've never been privileged like you, but I've hustled harder than what you could possibly believe to remain whole. I've carried my Harlem Pride. You need to know this."

"Alexis, has it ever occurred to you that it is that very pride that appeals to not my eyes or heart, but my soul and spirit? It's not been all about sex or my...dark predilections with you. I just need a rock. And you are so much that granite that balances me. Undoubtedly, there were times when I tried to break that inner strength to mold you to my liking, because I didn't understand it, but I learned very early in our relationship that it was impossible. There's a fire inside you I cannot put out, and I've secretly admired it...kept it to myself." He shook his head, clearly realizing his faults. Then he turned back toward me. "But these past few weeks have had me thinking..." There was another pause. "I want something new with you. A new start—fresh beginning. I want to start all over and come to a new agreement."

I couldn't help rolling my eyes, not caring if he could see it.

I sighed, "What? Another covenant?"

Ezra quickly stood to his feet and moved in closer to me, but didn't touch me. I could now see the redness and pain in his eyes.

"A bond," he rasped. "I want to bond with you. Forever meld my soul to yours. Because I never want to know what life is like without that fire. Your fire. I need that inner strength you possess to survive. I have this ministry, this job. I have to do this ministry—it's my calling. You are the ultimate helpmate that can help me carry out this charge and flourish. I don't want to just survive in life. I want to thrive. I've told you many times before, you're it for me, Alexis. My motives may have been misplaced when we made covenant, but you on your own merit have made an impression on me I could never do without. I just need to bond with you."

I couldn't think to breathe. I'd seen quite a few Ezras since meeting him. I'd been seeing warmer versions of him over the past few weeks—new masks. But this… This was no mask. This was a side of him he didn't want hidden from me. This was his exposure. The real Ezra. I had no doubt in my mind about it, my heart. He wasn't the pastor, scientist, therapist, or dominant. Ezra was a man.

"Ezra, I think we're bonded more than you think, whether I like it or not." My hand went to touch my stomach, but held suspended in the air. This would not be how I told him. Not when he's this vulnerable. I knew Ezra well enough to know he'd reached his emotional limit by exposing his true essence tonight. He didn't like surprises. "I've never been closer to a human being in my life, except for my mother. I don't have her anymore. I don't wanna be so dependent on you—"

"You can be," he spoke quickly with assurance. "I can depend on you, so I want you to be able to depend on me, too—"

"But!" I spoke over him. "You may not have broken me, but you've roped me into your crazy and freaky world, and I've survived. I guess it wouldn't be so bad being bonded."

A lopsided smile appeared on his dejected face, his left cheek hiked. I wanted to say more to comfort him, but knew we needed to take things slow. Ezra had to prove himself worthy of this bond. But I wanted it with him. We had covenant, I loved him, and was deeply in love with him. I wouldn't refuse being bonded.

With Ezra…and the beast.

~Ezra~

"Christ, kitten!" I droned over her as my forceful seeds burst through me.

My back caved and goose bumps covered my damp skin. My throbbing cock lodged deep inside the sacred place for me. The most relieving and therapeutic. I held onto her warm frame, clenching it just as much as the walls of her goodness gripped my pounding dick until I could gain my equilibrium.

We were down in the sandbox tonight, ending an extensive and lively evening of sensual exploration. Alexis had been taunting me since we returned from Kamigu yesterday. We arose early on our day of departure and endured an emotional episode of goodbyes from the people of the island. Jarabu's typical pleading 'see you sooner than later' was expected. He'd always make a show of inviting me back the day I was due to leave him. However, what was extremely unusual was Alexis' tearful farewells to Jarabu, Yanti, and conspicuously Ida. My wife's towering frame squeezed Ida, who was nearly a foot shorter. It was also at that time that I'd seen the rare smile that flowered on the older woman's face.

The flight home was expectedly long, but not as unbearable as the one out. I filled in the time with work, reading, preparing a sermon, praying, chess, sleeping, and watching a movie with Alexis. We landed at nine in the morning Eastern Standard Time. Extremely exhausted, we showered and stretched out in bed for a few hours. We slept most of the day in between unpacking, laundry and work for me. I ran out for meals as Alexis worked around the house when she wasn't sending me messages of her sensual desires. She didn't outright ask me for sex; however, since the top of the morning, she'd been throwing me long glances and lingering touches. This morning turned out to be a day of resisting my siren wife.

By the early afternoon, I couldn't take it any longer. When I threatened to bend her over for a good spanking, while she stood at the frame of my office door, I saw her pupils dilate, breath hitch, and thighs squeeze together. That's when I'd had enough and ordered her down here to the sandbox. I made her wait for over twenty minutes, punishment for her impatience. To start us off, I strapped her to the St. Andrew's cross where I delivered her first orgasm with lightning strikes, using the flogger on her nipples. We moved on to the horse bench where I tied her and slowly fed her my erection, torturing the both of us until I returned the favor. Afterward, I stretched out on the bed and explored her entire sienna frame with my tongue and fingers. That was where she began perspiring from the deliberateness of my patient speed and varied oral pressure.

We'd just ended the session with her on the wooden workbench covered in padded microfiber where I had her wrists gathered above her head, attached to the ceiling hoist while her endless meaty thighs were spread to me at the edge of the table. I pounded two more orgasms from her before succumbing to my own. The moment I released her arms from the air, Alexis sighed a satiated breath and moved her hands straight to her abdomen. The moment she realized I had been watching, her lazy eyes blossomed. I felt the squint in my own in reply.

Interesting...

More than that, this behavior was bizarre, and had been occurring far too frequently. Admittedly, I'd been caught up in a haze of delight and passion in having my wife back—absorbing the full fruits of my gift—then experiencing the unexpected death of my mother. However, now that I'd gotten away, gained a healthy grasp on my grieving, and was back at home with her, I could appreciate the peculiarity of her new behaviors.

"Can I pour you a glass of wine while we wait for the tub to fill for our bath, kitten?"

If it were possible, her expression turned even more aghast.

I lowered my chin. "You may speak to answer, kitten." My voice uncontrollably patronizing.

"I-I… I'm still taking a break from alcohol…" Her dark orbs danced in mine. "…sir," she amended.

"A break?" *Huhn…* "Like a fast of sorts?" I asked, reaching for the remote to retract the hoister to the corner of the room. I didn't like having it dangling over her head.

I watched the dip in her delicate throat as she swallowed then licked her lips.

Nervously…

"Uhh… Actually…" She scooted off the table, holding her bare breasts. "We've been down here for a couple of hours. I'm starving. How 'bout I go shower real quick and figure out dinner while you clean up down here?"

She quickly kissed my lips, not giving me a moment to reply before skirting up the stairs.

~thirteen~

~Lex~

After my shower, I dried off my still vibrating body, and spread lotion all over, doing a quick job of moisturizing. I had no idea what to throw on. It wasn't like I was going anywhere or expecting company. Hell, Ms. Remah wouldn't even be popping into the main house. I flew through the walk-in closet, eyes perusing the many bags and suitcases peppered all over in search of something to just toss on. Frustrated by the prospect, I headed straight to Ezra's drawer and pulled out a fresh V-neck t-shirt to toss on, and found ankle socks of mine to keep my feet warm.

I could now hear my hunger pangs, while stomping down the back stairs, en route to the kitchen. I tapped my nails on the open refrigerator and freezer French doors, deciding on ingredient combos to create a meal. I pulled out a few things then toed over to the pantry to do the same thing.

"Everything all right in here?" I heard his rasp from the entry of the kitchen nearest to me.

"Yeah," I answered distracted, my eyes roving the shelves. "Have you hit your beef limit for the month?" I backed out of the large storage closet to catch his answer.

Eyes fell and bushy brows met as his hands gripped either side of the doorway.

"I don't know, honestly. It's been an awfully loaded month." When his eyes met mine, my chest twisted and sex clenched, a common combination when Ezra was concerned.

It had been a hell of a month for my control freak. He'd been absolutely powerless since Valentine's Day.

I cracked a smile and winked, "I think your body would forgive you for the little bit of beef in my tacos."

Ezra snorted before turning for the stairs. I located hard shells, but had no luck on the soft ones. Instead of being disappointed, I decided on gratitude for some semblance of a meal considering the circumstances. I went about preparing the meal, pulling out a frying pain. I plopped the frozen block of meat inside, and then went for my phone for Pandora. Blackstreet's *Joy* flowed through the miniature speaker, creating a comfortable atmosphere for meal preparation. I focused on the meat, needing to defrost it while cooking. In between chopping it up with a spatula and covering it to thaw, I cut up lettuce, tomatoes, and red onions. My body somehow forgot about being pregnant-hungry—a different experience and far more detrimental than simply starving—and zoned into my own head as I cooked.

I thought about how tonight would be a good time to tell Ezra about the pregnancy. At this point, there was really no good time. I was twenty-one weeks today, and couldn't believe I'd been able to keep it from him this long. Ezra was the most perceptive man I knew. He'd call people out on their shit all the time, but I, without a doubt, believed he had no clue about my nestled bundle of joy. The little bump I'd developed over the past week could easily be blamed on my horrible and frequent eating of late. I explained to Ezra I'd been stressed, and food had been the way I decided to deal with it. And he'd bought it. When he learned the truth, I knew there would be hell to pay. No one liked being lied to. It was plain wrong.

And then there was the other part of it. As I finished slicing the tomatoes and moved on to the onion, I thought. Ezra may have had a change of heart where I was concerned, but I had no grand fantasies of him wanting a baby. He was a baby himself in many respects: territorial, demanding, wanting things only his way. All of these attributes mostly reflected how he was with me. I was like his damn teddy bear that he was emotionally dependent on in his underdeveloped mind.

See? A baby.

I didn't mind, though. Shit, I didn't mind finally putting my heart on the line for someone who met me half way. I now understood my husband, the man I'd made covenant with, was in love with me, and now bonded. He needed me. I believed this. But putting a baby on him would be too much for his underdeveloped emotional mind.

The meat was done, veggies cut, and now everything needed to be plated in an organized manner. I loved tacos, and preferred them homemade. It was one of my favorite meals with my mother. I recall it making me feel fancy, having to build my taco from communal bowls between the two of us across the small kitchen table. I chuckled as I placed the veggies and meat in pretty glass bowls we'd gotten as wedding gifts with all the other fancy shit we had still to use. When I turned from the center island to clear the table I almost lost my fucking bladder.

"THE FUCK!" I shouted. My body shooting backwards to the marble island, and my hand searched for the knife I used to cut the food. I saw a man in the window of the back sliding door, standing in plain sight with his arms folded against his chest. Then one hand slowly rose, stroking his chin while he stared at me appreciatively. A bitter tang covered my tongue, and my throat closed for a moment as I braced myself. "What do you want?" ripped from frozen lungs.

He didn't answer, only cracked a smile. Then he had the fucking nerve to raise his hand and wave while wiggling his brows.

What in the holy hell? My first thought went to my baby, my hand slipped to my abdomen.

"You have got to be kidding me!" I heard Ezra emit with a mixture between a growl and a scream. He marched over to the door, and I grabbed the little steak knife. I couldn't believe he would yank the door open so hard it bumped off its track when it hit the end. "You do know there is this thing called a front door and doorbell, right?!" Ezra yelled into the guy's face, the muscles in his neck and bare back flexed while he did it.

What struck me as stranger than him charging the guy instead of calling the police was how when he spoke, Ezra used his hands—more of his fingers. The guy's half amused, half frightened eyes bounced between Ezra's hands and face. When he could no longer hold it in, he snickered.

"You find this amusing, Mark Anthony?" Ezra continued to use his fingers as he grated words. *What the hell?* He knew this guy! "Did you not think you could startle someone? I'm not by myself anymore! You know this!"

"*Nou*," the guy responded, a very monotone and robotic sound as he used his hands to say more. "*Youau…*" he tried, but it came out weird, too. "*Marweed!*" He ended, now his face filled with anger.

Things went quiet between the two. It seemed that the guy had gotten one off on Ezra. Mark Anthony's eyes softened when they hit me, making me feel weird. Ezra exhaled hard, pivoting over his globular shoulder following the guy. His eyes fell from my face to my toes that were on top of each other from my frantic pose. My legs crossed, thighs naked, belly hidden behind the tee, and up to my nipples peeking through the thin material, thanks to the wind blustering through the door.

Then I caught the implication. The guy was checking me out, and Ezra didn't like it.

"Beloved, please go put some clothes on," Ezra almost squealed, his chest flexing.

"I didn't exactly dress for a damn peeping Tom to creep up on the back porch!"

The guy made some type of gesture with his fingers as he licked his lips then produced an appreciative whistle.

"She's my wife, man!" Ezra shouted as he charged the guy again, who was nearly as tall as he was.

I had to measure all of this for when I lanced him with the knife. I had my game plan intact now that Ezra was here. He was my second concern. I had to protect him, too. I would follow up whatever he hit the guy with.

This time Mark Anthony squealed helplessly and ducked for cover. He made some type of plea with words, but I couldn't understand them because they were rushed and, again, unclear to begin with. But he accompanied them with gestures from his hands.

"Look! I'm sorry I haven't checked in in a while, but I've been busy, and as you can see with what! And yeah, we're still buds, but if you continue to flirt with my wife that way, so help me God, Mark Anthony, you will be walking back to the house, in the pitch dark with one eye swollen shut. Get yourself together, man!"

"Oaukaay!" the guy shouted, trying to stand from his knees. He glanced over to me, hardly able to give me eye contact. "Sowee…" He scowled at Ezra, his brown hair ruffled on top of his head. Pain growing in his eyes.

"Oh, my god! Ezra, did you just make him cry?" I asked, toeing near them.

I couldn't help my concern. Within two minutes this guy went from an intruder, to a peeping Tom, to a freak, and now a defenseless punk against my beefy husband.

"No, I didn't make him cry!" Ezra screamed, not facing me, going to close the door behind the guy instead. "If you shed one tear, I'm taking you down the road and telling Tony and Ulysses you're a sucker, who cried in front of a woman!"

Speaking of him being a child: Why did my husband suddenly sound like a teen?

"Ezra!" He turned toward me, still seething. "What's going on here? Who is this?"

It was now clear to me, this guy was harmless as he replied to Ezra's threat, using no words this time, just his fingers. His face turning red with each passing second.

That's when it hit me: Mark Anthony was deaf.

For a second or two, Ezra said nothing, trying to regain his composure. And my muscles began to relax. The guy scared the shit out of me, which, in turn, rattled my protective husband.

"Mark Anthony's one of the kids from the group home down the road," he finally answered.

"A kid?" I trilled with wide eyes.

Mark Anthony winked and waggled his eyebrows again, a wicked grin folding onto his face.

"Yes." Ezra turned back to face him. "One that I'm two seconds away from treating like a grown man," he grated at a lower tone.

"Haaay!" Mark Anthony yelled before using his hands again. His chest heaving with resentment.

Resentment? But *he* was the snooper!

And cute. There was something cute about the kid, now that I knew he was just a kid. Apparently one Ezra had a relationship with.

"Don't be so violent, Ezra." I murmured, suddenly extending my protectiveness.

Ezra's eyes widened, cautioning me. "Don't."

"But he's cute. And you said he said he came by to check on you because he hasn't seen you in months, Ezra." Ezra's wide wings inched closer, closing in on me. "Leave him alone. And you can do sign language?" I lowered my voice not wanting to rev him up again.

"Yes," he said directly in my face, blocking Mark Anthony from my view. "And he reads lips, so be careful what you say."

I pushed against his steely frame and shifted from under him. "Oh, stop it. He's harmless. You're going to make him piss his pants with all this flexing." I smiled at Mark Anthony, who giggled like a damn teen.

"Beloved, please watch your mouth. He's already commented on you being too 'real' to be my wife from your earlier language."

"Why?" I asked Mark Anthony. "Because he's a pastor, or because he's a preacher?"

He signed with his hands, and immediately Ezra replied, "I'll show you 'a lame'!"

I couldn't help but laugh. "You ain't gonna be bustin' up in here clownin' my guy, Mark Anthony. See! I was just going to invite you to stay for tacos." I waved to the island countertop behind me. Mark Anthony's appreciative gape returned at the mention of dinner. "Tacos I have to warm up again now."

"Uh…" Ezra swung his thick chest in front of me again, shielding me. "After you go cover yourself. It's really too much for a fifteen-year-old boy to see, and know how to handle himself, beloved."

Oh…

"Fifteen?" I asked. "He's that young?"

Ezra didn't answer. He maintained his glare, boring into me. I knew in that moment he was admonishing me to put on more clothes. Without a fight or feeling clipped like I did when his parents visited last summer, I made my way up to the bedroom.

~~~~~~~~~~

Mark Anthony didn't slow on his chomping. Traces of his fifth taco shell shooting from his mouth. I fought my giggle at how cute it was. Ezra sat next to me, biting into his third taco slowly, while his eyes guarded over our guest. I just swallowed the first bite of my second, my belly no longer yelling in protest.

"So," I elbowed a stiff Ezra. "How long have you two been 'buds'?" I asked, using the same term as Mark Anthony.

Ezra scoffed, still upset about earlier. "I've known about the group home since I was a kid. I met him four years ago when I was at a lake fishing, and saw a group of kids plunkin' a shrimp into the water."

Mark Anthony's hands shot into the air, firing off his response.

"Yes, you were a shrimp. You couldn't have been more than five feet even," Ezra argued.

Mark Anthony thought about that for a moment. His eyes going into the distance before he shrugged and went back to his taco.

"What's the name of the group home?" I asked.

"*Love's Haven*. I've known Maria, the owner, for some years now. She takes in minor illegal immigrants with learning disabilities who, for whatever reason, the government doesn't turn away with their parents."

"Like...why are they separated from their parents?"

Ezra gave a slight shrug. "I really don't know. Sometimes their parents are still here, but in limbo with their status, and the child needs special medical care. Once, Maria told me of three sets of parents who'd abandoned their kids when thrown off soil. I didn't ask for details, understanding her position required discretion. But now with illegal immigrants being a hot topic, there's an even smaller pocket of this population of children. She receives special funding to care for them; place them into needed medical and educational services; and to board them."

My heart melted. I couldn't imagine being separated from my mother by anything but death.

All of a sudden, Ezra chuckled. I glanced up to see Mark Anthony signing again.

"What's he saying?"

"He's telling you that is why you should feel sorry for him and take him in. He needs love."

I sucked in air. "Are they mistreating him?" I got angry at the prospect.

"He's running game, Alexis." Ezra chuckled again. "Mark Anthony is one of about fifteen residents there who get a safe, nurturing environment here in the rurals of New Jersey. Maria runs a tight ship and has no tolerance for the gruesome tyrannical behaviors you hear about in a typical group home. She even facilitates dating with outside residents to cover all of their emotional needs, without promoting sexual activities, of course." He gestured across the table. "You're looking at a fifteen-year-old junior in high school. He's been skipped ahead; he's done so well in her program. Don't be fooled, beloved." Ezra turned back to his taco.

Mark Anthony signed again. His wink let me know he was being charming again.

"What did he say?" I asked, impossibly curious.

"He said but he'd do so much better here with one-on-one care from you." Ezra signed back at him as he spoke, "That offer to tap your eye is still on the table if you continue to flirt with her."

Mark Anthony waved him off and scoffed. That made me realize how comfortable he was with Ezra. What connection could he have with kids with learning disabilities?

"What do you do up there at the group home?" I asked.

"I do Bible class, play basketball or chess."

Mark Anthony signed again, smiling proudly as he chewed.

"You beat Ulysses? That's awesome, man!" Ezra praised. "But you're no real champ until you beat me."

Mark Anthony laughed at that. Ezra did not. I rolled my eyes at how he was still flexing from earlier when his friend showed unexpectedly.

"Did you teach him sign language?" I asked Mark Anthony.

"*Yeau…*"

Mark signed something new to Ezra.

"I may suck at signing, but I'm the king on the courts and chess board," Ezra replied to what I assumed his friend claimed, that he sucked at signing.

I laughed so hard, I had to cover my mouth. I'll be damned. My husband actually connected with a kid. Not only was I amused, I was now more intrigued by him and his revealing heart. I was also more hopeful about him not throwing me out on my ass about this pregnancy. I was going to tell him tonight over dinner, but yet another interruption intercepted my announcement. I didn't want to ruin this moment for him. Ezra had a friend: a fifteen-year-old who he played games with.

I waited until I found Mark Anthony's eyes on me to speak. He kept stealing glances. "Wanna stay for dessert, Mark Anthony?"

His face brightened with excitement.

"No! You've already fed him. If you give him dessert, he'll keep creeping over here." Though Ezra spoke to me, his eyes shot into a chuckling Mark Anthony.

I shrugged, collecting my plate to stand. "It's all good. I could use more friends than bears in these rural parts." I turned to be sure Mark Anthony could see my face. "You just don't pop up at the back door unannounced and you won't have to worry about me going Harlem wild on your butt," I warned.

I turned for the sink, but didn't miss Ezra's smug grin at Mark Anthony as he licked his fingers.

~~~~~~~~~~

~Ezra~

My body was completely shattered by the time we pulled into the garage after dropping Mark Anthony off at home. Of course, that wasn't a simple feat. Alexis wanted to see him in and meet Maria, and I sensed it was for peace of mind. Mark Anthony imposed on more than my privacy: he won my wife over. Alexis was especially caring, and even after the way he breached our privacy. Though completely unplanned, it was good seeing him. I was sure to express he could no longer show up unannounced at the back door. Hearing Alexis' panicked screech all the way upstairs, just after leaving the shower was not something I wanted to relive. I conjured murderous thoughts as I hopped down the steps, three at a time. It took a few hours for that violent energy to dissolve in my system. My simmering during dinner only made Alexis fall for Mark Anthony even more.

The fraud.

I cut the engine and closed the garage door behind us, but we remained in the truck. Alexis gazed into the distance with her elbow resting on the door. She eventually turned to acknowledge me with a soft smile.

"Long and unexpected night, right?" Her smile was wry.

"I would say," I murmured, exhausted.

"But it was good. I got a crazy sandbox session and made a new discovery about my mysterious husband."

"And what's that?"

"That you have a friend that doesn't work for you or with you in any capacity. That means you can't boss him around. He's a strong friend, deaf, and gives you a run for your money."

I snorted. "I wouldn't say all of that, beloved." I rubbed my heavy eyes.

Christ! This is a different type of exhaustion! I'd been debating going to see a doctor about it.

She emitted a dry chuckle. "It's like having a child."

"That isn't a pleasant thought at all." I sighed dismissively, my sight going over to the corner of the garage where I see I left my overalls hanging from the last major snow. "How's my relationship with Mark Anthony remotely akin to having a child?"

"He doesn't take your shit, Pastor." She peered into me decisively. It was bizarre.

My forehead furrowed. "And neither does my wife, last I checked."

Alexis' eyes retreated anxiously. There was a stretch of silence between us. Something was most definitely off.

"Beloved, something's troubling you. I can more than tell. I can feel it in my spirit." I paused to re-gain myself. This was the difficult part in totally submitting to her: I had to tune into my wife, not just gauge her moods and emotional needs. I essentially had to decipher them. Identify what they were, what they meant to her, and try to address them. How could I express this to her? "I want to meet your needs and can only be better at it if you share them with me. Could you do that?"

Suddenly, I could see the tears building in her eyes. Tears she refused to let fall. I leaped to grab her hand for comfort.

Stay with me here…

After several attempts, she finally whispered, "You're not going to like it." She then sputtered, "*I-I want to… I've* been wanting to tell you for a while, and it seems like every time I'm ready to, something happens."

I nodded slowly, trying to follow her. To comfort her and not allow my natural inclination of frustration from being out of the know. I swallowed hard and took a deep breath.

"Like tonight?" I asked calmly. "You were going to tell me tonight over dinner, but Mark Anthony showed." I'm more than confident in my assumption.

Alexis quickly nodded, profusely confirming. I understood it was not a good time to demand answers, but we needed to set a timeline for her avowal.

I peered directly into her swelling eyes. "Beloved, you do know I belong to you…I'm committed to you in every sense. That there is nothing—short of turning my back on my Creator—that I wouldn't do to keep you safe and happy with me. It's a term in our bond. You understand this, correct?"

She nodded again. My chest flooded with relief.

"Okay. Tonight, we rest. I have a member to eulogize in the morning. I'll bring lunch home and we'll curl by the fireplace to talk. Is that all right?" I didn't want to demand.

"Okay," she whispered.

Her vulnerability gave me a vision of the young Harlem girl no one protected beyond their own ego in a street fight. The little one who covered everyone around with no reciprocity. Here was the dark, tall, skinny girl who needed security and assurance. She had it with me, and always would. She was mine. We were bonded.

I cupped her face. "Very well, beloved. Can you promise me to stay in tomorrow and just relax? Things have been non-stop for us for months now. I want you comfortable and decided when we talk."

After another nod from her, I placed my forehead on hers and breathed a silent prayer of grace. Something still felt very off about this conversation. It was something I would carry into my final prayer of the day before falling into slumber with Alexis in my arms.

~Lex~

Lying on the couch in the den, I flipped through channels, trying to find something good to watch on television. This was a room I didn't frequent much outside of playing chess with Ezra. It could have been because he rarely came in here himself. The room was so damn cozy: oversized plush sofas, long and wide wooden coffee table, high windows permitting the sunlight, and a big ass flat screen mounted over the fireplace. The furniture smelled new, and I had an idea why. Ezra said he'd gotten lots done to the house about a year ago. The house, itself, was not even ten years old.

I relaxed more into the sofa, smearing my scent on it. I guess you could say leaving my mark. As cynical as it would have once been, even a year ago, I knew what my heart felt. It felt at home here at Ezra's house. My home. I was grateful he insisted that I not rush back into work today. I swear, if I were not the pastor's wife, my superiors would be looking to let me go for the number of days I had taken off this year. It hadn't even been a year since my hire. Thankfully, Ann worked out a scheduled leave for bereavement and distant working for my time off. I needed to enjoy this day, relax as much as possible because this would truly be the last day I would take off. I had a baby to think about. I had to consider time off to deliver and care for him.

Him...

That was the first time I thought of the sex. Why did I say 'him?' Did I want a boy? I didn't have any business having a girl. *I wouldn't know what the hell to do with a damn girl!*

The phone rang. I reached for the cordless.

"Hello..."

"Beloved."

A bunch of butterflies took flight in my belly, my core heated at that rasp.

"Hey, E." I was too glad he couldn't see the stupid grin on my face.

Shit! Is this what this love shit feels like? He just calls and I'm melting to damn goo?

"I am just calling to...check in on you."

"A.K.A. make sure I'm being the obedient submissive you're training me to be?" I hissed, using manufactured sarcasm.

I was happy as hell he called.

"Would you mind assisting me with the correct answer?" His question was genuine.

I rolled my eyes, more at myself for being unnecessarily cold to him.

He called just to check in, Lex, damn!

"Just say you'll prepare yourself for my jerk turkey wings tonight. It's not as authentic as Ms. Remah's sauce, but she's had it a time or two and didn't upchuck."

"I wouldn't miss it for the world. Just try and get some rest. Don't slave over it. I could always pick up something on my way in."

Was this Ezra? Ezra-fucking-Carmichael, calling in the middle of the day for no reason at all and offering to cater to me?

I cleared my throat. "No big deal at all. I have them in the crockpot already."

"Okay. Then I look forward to having them." I could detect the cheer in his deep voice.

My brows met. "Cool."

"I'll see you in a few, beloved."

"Okay…" I was stumped, so unaccustomed to this type of call that I didn't know what to say.

Then I heard the chuckle under his words. "Goodbye, Alexis."

"Bye." I clicked the phone off, wearing a big ass Kool-Aid smile.

I lay back on the oversized pillows, sighing. Not even five minutes later, my cell sounded.

Tasche: Yo wuts the move yo. Tried hittin' you up last week. I ran into Peaches. She good wit chu. I'm ready to body this broad. Hit me back.

I rolled my eyes. That was the last thing I wanted to think about. I decided when it all went down around Valentine's Day to not think about Nyree. Because if I did, I'd want to body that bitch. Right now, I had to focus on my baby.

Nobody's worth his health.

There was that guessing thing again. Rolling my eyes at myself this time, I tossed the phone on the coffee table and settled into the couch again. *Boomerang* was on. One of my mother's favorites. A smile spread on my face at recognition. Although gone, my mother was always a pleasant thought. I was good. I felt myself dozing minutes into the flick.

My cell ringing startled me, though I didn't realize I was that close to sleep. I looked at the caller I.D. It was my father. I hadn't seen him in over a month. At first it was because I was busy, then when I left Ezra and found out about being pregnant, Rasul fell completely off my list of priorities. It didn't help that Snoopie texted me about cutting my father off because of the new shit he got himself into. I didn't ask for details, didn't even return his text. I just took the information as a sign to give my father room to be an adult for once. I damn sure had to be one with a rocky ass marriage and an unexpected baby on the table.

"Daddy?" I answered, dazed.

"Yo…" I heard the moan in his voice. It immediately tripled my heart rate. "Lex, baby… *I-I…*"

My eyes shot open. "What the fuck, daddy! What's going on?"

"I can't talk over the phone. You could stop by the apartment?"

"Yeah, but I'm not at work. I called out today. It's gonna take a minute for me to get there."

I was already halfway up the stairs at this point.

"How long?"

I sighed. "Shit, I 'on't know. An hour?"

"A'ight. Hurry up, man."

I rolled my eyes as I hung up the phone. It didn't dawn on me until I was over the damn GWB that I left the crockpot on. Ezra hated that shit. He'd yelled at me enough about leaving appliances going while no one was there. I exhaled hard, slapping the fucking wheel. Something was off. I could feel it in my gut. There was a cry in my father's voice. He didn't say much because he couldn't. I just hope whatever fire I had to put out could be done before my bossy ass husband got home. Or what if he got home before the pot turned off. I slapped the damn wheel again as I turned onto my old street.

I jumped out to a quiet block. It was the middle of the day, most residents at work or in school. I made my way to the door while fishing for my keys until I remembered it was no longer my home. I knocked. After a few seconds of waiting, I knocked again, this time harder.

"No he didn't have me fly out here for him to leave!" I mumbled, knocking again.

On my third hard knock, the door swung open. A dude I didn't recognize was standing in the middle of the frame. He had a dead eye and a black skully coming low into his forehead as he scowled at me. Initially, I was intimidated when he just stood there like I owed him something. Then I recalled I was at the place I paid the bills.

"Who the fuck're you?" I asked, my face just as screwed as his.

"Oh, you 'bout to learn real quick, sweetie," someone behind him informed. "She by herself, T'wan?" The big guy in front of me nodded. His nostrils flared with anger. "Snatch that bitch ass in here then."

My face rose with my lungs at his audacity.

"Who the fuck you calling a—"

I was snatched at the throat before I saw it coming. The dude yanked me in, slamming the door behind me, and then tossed me onto the floor with what was probably a nudge to him.

"Shit!"

I screeched when my elbow slammed into the floor in an attempt to break my fall. The shock of pain blasting from it had me immediately ball into a fetal position. That's when my fear kicked in, and reasonably so. There were four men in the living room. One had a gun to my father's head as he sat on his haunches against the wall, looking scared his damn self. At that sight, I clambered to my ass and skirted to the corner of the room.

What the hell...

"Yeah. You smart as hell, all right. Now is the time for you to shut the fuck up so we can all settle this and go about our day."

I glanced over to my father, who was a few feet away. He couldn't even look at me. My hands went straight to my belly.

"Grab her bag, T'wan," another guy ordered.

T'wan stomped over to me in what seemed like slow motion. I could have shit myself. Only once in my life had I seen pure evil in someone's eyes. That empty look that told you they were unaffected by your evident fear and would hurt you without remorse. I knew this T'wan dude didn't give a fuck about pleasantries, seeing I was a defenseless woman. This proven when he yanked my bag from me, jerking my shoulder along with it until the strap unraveled. That was painful, too.

I yelped in pain.

"Shut the fuck up, or I'll give you something to cry about!" the first guy with cornrows warned. "T'wan, she got cash in there?"

"Thirty dollars," he growled.

"A'ight." The ringleader sighed as he eyed my father. "Debit card?"

"Credit card."

I watched as the guy tossed out the contents of my wallet. I was being robbed.

"What the fuck, Daddy? What's going on here?"

"Lex, man—" my father started.

"Shut the fuck up, Grier!" the ringleader demanded. "I ain't got time to explain to this bitch how you told me she would be ya pay off. You said she was rich. She 'on't look like shit to me."

"I said her old man," Rasul mumbled, face tight with anger.

My eyes collapsed at the revelation. He set me up. Fucking around with Rasul, I'd been set up.

"I just need my fucking money or it's about to be a double code red up in dis bitch. The god already told me if you slipped, to do what I gotta to make sure you don't breathe another day."

"She got a bank card, G!" T'wan announced.

My heart dropped to my bladder.

"Give him ya PIN, yo," G, the leader ordered.

I sucked in air. "No."

"Lex!" Rasul yells. "Just do what they say, man, so we can get outta this shit!" *Do what they say? How fucking cinematic!* "Take them to the bank and get them what they need!"

"Listen to him, lil bitch." The guy shook his head. "This some real beef. Bigger than that bet he lost to Artie—*rest in peace to the O.G.* Nah, this a real boss up in the pen. Rasul roughed up the lil homey, Young Killa, because he lost a bet to him. That's the god's seed, ya heard?"

I was confused. My father had killed Artie. That's what he did on his last bid. He caught a lesser charge because it appeared as a street fight gone bad versus premeditated murder since Artie came looking for my father at a bar. My father's sentence was lighter for that one fact. Okay, I see now the reason my father fought Young Killa was because of a bet: that was nothing new. My father made a living from bets. But what did a bet have to do with Artie?

"So, now the number done upped," he continued. "You got fifteen G's? Or," he snorted, "ya old man? 'Cause I got shit to do." He lifted his shoulders, widening his stance as he sniffed, a sign of boredom.

"Fuck you!" I said to him. "Fuck you and you and you!" I dipped my forehead in the other's direction. I finally looked over to my punk ass father. "And the biggest fuck you goes to yo—"

I didn't get my last words of declaration out. Didn't even see T'wan approach me when he backhanded me, causing my neck to snap back and my head to bang against the wall, knocking me out.

~Ezra~

"Come again?" I asked, my attention being caught while peering into the *Olympus BX51.*

"He's running for New York Supreme Court judge. You believe that?" Geoffrey grinned. "I mean… I'm happy for him and all, but that's an ambitious seat."

"I sense your reservations." I went back to examining the plastic material under the microscope, absorbing this information.

"Yes." He snorted.

The lab intercom rang.

"Mr. Carmichael, you have a call on line six."

I nodded for Geoffrey to hit the return button for me.

"Please take a message."

"Okay, sir."

Geoffrey continued, "My uncle's extremely..." He took half a second to choose his words. "Messy. They both are, he and Taylor. I just hope they can keep it together to get him elected and stay in there."

I scoffed, half amused. I knew nothing about legislation policies. It was interesting hearing legal banter from Geoffrey. It was in his blood, and I wondered if he had any regrets of not pursuing it.

"This isn't solid," I noted, going to my laptop and typing in my findings.

"Oh, no? That's *Bio-tech's*, the ones pitching to *Coke*, correct?"

"That would be the very one. I'm concerned about how the material would perform under extreme temperatures. With the size of the micro-pores, matter could leak under high leveled heat or seep in low temperatures."

"You would think they'd be smarter than to send flimsy products to be tested by an independent lab."

"Yes, but you've been here long enough to know they do," I replied, typing away. "Send this up to McDowell for second phase testing. As far as I'm concerned, we won't need to push it any further—"

The phone rang again.

"Mr. Carmichael, the caller is insistent they speak to you."

"Is it my wife, Craig?"

Who else would be calling here? I left my mobile phone in the office, perhaps she's changed her mind about cooking.

"No. It's a Detective Montgomery."

Montgomery? Insistent?

"Please put him through!"

Geoffrey's head shot up in my peripheral at that demand.

The minute the line switched over, I heard his heavy breaths. He was in motion.

~~~~~~~~~~

"Pastor Carmichael!" I heard shouted from behind me. "This is an official police operation! You cannot go in there—"

I'd already bounded the doorway of Alexis' former apartment. My eyes went wild in search of her. I saw dozens of moving bodies, none looking familiar. A few of them even in cuffs. I felt a push against my arm as one male with braids was being led out of the apartment. He jerked around, losing his balance. I moved out of the way, still scanning the room for her. There were three officers on a rather large male, possibly six inches taller than me and twice my size. He was less animated when being lifted to his feet.

"Carmichael, you cannot be in here, sir! I understand what this means to you, but we just got this place cleared!" Montgomery warned.

I could hardly hear him over the adrenaline. My sights went to the corner of the living room where there were a mountain of people hurdling.

"An ambulance is on its way! You have to wait outside, sir!"

That was when I noticed Rasul. He wasn't cuffed. He sat in a chair, near the window, speaking to two officers.

I leaped over to him, didn't feel my feet until I was at his, grabbing him by the neck.

"I am going to give you the Roman Road to Salvation then kill you!" I grated, my hands tightening around Rasul's neck while he was on his toes, against the wall.

The pulls from the men behind me felt like slight tugs.

"No!" Montgomery shouted. "Man down! Man down now!"

I had no idea what that meant. I just knew they would have to literally peel me from him if they were lucky enough to spare his life.

"You are literally the scum of the earth," I spoke through gritted teeth at his nose. I could see the sudden terror in the other man's eyes. "I have no idea why God has spared you this long, but I can tell you, you've put her in danger for the last time."

"Listen, Carmichael!" Montgomery's voice turned pleading. "You're a very important figure in this community. I swear to you, sir, I can make him pay. I already have the list of charges I'm sure the D.A. can make stick on this joker. But you!" he stopped short with his words. That's when I realized the tugs had stopped. I had more muscle power to concentrate around his weakening pulse. "Please, Pastor! Listen to me!"

I was fading, going into an isolated place of deliberation. The problem was, I wanted to be there, propelled myself there to get this out of the way. It was what I promised myself I would do if he brought her any harm, and today was the day.

I took a deeper look into Alexis' file a few months ago when Montgomery notified me one Sunday, between services that Rasul's name had come up in an attempted murder case concerning a young adolescent last fall. He was able to wiggle himself on the case just to keep an eye on Rasul. When I asked him why was Rasul so much of a concern at this point, he answered with asking me to look more in the file he'd given me on my wife last year, just before I left for Dallas, the night she agreed to be my girlfriend. I was so smitten at the time, I didn't care what was in her past, so I stored the file until just before proposing to her. What was inside the second time around deeply appalled me.

I was disturbed learning of my beloved's rape the first time I'd taken a cursory review. But when I fought to read through the recorded details of the players behind it, it sickened me. The rape wasn't, alone, the most disturbing news of her past. Apparently, the man who led the attack, had done so as payment from a bet he won in prison. Against Rasul. The nature of the bet wasn't detailed. Though, it had to do with a fight between rivaling gangs, neither of which Rasul was a part of. He just had a penchant for betting. For this particular one, the wager was his daughter, Alexis. As sick as it sounds, these men bet on livestock, and the victim in this instance was my gift.

Quickly, I decided not to discuss it with Alexis. She hadn't so much as even mentioned her attack; I wouldn't dare give her more details on it. It was a huge risk I took, one that nearly cost me my marriage. And it was this man who caused the terror in her that she would likely live with for the rest of her life.

Alexis thrived from pain because, when experiencing likely the most stressful physical discomfort in her life, she was able to endure by mentally tuning it out and escaping into a more pleasurable place in her mind. It was easy for me to detect her peculiar pain endurance. The link to masochism was a canny connection with me, a man who had demonstrated knowledge on the subject. In other words, it was either of divine orchestration or a stroke of coincidence that we intersected and held a palpable chemistry.

"If it weren't for your will or consequence, she wouldn't be here today." I whispered in his ear when I watched his eyes roll back.

"Ezra, no!" I heard a familiar shriek to the left of me. "Please don't!" Alexis screamed, terror in each syllable.

She's conscious! Relief undulated my body. However, not even my beloved could spare her father. As long as he was alive, she wouldn't be safe. Never bet on a man who bets on his innocent children.

"There is nothing you could say that would deter what is coming," I spoke in Rasul's darkening face, but speaking to Alexis.

"Ezra! Please!"

"Why?" I shouted rhetorically. "Why should I let him live another day?"

I felt Rasul's feet kick against the wall, liquid trickling onto my shoes. His urine.

"B-be-because *mi*-my…" I could hear the chatter in her teeth, but not even that could deter me. "…*bi*-baby's father will be in jail for killing *hi*-his grandfather!"

In the next moment, Rasul's near lifeless body hit the floor.

"Christ…" I breathed.

~fourteen~

~Lex~

"Christ..." he muttered so low, I hardly heard what came next. *"It's true."*

Those words played in my head for almost two weeks. What did that mean? I hadn't asked Ezra because things took on a crazy path since that day. I began living by the moment instead of planning a future with Ezra and our baby.

Ezra called Ms. Remah back to the States, cutting her vacation short. He didn't demand her. It had been apparent since the day she walked through the door that she wished she would have come home sooner than two days after the botched robbery.

And that...

The night it all went down, I learned my father didn't tell me the whole story of his beef with Young Killa. He lost a dice game to the kid and refused to pay up. The detective guy, Montgomery, aka Anushka's 'Fugly,' who was the head of Ezra's security team, was also some big time detective and gave me a rundown of my father's fuckery at the hospital.

According to him, my father's debt to Young Killa was one thousand dollars. That turned into fifteen when his father, who was incarcerated, got involved because my father almost beat him to death, hence him calling me to find a place for him to lay low for a few days last summer. I was able to get him on a train to stay with his great uncle upstate, just outside of Quaker Hill, near the Connecticut state line. He thought he'd escaped the police when the kid was out of the coma, but apparently, he had the kid's father on him once he returned to my apartment.

All these months, Rasul had been holding off his payback, by allowing Young Killa's father to use my apartment to sell drugs until he could come up with the money. It was hurtful to know once shit got thick for him, I had become a part of his plan, without my knowledge. And not to mention my husband.

Ezra was taken into custody that day and held for a few hours before he was told he could leave on his own recognizance, pending further investigation. It was an unofficial arrest because he interfered with an official police operation. I was told he ran into the apartment seconds after the dudes who were trying to rob me were cuffed. The place was hardly secured at the time, much less safe for a citizen to interfere. Montgomery had to explain to his commanding officer that Ezra was not a loose cannon, but in fact a newly married man, who lost it once he'd been notified of my situation.

And speaking of that, Montgomery could've gotten in big trouble if his boss knew how in the loop he'd kept Ezra all these months on this case. I was being watched for all this time and didn't know it!

When Montgomery learned through the department that my father's name had come up in an attempted murder case, it alerted him to look into it. He was able to wiggle his way onto the case, in Ezra's best interest to keep me safe. They had known all this time about my father's reckless behavior and how it put me at risk. Montgomery put a lot on the line to help Ezra look out for a clueless ass me. Even when I'd left him on Valentine's Day. I was still processing these facts. No, Ezra didn't disclose what he'd known about my past, but he worked hard at maintaining a security I had in not knowing all the shit that had been going down. The details they shared that night at the hospital made my head spin.

The most betraying discovery of them all was Rasul's involvement in my attack. He'd been the reason Artie targeted me. I remembered trying to get those detectives to believe I did nothing to provoke them that night. But of course, because I'd known him before that night, they thought I was hiding something. That hurt on top of the physical pain. The judgment.

Those solemn thoughts rang in my head that evening as I lay in the hospital bed, waiting to go home. I was sick for hours, being there alone when I first arrived. I was stressed the hell out about Ezra possibly being arrested. They didn't take him out in cuffs, but they threatened to had he not gone willingly. My beast didn't give them any problems because he'd turned subdued after I blurted out being pregnant in such a corny ass manner, but with the desperation that ran in my veins. I'd done more than half my life without Rasul, I could do more. On the other hand, I could not do without Ezra, and certainly couldn't live with the guilt of him going to prison behind some shit between my father and me. Ezra had too much to lose.

A chill still coursed my spine at the image of Ezra's eyes, pitch black and empty. I didn't recognize him while he held Rasul at the neck, completely off the floor. I saw the terrorized fear in my father's face. I could also identify the moment he understood he'd die, because it was in that same moment I knew my husband would kill him. I literally thought Ezra was going to kill my father. *Rasul pissed himself at Ezra's feet!* That's when I flew into a begging panic. In the days since, I realized Ezra stepped up for me in a manner I thought my father should have all my life. He was willing to lose it all for me. Simply to protect me.

What had been most heartbreaking was how Ezra had shut me out since that day. These near two weeks had felt similar to my first weeks at the house after we married. Ezra had turned clinical on me. When the doctors determined I'd only suffered a bruised face, and sprained elbow from when I used it to break my fall, they recommended I stay overnight for fetal observation. I objected only to have Ezra speak over me, telling the nurse I'd stay. He remained at my side that night, and until Ms. Remah took over at home. Since then, he kept his distance, and only checked in a couple times a day outside of the meals we shared together throughout the day. He'd been working from home, and I had a few more days to go until my face looked presentable to return to work myself.

This morning, as I wobbled down the stairs, taking my laptop and cosmetic products down to the den—my dayroom as of late—I decided to detour to the kitchen to put on the kettle for tea. It was eight, still early in the morning. Ms. Remah was in there, washing out her coffee cup.

"Morning," I greeted, dropping my things on the colossal island countertop.

She grunted in return. "How de baby?"

My face wrinkled. "Ummmm… Fine, I'm guessing."

"Can't be if you nuh eat breakfast."

I turned on the eye of the stove then looked back to her. "I'm not hungry. I'll grab something when I am, though."

"You may not be, but de baby need food, yuhnuh."

I turned up my nose at the mention of food. For a week now, I couldn't stomach breakfast. It seemed to be too much for my system in the first few hours of the day. Pregnancy made me crazy with all the changes. I still hadn't experienced much morning sickness, but I'd been experiencing exhaustion more and more since Kamigu. I now required daily naps to stay functional. That was the only thing concerning me about going back to work next week.

"Tea'll be fine." I reached for a mug from the cabinet. "Food is the last thing I need right now—"

The back door chiming stopped my words and thoughts. Ezra sauntered in with a stained dri-fit shirt, tights under basketball shorts, and running shoes. His pecs were round and pronounced, abs just as conspicuous, and thick long arms swung wide with each step he took inside. In slow motion, it seemed, he glanced my way and gave a quick neck bow while passing through. Sweat tracked down his face and neck as he whisked through the room without a word, earbuds hanging from the neck of his shirt, the wires tucked inside.

Fucking lucky ass wires…

I couldn't help but lick my lips, mouth suddenly salivating and clit pulsating at the masculine sight. This had been my latest pregnancy craving: wanting to be fucked by Ezra. And he walked right pass me without a lingering glance. This had been his thing lately. He stayed near, but didn't interact with me much at all other than asking how I felt. Some days, I took it on the chin, others I'd cry silently in my palms. Today, I had to devise a new reaction. I really missed him.

The kettle whistling interrupted my thoughts. I reached to turn it off and placed the mug down, changing my mind about having tea. Taking a deep breath, I willed myself into action, before grabbing my things and taking off.

"Nuh food for baby. No tea fi mommy?" Ms. Remah taunted.

I could hear the sarcasm in her question.

No. Mommy needs some of daddy right now.

I dropped my things off in the den before taking the steps to our bedroom. By the time I got there, I could hear the shower going. I stripped down naked and toed into the bathroom. I could see Ezra's thick silhouette through the fogged glass casing just before opening the door. He was wiping lathered soap over his shoulders, arms, and chest when I stepped in. I studied his tight ass as he faced the large shower head. When he turned and saw me gaping, I caught the flash of startle that passed over his face, but he quickly rebounded. His head and beard were dripping, eyebrows tenting his scowl. But when his eyes scanned my body, his dick sprang to life. Once he realized it, his eyes rolled to the side angrily.

"What can I do for you, Alexis?" he rasped against the echoing walls of the shower.

I stepped closer to him, placing my palms on his hard chest.

"Let me be kitten."

I dropped to a squatting position, knowing better than to get on my knees. The stony flooring makes for bruises after giving head. I learned the hard way. I sucked him in my mouth, immediately cupping his balls greedily just to feel him in the most intimate way. My damn hormones had definitely taken over because I could smell the musk from his workout and the scent turned me on instantly, causing a tingling sensation in my nipples. I couldn't help the moan shooting from my belly. I also caught the sound of Ezra sucking in air. I gripped him firmly, stroking, and rolled my tongue swiftly over his mushroomed head. My breasts pushed against his thick ropey thighs, purposely stimulating my sensitive nipples as I bounced on my toes.

But Ezra wouldn't touch me. So, I thought quickly. I brushed my palms up his thighs, pelvis, and bubbled stomach until I reached his chest. As I peered up at him, keeping my mouth busy on his cock, I offered him my wrists. He knew this maneuver: he'd taught it to me. With strained eyes, I watched my husband consider my proposal. That one act reminded me of his anger for me. His resentment. The shit hurt. But I was determined to do this. My eyes begged as my lips tightened around him.

I moaned again when Ezra took my wrists, pulled on them while he pumped his dick in my head. He controlled the depth and speed this way, I knew. He'd use this method to issue punishment to me instead of my preferred spankings. For me, it was a head-spin. Further manipulation and torture, detouring from what I wanted. Just like the few times he did it in the past, my eyes popped as his pelvis slammed into my face, his dick reaching my throat until I opened for him while trying to breathe. My healing elbow ached in protest, but I managed through it, thrilled by intimacy with my husband again. It had been almost two weeks. This challenge could go on and on and on. When it would stop depended on him, my dom. My eyes would tear from the pressure and lack of air if I didn't focus on the task and stay ahead of his rhythm.

When I saw his tongue rove over his teeth from canine to canine, I was alerted of the beast being present. It frightened me for a split second.

That was until I felt the first deliciously slimy taste of his precum. That distinct flavor boosted my stamina to stay the course. And I did, until Ezra pulled all the way out of my mouth, leaving my lips swollen and throbbing. I couldn't speak, but could feel my face open to a questioning expression.

"Stand and turn around." I rose to my feet, quickly spun around. "Foot up." He tapped my right thigh and I placed it on a middle shelf in the built in corner shelf.

I felt the heat of him when he inched closer. His big hands pulled my hips back, and he guided himself into me. The pleasure/pain sensation I felt from the pressure had my left knee buckling.

"Stand still!" he grunted angrily, though I knew he was just as wrapped up in lust as I was.

I could hardly breathe, I felt so full, and Ezra wasn't fully inside. His small thrusts grew deeper and deeper, faster and faster. Before I knew it, I felt my core tightening. My head swung back on his big knotted shoulder. It bobbled against his coarse movements. I tried tensing to anchor myself against the brewing storm.

"*Pa*-permission to come, sir!" I breathed, trying to hold off.

"Come, Alexis." He grunted behind me.

At the word 'come' alone, I exploded. My neck gave out and this time both knees buckled while my orgasm ripped through me. As I held steady to survive my groin imploding in pleasure, the echoes of the name he referenced me as sounded in my head, lost to the orgasmic siren going off. I screamed over it all. Hearing Ezra come behind me extended my orgasm. Feeling him clutching my frame just below my breasts like he needed me to stand was fucking everything. He groaned helplessly in my ear.

"Oh, god..."

That slip of emotions reminded me it had been just as long for him as it was for me. He needed this. We needed it. And I needed him. Once he was done shuddering over me, I winced as he pulled out. My heart was overflowing with emotions that suddenly surfaced. I felt intoxicated with my need of him to let me back in. Quickly, I decided to get over that slip of the wrong name—the non-preferred name—Alexis.

I turned to Ezra, my heart in my throat wanting to burst through with words of love and appreciation of him. He'd already backed up under the stream, chest heaving, out of breath, too. My arms rising to open before I took my first step. I saw his eyes scan my full frame. His breath hitched when they landed on my midsection. En route to him, I quickly glanced down and saw my now protruding belly. Last week, my pouch had finally popped, though small. I didn't know how I felt about seeing it with Ezra in that moment. When my eyes rose to meet his face, Ezra's were stapled to my stomach, and he backed up further, hitting his back against the wall. The message was clear. He didn't want me near him.

My tears fell before his words came.

"Trinity…"

My eyes ballooned and heart burst painfully.

He safeworded.

Ezra's eyes fell back to my belly. It was almost as if he was afraid of me. Of my baby.

"During our first conversation about your sexual history, I told you to get on birth control." My eyes circled, recalling that conversation. He was right: I never sought birth control because I'd been so overwhelmed with the wedding last year. Plus, I didn't believe I could actually get pregnant. "You kept this from me for twelve weeks." He knew this because he'd heard the information I'd given the hospital staff and did the math. "You've sworn to have not known the real me all this time. You may not have known it all up front, but even then you should've known I am not one for surprises." His eyes darkened. "I showed you everything…unveiled it all for you. You've known all this time, had countless opportunities to share it, but instead, you deliberately held it from me." Still out of breath, Ezra delivered each word with perfect clarity. "You may hold a feminine power over me, but my heart feels betrayed. I need time to forgive you."

I couldn't breathe. Didn't even have the words to utter. I'd begged this man to love me. I cried and fought for this place in his heart, and he'd finally given in over the past few weeks. And now, I felt fraudulent at his words of 'heart' and 'betrayed'. I felt dirty. Disgusting. Downright trashy. There was no coming back from what I'd done. I had no words that could fix this.

"Get the fuck out, Lex!"

"But, Mommy! It was only one C! I promise, I can pull it up next marking period!" I screamed, my heart bleeding from guilt.

"Nah. You fucked up. You ain't ready for high school. You wanna be a damn floozy. Get the fuck outta here," she waved me off.

"I can fix this, Mommy! I swear. I can make it all be-better," the round of hot tears made me sputter.

"Fuck outta here, Lex!" she warned with a low tone. A scary one. She'd been off balance for a few days. I suspected she hadn't been keeping up with her meds. "The fuck you still here for? I don't love you! I don't even know you, bitch!"

My lungs only took in small amounts of air. I couldn't breathe. I backed away from him, trying to get out of the steaminess, believing that would help. I tripped on my feet, quickly leaving the shower. I grabbed the first housecoat in sight and ran out of the bathroom, jetted out of the bedroom. My tears broke the moment I hit the hall. I choked on a cry that made my knees give out the second I reached a guest room and slammed the door. I fell with my back against it, my sobbing face buried in the fabric of Ezra's robe that I could now identify because I smelled him on it. My soaked body lay against the wooden door and the cold carpet beneath me, curled in pain.

~Ezra~

Ten thousand daggers searing my chest at once. That's how it felt. The pain didn't lighten. The confusion as to how it happened wouldn't slow. Is this what it felt like? Is this the reward of yielding to her? I'd done what she asked of me although I didn't quite get it.

This 'in love' phenomenon was the most compromising and painful I'd experienced by far. And it was a mutual vulnerability. I saw the pain in my beloved's eyes when she backed out of the shower like a haunted vixen. Her chocolate thighs and now recognizably larger breasts vibrated as she stormed out. And here's the trickery with that state of being 'in love': half of me wanting to chase her down and comfort her. But the other half won over my weakened self. I stayed behind. What Alexis did was wrong, and I couldn't excuse that.

I'd had an inkling of a pregnancy—a wild and hyper-imaginative suspicion. There was no way a woman who thought she couldn't conceive *and* who had challenged me to open to her could keep something as significant as a pregnancy from me. What sensible person would?

I had no room for a child. My lifestyle barely yielded to include a spouse. How could I spare the time for another little being? One that would be dependent on every weeping request? The unbelievable adjustments I would have to make to pursue this venture of parenting was overwhelming. And not for one minute did I blame Alexis, outside of not getting on birth control like I asked her to that day at *DiFillippo's*. I also understood countless people experienced unexpected pregnancies every day and endured. I had counseled enough to know. My issue was the secrecy. The ultimate lie. That was not covenant. I was new to it, but I suspected it wasn't a component of being 'in love' either. It certainly had no place in our bond.

What Alexis couldn't understand was I'd just experienced a series of surprises: her leaving me, my mother's death that I still hadn't quite settled, and now this. A baby.

And the pain was debilitating...

I was now able to identify I hadn't 'fallen in love' with Alexis over the past few weeks. I'd long before been locked into this exclusive helpless, needy, and interdependent place with her. I knew this because the pain I had been feeling for close to two weeks since her attack at Rasul's was similar in intensity to what I felt when she left me on Valentine's Day. It was bone-chilling, powerless, soul-wrenching pain.

She felt different all these weeks, and still I had no idea it was because she'd been with child. Yes, I was very much in tuned with my wife's body; it had been an obsessive passion of mine. Call me crazy, but I attributed the external and internal changes to blissful wedded reconciliation. Sex may not have been a focal point during our brief separation; however it was a welcome return once we touched.

That explained my unusual exhaustion over the past month or so.

I spoke with my doctor a few days ago concerning the ongoing fatigue, sudden cravings, and loss of appetite, and he advised I could have been experiencing a light case of Couvade syndrome, an unofficial condition some expectant fathers endured. *Go figure.* Alexis and I were bonded before we agreed to it in Kamigu.

So, there I was. In love, maddeningly. Love reduced you to your mortal status. She had me by the balls and the heart. Literally. And I didn't see it coming. Any of it. That was most frustrating. This woman affected me to dangerous degrees and unlike anyone before her. This was not a comforting revelation, but one I had to acknowledge.

Incidentally, my perceptive eye *had* identified the security in Alexis not having an alternative living plan. I knew she wouldn't up and leave me like before. She'd started the process of resigning her lease at the apartment in Harlem days after being discharged from the hospital. And if she absurdly decided to leave, I knew she wouldn't go far from the house because during one of our intimate conversations after sex, she admitted to choosing the hotel over returning to Harlem, not wanting to be too far from me, her love. That revelation was how I could easily rebuke her for the decision of withholding significant information from me.

I could discern her current torn state. I knew, similar to me, my beloved was in a maze of pain as well. But just as I had allowed faceless patients, whom I've counseled during their time in pity, I'd take mine. It was only right.

And that's what I did. Over the next few weeks, I took my time processing my life and its options until I could see through the fog of my latest circumstances.

"That's quite a number!" my father scoffed, impressed while he passed the document he'd just signed to the right of him.

"Yeah, it is!" Elder Levi Johnston, my father's assistant pastor agreed with a huge smile as he signed on the respective line.

"It's a blessing to see what my closing budget is. I'm leaving out on a high note, here." My father gloated.

He tossed a wink over to Marva, who giggled lowly in her seat. We were in the *Grace Room*, formally changing the pastoral hands of *Redeeming Souls*, though the ceremony was weeks away. My incoming assistant pastor, John Weaver, and I sat at one side of the table for the event. My father and his assistant pastor on the opposite side were essentially handing over the keys, though we'd had them for almost a year now.

Marcus Devereaux, my logistician acted as the mediator with two officials from the *RSfALC*'s governing body, *COOLJC*, overseeing the entire event. Over us were two photographers and a few administrative bodies like Precious, Sister Stacy, and a few others. I still hadn't quite worked out what Marva's purpose of being present was. Nonetheless, I was sure my father would justify it no matter how egregious the weak explanation would be.

"Well," Marcus hummed, sliding the paper over to me for my signature. "I wouldn't get lost in the dates of these numbers, Bishop." He cracked the antagonistic grin I'd become accustomed to, expressing mockery. "Let's not forget about the labor your astute bairn has provided to increase those numbers."

I sighed inwardly as I provided my signature. I was not in the mood for a pissing contest between these two. Marcus could run witty laps around my father before he recognized him coming.

"What's that s'posed to mean, Devereaux?"

I slid the paper over to John to sign.

"Well, sir, a significant portion of that budget comes from tithes. Stenton Rogers and his wife's recent addition, along with a few other hefty earners on the roster, give it quite a boost, wouldn't you agree?"

My father sucked in a breath. "Yeah, but Trent Bailey and Ragee been here before Pastor Carmichael took over," my father argued.

I sat silently, wanting to get this over with.

Marcus continued, "Trent would have never stayed without the spiritual mentoring Pastor's provided over the years, especially during his trial and incarceration. And Ragee himself would tell you if it weren't for Pastor connecting him to the new strong music ministry, he would be in Jersey, at his grandmother's storefront, bringing all his fanfare and money there instead of *RSfALC*."

There was a pregnant pause at the table. My father glared at Marcus, issuing his famous authoritative method of leveling. It worked on countless people, even me at one point in my youth. It, however, would not work with Marcus. I strategically kept these two apart over the past two years since hiring Marcus. Though a middle-aged man himself, he had a youthful arrogant flair that could rival the best of them. Also, Marcus wasn't a Christian man, and generally didn't respect those of that faith, particularly African Americans. He alleged the religion taught to black slaves from white supremacists was the biggest trick on a strong indigenous people ever played. He believed many leaders of the church didn't have the intelligence to seek education rather preach a third handed religion. That was until he met me.

"We're in the business of souls here, gentlemen, not high tithers," I spoke lowly, but with quieted warning.

"Of course, Pastor," Marcus' inflection changed at my title while his eyes shot into my father to the left of him as he sat at the head of the table. "Well," He glanced around the table with a satisfied smile. "I guess this concludes this portion of the business." He began packing up the papers.

We'd been signing for nearly thirty minutes this afternoon. I was hungry and...exhausted, though this wasn't new for me. I let go of a trying breath.

"What's next on the agenda?" I asked Brenda, one of our *COOLJC* representatives.

"Uhhhh... Let's see." She studied her writing pad. "Ah! The official ceremony. We've taken care of things needed on our end: the save-the-dates for all board members and its affiliates, appointed roles, and assigned task at the top level. I have the invitation list here with me for when you're ready to send them out."

"We haven't sent them out yet?" my father asked angrily, his regard leaping over to Sister Shannon.

"No, sir. They just arrived this morning," she replied calmly.

"Well, what was the hold up?"

Marcus quietly headed for the door, leaving us to other matters and my father's ruffled feathers.

"Well, sir, we had a significant change in planners." She coughed into her fist. "First Lady Carmichael's passing left us spinning. Even before then, for months now, she had lots of responsibility."

"Like what?"

"The guest list, for one."

"You could have had Marva or Precious pick up those pieces months ago."

"I couldn't, sir."

"Why not?" his voice rose, exposing his poor temperament.

Sister Shannon nodded toward me. "Pastor Carmichael didn't want extra hands on it. He was specific."

My father's glare turned to me. "Your need for specificity slowed us down, sir."

Believing he was right, I asked Sister Shannon, "Do you need assistance with the guest list on my behalf?" I didn't have room in my schedule, but would have created it to get this done.

"No, pastor, I actually have yours and Bishop's now."

I felt my face fold. "And who assisted you?"

The moment my eyes traveled over to Precious, who hadn't uttered a word for most of this meeting, Sister Shannon answered, "Sister Lex."

My regard snapped back to Sister Shannon.

"Really? When?"

"She got it back to me just before you two left for Indonesia. Here. I have a copy with me. She wants you to approve it first."

Who did Alexis put down as guests? She hadn't been acquainted with all of my friends and associates as of yet. I studied the list Shannon handed me, impressed by the names.

"She helped me with yours, too, Bishop," Sister Shannon added. "She sent me their wedding guest list and we worked together to alter it. I took your portion to Sister Graham, and she— Oh, wait! There's Lex there!" Sister Shannon informed.

All eyes peered out the window viewing out in the hall.

"Lex," my father scoffed with disgust, sitting up in his seat. "She's First Lady now...like it or not."

I quickly decided to allow that comment to slide. I was too captivated by the view. Alexis stood in a huddle with Ann Bethea and a young gentleman I quickly recalled they interviewed for a position at *Christ Cares*. I didn't remember the exact role, because I didn't concern myself in such matters. Now that Alexis was in place, the subdivision could function independent of my input. However, suddenly, I was curious about the role in question and how closely would the young man, who was clearly attempting to charm the two women, would work with my wife…*if* he got the position. He spoke animatedly with his hands, engaging Ann to the point of exposing her gums. Alexis' smile was more reserved though her eyes were soft. *She's comfortable with him.* Suddenly, Ann tossed her head back and cackled hard. Alexis angled her head and supplied a deep grin.

Such a soft and feminine expression.

Although through a partial view, I could make out Alexis' long fitted blue dress with a long matching cape. She had several of these ensembles; same style, just different colors—and two of the same shade, ironically. She'd been wearing them since her return to work. Alexis was showing now, but could façade her small protruding belly with this style of dress. Her face now fully healed and elbow, a distant injury.

Praise God.

Just when I decided to return my attention to the room, Alexis turned around. Her dark orbs scanned the conference room slowly. When her eyes met mine, they dilated and her lips slowly parted. I could see her shoulders ascend as she took in a deep breath. I strained my eyes, wondering what could have brought about that clear sensual response from her, and so abruptly.

Then it hit me.

I reached up and removed my glasses. I'd been peering over them when not reading paperwork. Alexis then nervously turned back toward her party, eyes bouncing about as she did. I studied the black plastic frames on the table thinking of the apparent power they had. My wife clearly found them to be an aphrodisiac, and I was now sitting at the conference table with a raging erection.

I cleared my throat. "This is good, Sister Shannon. I'm fine with it." I pushed the list over to her. "What's next on the agenda?"

I caught Precious' eyes whip from Alexis outside to my glasses then to me. She bit her lip as her eyes rolled away.

~*Lex*~

He has a limp…

I watched as he approached me. His shoulders sagged, eyes were tight and red, and his braids were scraggly. The grays of his roots growing out of the cornrows. The most striking notice was the uniform. When did inmates start wearing uniforms at Rikers?

He sat down and picked up the phone without looking at me, his eyes cast somewhere behind me. I tried studying his condition above the scratched partition. I had to rein in my instinctual budding of emotions. I had my purpose for being here.

"I would ask why you did it, but it doesn't even matter." My tone was as calm as I practiced it. I didn't want to kick off my message to him with tears. Once I started, I knew I wouldn't stop. "What matters is that you know that was it for us. I don't have your back anymore. You can go find another fool to pick up the pieces of your next fuck up. That one won't have the benefit of being of your loins, someone trained as a child to cater to your fuckery." I sucked in a breath, catching my liquid pain trying to escape from my schooled expression. "They call women stupid as hell for doing what I've done for you, for a man they're fucking." I scoffed. My father finally acknowledged me with his eyes. "What do they call daughters who ride for their Dads time after time when they've made it clear they value themselves over you? Did you ever try to take care of me? I mean... Was I always just someone who was supposed to take care of you?"

Things went quiet as I observed the blank look in his eyes. He wouldn't speak, so I did.

"I thought what you did to Artie was for me. Was it? Did you ever ride for me?"

I stopped. I told myself I'd keep it brief. No need to waste time on someone who's made it clear for decades I'd never be worth protecting in his eyes. I shifted to move.

"When I was out the last time, I ran into my old eighth grade teacher. She remembered me after all these years. Ms. Blasso. She was in the library and I was just coming in there to use their computers and shit. She told me when I was in her class, I wrote a paper on what I wanted to be when I grew up. Ms. B said she never forgot mine because it was so different from everybody else's. She said I said I wanted to be a dad when I grew up." He snorted, scratching the side of his nose with his long thumbnail, eyes cast in the distance again. "I remember that shit—wanted to be a dad so bad. I wanted to be what I ain't never had. I wanted to do the job and do it right. I mean, it couldn't be that hard, right. I was a good kid. Good enough to be a daddy, too, I figured," he scoffed.

He shook his head.

"After Tiny had you I thought the shit would be breezy." I tamped down the smile that wanted to spread on my face at that name. It brought with its mention fond memories. They called my mother Tiny because she was anything but. I may have gotten the mass of my hair from my dad, but my extreme height and dark shade came from my mother. She was a true amazon figure, but beautiful just the same. "I kept saying, "When she get a lil bigger, I'll do better. Do shit with her." But I got so caught up in the streets: hustling, fighting, getting locked the fuck up like every other year that…" He shook his head.

I swallowed hard, studying his troubled profile.

"You was like…nine, ya moms came home from the psych ward." He chuckled in the air, eyes took flight along with his memory. "It was crazy 'cuz we both had the same release dates and ya' grams was keeping you while she was in there. But she was 'bout to go down to Atlantic City and had to catch the bus by like three. My release got held up like always and she ended up leaving you with ya moms, thinking it was only gon' be a hour before I was due to touch Harlem World." He took a deep breath.

"I ain't get home till like ten that night. The phone was off at the time, so it wasn't like I could have my social worker call the house to check in on you. I ain't gonna lie, I was panicking like a mufucka', tryna get home. When I walked through that door, you was in the kitchen and she was—"

"In the chair while I combed her hair." I swallowed hard at the crisp vision of playing dress up to a comatose-like mommy.

They had her so drugged, but I had always been tall for my age and I managed to get her from the living room where the hospital transportation people left her, to the kitchen so she could eat something.

"Yeah," he breathed, eyes now on me again. "You had a big ass bowl of Oodles of Noodles sitting there in front of her with her favorite—"

"Can of grape *C&C* soda," I interjected again, lost back to that night. I remembered.

"Yeah," he emitted a dry laugh. "Lex, you was a kid taking care of Tiny. When I walked in, you was talking to her like you was the mother and she was the daughter. Like you was tryna soothe her and shit."

My eyes danced around his face, unable to focus in on his eyes or I'd cry.

"I knew from that day, wasn't much shit I could do for you. You was always so brave and sweet and mature. No matter how much me and Tiny fucked up, you always stayed to the ground, holding us down." I saw when he swallowed, his brows narrowed. "When she got outta that fog, Tiny got pregnant. It was like two months later. I told her to get a abortion. I ain't need no more kids." His voice broke and he graveled, "I already had a seed—a super kid. I accomplished everything I wished for as a kid. I was good with just you, Lex. I ain't need nobody else—"

He couldn't continue, and I felt my lips part slightly. For seconds, he didn't speak. My brain couldn't work fast enough to determine what his trip down memory lane really revealed about his parenting.

"I'm sorry, yo," he murmured so low, I almost missed it. But I caught it. This was the second apology I'd gotten from the only two men I'd ever loved. And I'd be damned if they were both unexpected, unusual, and…genuine. "I fucked up so much, and you just fuckin' with ya pops no matter what. I ain't never see that type of G in nobody. I promise—" He choked up again. "I won't press charges on your ol' man. I won't call you or contact you at all on this bid. If you ever hear from me again, I will be a real man at that time. No bullshit. No sob stories. No game. I may never get a chance to be a father, but if I could get a chance to be a man for you…"

He couldn't finish. Didn't need to. It was never my practice to emasculate my father. The corrections system did enough of that. For the majority of his life, my father had been told when to eat, sleep, and socialize. Arrangements had been made for his care: food, bedding, clothing, grooming. It didn't matter if he was in here or out there with me, Rasul was always provided for. The moment those systems—me or corrections—would release him, he'd turn around and run amok, making high risk decisions that would cause us to absorb him all over again. It was a noted dance. But here's where I abandoned the troupe. I was tired, and had a new dependent to prepare for.

"God bless you, Daddy. I'll keep you in my prayers."

Rasul's nostrils flared as he nodded. It was clear that was all left to say between us, and I was okay with it. I turned, facing the opposite way.

As I stood and began to pivot, I saw my father's final sweep of my frame. In a matter of seconds, his eyes went from heavy and tight to bright with a spark of cheerful discovery when they landed on my midsection. He pulled in his emotion like a flash of lightning. Then he nodded his acknowledgement. I took in a shaky breath and turned to leave. And that's when the tears fell, clouding my vision as I turned my back on the first man I ever loved and the last I would allow to use me.

I stirred from sleep feeling drowsy, almost drugged. This wasn't new: It was my new norm when awakening from a nap. I'd always come through dazed. It was another symptom of pregnancy for me as of late. It was Saturday evening, and my last memories were coming home from visiting Rasul. After crying my eyes out, I pulled into the driveway, deciding I would put away the depressing thoughts of my father, and behave as a thirty-year-old pregnant woman in her second trimester, and sleep. That one common activity was a big deal around here. Even Ezra now napped, something I'd never seen of him before—I didn't know.

I stretched, hearing the faint volume of the television still running from my nap. The news was on, and I could also hear distant clattering from the kitchen. I knew that was Ms. Remah. I hoped she was cooking up something good for tonight. I hadn't eaten since coming back in from Rikers; because I was so exhausted.

And there was the tingle of my ever-engorged nipples. It kicked off the frequent throb in my clit. Another symptom of pregnancy for me: I was horny as fuck! It didn't help that Ezra was still upset with me. Still on his bullshit with locking me out. I couldn't lie. If this was before Valentine's Day, I'd leave his ass again and for good, but when you were bonded with someone like we were, you knew he was simply in his feelings and as foul as Ezra being in his feeling was, I knew he didn't want to end this. Even with that strong inclination, I couldn't deny feeling lost in this, and at times alone.

A familiar name disrupted my groggy thoughts.

Huhn?

Lazily, I turned to face the mounted screen.

"Yes, NBC Nightly News received the footage just hours ago. Apparently, Lester, this video was taken by a party-goer at Diamonds, a long-standing adult entertainment club in Harlem. It's right here behind me. We tried to speak with the owner for more information, but he declined, not wanting to compromise the privacy of his clientele. But here's what we do know: New York Supreme Court hopeful, Justice Timothy Griffin's son recently married thirty year old, Nyree Scott. Well, this video of her behaving suggestively with what people are saying is an employee of Diamonds, surfaced earlier today and has all of New York's high society questioning the nature of Nyree Griffin's relationship with this woman. Take a look. Now is the time to provide a warning: if you have under-aged children in the room, either remove them or change the channel."

"Ms. Remah! Come here!" I shouted at the top of my lungs.

That formal disclaimer made me nervous. A grainy video began to play, and I could right away determine it was from the inside of a club, based on the darkened room, half naked bodies moving about, and the hard bass shooting from the speakers.

"Oh, my god!" I breathed, covering my mouth.

After being flipped and zooming in enough, I could make out Nyree, bent over a couch in a short, tight nude dress. Her ass scooted high in the air, and the small of her back dipped low as she leaned on her hands and knees over...

"Peaches?"

"Dat Nyree?" Ms. Remah asked from behind me, aghast herself.

I didn't answer. I was too busy sucking in air at the sight of Nyree cooing in Peaches' face, sticking out her tongue to trace Peaches' lips as she giggled. Peaches seemed disinterested as her eyes were set in a different place in the room. Nyree seemed challenged by that, continuing with her seduction. She ran her tongue down Peaches' chin and bountiful cleavage then waggled her tongue. That's when Peaches nudged her away, clearly not in the mood.

"Quit, Ny," she could hardly be heard over the music.

The show provided a closed caption at the bottom of the screen.

"C'mon, baby. You know I don't like being ignored!" Ny pouted, begging. "Let me eat it."

Then she put her mouth over Peaches' bikini top, licked then sucked where it could be understood her nipple was. My body cringed tighter each second they allowed this video to play.

"Oh mi gawd!" Ms. Remah sang behind me.

Peaches pushed Nyree completely off her. "Stop playing, Ny! Damn!"

The video ended with Nyree's torso in the air, her arms positioned behind her to try to break her fall.

"Yes. That was the racy footage floating in inboxes across the city today, Lester. We're told Griffin's people deny this is, in fact, the Justice's daughter-in-law, and say they're looking into it further to see who would release such a video, making the allegation."

As the reporter spoke, there was an inset photo in the frame of Nyree in more formal wear.

"This shit is crazy!" I shrieked high pitch.

"Dis social media gon' send all a' ya to hell, yuhnuh?" Ms. Remah angrily charged.

"I didn't do this!" I wanted to say this wasn't social media. It was the fucking Nightly News, way bigger than social media. "You know me better than that. My plan was to beat the shit outta her after I dropped this load."

"Den who did it, huhn?" she asked with her fists on her wide hips as she stormed out, fussing in her native tongue.

I had to understand her frustration. Too much had been going on in my world between moving up here, the emails of my rape being sent to Ezra's church, me leaving my husband, my pregnancy, and then my father using me as bait. The woman's nerves were fried. Mine were, too.

But her question was valid: Who did this? Several names coursed my mind as I considered that.

Tasche had been beasting to get at Nyree. She even said Peaches was down. In that video, Peaches didn't seem to want to be bothered with Ny. Did she set that up? Who recorded it?

"So, what we gonna do? Go through the front or back with this one?" I recalled Tasche's words. Then her text: *I ran into Peaches. She good wit chu. I'm ready to body this broad.*

But this played on television. Tasche wasn't that clever or connected, at least not alone. My mind continued to spin. Who sent it to the media? I only knew of one person whose arms were that long.

"So, Timothy Griffin, the criminal court judge who's running for Supreme Court, is Nyree's father-in-law," she'd shared, though not asked that day Ezra and I addressed the congregation about the emails Nyree sent.

But if Elle was involved, who put her in charge?

"Beloved, I don't want you to lift a finger or waste a breath on her or anyone else that offends you, moving forward. I'm still angered by her actions, but I assure you, Nyree will get her just due." Ezra's words when he asked me about her last month were threatening, too.

Well... Kinda.

Maybe I was reaching. Maybe this was another candidate's way of getting Taylor's father out of the running for the position. Either way, Nyree had just gotten the payback she deserved. She now knew exactly how betrayed I felt from having people who didn't know shit about me, judge me about a matter I wanted kept quiet.

I sat back on that thought, raising my leg to tuck under me. I realized there was no way this was not payback for what she did. And if I were right about the players involved, they did it on my behalf. They were riding for me. Finally having someone have your back after a lifetime of taking care of others felt good as shit. It felt like a huge weight had been lifted. But I wasn't totally stress-free.

I still had a marriage that was out of order. Ezra still shut me out, hardly speaking to me other than general pleasantries appropriate for Ms. Remah. Even she got him to smile or laugh when they intersected. But she wasn't the one he tied up and spanked. She wasn't the woman he spoke different languages to as he shot his hot and clearly potent seeds into. She wasn't the one he married and drug up here to the woods.

I had to remember my feminine powers. It was something Ezra often referred to. I had influence. As shallow as the idea of sex was to repair a marriage, it was completely plausible when it came to my controlling husband. It provoked the beast within him. The one who ravished me. The one I had a love/hate relationship with and decided long ago I couldn't live without.

At the end of the day, Ezra was a church boy—as he once said. His exterior may have seemed steely, but among his layers was that soft and flexible man of God he couldn't help but be. It showed those nights when he'd come to bed well after me, thinking I was sleeping. He'd place his palms over my stomach and pray. I'd hear the tiny movements of the wet portion of where his lips met as he spoke to God about my baby. Our baby. He didn't do it for long, but he'd do it each night I'd fall asleep before him.

This was the Ezra I'd forgotten about, so wrapped up in the rejection of my baby. It then became clear: Ezra wasn't rejecting my baby. He was rejecting me. He believed I betrayed him by not telling him about the pregnancy all this time. It was almost as though he accused me of hiding it purposely all the time he was trying to win me back. The time he realized he was in love with me. And if I would be honest, I did keep it from him for selfish reasons. I thought if I'd told him, he'd be completely turned off and not want to stay married. Every insecure inch of me savored his attention those weeks in between that period of dating him at the hotel and Mary dying.

I stood, feeling refreshed and challenged. My eyes cast the room for my belongings. I was horny as fuck and lonely, sleeping next to a preacher who was sexy as sin. Tonight that would change. I couldn't handle this silent war of wills taking place between my husband and me. I knew he was preaching at a church here in Jersey tonight, and wouldn't be home until late. That gave me plenty of time to prepare for him.

"...but I'm fuckin' you tonight." I hummed on my way up the stairs.

~fifteen~

~Ezra~

"You were like David."

I chuckled wryly. "And she was his Abigail. In this case, Nabal had a *daughter* that showed more courage than he did."

Bishop Jones let out one of his customary spirited cackles. "But in this instance you didn't give the grace David granted to Abigail to your—" he hesitated. "What are you calling her nowadays? Beloved...Alexis or Lex?" Humor never left his chords.

I chuckled silently. Bishop could always make light of a grave situation.

It's what I'm not calling her.

Kitten...

"Well, sir," I strained, sitting up in the back seat of the truck, prepared to collect my things. Carlos had just turned into my driveway. "I hate to bring this fellowship to an end, but I have an early morning, and a strong inclination that you do, too."

It was late Saturday night on the East Coast. We both had to preach in the morning, even if he had three extra hours to prepare.

"Oh? Do you have makeup first thing?" Bishop teased. "Don't let them tell you bronzer is needed for the new lighting you guys just had installed!" He continued to laugh.

I wrinkled my face. He was referring to our broadcasted services. "Just so we're clear, I've never worn makeup and don't plan on it. Is that what you fell for? Your contemporaries?"

"Me?" He gasped in his theatrical Caribbean pitch, sticking with humor. "I don't need makeup. At sixty-six years young, I'm still flawless, son."

"Then I'll take that to mean one of your preaching, pastoring peers likes paint on his face while delivering the Word from on high."

Being one of the most adept, fluid, and popular evangelists in the world, what most didn't have privy to was his humoristic nature. Bishop found drollery in just about everything. It was a part of his charisma.

"Aye," he returned, more soberly. "I never said."

He'd never say, but loved to pull my leg on such matters. He'd been in ministry since his late teens and as one of the most sought after speakers in the Kingdom, he drew droves of admirers in fellow-preachers, young and old. He knew the good, bad, and ugly in them. This was when I'd turn the joshing tables.

"Yeah, just be sure they're not *saying* that about you." I observed the tall trees aligning the long driveway as we approached the house.

"It's nice being reacquainted with your never-seen sense of humor, Pastor."

"Watch out. You're starting to sound like my spouse."

When I was expecting a witty comeback, I was given a spell of a silence.

"She's good for you, you know?"

"She's a lot of things."

"And good for you. She's your 'good thing'."

We rounded the circular tip of the driveway, stopping in front of the house.

She's my everything.

"I guess what this seasoned, single, de-coupled fool is saying is, it doesn't matter the origin of her induction to your life, the purpose of her nature is the same. She's yours to cherish. She adores you—clearly primed for your leadership, care, *and partnership*. Honor your gift, sir."

My chest tightened at his unanticipated adjuration.

"Amen."

"Go rest. You'll need it before your chair time. I hear the new eyeliner they're using works well with those lights."

I snickered at his high-pitched cackle.

"Good night, sir."

I watched Carlos climb out of the front seat. I'd just preached at one of our sister churches in New Brunswick, here in Jersey. It was a packed house, and the closing of their annual convocation. I was pleased to see Stenton and Zoey present, though it was her home church. Elle attended as well; apparently, as Stenton's personal relations representative. They did events together and had one earlier for his organization based in Newark, and she followed him down to New Brunswick after for service. I stayed behind to catch up with them. This was Stenton's last season in the NBA. His schedule was impossible, yet he found the time to come to church. It spoke a lot about his character.

Of course, having your friends support you at an event meant staying behind to catch up, even if for just a little while. I began to slow my mind, to prep it for sleep. It had been a long day and tomorrow was usually my most brutal out of all the days of the week. I offered my goodnights to Carlos and entered the mildly lit home. It was quiet as expected, and I could smell faint fumes of food. After dropping my things in my office, I took to the kitchen to find a plate of food in the microwave. Alexis and Ms. Remah regularly saw to it that I had food awaiting me every day. Tonight's baked chicken and steamed vegetables were a welcome feast to break my fast.

After cleaning my plate, I headed up to my bedroom. The room was pitch black, and I didn't want to disturb Alexis' sleep by turning on the lights. I found my way into the walk-in closet to doff my clothes, then quietly padded into the bathroom to wash up for bed.

Once done, I made my way to Alexis' side of the bed, a recent habit of mine that was done without premeditation. I was that drawn to her, and seeing that we hadn't been on the best terms, the favorite part of my day was the time I turned in because it was usually after she'd fallen asleep. When she slept, I could touch her, smell her, and pray for my incubating child. I still hadn't accepted her elision of this pertinent event in our lives, but I was fully aware of the deed at hand. There was life inside of her. The line blurred at accepting my wife and my child as one. The unborn child was innocent: its mother had been deceitful. Either way, they were both my responsibility. To say I was torn, wouldn't fully speak to the internal battle taking place in my heart every day since learning of her pregnancy.

Nonetheless, I was irrevocably drawn to Alexis. That inclination hadn't faded one iota. It may have slightly intensified from the distance wedged between us. So during the late hour, I stole touches of her soft mocha skin as I prayed over the tiny being inside of her. Then I'd torment myself by getting in bed next to her, and begin a six-hour stretch of torture from the painful erection that would soon inflict me.

I sat on the side of the bed, but couldn't detect the natural heat of her body or the familiar scent of her woolen hair.

"Alexis?" I spoke into the dark air.

Perhaps she's on my side of the bed. I couldn't tell in the dark of the room.

I stood to turn on the lamp of the nightstand. My eyes strained to adjust to the sudden illumination, but I still managed a gander of the other side. It was empty.

My throat closed against the air my desperate lungs tried to pull through. Each joint in my body tensed with a burning clench, quickly going into panic. Slowly, I closed my eyes, willing myself to relax just enough to think.

That's when I heard the faint sounds of music. Right away, I could identify it was being played from a small device. Less than seconds later, a tall figure appeared, strutting from my closet. I'd already begun the path of heightened awareness, so I didn't so much as leap on first sight.

With my lips still meeting and my eyes impassive, my jaw dropped.

Christ...

She'd straightened and curled her hair, big uniformed locks of wool, shining and forming long ringlets down her shoulders, breasts, and back topped with a blue Yankees baseball cap. Her upper torso was cased in a denim shirt that was tight at the waist over blue lace panties that matched her hat. Her thick thighs were glistening, legs wouldn't end. Her feet... They were covered in classic wheat *Timberland* construction boots.

She swayed her hips, clearly dancing rhythmically to the tunes pouring from her phone. The song rang familiar, but I couldn't quite grasp it. I sat motionless, observing her spectacle. It was clearly calculated, and I wouldn't interfere with that. When her sensual moves transitioned her to face away from me, I caught the obscene view of her rear. The first glaring notice was the word *'Sir's'* stitched in the panties that exposed the dip in her round rear. The curd like ripples in her cheeks vibrated with a simple move of her legs as she clapped her cheeks together while gyrating her pelvis midair.

Lock. Stock. And. Barrel.

My dick ballooned, tripling in size, my balls leaped in heavy arousal. But I sat unmoving, fighting the urge of my very nature to devour her. I tamped down the urge to punish her for plotting to seduce me with this course, urban version of her femininity, and for what I could now detect as heavy vulgarity in my home. It was hip hop—Notorious B.I.G...and that ever-belting of sexual undertones, R. Kelly.

She neared me still strutting rhythmically. Entering into the light, I could detect her made up face: eyes sensually darkened and full lips painted in a dark red shade.

Just before cupping my beard, pulling my mouth toward hers, she mouthed, "...but I'm fucking you tonight."

As I gulped in the evidence of salivation, my lips parted in shock. I wasn't offended, by far. I was however, pleasantly appalled by her uncut nature. Once again. She smelled like heaven. Alexis kept her mouth ajar while she stroked her tongue against mine. Her eyes never closed, telling of her stern determination in seduction. She used her fingers to comb through my beard, yanking it down. That maneuver hardened me even more.

She withdrew, holding me in her close regard as she pulled her arms back to the band of her panties and pushed them down. I watched as she kicked off the boots, making a show of that, too. She then reached for the band of my briefs. I lifted to allow her to pull them down, though I couldn't do much about my standing dick getting caught in them, obstructing her attempt. Her stunned eyes shot up to me. I didn't react, kept my regard deadpan.

The track repeated by the time Alexis mounted me. She made a show of tossing her hat behind her and took to my mouth once again. This time she used her lips as well, sucking on my tongue. Under normal circumstances, I wouldn't be able to ignore the obscenity of the lyrics streaming from her phone next to me, but this was when my flesh embraced her. I grabbed her bare cheeks and squeezed them.

Alexis moaned and pulled back. "You get where this is going, Pastor?" she taunted with that familiar line, her eyes dark, lids narrowed.

When I didn't answer, Alexis pushed me down onto my back. That's when I realized she hadn't removed her denim shirt. I didn't inquire, never spoke a word. When her palm wrapped around my erection, I inhaled deeply. My eyes left her emotionless face when I felt the first swipe of her creamy essence against my cock. Another deep breath. I watched her rub the head of my erection back and forth, covering me in her sweet juices. When my eyes roved back up to meet hers, I saw the infinitesimal flutters of her lashes. My kitten was crashing so soon in her acts of seduction.

Her eyes slammed shut, squeezing when she finally guided me over her opening and pushed down. She grinded on me until I was buried deep. My tongue swiped my lips as I exhaled deeply again. Alexis found her rhythm on top of me and I enjoyed the undoing of her cool seductress veneer. My kitten was fading into the waters of bliss. I could feel with each thrust she made, and her increased lubrication.

Her meaty thighs flexed against me, lifting as she squeezed me. This went on until her neck gave out and her head swayed around her shoulders. So badly I wanted to strip her, needed to see all of her to see the total helpless response to me. I wanted to see the tautness in her chocolate nipples and how they bounced with every dip she made on top of me.

Her sexpert resolve was eluding her. And that's when I thought to push her to the edge. Pressing back on my shoulders and heels, I lifted my hips, pushing further into her, increasing her cautious pace. My kitten didn't want to explode too prematurely, but the sinister lover in me wanted to level her in that very manner.

Alexis' eyes flew open and her palms clutched my chest as I tossed her in the air and seared her on the way down. The track started for the fourth time when she began to whimper. I kept with my hyper-pace, biting my lip to deter my own explosion. The moment she opened her mouth, my tongue roved over my teeth.

"Oh, no!" ripped from her lungs.

Her eyes rolled back and hips suspended, giving me full rein of her pussy. I pumped into her until those shouts waned into moans and then whimpers. When my kitten was able to open her heavy eyes, she sucked in her bottom lip and her sights fled into the distance. She was ashamed. I was impressed...and delighted with her submissive slip.

"Up." I patted either side of her hips.

Alexis quickly moved into action.

"At the top of the bed, back against the pillows."

While she shifted in position, I reached for her phone and silenced it. That was her speed to get her off. Now that I'd accomplished her mission, we had no use for it. I placed it on the dresser, across the room. When I turned for her, Alexis was sitting against the pillows against the metal railing of the headboard. Her limbs were shaking and she heaved out of breath. That element of fear she'd always try to conceal was present as her eyes shifted back and forth, bouncing all over my frame. Taking full advantage, I slowly approached the bed, flexed every visible muscle as I climbed on top. While I wanted to return the seducing game, my body's erratic muscle movements were an involuntary response to her sienna frame bared to me from the waist down.

When I approached her, I made quick work of her shirt. I untied and opened it to find she didn't wear a bra. Her breasts... The skin around her areolas darkened even more, and the path to them was veiny. And they were just…bigger.

My beloved was pregnant. Each time I explored her body since learning of it, there was new evidence of the secret she kept from me. Just when I'd planned to take her slow—more vanilla—there was a change in course. I wanted to be rough with her, and couldn't make that happen the traditional way.

"Shirt off," I demanded, full snarl in my tone.

Quickly, she shifted to remove it. Doing that, caused her to become self-conscious. Her regard bounced between me and her growing belly. Alexis bit her lip bashfully. I didn't want to stay in the awkward moment, so I stood on my knees, scooted up closer to her before straddling her belly without touching it. She sucked in a breath at the proximity of my dick to her face. I nodded, confirming the juxtaposition.

"In your mouth," I groaned, my arousal returning tenfold. "I want you to stain me with your lips."

I loved the new lip color and this was my way of expressing it. She opened for me and I pushed ahead, moving my length into her mouth, against her soft lips. I pulled out slowly and pushed back in, warming her up. Then I grabbed her hands, gathered her wrists over her head, and held them with one palm as I thrust into her mouth. Electricity shot through my balls by the time I'd worked mid-way in. I was so close to her, I could feel the strands of her curly hair against my thighs. And it felt incredible as I pumped into her. Some shallow, others deep with speed variations.

You can't top me from the bottom, kitten…

I pumped at the excitement of having her helpless on the bed, against the headboard, into her face, making her take all of me. My motives marked by the dark depravities as I was soothed by the slurping sounds of my movements. I wanted to punish her for being so alluring and deceptive. For making me fall in love with her to the point of losing control of myself, my moods, my desires, my life. But when she moaned, I remembered she enjoyed tasting me. Pleasing me. She yanked her arms, signaling for me to release them. I did, knowing I was on the brink of my release. Her hands went straight to my hips pulling me further inside her mouth, my head feeling the cervix of her throat.

That's when I felt the flutter in my groin and I scooted back, careful of not rubbing against her belly. The first squirt landed on her chest, above her nipple line. The second zagged across her right nipple, and the subsequent ones hit her belly. *My child.* I grunted until I was unloaded, struggling to clear my vision so I could see my markings.

Alexis was out of breath, her lips swollen, and eyes dilated. I waited for her to speak with my hands on my thighs, trying to gain my breath. I needed to be sure she was okay with what I'd just done. That quickly, guilt began to build in my chest, reminding me of one of many reasons I wasn't ready to become a father. I was too selfish with her body. It belonged to me and I hated the thought of sharing it with anybody. I had no idea what was appropriate sex with an expectant woman. All I knew was that the swelling and expansion of her body appealed to some subconscious part of me. Now that I knew what she felt like while pregnant, I wanted to explore more of her. I also feared hurting her and the baby.

Jesus…

I was turned on again, flashes of possible acts shot through my head that quickly. But I knew she'd reject them all. This was her first pregnancy and I wouldn't want to risk it any more than she would. What was I going to do? How was I going to survive this period in our marriage? Could this work?

"I missed you," she breathed. My eyes flew to her face. Alexis was still out of breath, clearly still coming down. "I don't like fighting. We're bonded now. We need to be doing more of this than fighting."

My lungs sucked in more air than I could control and my chest expanded with relief and joy. I reached over and kissed the lips I treasured more than she would believe. I adored this woman and it frightened me. Her hands immediately palmed my shoulders as her tongue rolled against mine. I kissed my wife until I needed to breathe. Pulling back, my attention went to her small, but very hilled belly. Alexis' eyes followed. As they had for weeks now, her hands reached down and rubbed over the sides. I heard her giggle bashfully. That timid sound had me observing her expression again. I didn't want her to be ashamed of her body, and certainly not in front of me.

It was here. The space between us. The element of our lives that drew the boundaries I still struggled with no matter how well I could ration it. Ready or not, Alexis was pregnant, and I was going to be a father.

"Are you happy?" I could barely hear myself, but I studied her face for an answer.

Alexis bit her lip, sucked in a breath, and nodded emphatically. Then out of nowhere blubbered, "I didn't think I could have kids."

Tears sprouted from her eyes, her bare breasts shook as she let go of what seemed to be a burgeoning sob.

I rubbed her upper arm. "Why are you crying, beloved?"

Her cries were verbal, from the bowels of her belly as she covered her face.

"Be-ca-cause I want you ta-to be happy, too," she wailed her words. "Isn't that why you had that lady pray for me that day?"

I'm trying, beloved…

I know… I should have used those words to assure her. As a licensed therapist, I understood the value of communication. But as she'd once apprised, I was a flawed man. I battled emotions I could hardly manage, feeling strong passions for this woman I couldn't identify. Clearly, I wasn't settled. I'd gone from panicked, to relieved, to impressed, to aroused, to jealous, to angry, then to expressing empathy in the span of thirty minutes. Internally, I was crashing, burning with the need to hold her. I grabbed her into my arms. I needed to touch her for my comfort. Alexis continued to shield her face. To me it was rejection. I wanted to be in each moment of her sadness, especially if I caused it.

"Didn't I tell you not to hide them from me? If you need to cry, do it with me. Don't hide it!" I spoke with a tone viler than she deserved, but I meant every word.

I may not have been the best husband, but Alexis was mine. We were bonded.

That night I held my wife until she released her last tear then walked her into the shower to clean us before having her fall asleep in my arms.

The following morning, I rose at five-thirty. As I slugged into the bathroom to prepare for my 'main job,' I began to pray to awaken my spirit. It had been a late night for me, an emotional one that unpleasantly reminded me of my limitations. I tried not to focus on that as I let the streaming water beat down on my body, assisting with my consciousness. I nearly leaped in place when I felt soft hands round my waist and warm skin press into my back. She didn't speak, but her hands did when they found my dick already awakened.

My lids slowly fell, and I relaxed into her touch. I was doing it again. Helplessly yielding to her needs, moods, and preferences had become a natural inclination for me.

"Good morning, Alexis."

She didn't speak right away, instead using the digits of her hands to speak for her. I cupped my hands to create a pool in my palms and splashed water into my face. I needed a distraction or else I'd be late from putting my temptress back to bed. I couldn't be late for today's job. It would throw my entire week off, and other's.

"Did you catch the news clip about Nyree at the strip club?"

I froze all movements at that muttered question, almost missing it.

"Yes. It was emailed to me."

"Did you do it?"

I glanced down at her blue painted nails, stacked together, jerking me with coordinated strokes. Alexis was trying to unman me for the purpose of seeking answers.

I swallowed, my eyes closing again. "I don't contact the media, beloved. I hold many occupational positions, that type of work isn't a part of any."

"Well, someone did. And whoever it was, had to get the order from someone."

"Don't worry yourself over who. It doesn't involve you. You've moved on, and that's all that matters."

"Hmmmm... Oh, yeah?"

I nodded.

I knew she'd moved on, considering her seductive dance number last night. She wasn't afraid to do it, and I was grateful. She wanted to visually please me, and nothing made me happier.

My jaw clenched, her movements increasing.

"You know the drill, kitten," I droned in the stalls of the shower. "I'm preaching this morning."

Alexis' hands stopped immediately to my displeasure.

"Oh, no..." I could hear the smile in her tone as she turned me around to face her. "If you're trying to say you're fasting"—an alluring grin broke on her face, a mixture of humor and irreligious sensualism as she lowered to her haunches—"you broke it when you came in late last night. It was after midnight before we were done."

I watched her tongue swipe around my swollen head slowly. She traced the veins down to the base, stroked me while sucking on the head. Immediately entranced, I couldn't believe she wanted me in her mouth again after last night. Nonetheless, I was thrilled. She wasn't the only one suffering lately. I enjoyed having a companion, more than I originally thought I would.

"*You* broke it." I swallowed back a moan.

My kitten's mouth was a wonderland, even when it spewed profanity. This mouth got her in lots of trouble. Me, too.

"Uhn-uhn," she hummed with me in her mouth. She quickly pulled back and muttered, "You did," having to have the last word. I gave it to her, already lost in her morning ministry. This morning, I had her from the back, needing to feel her come around me.

I eventually learned she was up that early to ride into church with me. Her desire to spend the entire day with me surprised me, and would be the first. Our ride into service was my usual preference for quiet but for worship music flowing in the truck. I went into my own head as was customary on Sunday mornings to prepare myself for the day. At some point in the commute, I felt a soft hand clasp mine on the center armrest in the back seat. My gaze went from our joined hands, up to her face. She offered a soft smile of grace, something I'd never seen on her before. She wasn't expressing displeasure at the silence of the commute, neither was she demanding I talk to her. When her attention went back out the window, I knew Alexis was simply sharing her pleasure at being with me this morning. It was...nice.

Coming in with her was different. I was aware of her every movement, and didn't know if that was a part of my admitted obsession or the 'love' thing. Nonetheless, there was something natural and satisfying about her presence at this hour. Alexis took to her seat before I left the *Bishop's Office* for the pulpit, but not before staying for my morning staff prayer. She winked at me on her way out, communicating encouragement.

Her attendance delighted me more than I cared to admit. After first service, I arranged with Sister Shannon for Alexis to have a snack to hold her over until after the second. I also had Shannon contact Ms. Remah to let her know I would be taking Alexis out for dinner here in the city after church, so she could adjust her meal preparation. Alexis talked with me briefly in between services, asking questions about my sermon afterward, and what I felt when I prayed for people. She allowed me time I needed to provide guidance to my staff to better the second service, all while by my side. It was something I could get used to.

All went well with the Spirit, atmosphere, and my sermon throughout the day. I was happy with the number of souls asking to be saved, and thrilled to see Alexis in her usual row each time I hit the pulpit. However, something changed in the span of the time before the first service and after the second. Alexis was by my side or as much as appropriate considering my charge, but her quieted affection waned by the time we left for *DiFillippo's* for dinner.

We talked throughout the meal, and even made plans to see a movie later on in the week. The food was gratifying per usual, and the crème brûlée topped off the culinary experience. The fact that we shared the fondness of the dessert felt emasculating. *I actually have cravings like a woman.* Only now I understood why.

We stood to leave the table when Alexis stretched, her long arms in the air, on either side of her frame. She wore her usual ensemble: long fitted dress with a matching cape. Today it was off white with a pair of *Tom Ford* pumps I couldn't wait to have her in alone. Even more striking than the heels was the little bump in her abdomen. It was more pronounced with her body stretched like an octopus. Strangely, I felt a pull in my groin.

"Oh, my!" the hostess appearing out of nowhere gasped.

I followed her line of vision to Alexis' exposed posture. A panic struck inside, and as I saw her near my wife, I rounded the table in double time until I was at Alexis' side.

"I didn't know we were expecting!" she trilled, her fingers wiggling in the air as she lowered herself, belly level, gaining on Alexis.

Quickly, I wrapped my arm around Alexis' waist, my hand covered her small bump, and I pivoted her backwards. Alexis stumbled into my ready frame and she let go of a nervous giggle before covering my hand at her abdomen.

"Oh!" the hostess chirped, realizing my maneuver. Her brows hiked in the air.

"Not yet," I provided. "I'm not ready for the touching of the belly."

I felt Alexis freeze in my arm at that declaration. It may have been crisp, but not intended as rude.

"Oh," she repeated, but in a new pitch this time as she straightened. "I understand. My daughter was the same way with her first." Her delivery was wry, but she tried to maintain her smile. "Well, congratulations. I can't wait to see the new bundle come in and dine with us." She waved, walking off.

"Don't you think that was rude, Ezra?" Alexis' eyes went between me and the fleeing hostess. "I thought you liked her."

"I do," I admitted while grabbing our leftovers bag. "I just don't want to share the feel of your body with anyone." I tried to keep my tone pleasant.

"But people like to feel pregnant bellies. It's a...thing."

"Not mine." I smiled tightly and dismissively. "And not for my belly or baby."

"It's my belly," she argued, still in the same place when I'd begun to walk off.

I turned and reached for her hand. "You are mine. Everything about you, down to the baby you're carrying. I will not have people who are not spiritually cleared by me touching you. You'd do well to practice the same in my absence, beloved."

I didn't wait for her to join hands with me. I took hers and gave a little tug to command her into step. Alexis took the cue and continued with me.

On the way out, I provided a generous smile to the hostess, to emphasize my neutral ground with her. During our commute to Jersey, I rubbed Alexis' feet to relax her until she nodded off. Watching her sleep, I began to brew about people touching her belly all this time when I didn't know about the baby. *Just another reason I should have been told from the beginning!* I may not have been prepared to be a father, but I am provider and protector. I'd never considered until this incident in the restaurant how intimate a woman's incubating womb is. There's life inside, a delicate one. I would not have anyone questionable spirits touching my wife's belly. I'd never been a man of demonic fear, understanding the omnipotence of my God could destroy any dark spirit. Except in that moment, my vulnerability had been revealed. I had no idea what spirits could pass on to my wife or innocent child. I couldn't be with Alexis all day, but I could certainly direct her as it concerned my child.

No.

I did not verbalize this to her when I had the opportunity later that night as I made love to her and could feel her apprehensions, confusion, and frustrations while deep inside her. I did not, because doing that exposed my vulnerability and lack of control. Speaking my fears into the atmosphere was not something I did. I just had to find a way to get through this pregnancy safely, and accept the fact that I would no longer have my beloved to myself. I'd have to share her with someone else. Forever.

~sixteen~

~Ezra~

"According to Montgomery, at his arraignment he received the same felony charges as the other men at the apartment. They're not treating him as a victim in the least, which pleases me. He's been appointed a public defender."

"Yeah, and hopefully he or she will not motion for continuance. That has become a common move for PDs, and allowed because judges know how overwhelmed they are," my attorney, Jack Kalwoski advised. "What are the charges?"

"Conspiracy, kidnapping in the second degree, assault, robbery in the first..." I stalled to recall the other category. "...and possession of firearms by a convicted felon."

"All class B violent felonies. Robbery in the first comes with a mandatory minimum sentencing of five years with a maximum of twenty-five. I don't think your father-in-law will be at holiday dinners anytime soon, Carmichael," he joked dryly.

Little did he know, Rasul Grier had never stepped foot in my house. I'd considered that during the period Alexis left me. When she spoke about putting others' needs before her own, I wondered did that include her discerning my preference for her father to stay as far as possible out of my life, which included my home. Alexis had treated it like a haven for the most part.

There was a knock at my office door.

"Come in," I shouted. Though the room was small compared to all my other offices, it had become one of my most frequented because it was where my wife spent her working hours.

"What about that other matter?" I asked Jack.

Precious strolled in with a file in her hands. She smiled and gestured that she'd wait.

"According to my firm's P.I., the Griffins hired a P.I. to find out who's responsible for that video. He's been knocking on doors, yours included, probably at the advisement of the young woman."

A private investigator had been to my lab and the church office, asking for me a few days ago. He left a business card that I handed over to my attorney.

"I'm surprised she's cooperating and not denying it."

"Those judges aren't the bears to poke. They take their reputations seriously. If a blemish is exposed on their white coats, heads are rolling with countless casualties to follow. Doesn't seem that the new Mrs. Griffin stands a chance against them. That was quite evident at her press conference."

Nyree made a public apology by way of an unusual press conference two days after that video was leaked. I would have never guessed this would make the airwaves, but it had been becoming clearer to me that Elle was onto something when she advised Nyree would pay. Nyree's tearful reaction to addressing the tape was so overwhelming, her swollen face was almost unrecognizable in the camera with Taylor silently at her side. Elle also advised it would all blow over the moment the next scandal was discovered. It was the business of media. The question was how long would it run. It had been two weeks now.

I motioned for Precious to hand me the file.

"Yeah, well," I exhaled. "I'll handle the P.I. and keep you posted. I don't foresee that encounter being a problem at all."

Jack chuckled. "Call me crazy, but I believe you, Carmichael. You're the only client I could trust to provide a mind fuck to a P.I. I hope he's well trained."

"For his sake, so do I." I chuckled along with him. "Listen, I have to go. I'll call you as soon as I learn something."

"Same here. Enjoy what's left of your morning."

I hung up the phone and paid a cursory glance to the file. It was a report from the last board of trustees meeting, more specifically the results of our votes for various proposals. One of them was Alexis' for the safe house she wanted *RSfALC* to undertake. I'd told her it would have to wait six months for the next review meeting, but after seeing how broken her spirit was at that information, I pulled a few strings to have it on the agenda for last month. The majority approved it.

I closed the file. "What was her response?"

"I haven't told Lex." I couldn't miss the coy smirk she tried to hide because her cheeks were heating.

I removed my reading glasses.

What is it with these things? They drove Alexis crazy. Evidence of this was how many times I had sex or gotten blown in my home office at random hours of the day since getting them.

"Why not?" I asked. "She's in today."

I knew this because I always knew where my wife was. I had to stay aware of her whereabouts when she wasn't exactly the most forthcoming. She'd been off for weeks now. I struggled with going over each detail of that Sunday she accompanied me to church for the first time. Oddly, she'd done every Sunday since. The most bizarre part about that is she doesn't sit out in the congregation. Alexis stays in the *Bishop's Office*, doesn't even go to the lounge to eat with other members of the clergy and staff in between services. She stays in my office, prays, asks questions, and even gives feedback on my sermons, but she doesn't leave until I do for the day. I asked her about it twice since it began. Her response had been she didn't feel like being 'squashed'—her word—between people now that she had begun to show.

I thought it was odd seeing that depending on what she wore, Alexis could hide her belly well. According to her doctor, this is possible for some women with their first pregnancy, and that she was perfectly healthy. I didn't badger her over it, but could still feel in my spirit something was wrong. When we made love, Alexis wasn't as forthcoming as usual. Even when she initiated sex, which was quite often, she wouldn't linger in the after cuddle. She'd get up and head to the bathroom without so much as a flirty smile. Her behavior had been peculiar, but I couldn't develop a case because she would still speak to me, and even thank me for flowers I'd sent or lunch I'd surprise her with here at *Christ Cares*.

"Because I just got the report from Sister Shannon and printed it out. When I passed the conference room, I saw she was busy so I came here."

But why would Precious make such a big deal out of this report? I was sure the same email was waiting in my inbox.

"I wanted to know if you want to tell her."

"I don't think she'd care who delivered the news. Her hopes are high for this." I closed the folder and tossed it in a basket at the corner of my desk.

"I just know there have been problems with you guys and hoped you delivering this bit of news would..." She shrugged. "You know."

"Problems?" I lowered my chin.

"Yeah. I see she hasn't been in church for a couple of weeks. And that guy came by the church looking for you last week. I'm not saying it had anything to do with Lex, but maybe. And she's been to herself a little more than usual around here...a lot of closed door meetings with her staff..."

She's been out of work a lot over the past month or so, so of course she's been busy working with her staff. It was her job.

It disturbed me to see Precious blatantly probing into my personal life. She used to act with a level of subtlety before I married Alexis. Now that her mother and my father had put so much pressure on her to remain 'faithful' to me, believing one day I'd crack, she'd dropped to new lows. It had been concerning me more than I addressed it because I'd been so wrapped up in my own world. Seth had been spending more time in town, presumably pressuring her for a formal relationship. One she clearly wasn't open to.

Precious was pushing here, applying that same pressure she was under. I was not one for games.

I grabbed the folder from the basket and tossed it to the end of the desk. Shifting to engage my computer, I advised without my eyes, "Go give it to her and let her know she can contact you or me for more information."

"I can't. I think it's a very important meeting based on who's in there with her."

I took a deep breath. I could smell the manipulation wreaking from her.

I sat up in my chair. "Who could possibly be in there that you could not drop off the file and leave? de Blasio?"

A wily beam filled her eyes. *"Neighborhood Defenders Office."*

"Who?" I was confused, not by the organization, but the reason their being here would be an event.

"Bradley West."

And there was the hook. Never mind she'd deliberately and unnecessarily made me aware of his presence on my property, but what business did he have here, and why with my wife?

I jumped to my feet and charged to the door. Taking large lunges down the hall to the conference room in the middle of my and Precious' office, I couldn't get there fast enough. The door was ajar; I could tell as I neared it.

For what? Privacy?

Adrenaline shot to every cell of my body. My fists clenched and jaw tightened. She hadn't been right with me for two weeks and had the gall to invite a former lover to our place of business?

What did she wear today?

Was it revealing of her body?

Her belly?

Did she allow him to touch her belly?

My child!

The door hit the wall when I pushed it open. Gasps and squeals sounded in the air, and necks pushed back from the table. A baby wailed, and one male body shot into the air. I counted heads: five in all.

"Oh, my gawd!" Kim Baker sighed in relief, holding her chest.

"Shit, man!" The young fit man wearing an ultra-fitted suit shrilled.

Alexis' regard immediately went to a woman who appeared familiar, comforting a toddler. They both rang recognizable to me. Alexis sat across from Bradley, who sat on the side of the room closest to the door, next to Ms. Baker. It quickly became apparent this was a work-related meeting.

"Who is this?" Bradley posed to Alexis, demanding an answer.

"I think the more appropriate question is who are you?" I countered.

"Bradley West from *NDO*," he provided with flared nostrils. "And you?"

"This Mr. Carmichael," Kim Baker answered out of breath. "He runs *CC*." She could detect the tension bouncing between the two of us.

"Oh," Bradley replied to the weight of my title.

As he should.

Alexis' wild eyes went from Bradley, to me, then to the back of me. Precious. That's when they tightened with revelation and fury. She reached across her chair and grabbed the bawling child then stood to her feet.

On her way to the door, passing me, I asked, "And where are you going?"

"To calm down the baby you just scared the shit out of," she grated. Behind me, when she approached Precious, she blurted, "This is a crisis meeting you just interrupted. I told you I'd get back to you as soon as I was done. We have someone who's about to turn herself in." I leaped around, in just enough time to catch the drainage of blood racing from Precious' face. She'd set me up. "Are you happy?"

Anger coiled in my chest, seemingly aimed directly at Alexis. The seconds were fleeting before she'd be out of the room. I didn't think, just fired off.

"Please don't hold him on your belly. It's not safe for the baby!"

Alexis stopped. I could see the deep inhale she pulled from her nose, shocked by my outburst. I could even see the tears pooling in her eyes at my uncouth announcement to the room.

"Go the fuck to hell, Ezra." she swore so low, yet so vehemently.

Then I heard the final gasp, probably the loudest of them all. My sights went to Precious. She covered her mouth with a shaky hand.

"Oh, wait…" Bradley trilled, with a new ring to his vocals, this one more casual. "Lex is pregnant?" His face lined with wonderment.

"Very." I confirmed with emphasis, squaring my shoulders.

Ms. Baker's eyes widened like saucers. The woman who sat next to Alexis had red and swollen eyes that were just as expressive.

That's when it all crashed in on me. No one knew she was pregnant, and I'd made the announcement in the most dramatically crude manner.

~~~~~~~~~~

I learned later on that the young woman, Kema, had stabbed her son's father's lover during a heated argument in the early hours of the morning. Knowing Alexis as a trusted associate, she came to *Christ Cares* for guidance. She threatened to kill herself and her baby so his father wouldn't have custody of him. Alexis was able to talk her off the ledge and into turning herself in, which created a need for Bradley West from *NDO*. She called in a favor for him to help legally advise Kema. With Ms. Baker's assistance, they were able to find emergency placement for her son.

As plausible as that sounded, it bit at me that it was Bradley, a former lover, she called on for help. It also pissed me off that Precious deceptively pushed the right buttons to inform me he was on the property. I demanded that she leave for the day before taking off for a meeting at the church.

~Lex~

"Well, now that I know you're not calling me for more of those god-awful gothic dresses, we can end this conversation."

"*Wha*-what? End the conversation? I don't think so!" I snapped, trying to keep my voice down. "Why the hell are you being be so damn evasive, Elle?"

"Because this is the second time you've called me about this shit and I don't know how many times I can tell you that even if I had something to do with your girlfriend, I don't have the privilege of discussing work matters with non-clients. My answer won't change."

"First of all, she's not my girlfriend. Second, your answer won't change, but our relationship can," I threatened.

My eyes fell from shame. I was desperate to know.

"First, we're not friends, Lex. Second, you aren't even a client of mine. Please don't try to use a gun without ammunition."

The doorbell rang, scaring the shit out of me. I jumped from the piano bench toward the foyer, having no idea who it could be on a Wednesday night. We never got unexpected guests except for Mark Anthony, who had the privilege of being cussed out by Ms. Remah the next time he popped up.

"Fuck you."

"And fuck you, too." My mouth was balled up, not having gotten anywhere with her. Again. The woman was ironclad. "Oh, and by the way, I think it's really cool that you agreed to being little Ms. Amora Ardell's godmother on Sunday. Zo was relieved. She thought you'd say no." *Why?* I found myself rubbing my belly defensively. "Isn't she adorable?" Elle cooed in the phone. I'd never seen her so affected—other than when it came to Jackson.

Weird.

I arrived at the door, unable to believe who was on the other side.

"That she is, but you're fucked up. Thanks. Gotta go."

"Bye."

I rolled my eyes while tapping to end the call. Taking in a deep breath, I opened the door.

"Bishop Carmichael," I tried for pleasant. "Wasn't expecting you."

He never came unannounced. He never came at all.

The man hardly looked my way, instead he scanned the foyer. His cologne was loud enough to be offensive. But he looked the part: slacks, nice leather shoes, a Kangol flat cap, and spring jacket.

"I didn't think I needed to call ahead to visit my son's home."

"Our home," flew out before I could think. My heart rate took off, too. "Your son doesn't live here alone."

I was sick of his shit, and without me trying, it showed.

His eyes went from my head that was up in a messy bun, slowly down my body covered in tights and one of Ezra's loose fitting t-shirts until he reached my bare toes.

"Sweetheart, this is my son's home. You may have married him, but I'm aware of the pre-nup in place; I made sure of it."

"The pre-nup that says I get this house if we split?"

His neck snapped back. This evening was not the one to challenge me. Since coming back to the house, Ezra showed me the documents to confirm I was indeed the sole owner of the property if Ezra and I were to split in the first five years of our marriage. After that, I would decide if I wanted the burden of the taxes, as the home was paid off. So, I could say it now with confidence. I'd already been fired up from his son, and the conversation I just left with Elle didn't help. Bishop Carmichael may have been intimidating, but not tonight on my home base.

Fuck that.

"Young lady, go get my son," he commanded dismissively, eyes rolling in the distance. "I'm here on an emergency."

I froze in place, giving myself a few moments to think. Had I reacted to that, my next move would have been cussing him the fuck out. I couldn't do that to Ezra. I wouldn't do that to myself. I was not trash. No matter how much he deserved it, I had to remember who I was now. Like it or not, I was married to a man of God, and this was his father, who had high ranking in a religious organization. I may not have been able to appreciate all the happenings of the church, but being in this family for almost a year, I knew this man was held on a high pedestal whether he deserved it or not.

I took a deep breath.

"Down the hall, hang a left past the kitchen," I instructed before walking off for the den.

Bishop huffed, realizing my sass. Once I could hear his footsteps taking off down the hall, I came out of the den and made my way to the powder room. I needed to take a leak. By the time I was done, I padded down the hall, barefoot, on my toes, and just before I reached the kitchen, I could hear voices.

"And what do you expect me to do?"

I toed closer to Ezra's office.

"What do I—" Bishop stopped, stunned by Ezra's question. "Son, you are her leader, the pastor of the organization she's devoted her life to. You have to think about more than yourself for once!"

"If Precious were another member of *Redeeming Souls*, I would certainly have a course of action. But we both know her placement in my life is more complicated than that. She has her mother, a boyfriend, and clearly, you to comfort her at this time."

"She should have you, too, especially because you're the one at the center of this breakdown!" Bishop shouted. "Did you have to blurt out Lexus' pregnancy like that? Don't you think Precious deserved a more formal notification—I should have had notification?"

Things went quiet. My eyes skirted around the hallway nervously. I was sure the beat of my heart could be heard. I couldn't believe I was in the middle of this drama. Did all church people keep this negative energy around them?

Afraid of what I'd hear and of what more he'd say about me, I took off to the kitchen.

~Ezra~

"Lex," I advised, with a tight throat.

"Pardon?"

"My wife. Her name is Lex."

"Whatever her name is, she ain't been nothing but trouble since day one. Don't think I don't know about that foolery with her father. You may be able to keep some things from me, but don't forget I had all the resources of a respectable pastor at my fingertips less than a year ago! Your priorities are misplaced here. I get it. You have a wife. You slipped up and got her pregnant, but let's not forget the people who have been here from day one. You need to pull it together!"

I stretched my lips up toward my nose, fighting for fortitude.

"The same way you did with my mother?" Silence fell over the room for a spell of time. "Are you still under the mentality that just because I'm your offspring, I share your reckless conduct?"

Slowly, I rounded my desk, approaching him.

"What are you say—"

"She was sick for years and you had no idea because you were so busy gallivanting with Marva Graham to even care! Then you have the nerve to bring that woman to her burial. It was disgraceful! Haven't you gotten the memo? I am not like you. I minister from the inside out. It starts here in my home and then extends out."

"This is about that mess when you was out in California. You need to get over it! You're forty years old now, son!"

"And she will soon be forty. Precious should be past this. I am married—decidedly devoted to one woman. Understand that I empathize with her. I really do, but this 'breakdown' has less to do with her pining after me, and more to do with the undue pressure you and Marva have put on her all these years. Have you ever considered she may have finally come to the conclusion that this sick fantasy you and her mother have been feeding her about me is untrue? But you two continue to push and push."

"Hear me." I lowered my voice to express the gravity in my coming warning. "You and Marva will be held responsible for what you've done to her, to my mother, and to the people you're supposed to be serving instead of creating the unholy world of adultery and confusion. You"—my index finger rose in the air—"especially because you'll be held to a higher standard for your pastoral role in the Kingdom."

There was a flip in his pupils. When they'd filled with fear and judgment, they quickly switched to arrogant amusement.

"I cancel the power of those words." A clever smirk curved on his face. "Don't forget my ranking, son. Do you remember my declaration to you when you spoke against God?" He scoffed. "Yeah, you're not the only person hanging on to what was said and done over fifteen years ago. You are cursed, and so will your offspring be. It shall come to pass."

Casually, I gestured with my chin. "Leave my home. Now."

He chuckled, slowly turning for the door. "At least one of you knows who this place belongs to."

I didn't know what that meant and had said all there was to be said between us. This was my father's second visit to my home. The first was to assess my wife under the guise of appeasing my mother. This subsequent and unannounced visit was on behalf of Precious as he disrespected my wife. The common denominator? My wife. Alexis was mine to love and protect. She was no burden to him or anyone else. He would not disrespect her. No one would.

"Well, my scholarly brothers," Amare supplied a knowing grin, understanding he was trying the group's patience collectively. "My last point of the evening is that this presidential election is very telling of our, quote/unquote, culture here in America. A man who has no experience in political science, no deep religious roots, is on record for his bigotry and hatred towards a combined major population of this country—women and

Latinos—can make it to the primaries is revealing of America's true values. And why? Because he's been a millionaire, and sometimes billionaire, all his life." His eyes perused the table. "Even your Bible, Bishop, tells us money is the root of all evil."

Bishop Jones cackled at his dramatic argument in a similar fashion to what he usually did when not willing to engage in a debate with him. My sentiment wasn't too far off of Bishop's.

Dr. Amare Williams was a passionate Pan-African. His zealous and compelling delivery mixed with his education and clinical experience made him an expert on the welfare, mobility, and uplifting of people of African ancestry. He was one of my closest friends, and a regular religious and sociological sparring partner.

In fact, my closest friends had opposing religious, political, and cultural views and practices from me. One thing we all had in common was our professional commitment to, practice, and experience in psychology or psychiatry. Though it used to be more frequent until years ago, we'd gather together annually to discourse. As Bishop Jones would say, we pursued the concept of iron sharpens iron with our opposing banter. These discussions, while dangerous, never got out of hand, but for when Dr. Amare—as he was referred to in his professional realms—would unleash his passion and use provocation to assert his arguments.

Tonight, we were wrapping up our latest gathering at my place. I rearranged the den to accommodate the makings of a game room where we'd play chess, Go, and when we were feeling less competitive, Scrabble. There were only five of us in attendance tonight, and they'd been over for hours. It was a big deal because not everyone was in the New York tri-state area. Bishop Jones lived in Malibu, though he traveled the world, pursuing ministry. Amare had similar occupational mobility to his schedule, but was based out of Brooklyn. Caleb Adler was a renowned psychiatrist in the Jewish tri-state community. Theodore Barlow, a psychologist, headed up a team of clinicians in the Department of Justice of the Northern District of Illinois. There were three members of the gang missing at this event, and none of them were of African descent. And that rattled Amare, who never turned down a debate on race and/or culture in America.

"What do his religious roots have to do with his presidential qualifications, Amare?" Adler asked, his neck red from the uprise of his anxiety. Amare brought it out of the best of us.

Even now, as they were gathering their belongings and putting on their jackets to leave, we were barely missing the rare occasion of ending the fellowship without heated debate.

"What do they have to do with it? America doesn't elect non-Christian candidates."

"Nearly eight years ago, your argument would have been we don't elect non-white ones either," Barlow snorted, pulling a strand of his blond locks behind his ear.

Amare squared his shoulders while tossing him a glare. "Well played attempt at deferring the argument."

Bishop saddled up beside Amare, placing his hands on either shoulder as he belted his high screeching laughter. "I don't believe we were about to perpend this topic. It is my understanding that we're about to leave the Carmichael home. You know he's taken on a wife recently?" he presented rhetorically.

Barlow's palms rose in the air, a peaceful gesture. "Listen, Amare, I'm just saying, religion doesn't matter. It isn't as much of a divisive issue as it used to be. You're of Muslim faith. You could run, and with a strong political platform, could probably win in the current cultural climate in America."

"To answer your question, religion very much matters," Amare insisted with flared nostrils. "Christianity has been supported by white supremacy in all its history. Even your Jesus has blond hair and blue eyes like you, according to your contemporaries. I was raised in Islam. However, I am an African, who is coincidentally Islamic. My religion is secondary to my racial identity."

"I think many in America have progressed far beyond the Baltic Sea-habitant...Nordic characteristics of Jesus Christ." Adler chortled at the absurdity of that comment. He began walking sideways toward the door leading to the foyer, and we followed. "We all know His biblically documented features, and how they were parallel to African descendants. That argument is archaic and impotent as far as I'm concerned."

"That's a major development coming from a Jew, Adler." Adler responded by way of a flippant wave, humor still playing on his face. "One of these days, you all will realize Jesus was not the Messiah. Today he's used as a supernatural force to fatten the wallets of pastors at the expense of their poor congregants. Or for some Christian segments, a statue thought to have reverential powers for prayers and supplication."

"And what guides your morality, Brother Amare?" Bishop asked, now in the center of the vestibule.

"Mobilizing the systematically oppressed Africans here in the United States into a place of empowerment and mental, physical, and socio-economical wealth. We deserve it—have been stolen, beaten, abused, and generationally disenfranchised at the hands of our oppressors. No more."

I contained my humor at the physical wealth part. I'd assisted him in reprogramming the way he viewed his body as a dumpster. As he'd been in school over the past decade dumping in knowledge, he'd also been dumping in convenient junk foods, and not unloading it through proper diet and exercise.

"I've contributed to your visions and initiatives, Williams, and I'd be willing to do it again," Adler offered.

"Not for the one I'm working on now. I don't want Jewish blood on any of it. The funding needs to come from our African brothers and sisters who have the disposable income to sow into our own people, Adler. The Jews have done it for generations. It is now time for us to step up...seeing how they let Africans into the oval office and all." His mouth twitched into a sleek grin.

It was a wise crack. Adler seemed to have brushed it off easily. We were all accustomed to doing so.

"I know of a guy, out in Cali...a Muslim brother by the name of Azmir Jacobs." Amare gestured to me with his chin. "You familiar with him, Ezra?"

"I've heard of him." I shook my head. "But I can't say I know him. Never met him."

"Well, that's who I plan to target. Being a fellow Islam man, he would understand the importance of this venture."

I nodded. It was good to see him so strategic, another trait of his I'd always admired. Amare was resourceful, influential, and tactical.

Bishop chimed in, "I'm aware of Brother Jacobs. His wife has a foundation members of my church engage in. He's actually a reformed Christian. His pastor," Bishop regarded me. "John Edmonson and I go back a ways."

I was familiar with Pastor John and his wife, Twanece. They were not only peers in ministry, but in the field of psychology as well. They, too, merged ministry with their traditional careers. It was a nice connection.

Amare gave a slight rolling of the eyes. He would never say it in front of the others, but his wings had been slightly clipped by that conversion mentioned. He was a true advocate for blacks evolving past Christianity, and Allah had been his answer.

"Well, as for me and my house... I just want to stick with Jesus. There has been no friend that has stuck closer than a brother," Bishop chimed in, clandestinely closing this chat.

"Is that all that could be said about Him?" Amare smirked.

"That and He doesn't discriminate based on past transgressions or color. Not many beliefs can argue the same," I added. "Also, not many can claim the supernatural powers of their god the way we can the great I AM."

"Oh…" Bishop rumbled in his best preacher cry, not skipping a beat. "…the power of El-Elyon!"

"The most high God," I interpreted for Bishop. Then I continued. "All praises be to El-Olam!"

"Aye!" Bishop shouted joyfully, swaying his shoulders. "The everlasting God! Now, I feel my Help coming on! I'm getting ready to preach up in here!" He stomped his feet and clapped his hands.

Amare, knowing the tactics we used to quell his passionate attacks, stifled his laughter, unlike Barlow and Adler. They were red-faced in laughing fits. We all took a minute to share in the good natured joshing. The other three gentlemen knew if given a moment more, Bishop and I would have had proper church in my foyer. Alone. It'd been well-documented.

"Now, if that is all, my scholarly peers, I must be leaving."

The lights of several waiting cars shined through the front windows of the house. Two of them had drivers, Bishop's being one. It was a common occurrence for them to message their cars when preparing to leave.

We all took turns bidding each other a good night.

Then Bishop turned to me. "Please give the matriarch of the home a note of gratitude from me. And tell Ms. Remah the ackee and salt fish brought back warm memories for me. It was fantastic meeting her."

"Oh!" Amare screeched animatedly, clearly hit with oversight. "I haven't had the pleasure of making the acquaintance of Mrs. Ezra Carmichael," Out of the country, speaking at an event, he wasn't able to attend the wedding. "Think it's too late?"

This was the Amare I knew: mannerly and humble. He had not yet arrived when Alexis and Ms. Remah brought the last of the food into the den. They'd been working the menu since yesterday. I was truly grateful to have them be so hospitable. Typically, I'd hire a contracted caterer for this event, too.

The other gentlemen were leaving out of the door when I checked the time on my wrist. I turned to the back of the house.

"I don't believe so. Let's see if she's back here waiting on me."

En route, I scanned rooms and listened for movement. Ms. Remah was usually tucked away in her suite at this hour. It was a Friday night, and if I were not working late or at a speaking engagement, Alexis would wait up to go to bed with me.

We finally entered the kitchen, and I noticed the back sliding door was open. I knew then she'd be out on the deck. Amare followed silently behind me. When I stepped outside, I caught her on the far right, curled up on the lounger, reading a book. Alexis' presence since leaving me quickened my heart rate, spiked my body temperature, and thickened my throat to a close. She peered up when she sensed my presence. But when she registered Amare's, she quickly closed her book and scurried to sit straight, pushing it to the far side of her.

Odd...

"Beloved, I am sorry to surprise you, but I have a dear friend I'd like you to meet before he leaves to incite the next Civil War." Alexis stood and met us half way on the lit deck. "This is Dr. Amare Williams, a clinical psychologist, community activist, and long-time friend." Alexis cracked a polite smile I could tell was forced, but courteous. "Dr. Amare, this is my aesthetically pleasing, mentally and emotionally stimulating wife, Alexis."

Amare released a smile. "What an introduction." He extended his hand and Alexis obliged. "It's good to see Brother Carmichael has made a statement; sticking to his own. No self-hatred amongst my friends." His beaming eyes turned to me.

Alexis appeared confused by his covert statement about me marrying a black woman. It was clear to me he, too, admired my sienna temptress' beauty. No matter how friendly the expression, that didn't bode well with me.

To brush over that inside joke, I asserted a new one, "She's not partial to beards."

"But, my fair scholar, you don one so well. And if I'm not mistaken, you did so when she met you?" Amare's sinister leer was on full display.

"She was literally a gift sent from above. Or perhaps kismet is how you'd deem it, Brother Amare? What God has joined together..." I left open for his interpretation.

Amare was conversant with the Word in spite of his opposition to it.

"Yes...I see." Amare tugged at his beard contemplatively. "Well, anyways..." He turned to Alexis. "It's a pleasure, Alexis—"

"Lex," I corrected.

"Pardon?" His brows peaked.

"You can call her Lex." My beloved's bewildered eyes bounced between the two of us.

"But you just said her name is Alexis."

"Because it is her name, but you can refer to her as Lex. It's her preference."

Amare cocked his head to the side.

"It *is* nice meeting you, Dr. Amare," Alexis interjected with grace before pausing. "Your name rings a bell."

Amare scoffed, of course, thrilled by that admission. "Well, I should hope so. I've been involved in community mobilization for close to two decades. Where are you from?"

"Harlem—"

"Harlem World," she corrected me.

"Oh, okay." He straightened, folded his arms, and brushed down his beard with his right hand. "We've done lots of events there. Financial Empowerment…African Family Uplifting…American Boys—"

"To African Men," she completed with a docile smirk.

I hated witnessing every moment of it.

"Yeah. We ran that one a few times at the old rec there. I think it's since been closed."

"Yes. I ran it for almost ten years. I coordinated with your group to come in."

"Did you attend?"

Please say yes…

"No. It was at night, and I was taking classes at the time."

Christ…

Her saying yes would have meant she'd seen him and didn't find anything particularly intriguing about him.

"Well, that's too bad. Maybe Ezra can bring you to one of our events. We're all over now."

Alexis' eyes climbed up to meet mine. I didn't commit to it, but did offer something else.

"Beloved, you're familiar with Amare's kin. His grandmother, Mother Snell, is one of the longest standing members of the *RSfALC* community."

Alexis went rigid beneath me.

"Oh…" She blinked successively. "Okay. Good to know. Powerful woman," she murmured.

That was a partial dig, but not toward Amare. This insider was between my kitten and me. Anger bloomed in my chest. She'd been distant since that Sunday, two weeks ago when I thought we'd reached higher ground. I felt I was over the rash announcement of her pregnancy. And now we were back to dealing with her keeping something from me. It was my ministry to discern moods. I knew when something foul was in the atmosphere.

"She's that and more." Amare's focus then turned solely on me. "I want to say thanks for allowing her and her crew access to the sanctuary in the mornings. I can't say enough how much her disposition and vitality have improved over the past few months since." He rested his palm on his chest.

I knew it was a genuine gesture. He honored his grandmother greatly.

"Well, that's my job as pastor. We value her gifts and fellowship."

"I'm gonna get going. Lex, it was a pleasure. You take care of my guy. He's one of a few." Amare pounded his chest this time before requesting her hand. After their shake, he turned toward me for a shoulder hug, and I obliged.

"Let me walk you out, Doc," I offered then turned to Alexis. "I'll be right with you, beloved."

Just before we entered the house, I heard. "Aye!" I turned and saw Amare following me. "Down sixty-two pounds, sir."

"That's amazing."

At six feet two inches, he'd been nearing two-hundred sixty-five pounds: in the playground for heart disease, diabetes and the whole gamut. I had to pull him aside and address holistic transformation for better influence. You can't command change for the masses when you're lacking in an apparent area. Spending years in school, his focus had been his various degrees. He neglected his body in the process.

"Yeah," he affirmed, now shoulder to shoulder. "It's been twenty-six months. I still have a journey ahead, and you to thank for it."

"I think you're paying me back by extending the years of your life. That extends my time on earth with you. Where are you headed at this hour?"

"I'm gonna head in and get some research done."

"Oh, yeah? Grant funding?"

"Nah, man. Another Master's."

I slowed my stride in the foyer. "Really? Sociology?"

"Are you ready for this?"

My brows furrowed. "I suppose."

"Theology school."

"You're kidding me," I breathed.

At the door he stopped, sporting a perceptible grin. "I gotta have the wind in my sails to challenge Jesus enthusiasts like you."

"But you've studied Religion in your former education."

"Only in classes, not a full program. It's a concept now. I need to gather more information first."

"You only pursue ventures with excellence. I bid you well, Brother Amare."

"Thank you, sir." He nodded before leaving.

I locked the door and took to the back of the house, needing to address an egregious issue: my wife. As I entered the kitchen, Alexis was closing the back sliding door behind her. I was able to catch the title of the book she'd stowed away in a stealthy manner earlier. It read *What to Expect When You're Expecting*. After a few beats, I realized the correlation of her steeling beneath me at the mention of Mother Snell's name. But why she saw the need to hide her book concerned me.

Alexis stopped in her tracks, startled when she saw me. It was another characteristic of stealth.

"I didn't see you there," she breathed, clutching her chest.

"Do you think you're miscarrying?"

Her face contorted. "No!"

"Well, what are you keeping from me—and before you speak, just know I can read right through you." I lied.

It may have been true with countless others, but it was an established fact that I didn't know the first thing when it came to my wife.

She sighed, rubbed her eyes. "I'm tired, Ezra. I've been waiting on you to go to bed."

My stomach curled in anger. She would not dismiss this issue again. Just like two Sundays ago, at Stenton and Zoey's reception at *DiFillippo's*. We were there celebrating their joining *Redeeming Souls* when just before it was over, the Rogers' asked Alexis and me to be their daughter's godparents. She was being christened next week. To the naked eye, one would have thought Alexis' reaction was a pure shock. And while that was partially true, I knew there was more to why she gave a slow yes. I asked her about it on the way home, but she gave the convenient explanation of being surprised.

Could it have been because she was having thoughts of leaving me again? For good? Could that be why she had been reading books on pregnancy and parenthood? Was she planning on raising our baby alone? Did she think I'd be okay with that? Life without her? I grew lightheaded with endless questions.

This would end tonight. The air would be cleared before we went to bed. Together. Alexis was going to finally tell me she wanted to leave. And I would make it clear she couldn't.

"We're going downstairs." I felt my lips curl. "Sandbox. Now."

~seventeen~

~Lex~

"*Beat it like a drum...*" I struggled to recall the matching cadence to the lyrics against that on my wet flesh, so desperate to escape another stirring in my groin. I swallowed hard, lips swollen, and eyes shifting under low lids. The lyrics played faintly in my head.

"*Bom...bom...bom...bom...*"

Yes! That was it.

It was a Jamie Foxx track. Which? I couldn't recall. My damn brain was mush. Pores pushing out sweat, heartbeat irregular, and body temperature spiked.

"I can go all morning long, kitten. In my mind, my training is canceled," Ezra threatened again.

He was referring to the martial arts class he attended on Saturday mornings. We'd been at it for at least thirty minutes, possibly more. While that may not seem like a long stretch, try being on a big ass workstation with black candles lit all around your wet, naked, and trembling frame. Lying on your back with your arms stretched and tied over your head, ankles spread as far apart as possible by restraints with your pussy open for your maniac control freak of a dominant husband to beat methodically and teasingly after midnight.

He made me wait all of twenty minutes on the purple pillow, naked, with a quaking spine until he came down the basement stairs dressed in low riding lounge pants. The minute I saw the swollen 'V' of his pelvis, the salivation began. His glaring erection played the background of my torture the entire time under his torment. And now, edging toward forty minutes later, I still had trouble swallowing the collecting saliva in my mouth. My muscles screamed from the tightness I held them in to fight against failed orgasms. My nipples were huge, swollen, and teased by the damn mere air that moved past them as I trembled under him.

Ezra pulled out a riding crop. A long one that kept him at a distance I wasn't comfortable with as the flabby end of it smacked the juices of my pathetic pussy that cried for him. For me. He was withholding my orgasm. *For over thirty fucking minutes!* There was no way wives could be this turned on by their husbands, especially husbands like mine, who was half past insane at times. It was torture. It was always torture when he pulled out a riding crop.

When I saw it at first, I was scared as shit, thinking about his first time spanking me. It didn't help that his anger matched that time and the night I'd met Seth Wilkinson for the first time. Ezra had been harsh then, too. Initially, I feared for my safety for the baby's sake. But after the first few biting and tingling thrashes of my inner thighs, I felt foolish for even thinking Ezra would ever risk the health of my baby. He never neared my belly. Ezra only lashed my inner thighs, heavily tapping my labia to a pleasurable sting until he landed deliciously on my clit. Once there, his taps were quick and firmer, but in shorter measures. He was sure not to send painful thrashes to likely the most sensitive member of my body. The ones there weren't meant to ache: they were for the purpose of erogenous torture.

And oh fuck, did it feel good. The asshole knew what he was doing. The slight sting on my nub burst in a gazillion pleasurable bites that had me ready to burst in a wet, gooey response. But Ezra wouldn't allow it. He'd lead me to a building orgasm just to stop.

I grunted tearfully this last time, only to hear Ezra snort.

"You know why I like you in this position, kitten?" he spoke slowly, concentrating on keeping with the rhythmic swatting between my legs.

No, mind fucktard...

Choose a fuckin' room, Lex!

There were too many voices in my head, including Ezra's. I needed an escape. So, I checked into the first door I could find in my mind.

"*You good, Lex?*" *My mother asked as she tossed the third blanket over me.*

"*Ummmmhmmmmm...,*" *I hummed my answer, fighting the urge to break loose.*

I was beyond hot under the layers. It was after midnight in my parents' room. My father was home this particular summer. My mother had been just days off her medication, a week or so after being home from her stint in the psych ward. She called me into their bedroom out of nowhere. An odd request for her, but I obliged, happy to be included.

I was hot, sweating more than I ever recalled doing. My breaths started out short. It was the middle of the summer, too hot for blankets.

"*Damn, Tiny! I'm sweatin' looking at all them fuckin' blankets over there,*" *he grumbled on the other side of her, she was in the middle.*

The windows were open and two fans were going to ward off the incredible heatwaves of the season.

"*Shut the hell up, 'Sul,*" *she hissed without turning to face him.* "*You sure you good, Lex?*"

She'd been so balanced for days, mood-wise. My mother catered to my every need. When I came home hungry from playing with Tish down the block in the middle of the afternoon, she'd jump from her La-Z-Boy and fix me lunch. While I ate, she combed my hair back into two neat braids. I'd seen the improvement from her zombie like disposition to the one where she'd dance and laugh with my dad all night long. I didn't want to disrupt that. I'd had my mommy back while my daddy was home. I didn't know how long the euphoria would last, and I sure knew I didn't want to be the cause of it ending.

But in that bed, I felt the clammy layer of sweat between my blanket and legs as I tried to twist. My chest felt confined and arms restrained. My damp scalp itched from the heavy moisture that excreted between the follicles.

"*Mommy,*" *began my bursting cry.* "*I'm hot.*"

It was like in slow motion when she sucked in a breath. "*You just said you was good, Lex! What the fuck is it?*"

My heart dropped beneath the lumpy mattress we laid in. I was doing it again. I disappointed her. And when I let my mom down, she got mad. She didn't always hit me. It was usually when others did and I didn't retaliate. Either way, I didn't want to disturb this family we seemed to have going. When my dad was home, my mom seemed healthier, vibrant. But I didn't know what I could say to tell her the blankets were too much. I started to feel weak and dizzy. So, I didn't. The tears started to fall and my stomach turned over. I could feel the upchuck of my belly.

"Goddamn, Tiny! She ain't leaving! Them people ain't taking her! I know you scared and feel fucked up about what happened, but Lex told them she was good here. Let her up!" my father roared in the darkness of the room.

My whimpers grew to a higher pitch. I couldn't help it.

Child services came two days ago and interviewed us as a family, then me separately. They were late about it. The cause for them coming was a neighbor hearing my screams the night my mother beat the shit out of me for losing a fight to Rocky from around the corner, who was two years older than me. I wailed so loud that night before being knocked out, my grandmother was called. It was so bad, an anonymous call was made to the city, and resulted in a visit over a month after my mother was committed from that breakdown. In my one-on-one with them, I made it clear, I was safe and happy with my mother. I even made a plea of now that my father was home, I was extra safe if she were to go off her meds.

That was the event that I learned, despite my mother's head trips— that I never fully understood—she loved me. Yeah, she beat me, and while most were senseless, none were ever random. They came from a place of her illness. Her limitation. People can't give more than they have. My mother loved me. I was mishandled, but loved.

Bom...bom...bom...bom...

That now familiar rhythm snatched me out of my head.

My slightly swollen belly sunk downward as my lungs seized loudly in my chest. Ezra's eyes were wild with anger by my inability to speak.

I'm so fucking far gone!

"You left me for a minute there, kitten. You know you'll be punished for that." There was a stretch of a pause while he examined me before continuing. "As I was saying, it's because you're exposed to me." My heaving chest dropped. "I can tell by the increase of secretion or dryness of your pussy if you're with me or not. I see it all, kitten. I know when there's something in the air—"

"I'm not leaving you!"

The words shot from some unknown place. It was a new revelation to me, but felt so right, and fell from my lips like a plea. This had to stop. I couldn't last any longer, and needed him physically and emotionally. Right now, Ezra was angry.

He skipped a beat and his eyes fluttered, affected by my assurance, but continued with the swats. I needed to keep him distracted enough until my next stirring. Then I'd come and be done with this crazy state I was in.

"Oh, that wouldn't happen again anyway, but I'm glad to hear you won't even try." He didn't look at me when he spoke. "Then why the subtle coldness?"

His concentration stayed on the task at hand. Ezra didn't want to believe I wouldn't leave him. He wanted to catch me in a lie. The fucker had some nerve considering his major fucking oversight lately! This wouldn't be a one-way blame game.

Fuck begging for an orgasm. I was now pissed at his arrogance coming into full view again.

"Talk to me, kitten!" he demanded, lips tight with concentrated anger. *The fucking nerve!* "You owe me an explanation. I won't continue this way. We're bonded. You're mine for life. I need you to open all the way to me. That means—"

"*YOU DON'T WANT MY BABY!*" I screamed to the point of feeling a stretch in my pelvis.

Ezra steeled over me, his eyes roved over my puckered belly. Silence showered over us, but I could see the reflected flickers from the candle flames dancing in his eyes as he processed my words. Ezra's lips parted, brows met, and eyes swung left and right.

"*Christ!*" he breathed. "Is that why you've been so elusive? Why you don't sit out in the congregation anymore?"

Delirious, I yelled, "It's like you don't want him! Why should I sit out there where people can see me like this, and you haven't even told them about my baby?"

"It's not *your* baby. It's of our creation...my baby, too," his rasp was gentle.

"You don't act like it!" I yanked too hard at the wrist cuffs. "Fuck!" Pissed the hell off by the sting, I lifted my neck and yelled, "You didn't even tell your friends! Amare doesn't even know I'm pregnant! You didn't even tell your father about him!"

Ezra's eyes went even wilder. His mouth dropped as though I'd just told him I was born a man. His lids collapsed and he mouthed something silently. My heart felt like it was being ripped from my chest, waiting for confirmation of what I'd been feeling for weeks now.

"First off, that's no boy incubating." He lowered his chin for emphasis. "Second, and most importantly, why didn't you say something weeks ago when this began?"

"Because when the topic of my pregnancy came up after the first time we had sex in the shower, you safeworded! You locked me out! Why would I think you'd do something different over telling your church about it?"

Ezra backed up before turning in the opposite direction and walking over to the wall. With my head lifted even higher, I watched the flex pattern in his muscles on the way. His left hand reached for the back of his head, clearly perplexed. And here was when the guilt would normally pour in. But not tonight.

This was my baby we were talking about. In my line of work, I'd seen too many sacrificed because they came unannounced. I never understood how innocent babies were short-changed in life because their parents were being careless. No one asks to be born. My child was a welcome surprise. Ezra had to get on board or he could kiss our bond good-fucking-bye. I was now a package deal.

I lay my head back on the padded table. No more of me suppressing the urge to go out and purchase clothes or look at the furniture section in *Target*, waiting on his acceptance. I was living a dream: having a baby, something I was told I'd never do. My baby was a blessing. I felt my first direct blessing from God.

My gift.

"I am trying, beloved," I heard the pleading rasp from below. I lifted my neck to see his broad back heaving. "It may not be apparent to you, but I am truly trying to accept this new development in my life—they've been coming so quickly and unexpectedly."

I could hear the cry in his chords.

"What do you mean?"

"I didn't expect you to leave me in February, and certainly didn't expect to feel the deprivation I did day after day after day after..." His words trailed off into silence and he ducked his head. It took some time, but he continued. "I didn't think you'd come back, but I wanted to let you know how repentant I felt even if you decided to really part ways. You're strong, Alexis, so brave and flexible to your environment. A survivor."

Lex is a fucking warrior! my father's mantra of my childhood echoed.

Ezra turned to me.

"That is what I've been using as an example all these weeks when experiencing my entire future—you—possibly not coming into fruition. I mishandled you, and I get that now. Then my mother..." His neck gave out on him again. More silence shredding my heart. "I was—and still am—angry! I did not see that coming."

I couldn't believe he'd turned this transparent. Felt I was infringing on his private confessions. But that couldn't be possible. I was his wife. Isn't that what our covenant was about? Being in love and bonded—our bond—was about sharing it all.

"Don't keep it from me!" I demanded through gritted teeth, my fists balled to a painful clench above my head. I repeated his words to me in the past, whole-heartedly. "If you need to cry, do it with me! Don't hide it!"

Ezra's head shot up. His eyes were tearless, but red with swollen rims.

"You didn't know because Mary didn't want you to know."

"But He should have told me! It's who I am in Him. Do you know why I came back to the States after all those years?"

I shook my head.

"It was because for weeks, while in Oman...Saudi Arabia, He appeared after years of silence, and began to trouble my sleep. Night after night, I had dreams and visions of people suffering—addictions, abuse, murders, betrayal, death—you name it. Then one night, He awakened me with the violent screams of a woman, clearly in agony. The high squealing of her chords tortured me. After twisting and turning on my cot for hours, a vision of my mother, on her knees, wailing came so clear. I jumped out of my bed, and ran out to a wadi, next to a stream of water, and proposed to surrender all to Him."

His eyes rose to meet mine. "But under one condition." I swallowed hard at what was coming. "That He'd send me you, the right one for me. I knew He'd been after me for years to do ministry. And I understood what my charge was, though I fought it through rebellion. But I accepted it...that night. We made covenant there by the water when He agreed to send you. It took seven years, but you literally landed at my feet."

Goosebumps rose all across my body, and my mouth went dry.

"Ezra..." Tears collected in my eyes. "Do you think the screams from that woman was me, and Mary's tears were for you to come home? Or maybe for the pain she survived in silence for years?" Ezra's eyes paced the room. "No, you don't like surprises, but maybe He *had* warned you. Maybe He disturbed your sleep to get your attention. If I'm your gift, Ezra, I'll be that. But you have to love me—"

"And I do! With every breath I take in!"

"Yes, now. After I left, and *that* got your attention. It may've been unexpected, but it served a purpose. We're here. We're in love...and now bonded. But imagine what *Redeeming Souls* would have been if you didn't come back. Mary worried about that, I bet. She told me the type of man her father was. She knew you could turn the church around—set it back to the high standards her father left it in, she said. What if her prayers were answered when you returned?"

"But why would she keep that secret? Why not tell me?"

"Maybe she didn't feel it was your burden to carry." I lay my head back down on the table, needing to rest my neck. "What if she was finally content with where you are in life. The covenant you made with God, without her knowing the details, satisfied her."

I really didn't know, just tried to offer peaceful revelations to calm him. They were all possible. I just needed my husband in a secure state again. Yeah, he skirted on asshole when he was his usual confident self, but I enjoyed that security in him. I needed it. It was a huge part of his dominant persona.

As I considered these things, Ezra, too, must have been in heavy contemplation, quietly.

"Mary was good at keeping secrets." Tears ran down the sides of my face. "She knew about my pregnancy." I could see in my peripheral when Ezra jumped and turned to face me. "Please don't be mad. It was hard not sharing it with her. She was going so hard to make sure I didn't quit this marriage...end things with you, is what she really didn't want. You were really special to her, Ezra. No matter what differences I had with that woman, she made it clear, you were her priority to protect. So, if it provides any comfort, she left knowing you'd be a father." I swallowed. "She was technically a grandmother...in utero."

There was a deafening pause. I didn't know how he'd take the news. I decided at her funeral I wouldn't open up this can of worms. I didn't want his wrath. Ezra thrived on control. He'd consider this sneaking behind his back. In some ways, it was.

"Thanks for sharing that, Alexis. I'm going to meditate on this. In fact, I am going to seek God on it—all of this, including how to be a better husband to you. It will include fasting and an enhanced prayer regimen."

I rolled my eyes.

Shit...

My head shot up from the table. "*Fa*-fasting? Fasting from what?"

My eyes brushed past his flat pelvis. He'd lost his erection, but my arousal was still lurching in my groin.

Ezra angled his head, face wrinkled. An incredible smile flashed upon his face, and he exhaled, rolling his eyes into the distance.

"I believe we just had our first spiritual meeting place, and what you walk away concerned with is sex, belov—"

"Kitten!" I snapped. "You have me down here, tied to this table...tortured me for almost an hour now." My eyes scanned the digital clock hanging on the wall. "I'm pregnant and horny. Did you expect something else?" His head shifted to the other side, and eyes squinted with humor. "I'm not playing, Ezra! Fuck me now!"

After a pause, Ezra's left hand went to his waist. That's when I noticed his erection had returned. It was beautiful and now throbbing against the thin material of his loungers. He dropped his pants, and when his thickness plopped out, my head fell back hard against the table. I tried rubbing my thighs together until they were yanked back by the restraints.

"You would do well to mind your mouth down here, kitten."

Then I felt him breech me forcefully with a bite of pain, filling me with the intensity he'd always had, literally and figuratively.

~Lex~

"And that's all of my reports from the past six months. The previous ones are backed up on the server." Richard patted the table. "Lex, you have access to that."

I sighed, not exactly responding to him. I couldn't believe I was getting emotional about this. I knew this day was coming for over a month now, but here at our formal separation meeting, I started feeling blue about him leaving.

"And you filled out the LOA paperwork, correct? I think the *Missions* organization should respond within a week with confirmation," Ann Bethea confirmed his documentation.

"Oh, of course. I spoke with a representative last week," Richard assured. "They explained the perceived delay in documentation processing."

"Well, I trust you more than *Missions*. I've been working with you since I've been here at *Redeeming Souls* Business." Ann smiled. "You just stay safe over there. I know challenged regions like this move you, but remember you have a family who cares for you here in the States."

It was strange to see Ann lay down her professional hat, but not at all unusual to see anyone do it for Richard. He was a dedicated member of the crisis prevention services staff, and would be missed for the next six months. He finally decided to fulfill his dream of attending a missions trip to bring crisis management to a needed region struck by terrorist attacks in Eastern Europe. I swallowed back a cry.

Fucking pregnancy hormones!

"I appreciate that, Ann. And I will return; my wife wouldn't have it any other way." He smiled his kind smile.

Richard's brown hair was still greasy, and his glasses still outdated. But his heart was always calm, his aura always peaceful.

"Okay." Ann exhaled loudly. "Anything from your direct supervisor?" She glanced over to me; Richard's regard followed.

I licked my lips, reining in my stupid ass emotions. "The first temp starts first thing in the morning. I'm working on the second now. Are all your tools—books, notes—easy to find on your desk?" I tried for professionalism.

"Yeah...yeah." He sat up in his seat. "I even have updated emergency response talking points hung around my cube."

I nodded, swallowed hard as I eyed the table.

"Then that's all, Romo. Go out and save the world." Ann smiled, I was sure meaning every word she spoke.

Richard was easy to bet on.

She stood from her seat at the conference table, there at *Christ Cares*. I didn't move as quickly, but did start collecting his reported cases on the table to carry back to my office downstairs.

"One sec, Lex," his soft voice commanded. "I do have one more thing for you." I watched as he pulled a smaller brown paper shopping bag from the chair next to him. "I know you haven't made the official announcement, but let's say a little birdie told me you were expecting."

Ann froze momentarily before speeding up her packing and heading for the door to leave. Richard was right: I hadn't made the formal announcement. After Ezra's childish ass broadcast, delivered with much bravado to Bradley West, the word spread around the office. It was yet another embarrassing event. When I started at *Christ Cares*, no one knew I was the pastor's wife. They found out in a scandalous manner. It was the same with my pregnancy. My husband spilled the beans to my colleagues while in a childish ass jealous fit. It was shameful; I couldn't stay ahead of my own business when it came to my staff. Apparently Ann understood this to some degree, which was why she left out so abruptly.

Richard continued, "It's no big deal. Just a book that helps you name your baby if you want to stick with a familial theme. Maybe you'd like it to be a namesake." He shrugged, pushing the bag across the table to me. "My wife thought of the idea." Then he stood.

"Thanks, Richard," I offered without my eyes. "I was taught as a child not to cry." I swallowed. "And as you can imagine, the combination of tripling hormones and losing one of my strongest staff members, even for six months, is challenging that."

"If it makes you feel any better, I'm not exactly thrilled about missing the birth of Ezra's first child. He's an upstanding guy, and I couldn't be happier."

That's when my eyes finally reached his.

"You better hope Ezra doesn't miss the birth. My due date is October 20th. I just may kill him before," I partially joked.

Richard laughed as he rounded the table for a hug. During our embrace, I caught Precious walking past the door. Her eyes all over Richard and me, no matter how formal our touch. I rolled my eyes at the thought of her stirring something up over Richard. Ezra was just as fond of him.

Richard left and I managed to make it through that exit meeting without breaking down. It was the end of the day, so I packed my things up and headed over the bridge. On my way there, I thought about my joke to Richard about my baby's father. It had been four days since the breakthrough we had down in the sandbox. I attended church with Ezra that Sunday, and finally resumed my seat next to Lillian in the congregation. I wore clothes that didn't make my belly so conspicuous, but people like Lillian knew. And just like old times, Sister Shannon came to collect me at the time of benediction in the service so I could wait for Ezra in the *Bishop's Office*.

Two services last Sunday, and Ezra hadn't mention one word of my pregnancy. I decided not to expect it and therefore not feel hurt behind it. He said he had been trying, and I believed him. Even through the bite of pain from rejection, I pushed through and enjoyed his sermon. That part wasn't difficult to do. Ezra's words were always poignant. He was a verbal illustrator, and when he laid hands on people, it chilled me. Grown men still passed out, and the unusual amount of women—thirsty and sincere—flocked to the pulpit each time my husband opened it up. Just as I had to accept that part of his ministry, I had to accept him not being ready to share the news with his church.

Big girl panties and shit...

I rolled my eyes, pulling into the long driveway. Once I made it to the horseshoe curve, I noticed a compact car with an image and logo on the doors. I parked behind it, and walked to the open front door.

Ms. Remah was standing there, talking to a short woman with a skirt suit and auburn hair. As I neared them, I caught her Hispanic accent. There were two men with jeans and button-ups behind her. They greeted me with smiles and head nods.

"Everything all right, Ms. Remah?"

"She for de guest room?" Ms. Remah asked, confused with her arms crossed over her belly.

"Hi, you must be Lex!" the woman cheerily offered me her hand.

I shook it. "I am. And you are?"

"I'm Lucy from *Baby Luxe*. We're located on Fifth Ave in Manhattan. Elle Jarreau scheduled for us to come in and assess your guest room for the conversion to a nursery." She ended on an excited smile, expecting that emotion from me.

Huhn?

"I wasn't aware of this." I tried to think quickly. "You mind taking them upstairs, Ms. Remah? I need to make a call."

Ms. Remah grunted before turning for the inside of the house. Lucy and her guys nodded with smiles as they followed. I didn't even know which room they were looking at, but knew Ms. Remah wouldn't let them roam around.

I pulled my phone from my bag.

"Hello, Lex…" she droned into the phone, annoyed.

I cringed inwardly.

"That's First Lady to you," I hissed as my eyes combed the front end of the property. Summer was here and Ms. Remah had done a gorgeous job, even with her back being out. "You are now a member of my husband's church."

"First Lady would imply it's your church, too. How can I help you, Lex?"

"I have strangers here, trying to get into my house. They said they were sent by you."

I waited a beat for her answer. It was apparent she was considering my words.

"Oh! *Baby Luxe*…Lucy!" she breathed. "I forgot that was today. Ezra asked me to set it up this week, between Monday and Wednesday. Today worked best for them."

Ezra? He was away in Chicago for a revival.

"Why would he arrange for this when he's away?"

"That sounds like a marital issue. Not exactly my area of expertise."

"But fighting my battles seems to be, and I still can't figure that one out."

"*Allegedly* fighting your battles. You can't prove that if you have no evidence."

"My evidence is up in my house right now." I swung my arm in the air, toward the house. "Inspecting my second floor."

"Again, Lex. That's not my problem."

"But it is your doing—"

"At your husband's request!" she yelled.

The fuck?!

I saw red, and knew I needed a breather. This wasn't us. I liked Elle when I first met her.

"How did we get here? What happened to the gorgeous lady that has impeccable style? I had no beef with her. I actually liked her!"

I'd seen Elle outside of church on two occasions since Nyree's spot had gotten blown up with Peaches. Once was at a fundraiser Stenton had in Newark for a basketball camp he was starting his first year into retirement. She worked the entire event, but did greet Ezra and me warmly upon arrival. The next time was at Stenton and Zoey's dinner reception at *DiFillippo's*, over two weeks ago, when they asked me to be their daughter's godmother alongside Ezra. Elle was cordial then—excited even. She smiled, and hugged me hello and goodbye.

"She's been getting cussed the hell out by her first lady over things she may or may not have done!"

I gasped. "I didn't cuss you out!"

I tried going over my words since we started this conversation. I had really been trying to lose the vulgarity in my vocabulary. It was a lifelong manner of speaking, but I'd been trying for the sake of my husband's reputation. It was one thing to cuss him the fuck out on occasion: he deserved it. But it was something entirely different to do it in public and have his image affected by it.

"You said fuck me the last time you called!" she whined with incredulity. I flinched again.

I did, didn't I?

Tears pooled in my eyes. "It's just that I'm not used to calling on nobody in a fight. I fight my own battles, Elle! Harlem Pride. I'm no punk. I could've dealt with Nyree properly!"

"Not that I'm saying I had anything to do with it, but how, Lex? You're pregnant—and by the way, I felt some kind of way that you didn't tell me yourself. I had to hear about it from Ezra when he asked for help with your nursery."

"You said we weren't friends!" It was my turn to whine.

"After you said fuck me—"

"No! Before, Elle! And that shit hurt my motherfuckin' feelings!"

"And here is that classy language served by my fine fucking first lady," she breathed.

The tears fell.

"I'm sorry!" I squealed, like a big fucking blubbering mess in heels, leaning against my *F-Type*, in front of my 4,500 square foot home that sat on five acres of land.

I was pathetic with this damn crying!

"You should be!"

I sucked in a breath. "Why?"

"Because I wanted to invite you to a show with me last week. I don't have a lot of friends, and didn't know if you'd like it, but we vibed so well last fall when shopping. And I just wanted to let my hair down and toss back a few with a down ass chick."

"But I can't. I'm pregnant."

"I know!" she breathed. "Now. After my pastor told me."

"Do you see how weird this sounds? At first you're accusing me of not being a real first lady, now you're yelling at me for not being able to go out drinking with you because I'm pregnant. I'm still your first lady." I wiped my eyes, sniffling.

Elle and I laughed together, and for a good while. My shoulders felt lighter when I was able to come up for air.

"See! Ezra was right! We could be good friends."

"Wait! He said that?"

She squealed, "Yeah. That's why he set up that shopping date. I don't do shit like that randomly. It was a part of my treatment plan: to get out with other women and start relationships."

That news made me cry again. Ezra thought I was good enough to be friends with someone he deemed in need.

That fucker is all right...

"Lex, that's my other line. I gotta go."

"Wait! What about these people in my house?"

"Call your husband. He set that up."

I had to ask. "Elle, is Ezra a client of yours?"

"I can't answer questions about my roster." *Bullshit!* "But I can say, Ezra said it wasn't ethical for him to be my client when I am his."

"Bye, Elle. And I'm sorry." I felt I rushed that huge apology, but she had to go.

"Me, too. I'll call you later."

I dropped the phone from my ear and took a deep breath. I tapped to make another call.

He answered in two rings. "Yes, beloved?"

He seemed as preoccupied as Elle.

"You arranged for a *Baby Luxe* to stop by today?"

"Yes. I knew your next visit was yesterday, and maybe you'd finally find out the sex. Regrettably, I couldn't be there, and thought you'd want to start thinking of ideas for the nursery."

I rolled my eyes, fighting a smirk. He left Monday morning before the sun came up.

"I don't want to know the sex." I hadn't told him that.

"You keep saying it's a boy..." his tone dropped.

"Because that's what feels right."

He'd also hinted at it being a girl.

"I don't need to know. As corny as it sounds, I'm just happy to be pregnant."

"I see..."

Things went quiet and I absent-mindedly scanned the compact car in front of mine. Something hit me.

"You were trying to be romantic with this?" A smile burst on my face.

"I was being thoughtful, I guess." He exhaled, and his voice dropped to that subterranean level. "And I also knew I'd be missing you around about now. I hoped you'd be missing me, too."

"Shit!" I breathed, excited. "You *are* being romantic, E!" I bit my lip, kind of turned on.

"Mouth, Alexis..."

I flinched again. I had really been trying. And apparently so had he. He initiated the designing of my...our baby's room. So, no. I didn't bring up the lost opportunity of him sharing the good news with the church. He clearly wasn't ready.

"Hey," I chirped, giddy.

"I'm here..."

"You remember today was Richard Romo's last day at CC?"

"Yes, beloved." I could hear when the memory clicked in his head.

"He gave me a book for naming babies." I smiled in spite of myself, moving past what could have been a painful moment.

"That was really generous of him. Truly indicative of who he's always been..."

I started my walk into the house, listening to my husband speak randomly about nothing. And it felt incredible. It had become a new thing for us: random talk. My second best activity with him. Of course sex was the first. Nothing topped sex with Ezra.

~eighteen~

~Lex~

I clicked the light off before toeing back to the bed, careful not to awaken him. He'd just gotten back into town this morning, and preached hours later at Bible class. He may have endured a heavy traveling schedule doing ministry all week, but when we came home from church, he was mine. I met him halfway in not demanding we do a scene—a term I'd learned from him—in the sandbox; but after dinner, once his belly was full, I let him ravish me until we both fell out from exhaustion.

Now, with my late night bladder activities, I would make these frequent trips to the bathroom. The upside to it was that with him back home, I'd fall right back to sleep against his big, hot body. As soon as my knee hit the mattress, my mobile phone lit from a call. It was after one in the morning. My head swung over to Ezra, asleep on his back, chest and abs free of the covers. It was an unknown caller, so I hit to dismiss the call and crawled into bed. Seconds later, it lit again. The same number. I turned to see Ezra had not stirred. My first thought of a midnight call from an unknown number was my father with an emergency when he was out, or on occasion, from a smuggled cell while in prison.

But he said he wouldn't contact me for a while…

I couldn't take the suspense.

"Hello," I whispered, checking over my shoulder.

"Well played, Lex. You got that off."

It was Nyree.

My eyes squinted and I licked my lips. "What exactly did I get off?"

"You know what the hell I'm talking about. Don't play dumb."

"I'm really not." I grew pissed that quickly, but kept my volume down.

"You and your choir boy husband set me up. I know it was y'all, so don't try to deny it. You got what's coming to you."

My eyes stretched receiving that threat. If I didn't know any better, I'd say Ny was flexing. But that couldn't be possible because the little she knew to do, I'd taught her, even backed her on it. Nyree was no gangster.

"I ain't have nothing to do with you getting caught out there with Peaches. That was your sloppiness."

"How did you know if you didn't have anything to do with it going public?" she quizzed.

That was a good question. I'd never known for sure they were lovers, only had assumed by the quick questionable exchanges I'd seen between the two over the years. But we'd all had suspicions.

"That's my point. I wouldn't have known to set it up. I'm in social services: I don't know media people." I tried using Ezra's claim. "Not for nothing, Ny. I still ain't get my revenge yet." I lowered my voice for this part. "I still owe you a' ass whoopin', Harlem style. I got one with your name on it." I found myself smiling at that taunt.

It felt good.

"And I got a lot of shit with your husband's name on it: receipts from hotels with random women. Oh, and a tape with booty play…another man." She laughed. "At least I'm letting you know ahead of time your man is really gay. I'm fair that way."

The fuck?

I felt my mouth ball, my shoulders tense.

"Listen, you stupid ass bit—" The phone was snatched from my hand.

His hot frame was almost on top of me.

"Nyree, don't ever call my wife again."

"Or what?" I heard her challenge him.

"Or I'll inform Sherman Hooks, the private investigator your in-laws hired, that I'll be filing an order of protection against you for harassing my wife." He paused for her rebuttal. None came. Maybe because hearing about her in-laws' involvement in this scared her. That Hooks guy tried visiting me, too. Ezra told me not to speak with him unless he was present, but the guy never tried again. I'd heard from Tasche, who heard from Peaches that the Griffins wanted Nyree out of their family. The only reason she hadn't been forcibly removed was because Taylor wasn't with it. Little did his parents know, Taylor had participated in threesomes with the two women. What he didn't know was Nyree had real feelings for Peaches. "Moving forward, Mrs. Griffin, this line will be monitored. Leave. Her. Alone," he growled into the phone. "I can assure you, I am not the type of man you want to take for granted."

There was a long stretch of silence before I heard the click on the other line, ending the call.

Ezra powered off my cell phone and placed it back on my nightstand. He clicked on the lamp, grunting when the light hit him. I lay stiff, coming down from the call.

"Are you okay?" I could hear the gravel in his chords from the late hour.

"No," I whispered, staring out into the darkness of the room.

"What's wrong?"

I licked my lips. "That was crazy. She's desperate, I can feel it."

"How?"

"By the bombs she tried to drop. It really..."

"Concerns you," he stated instead of asked. Ezra's left hand slid down to my belly and he rubbed it gently.

"Yeah. I can feel it. I know I should be mad and stay mad, but you know me...always feeling for people more than I should. I actually feel bad for her, feeling the need to drop those types of bombs."

"Well... What did she say?"

I finally met his eyes. "Are you ready for this? It could really damage our marriage."

Ezra lifted a brow, signaling me to spill it.

"She said she has copies of receipts from your creeping with other women, and a video of booty play with you and another man." I held my breath after that last word.

Ezra's eyes narrowed and neck rolled to the side. He shot daggers into me with his eyes.

When he rolled over to his side of the bed, ignoring my claim, I couldn't hold it in any more. I busted out laughing.

"Wait, E! So, you're not going to answer to those allegations?" I tried for serious, but couldn't breathe to pull it off.

Tears spilled from my eyes. Ezra tucked himself under the blanket with his back to me.

"I fornicate and am a homosexual: typical church-boy accusations. Alexis, see me in the morning when you've come up with something more compelling."

I couldn't help the sputter in my next round of laughter while trying to turn off the lamp.

The music played softly in the background of the packed auditorium. Dwayne directed the praise and worship singers on the other side of the pulpit in humming a soft and agreeable tune. It was hot on the stage of *RSfALC*; I didn't recall feeling this warm when I was last up here, convincing the people of a solid marriage I didn't have.

So glad we're removed from that place.

A flash caught my eye, and I glanced down at the professional cameraman, shooting away at the pulpit. It was a joyous occasion, far more special than I realized when I agreed to participate. I stood, unable to fight my smile at the sight before me. My hands were clasped at my waist and my heart swollen from the joy I felt.

"Ms. Amora Ardell Rogers, we present you to the world, your community, whom you will soon serve," Ezra professed as he shifted his back to the audience so they could get a view of the precious baby who drooled over his head.

Zoey leaped up and wiped her mouth before it landed on Ezra. He held her high in the air, his arms stretched as far as they'd go. It was a moving sight, seeing Ezra in an off white robe, holding this baby for the church to witness. I was to the right of him now, and Stenton, Zoey, and little Jordan were to the left, looking on their princess with beaming eyes. We all were. It was Amora Ardell's christening day.

"We declare victory over your passage that your life may be fruitful. Speak life into your mind so that it will bear ideas and creations with the mind of Christ. We command peace in your heart that will overflow for those in need. Even your little hands are blessed with favor to work in the Kingdom. Your feet will light the path for others to follow to their destiny and purpose as willed by God." His cadence was strong and words powerful.

"You will not succumb to the fallacies of the heart, give away your body, or close off your heart to the things God is calling you to." He turned her to face Stenton. Ezra's back to him. "You are a product of your father's loins, survived among countless cells for life."

The church reacted to that profession. My tears began to collect. I'd never witnessed a christening before. I had no idea of its rituals or how deeply it involved the community.

He turned her to face Zoey. "You are a Kingdom child, purposed in your mother's womb for ministry."

The church went up again.

"Here is your secondary parenting community. We're here to assist when your parents cannot or when they simply need backing. Our tutelage will never invalidate theirs, but will edify the blueprint of their parenting." That's when I realized his back was to me and there was a new line of drool falling from little Amora Ardell's mouth.

This time, I acted quickly, and without thought used the clean facial tissue I carried to swipe my impending hormonal tears, to catch it before it landed. I was careful to wipe her little pouty mouth, too. Zoey had added the right touch with a cute lace headband matching her fluffy dress that puffed around her chubby legs. She hadn't cried one bit up here, and we'd been up on stage for over twenty minutes during second service.

Man, she's gorgeous...

I noticed the stretch of silence. Ezra had stopped. His admiring gaze still on the princess. Amora Ardell ducked her neck and for seconds long, it appeared that they'd locked eyes. I wasn't alone in noticing the pause, Stenton's smile widened when he scanned Ezra's face, appreciating the doting on his daughter. Zoey hugged her small frame protectively as she quietly sobbed, apparently overcome with emotion. Then the church let off a round of applause for Ezra's entranced moment.

It was sweet considering not much affected the man, other than my vulgar language...or when I showed up plastered to a lunch with his spiritual mentor, or when I leave him...or when I disobey him and go see about my troublesome father...or when I blurt out I'm pregnant after keeping it from him for weeks while he's ready to kill said father.

I cringed and steeled at that. I'd done a lot to upset this man, and yet, he'd made it abundantly clear he would not let me go. I wanted to rub my belly, but knew I couldn't. So I kept my focus on the perfect little angel before me as she looked upon my husband, channeling something.

But what in the world was Ezra doing? He never stumbled up here.

"I am sorry for the interruption. I can't..." He struggled to speak.

My eyes popped open wide and I wanted to jump for him, but that would be doing the most. Ezra never lost his cool up here. It was one of the places he was a natural. I swallowed hard as my eyes swept the stage looking for Thaddeus.

What should I do?

"Life is precious…so delicately and specifically woven. It makes you experience God on new levels." The church went up in applause, affirming his words. I exhaled, relieved he was speaking again, though now choked up. "And there's nothing like God increasing you in a manner that makes all of your previous accomplishments pale in comparison."

The place went quiet. Like me, they didn't understand Ezra's direction. He and the baby were still sharing exchanges. Weird for a child so small. He spoke in a gentle tone as though communicating to her alone.

"My wife is at the end of her second trimester—"

The glaring response of shouts, screams, gasps, and gulps rang out all over the place. I couldn't move, couldn't even hear for a while. *Did he?* In slow motion and with muted ears, I watched as Zoey's lips parted and eyes widened across the stage from me, matching my sentiment, *but I couldn't move.* She covered her mouth with her hands and her eyes squeezed, tears shooting from them.

Oh, my…

I tried to breathe, and my body heated all over. I was embarrassed, shocked, and angry initially, and all at the same time. He'd done it. He told his congregation about my baby. Our baby. I couldn't believe it. All of these weeks and I hadn't planned on my reaction to it. I only wanted him to show some semblance of acceptance. His happiness would have been a bonus. And here, with how he announced it, it was clear to me Ezra was happy about my pregnancy.

I felt soft hands on me. I glanced down, and saw Zoey reaching around me to hug.

"Holy mother of Joseph! Lex!" she shouted, engulfing me in a hug. "Congratulations!"

Another set of hands were on me. It was Dwayne's wife, Lucy, whose hair was now dyed platinum. Her eyes were filled with tears.

"Glory be to God!" she sang in a sharp pitch, apparently caught up in her feelings.

My tears wouldn't stop, and I still hadn't fully regained my lungs.

In a more recognizable, more authoritative, and cautioning timbre, I heard, "I know you're all excited…and I will allow her to stay after the benediction, but we have to get back to the event at hand." Anxiety at that thought choked me at the neck. I never stayed behind. He'd made sure of it. "One last thing: please do not touch her belly. No hands are authorized unless cleared by me for spiritual purposes." Ezra now held the baby in his arms, his eyes still on her, cadence just as calm, but still admonishing. "And you know I'll know if you disobey me."

And just when I thought that arrogant demand would create an awkward shift, a resounding new wave of cheers rang out even louder. *Redeeming Souls* was not fazed at all. They knew their leader. He was incorrigible—a term I'd come across when we were separated—but still good at heart.

Ezra was able to calm the congregation enough to finish the christening. After, I took to my usual seat next to Lillian while Zoey and Stenton sat in a different section. The sermon was amazing. Ezra spoke on believing in God to equip you for the battle. He referenced a man name Gideon, and how he was charged to go into battle with a powerful opponent. God used his faith to select the men to take with him. Although it seemed like an erratic decision, Gideon trusted God not only to choose his soldiers, but to downsize his army. In the end, Gideon won the war, but it was first through faith.

It made me reflect on this latest battle with my incorrigible husband. I'd been praying about his acceptance of my baby. Our baby. I could have up and left again—for good this time. But I stayed faithful in my prayers, and exercised a little hope in God for Ezra. It had been a constant journey of battles and wars with the beast that is Ezra, and I was sure there would be more. But with this new tool of prayer that seemed to work, I had some ammunition to keep fighting.

As he promised, I stayed behind after the close of service. Shannon was posted to my left and Lills to my right. No one was pushy or aggressive, but the attention and desire to talk to little old me, was overwhelming. Ezra remained at the foot of the pulpit, entertaining his own crowd. It may have seemed he was carrying out his pastoral duties, but I knew he'd stayed to keep an eye on me. I didn't like the fanfare of being First Lady, but admired the community in *Redeeming Souls*. I was given telephone numbers and business cards for contacting, hugs, and countless well-wishes.

When it was over, Sister Shannon escorted me out. Call me crazy, but out of nowhere I had the desire to finally visit the *Bishop's Lounge*. It was the place she'd offered to take me the first Sunday we'd returned after being married. That was where the dignitaries went for refreshments and fellowship in between services. They had food, and I could use a snack. The room was almost empty with a few stragglers in conversation. It seemed like perfect timing to me; service had ended almost forty minutes ago. I made my way over to the food table and picked up fresh vegetables and spooned dip on a small plate.

"Now we're showing up in the *Lounge*?"

I glanced up from my plate and saw Precious standing next to me, pretending to organize the array of platters.

"Yeah." I bit into a carrot stick. "I'm hungry."

It didn't take her long. She exhaled loudly and turned to me, pushing her hip into the table.

"He won't be faithful." I frowned, more surprised than affected. "You may think because he's a preacher...or a church guy that he's safe. You think he's a safer bet than the thugs you're used to, but these men are bred to spread their loins. He's Bishop Carmichael's son. Need I say more?"

I chewed while eyeing her.

"Did you hear me, Lex? He won't be faithful!" She was a princess for sure, throwing a tantrum because I wouldn't give her the reaction she wanted.

"He doesn't want you," I garbled.

Precious gasped. "Excuse me?"

"He doesn't want you. I used to think your lurking was weird because Ezra made it clear he wasn't interested in other women. But I've been insecure about you still hanging around." I swallowed my food. "I just thought you were weird. I couldn't put my finger on it, but it's clear now. You want Ezra."

"I have options!" she damn near yelled.

In my peripheral, I could see people looking our way, including Sister Shannon. I didn't want a commotion, had caused enough of that in less than a year at my husband's church. My church. I wouldn't engage in a fight with princess Precious today. But I would rattle her a little.

"But you want him. And what I don't get is how you had him and lost him." I turned to walk off, but grinned slickly as I did it. "What's the matter, princess? You didn't like when he tried to tie you up and spank your tush?"

Before I could turn away, Precious' almond eyes went wild and her chest expanded wide, causing me to trip over my feet when I tried to turn back.

What the hell?

"You don't know nothing about me! I was a kid when he tried that demonic stuff with me!" she screamed at the top of her lungs. Precious' head started vibrating as she spoke. "Nobody believed me, but Bishop and my mother! He knew better! Ezra was a brat…always got into crazy things! That was devil worship!" she continued to shout.

I turned slowly, placing my plate on the table. It hit me. I'd opened up a can of worms. I assumed she was familiar with his bondage lifestyle. He said they'd slept together. But clearly she hadn't been that familiar. She'd damn sure been introduced to it, though it was clear she didn't like it. What confused me was how could she be with the guy, Seth Wilkinson, who clearly was into the lifestyle.

"So, what? You break up with him?"

"Lex," Shannon tugged at my arm from behind.

I shooed her off. Yeah, I saw Precious' honey complexion heat up. I wanted to know—needed to finally understand her fixation with my husband.

"Is that what you did? Break up with him?"

Precious huffed, eyes wild and haunted. I'd never seen her this way. She tossed her arms in the air and slapped her palms against her thighs on the way down.

"Like you don't know!" she trilled with suspicion. She didn't believe I didn't know. "Like he didn't tell you!" She gestured to my belly. "He married you off the street and pumped you full of baby. He stayed with you after your trash followed him to the house of worship, and don't think I don't know about the troubles with your thug of a father!"

"Wow." I sighed calmly, nodding my head. "He did, didn't he? He forgave all of that. But you couldn't forgive him for trying out a lil' kink. You were a bit extra about it, weren't you?"

As difficult as it was to admit that, I continued my pursuit of baiting.

"I told my mother I was going to press charges, yes! My professor told me to get a lawyer since I didn't call the police that night when he tried it. I was a kid; I didn't know the protocol. But you know what?" She placed her hands on her hips and cocked her head to the side, a little too hard it seemed, but she didn't flinch. This was all becoming so familiar. "I should have called the cops. I wish I had known what to do. I shouldn't have allowed our parents to talk me out of it. If Ezra would have, for once, faced the consequences of his actions, maybe he wouldn't have left the country, abandoning his family. Maybe he would've made better decisions." She gestured with her upturned palm to me and my belly.

Once again I nodded, understanding. She was fucking nuts. Sadly, Precious was having a meltdown. I'd seen it with my mother, only Precious wasn't violent…or predictably violent to me.

"But you participate in it with Seth. Why is it okay now?" I spoke as though I knew for a fact when I didn't.

I had no clue if they were fucking.

Precious' face hardened even more. Her eyes skirted around the room and she stepped closer toward me, speaking through gritted teeth. "I was more mature with him, and more into my body. By then, I knew more about it."

Bondage, dominance, and sadomasochism...

"You learned about it after Ezra."

"Of course! I wanted to know what he was into! I wanted to be ready in case..."

She knew better than to finish that. And that told me Precious was not totally off her rocker like my mother. She had simply come to a point in life where she lost her battle of trying to keep it together.

"Alexis!" Ezra yelped from behind, his voice laced with concern.

I felt him pulling at my arm, but I didn't budge. I was done being taunted by Precious' words long ago, and now felt satisfied with my question about her all this time. She felt she'd lost Ezra and had been around all this time, hoping to get him back in spite of him clearly having moved on.

"What in the dickens is going on in here?" It was Bishop Carmichael, wobbling in from the other door, fear etched on his face. "Sister Shannon, go get Marva! Now!" He tossed his index finger for emphasis.

"Nothing," Ezra replied with emphasis. "Precious needs privacy right now. She should rest."

Ezra didn't lose his grip on me. In fact, he pulled me back until his hands enclosed on my belly protectively. Still, I kept Precious with me via eye contact. Her expression seemed to be even more disturbed by the sight of Ezra around me. I didn't know how far she'd break; I wanted to keep her with us.

"Maybe you're right, Precious. But if no one else has said it—because we all know how stubborn, controlling, and incorrigible he is—I am truly thankful that you decided to let it go."

Ezra froze behind me. I could see Bishop's mouth drop.

Marva swept in from nowhere, and just in time. Precious stumbled backwards, so disoriented, Marva and Bishop both leaped to catch and lower her to the floor. She looked to be hyper-ventilating. I went to her, but Ezra pulled me back.

"You, Thaddeus!" Ezra barked from behind me, still pulling me back. "Call 911 now!"

Precious' eyes rolled back and her chest lifted and dropped at too high a pace. I felt more hands on me.

"Please, Lex, you shouldn't be upset by this," I recognized as Sister Shannon.

Marva started fanning her with papers. Bishop began praying over her, his shoulders tensed with palpable fear.

"Her mother's here to help her, beloved," Ezra informed softly. "Please...let's give them some privacy."

I stopped fighting somewhere near the door and walked hand in hand with Ezra to the Bishop's Office. I was happy to see the absence of the usual crowd in this area of the church. It was typically flooded with parishioners and staff. They'd all gone home some time ago. Ezra asked for privacy from those who followed once we passed through the double doors, his hand flat on my lower back guiding me into his office.

The second he closed the door, he turned to me, cupping my face with his big hot hands.

"Are you okay?" His speculative gaze speared through me. I nodded. "I am so sorry you had to see that. And I know I have lots of explaining to do." He dropped his hands and backed away.

Before I could say he didn't need to explain anything, especially not now since I'd already had my summary of it, he had begun.

"I've told you Precious and I dated—if that's the term we want to use—but more specifically, we had taken on a sexual affair in my late undergraduate years. She came to visit one break, and I thought to try her out on my latest pursuits of bondage." He paced the floor in front of me, similar to how nervous Thaddeus was that day we'd all been suspiciously summoned here by him. "And before you ask, I did not apply sadism, knowing she hadn't an ounce of masochism in her, much less sexual adventure." He stopped to examine me.

Again, it was unnecessary: Ezra, at least, now, wasn't big on sadism. He was honest when he told me last summer it wasn't his thing. As he advised, he'd only kept the lashes on my genitals, thighs, hips, and ass. I enjoyed it—embarrassingly craved it at times. I didn't want to hear more because hearing more likely meant detailing their sexual excursions. Doing that would be a major turnoff, if that's even possible concerning this man.

I shook my head, blinked and stretched my lids, momentarily overwhelmed by the possibilities of the level of passion she'd had for him.

"I don't need to hear more. As far as I'm concerned, those details are only of significance to you, Precious, and your families. You didn't hit her...or force her, did you?"

His eyes ballooned. "Absolutely not! I only tied her wrists. As soon as I saw she was blinking frantically, I uncuffed her! She freaked out the moment she was released...having a meltdown I had to endure alone; I didn't know what to do back then."

"Was it like today?" I was curious.

Did Precious have a history of breakdowns?

"No. This was different. She's been stressed for years now by those two I left to care for her," he rasped, yanking his beard, quickly lost in his thoughts.

"Well, what about Seth? He's into that. How could she date him if she didn't like it?" Precious had answered that, but I still didn't understand.

"The only significance Seth holds is the noted long rivalry between the two of us. He used her, thinking she was of interest to me for marriage and ministry. She used him, knowing his was the only feud I'd engage in with those I don't generally get along with. Precious wanted to rattle me, only it didn't work. Their affair has been on and off for a number of years. This recent visit of his where you met him, apparently he was trying to marry her."

"...knowing she'd be okay with his trifling ways, I bet."

Ezra didn't confirm or deny that inclination. He didn't have to.

"Ministry. You said ministry. What does that have to do with marriage?" I was now curious. I'd never heard of a correlation.

"Many marriages in the Kingdom involve joint ministries where oftentimes, wives support their husbands. Precious has been groomed to support my ministry by her mother, which contributed to her stress over the years."

I bit my lip, preparing for my next statement.

"I want to support your ministry one day...when I'm read—"

His warm lips hit my own before I could finish with my offer. His big hands cupped my face as his nose tenderly swiped mine. Ezra held there for a moment, his eyes closed. He wouldn't say it, but he appreciated my offering. Ezra still frustrated me, but I loved him wholly. I would do almost anything he asked...at least try.

"I'm going to take you away," he whispered in my mouth.

My eyes burst open.

"Away where?"

"Somewhere we can retreat. You deserve it. It's been a tumultuous year for you...since meeting me. I want to give you restoration."

My heart broke. When he said it that way, it had been a rough year. One of hasty yet serious decisions, a quick marriage to an incorrigible and controlling man, moving, employment, embarrassment, scandal, betrayal by loved ones, and a surprise pregnancy.

"Ezra, you don't have to take blame for all that's happened. You've brought some good things, too."

"Yeah, but I started off wrong," his rasp was solemn.

"What do you mean?"

Ezra glanced around the office, eyes scanning corner to corner. He located a box, picked it up and put it over on the coffee table.

"Come, beloved." I sidled up to him, wrapping my arms around his waist. I couldn't help myself. It had become a habit of mine. Ezra's body felt like home, not to mention the pride still bursting in my chest from his development today. "This box contains my life. The sides are barriers between me and the world. Only those things inside this box matter the most to me...the only things I truly value in life."

He pointed to gesture his point.

"Okay..."

"For a while after we married, inside the box," he pointed, "was just me and God."

I swallowed hard, slowly comprehending his point. I sucked in my bottom lip and nodded.

"Outside of the box was everything and everybody else." His eyes collapsed, brows met. "You were out there, too, beloved."

I took a deep breath, trying to survive the wave of dizziness that came over me.

He didn't love me.

"But now..." I slowly cracked my lids to rejoin him in the moment. "Now, there are three of us adjusting in there. We're in there under covenant, strengthening each other—loving each other, and perfecting our bond. We're also making room for a fourth." His eyes lowered to my belly.

Those damn tears pooled again, and before I knew it, had raced down my face. I let go of a breath I didn't know I was holding. I didn't want to cry again today, much less do the ugly cry.

"We're about to be a full house, huhn?" I sobbed as I spoke, a sputter of nervous laughter escaping.

Ezra stood from over the box and turned to me, placing his arms around my waist, and pulled my belly into him.

"I call it God's favor on my life." He was so close. I reached up and pulled my fingers through the hairs of his thick and dark beard. "Now, about going away: You may not know because I haven't done so in a while, but I am a man of frequent travel. You have to get used to it."

I didn't think my heart could take much more of this new and in tune Ezra. He'd been around for quite a while now, and I had to get used to him. I wanted to.

"Give me some time to clear my desk...and beg Ann Bethea for more time off," I whispered into his lips before including my tongue.

~Lex~

"Gosh, it's gorgeous out here," I murmured over a stretch the moment I strolled out the back door of the villa.

The sky was clear and the bluest of blue with not a cloud in sight. The ocean color, and pool beside it, were a hue darker, but just as crisp. There was a gentle breeze kissing my skin against the friendly glazing of the sun. I felt as though I'd walked out into aquatic nature; all I could see ahead was water.

"That's an improvement," Ezra rasped from the right of me, his nose in a book—a book I'd seen him read before.

"What is?" I moved to stand behind his lounger.

I leaned over and brushed my hands down his hard, dusted chest.

"You, using the term 'gosh' rather than your more conversant profane dialectal."

I grunted, stretching to reach the drawstring of his trunks that hung low.

"I told you, I'm getting better."

"You would do wise to, beloved."

A smile broke on my face. "Don't front, E. You like my dirty mouth. Especially when I put it on *your* mouth," my fingers crawled further past the band of his waist until I could feel the silky hairs and the trunk of his thick appendage, "and especially here."

"You're needling the beast, beloved." His delivery was calm, but I knew he was anything but.

Ezra enjoyed my affection.

My eyes left where my hands disappeared under his shorts and traveled up to his hands. "Why are you reading this...again?"

It was *Words for Turbulent Times* by Andre S. McCollum I. He'd read it last year, too.

"I like it," was his terse response. His voice low, chords vibrated through his thick chest. "I don't complain that you revere R. Kelly's historical catalogue."

My face cracked with a goofy smile.

"What?! Kellz is dope! You know you be feeling me when I be singing his stuff for you!"

Calmly, Ezra replied, "And so is Elder McCollum here."

Still giggling, I stood from over him and lazily dragged over to the pool.

"You've been in yet?" I kicked my foot in.

It was early afternoon, and I'd just awakened from my nap. I was now recharged and...horny as hell.

"Yes," he answered behind the book. "Before breakfast."

"Ms. Remah texted me this morning," I called out over my shoulder leaning against a big rock near the pool.

This scenery made me think about her time back at home, in Jamaica. It was July, and I was just into my third trimester. I mentioned to Ezra wanting her to have as much free time as possible before the baby, and the next day, he arranged for her to go back home. It was the only place she wanted to be. Her heaven on earth. I bet the sky was as blue there, too.

"Me, too," Ezra replied, still in the book.

We were in Ecuador, on a small private island east of Santa Cruz. Yup. I looked up the place last month right after Ezra told me we'd be visiting. We arrived yesterday, and had already explored a portion of the island. It was absolutely breathtaking. Just like Kamigu, Ezra had been friends with the people who owned the exclusive resort for years. They'd been gracious and welcoming, but no hospitality beat that of my Indonesian family.

"You haven't heard from Nyree have you?" I heard from behind me.

For the first time, my stomach didn't curl with hatred for that girl. I had a lot to focus on over the past few weeks since Ezra proposed this trip. *Baby Luxe* had begun stripping the floors of the guest bedroom to convert it into a nursery. I'd been busy at work, especially having to make sure little Noel Jr. was placed with stable relatives while Kema was awaiting her trial. I also had new staff coming in who needed situating.

And not to mention Precious' absence being felt by all. She really had been a huge asset to *Redeeming Souls* and their business wing. She abruptly resigned from every facet of the church, including its boards. Ezra told me she left for France days after that breakdown in the *Bishop's Lounge*. And since, she'd enrolled in culinary school there. In all honesty, I couldn't help but feel sorry for Precious. After Ezra explained the psychotic brainwashing of her own mother and Bishop Carmichael, I could see how stressful her world must have been. There was no way I could put my hopes and dreams into a man who clearly didn't want me. By the same token, I could understand the pain of not being loved or protected by those who should have. No one truly cared for Precious. If they had, she would have been off the track of helpless pining for Ezra long ago.

"Do you miss her?" I asked without thinking, lost in my thoughts. "Precious."

I glanced back over my shoulder at Ezra. He didn't move, for a while didn't speak. I turned back for the water, admiring the view.

"Actually," I turned my neck again toward his voice. "I do. I've been considering this all week. It finally hit me that she's gone." He spoke thoughtfully, his regard to the ground. Nothing prepared or glossed over to protect my feelings. Just real. "I have to find several replacements for her various roles in the organization. She's been proficient and wholly dedicated. It will be hard to find people to fill those shoes. Yet, I'm extremely proud of her. She's never stepped out on her own...spread her wings in life, so to speak. New place, new people, and perhaps a new identity. It should be good for her. I pray this is a successful move." Ezra shrugged his brow and sat back on the lounger.

I was grateful for his candor, his willingness to be open with me. I wasn't insecure about Ezra's fidelity to me. He may not have been perfect, but my husband's obsession with me was too thick at this point to share with anyone else. My private thoughts continued to run. Life had changed a lot in a year; some for the good and some with difficult adjustments. Overall, I was grateful. Happy. I rubbed my belly.

"Have you heard from Rasul?"

With my back to him, I shook my head. He said he wouldn't contact me for a while, and for the first time in his life, it seemed he'd been keeping his word.

"Are you worried?"

"About what?" I spoke over my shoulder, catching him in my peripheral.

"I don't know... About his mental state and overall health? I know you've been his sole support most of your life."

I sat and considered his question. "Nah. Rasul is very acquainted with the department of corrections—more than he is any system outside. Whatever he needs, he can get in there on his own faster than I can get from out here. I'm done." That last sentence dripped with melancholy, but I was all but sad.

My heart would always hold my father's best interest, but I had to start using my head when it came to him.

I turned fully, padded further into the lounge area, and oddly spotted his sandals. The thought of Ezra in sandals tickled me, no matter how many times he'd worn them while away. He actually had good looking feet for a man.

I slid into them and wiggled my toes.

"This is what the little guy is going to be doing about two years from now." I giggled.

Ezra looked over, and the moment his eyes hit my upper body they grew to the size of saucers.

"What?" I asked.

His face was hard, lips parted like he'd seen a ghost.

"You are absolutely breathtaking," he whispered, completely taken.

I glanced down at my open kimono robe. Underneath, I wore only black panties that had barely covered my ass in the back. My belly was on full display, and my tits. *Dang!* They were watermelons. I was now sure they were what caught his gaze.

"E...," I breathed as I rolled my eyes.

"I love seeing you like this. I want to take a picture."

"Like this? Why?"

"Because in this state I'm always evident. When people see you, they may not know my name, but know I've been there. In your womb."

He picked up his phone. A boyish-like grin of mischief playing on his face. As he focused the camera, his tongue protracted, and he bit it.

So damn adorable...

I sputtered a laugh as I held my belly. He took a few shots then put his phone down.

"Hey. Come here," he commanded.

I toed over to him. Ezra wrapped his thick arms around my hips and placed his head on my bare belly. Call me crazy, but I felt a warm energy emanate from him.

"You don't think you're beautiful this way?"

I ran my hands over his head.

"I do." *You make me feel that way every day...*

I was too afraid to speak those words, not knowing if I should be so affected by my husband's approval. Either way, I basked in it.

"I don't know what type of father I'm going to be. I'm deathly afraid, to be honest. But the insane beast in me wants to see you like this again, and soon."

My belly fluttered at that. Was he talking more babies? He couldn't be. Ezra still had been adjusting to this one.

"See, she wants a little sister soon."

"She? It's a boy, Ezra." I giggled. "Get over it!"

Ezra's head came up, and he peered deep into my eyes. "I hate to disappoint you, but this is a girl, Alexis. I know it."

My face balled into a frown. "Ms. Remah said I'm not ugly yet, so it has to be a boy because girls steal your beauty."

"Well, apparently you have more than enough to give because your beauty enhances every day."

I pushed him back and motioned for him to lay on the lounger. Then I straddled him, leaving room for my belly.

"It feels good to hear you talk about me like this. I could get used to it."

"Why? It's the truth." He squinted his eyes from the sun.

"I'm just not used to it." I inched closer to his face, centimeters away from his smooth lips surrounded by hair.

"Well, get used to it. I love you, beloved." And just when I thought I didn't recognize the man underneath me, he reminded me with a cautionary rasp. "You're mine."

I rolled my eyes. "Shut the hell up, Pastor, and fuck me."

"Mouth, Alexis," he growled, nostrils flared.

"Where?" I whispered, then pushed myself down his torso. I managed to release his thick and veiny rod. "Here?"

I pulled him into my mouth and heard his delicious exhale.

~epilogue~

~Ezra~

"...and you will be an asset to your community and the Kingdom. It was destined from your mother's womb," I whispered in the darkly lit room. "You will honor your mother, who gives you wings to fly. And as your daddy, I will be the wind to set your sails. You will be victorious at each thing you set your desires to." I stopped to consider that decree. "Be careful, that can be dangerous if not properly wielded. Trust me, as your ancestor, I can tell you how powerful your will is," I corrected. "You're not here by happenstance."

Though sleeping, a slow and abrupt yawn began. I'd seen this a few times over the past nine weeks. Those tiny lips parted and stretched wide, that button of a nose hiked, and that little tongue extended past the bottom glossy lip. But just before, my favorite part happened. A small push of breast milk flavored air rushed, and I lifted the little bundled body in my hands to have it hit my face. It was the best scent known to man...other than—I won't go there now!

I shook my head, trying to erase the salacious grin from my face.

"I get it. You're over your old man already. We have this same dialogue every night."

Well, since your fourth week of life…

That first month of fatherhood was difficult for me. I'm still embarrassed by my selfish transition where I didn't realize how much I'd be sharing Alexis. She had to devote her every waking moment to the needs of this little one. That's saying a lot considering she hardly slept. And because she wasn't rested, Alexis couldn't tend to me. She'd replaced Precious in collecting my things at the end of my sermons, before benediction, and I'd gotten used to her swollen belly and captivating gait, pleasantly distracting the congregation and therefore me. Then since she had the baby, before and after service when I prayed with my team, she had been right there petitioning along with me, but with the baby on her bosom. Everywhere I went, accustomed to my wife being there to aide, comfort, or release me, there was the baby.

It was clear that I hadn't bonded with my child. That was until one night Alexis slept in the guest bedroom in an attempt to take a nap in between feedings, and left the baby alone with me in the master suite. After wails that rocking the bassinet couldn't cure, I was forced to pick her up and comfort her. When that didn't work, I panicked and became frustrated by my inability to soothe. Just when I was prepared to go and awaken Alexis, I thought of something. I went to change the diaper on the bed—*oh, what a steep learning curve that was, nothing rudimentary about the application at all*—and as soon as I figured out how to tape it up, back in my arms, the crying stopped.

That small victory was where our bond kicked in. We'd been inseparable since.

"Don't be rude, Lisa-Mare. Daddy is almost done and will let you rest." A bubble of air pushed through her lips and she stretched out. My brow arched at her mutiny. "Defiant, like your mommy, I see. Where was I?"

This was truly an event I looked forward to at night. Putting my princess down for bed was absolutely precious. She'd been named a combination of Alexis' mother's name and mine. It was a concept she'd gotten from the book Richard had given her. Alexis' mother's name was Lisa, and I requested we give a twist to the spelling of 'Mary'. From there, we came up with Lisa-Mare, it worked well, seeing she was born on their birthday. Alexis' due date was October 20th, but she went into labor on the seventh, and endured an emergency caesarian section in the early morning of the 8th. I'd traveled the terrains of the most deathliest, dangerous souls while out of the country. Yet, never had I been so terrified of an event in my life. My wife, needing surgery to deliver our child? It was either that or risk the life of one or both. I made the call after a quick prayer. And now, I had life in my hands.

"Oh! I remember!" I whispered. "You were purposed, Lisa-Mare. Destined to the world. And I am privileged to be your daddy!" My chest expanded in stunning pleasure.

"Ezra…" I heard from behind. My gaze traveled the nursery to find Alexis at the door, wearing a robe. "It's getting late." From the lighting out in the hall, I could detect her undisguised lust.

I didn't answer, instead turned back to my precious little girl. "You know, your mom is a bit of a rebel, too, so I know how to respond to such stubborn spirits." Lisa-Mare turned her little head, still asleep. "Okay. Enough for tonight, but tomorrow, we have more to talk about after your nighttime read." I stood from the rocker and carried her over to the circular crib, knowing I'd be having the same conversation with her in four hours or so when she woke for her first night feeding and her mother handed her over to me for burping.

It was my thing: speaking life into her.

Quietly, I pulled the door, keeping it ajar.

"How long did you expect for me to wait?" Alexis demanded.

"Beloved, it's only—"

"Kitten!" she corrected.

I took a deep breath. We were outside of my princess' room!

"Kitten, it has only been ten minutes."

"Try thirty! Have you checked the time?"

I pulled my phone from my lounge pants, and saw it had certainly been thirty minutes, thirty-five to be exact. That had been the fashion of my life as of late. I get to Lisa-Mare, and lose track of time and space. She was mine, too.

Her mother here was a feisty siren.

I switched stances in front of the door, inching closer. "I don't like your tone when I'm putting my daughter down," I growled.

Alexis sucked in a breath. The size of her eyes doubled and her pupils dilated. I was reasonably sure she was bare beneath her robe, soaked with evidential need.

"Downstairs, on the pillow," I ordered. Alexis' glossed lips moved slightly, processing my demand. "Now!" I grunted.

She did an about face and padded down the hall to the back stairs. I dipped back into the nursery. Quietly, I crept over to the crib and softly kissed my baby. I then powered on her monitor before leaving out. I sent a text to Ms. Remah to let her know she was on duty for the next three hours. I went to our bedroom to take a leak and shed my shirt. By the time I made it to the main level, she replied that her camera was on and would be over to the main house momentarily. I went into the kitchen and took a few gulps of a bottle of *Pierre*, strategically killing time. Once I saw Ms. Remah's round wobbling frame approach the main house, I exited the kitchen for the hall.

The moment I opened the door, I could see her toes curled from that mixture of sensual anticipation and fear. Slowly, I plopped down the stairs, my excitement expanding in my pants. The distinctive structure of her spine caved and arched with aroused anxiety. I traced it with my index finger from the opening of her rear cheeks to her neck.

"*Uhhhhh...*" she grunted.

"Quiet!" I demanded.

That was met with an unintended moan from my kitten. She stretched back, exposing her rear cheeks in a lecherous manner. My dick leaped its readiness, eagerness. Tonight was a special event. This wouldn't be our first time together since Lisa-Mare's arrival, but the first in our sandbox. Alexis had been itching to get down here for weeks, but I'd been concerned about her regaining her strength and stamina. It was early December, but she was just eight weeks postpartum.

I moved to pull a wooden bar stool to the middle of the floor. I placed standing lamps around the circumference of the stool. Two of the lamps had designed kaleidoscopes circling around. I grinned, impressed and excited by my creative plans as I awaited this day. Next, I powered on the stereo. I created a soundtrack for her: a mixture of songs I'd shared with her along with those I'd noticed she was partial to. It was inarguably the corniest thing I'd done to date, but I took it in stride, as I understood my desire to please her using small acts of kindness was, in fact, evidence of me being in love with her. It had become undeniable. Faith Evan's *Kissing You* was the first to flow from the speakers throughout the room. My erection stood painfully on my way to her.

"Come, kitten." I helped her stand and guided her over to the centered stool. "Sit."

Her frame trembled as she scooted back on the seat. I pushed her thighs open wide, rendering her glistening pussy open to me. With black silk ribbons, I tied her ankles to their respective posts to keep her exposed. I secured her wrists behind her with purple ribbon. Her enlarged nursing breasts hiked to a torturing view. I now ached with an unbearable desire for her.

"Now, kitten, I'm going to cover your eyes for this," I heard the groan in my vocals as I pulled the gray silk mask from the workstation. Her bountiful chest heaved as her breathing could be heard. "Are you with me, kitten?" I asked from behind her, prepared to cover her eyes.

"Yes, sir," she answered without hesitation.

After blinding her, I moved in front to observe the various patterns from the rotating lamps reflecting on her cacao skin. She was an absolutely stunning sight to me. I couldn't believe my good fortune. How did I deserve a willing and devastatingly attractive wife? It was almost like a dream.

"Now, kitten, I have to address your impudence earlier while I was with my child," I informed on my way to the armoire to select my implement. I went with the usual black leather flogger; it was her favorite. She once told me she enjoyed the mass reach and stinging bites from it. "I will not tolerate being rushed when I'm with her." That comment was hypercritical at best: It was exactly what I did before bonding with my princess.

Alexis' head bobbed her understanding, her bottom lip sucked in her mouth as she grinned. I groaned at the revelation of her being so turned on.

Abruptly, I lashed her right breast. "That was not a proper response, kitten!"

She moaned, her head swung back and rolled on her neck. "Ye-yesssss, sir."

"You'll receive five more lashes for your breaches. And you will count them. Is that understood?"

"Yes, sir."

Then let the games begin...

I struck her left breast. Alexis caved in, sucking in air.

"Two," she grunted.

I gave her a moment to receive the bite. When her lips parted while her neck rolled, I knew that's when the pleasure was about to sprinkle over her body. So, I threw another.

"Ahhhhh!" She slurped in air. "Three."

The next I made sure to let up on the pressure. I had to measure the thrashes and watch for cues of discomfort or real pain. So far, only my cock ached from growing desire.

"Four," she delivered with more control.

I allowed her a moment to enjoy the onset of endorphins. She needed the reminder of chasing blissful sensations after the pain.

I struck again.

"Shi—" Her head swung forward. I applied more power to that one.

Seconds later, I noticed her lifting off the stool, rearranging herself. It was clear her arousal had collected on the seat.

"Five..." was more like a cry.

"Are you still with me, kitten?"

I had to measure her every move, sound, reaction to my strikes. If she was under duress for even a moment, all play had to stop.

"Yes, sir." Her breaths came in short stents. "Please, sir!"

Don't beg, honey. I won't last…

I lifted and quickly released the final whip.

"Uhhhhh…" she uttered with little breath.

Her mahogany frame barreled back and head swung back.

"*Sa*-six…"

It was over. I'd brought her to a place where I could measure her new limit. We hadn't played since the mid-summer when I concluded the clear line between my kink and my wife's advanced passage into motherhood. Alexis protested, but I kept to my decision.

I took note of my long breaths and tightening fists. My regard traveled across the room to pace myself. I wanted her to enjoy the intense orgasm she'd receive next. When my eyes returned to her, I saw opaque liquid squirt from her right breast and it leaked from her left.

Christ…

The sight of her femininity and evidence of motherhood turned me on, almost past the point of control.

I dropped to my knees before her, pushed her thighs apart even farther. My tongue pushed against her swollen and throbbing pearl. I paid a few swipes to clearing her wetness from her flesh. Alexis' thighs tightened around me. I could feel the vibration in them. And when I began long and broad strokes of my tongue over her entire cleft, being sure to add pressure once the tip pushed against her clit, my kitten screamed and shuddered over me.

"*Oh, god… Oh, god… Oh, god!*" she screamed insanely.

And I knew she was lost in bliss. The combination of the pleasure endorphins attacking her after the bites and clitoral stimulation shot her to a new stratosphere. I could feel her small pouch, still left over from incubating my child, against my forehead. I wish I could offer another this way, but our time was no longer ours. We had to clock ourselves down here. Alexis had to be ready for the next feeding. However, we had time for the next few tricks I had in store for her before we locked up the place.

I reached up, and released the mask from the back of her head. She was immediately blinded by the circle of lamps around her. I jumped up and turned them off before tending to her ankles and wrists. After untying her, I picked her up in my arms, her long thick legs wrapped around me. Her open mouth rested against my neck. When I lay her down on the purple silk sheets,

Alexis' eyes opened. She hadn't expected our next scene to be on the bed. I fought my amusement.

"You get to see this. I want you here with me," I attempted to explain as I parted her thighs for me.

She understood the sandbox wasn't the place for missionary of the vanilla variety, at least, but I needed it tonight. I wanted my wife to see my explosion into her. It was her thing, and now my affirmation as her supreme lover.

Her arms shifted to move, eyes lined with hesitation.

I nodded. "You may touch me, kitten."

Her hands reached up, caressed my abs, worked up to my chest. The hooded beam in her eyes heated my chest. My lids collapsed, taken by her soft touch. She sat up, pushing from my waist then fingered my beard. I was breathless when Alexis' lips met mine. This was not just sex; this was a celebration of intimacy at its highest level. It was communication and validation of dominance. It was also an illumination of my submission to my wife. When she took over and explored my body like this, it was worshipful, similar to my admiration for hers. It was our covenant coming alive, our bond strengthening. In no time, I was lost in her sensation, conferring my control. It was frightening no matter how settled I was on relinquishing it all to her.

I pulled back.

"I love you," I murmured.

Alexis' lashes fluttered, she was so far gone. For a while she didn't speak. I could only see the dip in her throat as she swallowed.

"I know," she whispered. "I know."

She laid back, making her wishes known. My kitten was ready for me.

I took my evident desire in my hand and glided it into her treasure. I pulled out, catching her pleading moan. I entered her again on a longer thrust. The moment I was fully cushioned, I could see and feel it all: relief, excitement, satisfaction, her unusual timidity down here, dripping lust, anxiety, and most of all, love. That acceptance meant more to me than them all. She was here, even if in just one facet. He'd kept His end of the bargain. Alexis was my gift. My covenant. My love. Our bond.

I reared back, and roared, "Mine!" before lunging back into her shuddering treasure.

The End.
####

~Love Acknowledges~

Researcher: Shumethia S. — I can't say enough how awesome of a human being you are. I can't wait to take our relationship to the next level. You may be flinching at that statement, but my heart is well knowing you'll be with me {in my best Shumster feel good voice}!

Love's Betas — Angela J., Corinne B., and Sabrina S. Scott, thanks for your dedicated patience and honest feedback. You have no idea how helpful your feedback is. Yorubia Ardell, you're unapologetically the best nagger, and just shameless. But I love it all. Thanks for your enthusiasm, Scoot.

Love Belvin Therapy Room — Regina, Linda W., Deidre, Dee, LaLa, Michelle M., Heidi, Artemysia, Tabatha, Roslyn, Diva Dee, Linda R., Rose, Michelle T., Monique H., Pamela, Sola, Teresa, Terri G., Gail (*what's your name again? LOL!*), Courtney, Doris, Kita, Tanya, Wendi, Tonya, Stina, Marshall, Andrea, Stacey, Angela B., Nikki, Deborah, Rakia, Ashleigh, Yvette S., Bonita, Kerry, Kim, Erica, Crystal S., Chameka, Vivian, Richell, Heather, Tesha, Tineka, Yolanda, Jessica, Sherri, Nicole, Deena, Ayo, Ayanna, Stacy M., Keyma, April, LaKisha, Katina, Sharon W., Ja'Nice, Brittany, Monique N., Natoya, Angela J.J., Crystal H., Shaun, Denise, Sharon L., Tara, Jalissa, Kamashia, Yvette H., Tiffany, Fennia, Katrina, LaKaya, Tanisha, Karmen, A. McClure, Ella, Teresa, and Robyn. "Ain't nobody fresher than my clique!" Thanks for riding with true enthusiasm. You guys rock! ***Jemeka*** & ***Rita***, thanks for supporting my brand. I am oh so fortunate for the real work you two put in daily to maintain a ~~simple group~~ circle of trust. It's unreal, and I'm grateful.

Christina C. Jones aka CCJ — You continue to impress me with your endless talent. Your brain is amazing! Thanks for being you. #AuthorBae

Interior Artist: Cedeara Ardell McCollum — Thanks, baby girl, for the imagery you've designed for my books! Love you always!

Proof Reader: Tina V. Young — Thanks for your patience, #petty eye, flexibility, and encouragement. So fortunate to have my own personal geek!

In House Editor: Zakiya W. — Welcome back! Thanks for the developmental eye you've kept on this baby. I really appreciate you!

Editor: Karen Rogers-McCollum of **Critique Editing Services** — This time I took six steps back. LOL!! Thanks so much for your magic eraser, flexibility, nurturing hand, and encouragement. Whew! Where would I be without your clean up?

MDT: I know... I know... *I know!* This one was tough for many reasons. But look who came through *again* doe! I guess it's me who needs to remember who's the producer versus the director, huhn. #BookTenAndCountingSir

Master, my ***Jireh***, my ***Rohi***, *Proverbs 3:3. "Let love and faithfulness never leave you; bind them around your neck, write them on the tablet of your*

heart." Thanks for giving me the man of God to bring into my eccentric creative world. #Ezra Thanks for Your grace, mercy, favor, and trust to present him flawed, but holy. *You've* blown me away! I will forever worship You.

~Other books by Love Belvin~

Love's Improbable Possibility series:
Love Lost, **Love UnExpected**, **Love UnCharted** & **Love Redeemed**

Waiting to Breathe series:
Love Delayed & **Love Delivered**

Love's Inconvenient Truth (Standalone)

Love Unaccounted series:
In Covenant with Ezra, In Love with Ezra & **Bonded with Ezra**

The Connecticut Kings series:
Love In the Red Zone & **Love on the Highlight Reel** *(by Christina C. Jones)*

Wayward Love series:
The Left of Love, The Low of Love & The Right of Love

~Extra~

You can find Love Belvin at www.LoveBelvin.com

Facebook @ Author - Love Belvin

Twitter @LoveBelvin

Goodreads: Love Belvin

Snapchat: LoveBelvin

and on Instagram @LoveBelvin

Join the #TeamLove mailing list to keep up with the happenings of #TeamLove at www.LoveBelvin.com

Made in the USA
Middletown, DE
26 June 2017